DEATH BY PEANUTS

DEATH BY PEANUTS

C A Shepherd

1

Got you, you little bugger! exclaimed Parlour, successfully lancing a whitehead on the tight skin between his eyebrows in front of the bathroom mirror. He washed his hands, then readjusted his navy pique t-shirt for the seventh time that afternoon. Taking a step backwards, he turned from side to side, twisting his head to contemplate his reflection in the mirror. Acutely aware of his skinny frame, the ginger-haired man pulled the t-shirt out of his jeans another inch. It wouldn't do to look too tucked in.

This was a ritual Detective Inspector Mark Parlour performed every time he left the house. And he was about to step outside that Saturday afternoon, to collect his wife, Juliet, from a church conference in nearby Lexington Green.

Five minutes later, Parlour swung out of Spatchcock Drive in his silver Mercedes SLK, frowning at the digital clock on the dashboard. Ten minutes to cut across Deverton, the designer town where he lived with Juliet, and out onto the Billock Road.

How long till they finish that bloody bypass? Parlour cursed, watching some men in fluorescent orange waistcoats hack at some foliage alongside a half-baked stretch of tarmacked highway as he pulled up at the lights. Much of the flimsy ring of green that surrounded the new town had already been sacrificed in the name of traffic management, but apathy was rife in the two point four car households of Deverton. It was not difficult to put your environmental conscience to one side when it took at least twenty minutes to get *anywhere* in the Deverton area. Whoever designed the elegant high street with its greenhouse style Melrose supermarket at the helm patently hadn't given much though to road congestion!

At thirty-nine, Mark Parlour had made steady progress to the rank of Detective Inspector. His surname, allied with a rather unfortunate habit of picking at his skin during moments of stress, had led to Parlour being nicknamed "Pizza" by close friends and colleagues. A late convert to Christianity, Parlour compensated for his religious beliefs with a healthy dash of secular cynicism, accrued through decades in the "wilderness" and a challenging professional life. Such world-weariness, whilst not always endearing him in church circles, helped him deal with the frequently shocking nature of his job. Only a few months back, he had headed the enquiry into the brutal murder of a Bangladeshi shopkeeper in downtown Billock. The young Asian lady had been strung up in the shop window for all to see, dressed in a ruby red sari, which on closer inspection turned out to be a heavily stained cream garment. He'd been pleased to nail the monster who'd done that one. Parlour hadn't felt quite as elated, however, when his garage door had been graffitied and Juliet's car sprayed with the words *Paki Lovers*, an episode that had accelerated their decision to sell up and move to Deverton three months ago.

The Parlours had taken advantage of one of those part-exchange deals, and had sold their 1930s three-bed semi in Billock's exclusive Chave area, home to the town's population of General Practitioners and overpaid sportsmen, to *HomeFromHomes*. In return, they had received the keys to a spanking new link detached property on the red-brick Deverton Estate. Admittedly, they could have got a lot more for their period house, had they sold through an estate agent, but with both Parlour and his wife putting in long hours as a police inspector and teacher respectively, there was little time left at the end of a draining day for showing prospective buyers around the house. And absolutely no time to keep the house in the decluttered, sanitised state required these days to "make that sale" to an increasingly unimaginative and anodine buying public. In Parlour's view, it wasn't worth all the hassle at this stage in their professional careers for the sake of fifteen or twenty thousand pounds, which they could, albeit reluctantly, afford to lose.

The inhabitants of the designer town generally fell into two categories:- young professionals with neither the time nor the aptitude for DIY in search of an up-together property, or retired couples desperate for a safe haven away from the petty crime and general grime of the city. Deverton offered its inhabitants a chance to start afresh with its newly turfed lawns and made to order fittings. And - as Parlour often thought to himself - most of the residents blended in perfectly:- a little bland, but essentially harmless. Even if it was a little twee, Deverton beat Billock hands down, in his opinion. Moreover, it was the ideal location for bringing up the family he and Juliet intended to start once she had got her Year Elevens through this summer's GCSEs.

They had been married some sixteen years now. They'd met at college in 1983, and Parlour had proposed within the year. Police secondments and teacher training college had contrived to keep them apart for a couple of years, but they'd finally made it down the aisle one sunny day in June 1987.

Cod, Parlour thought, adopting his favourite alternative to taking the Maker's name in vain, she'd looked beautiful that day, with her thick dark blonde hair resting on the pale shoulders exposed by her cream off-the-shoulder wedding dress. Bit skinny, mind, then. Preferred her with a bit more meat on her, like now. More up top, too, he grinned. They had been enjoying married life again since Juliet's transfer to Billock Community School, which shaved forty minutes off her journey to work. While the kids had been much easier to manage at Foxburgh High, at least she was home by five most days now, and teaching a refreshing combination of German and IT, too, rather than the standard two language combination she'd been lumbered with thusfar, despite her protestations she was no Francophile.

Hopefully Juliet's car would be ready by the time they reached the Fiat dealer on the way back from Lexington Green. Parlour frowned as the lights turned green – hopefully the MOT wouldn't throw up anything too major. He eased into second gear and turned right onto the Billock road. Two miles further up, the road forked and Parlour pulled off to the left towards Lexington Green. Zion House was about five hundred yards on the right, a salmon pink sign requesting visitors report to reception.

Parlour smirked to himself, as he had done that morning on dropping Juliet off for her Parochial Church Council Away Day. Two of the black plastic letters on the sign outside the shabby building owned by the diocese of Foxburgh had dropped off, leaving a rather enigmatic invitation to enter the Zion House Christian treat Centre! If only, Parlour thought, congratulating himself for the umpteenth time on his decision not to stand for election to the PCC, the committee responsible for running Deverton Parish Church. Pleading a busy work schedule, it was with some degree of smugness that Parlour left committee business to Juliet, reaping the benefits of inside knowledge of church affairs without the considerable burden of having to attend the meetings and – horror of horror – away days!

The Parlours had transferred to Deverton Parish Church, a newly created offshoot of St. Jude's in Lexington Green, six months ago. St Jude's, whilst boasting excellent teaching from Scripture and a talented lay congregation, lacked a certain intimacy which a smaller, more "amateurish" outfit such as Deverton Parish Church could offer in abundance. Billock, with its multicultural sensibilities, housed just three Christian churches:- a Brethren church that was decidedly Puritanical in outlook, an Anglican church with a regular congregation of pensionable age you could count on the legs of a Zimmer frame and an overtly jolly church that met at Billock Community School and called itself The Wineskin Fellowship, where Parlour and his wife had felt distinctly old the first and last time they'd attended their 10.30 worship! It was therefore with some relief that the Parlours accepted an invitation to join the

Deverton church plant team last autumn. It tied in neatly with their plans to sell up and make the eight mile trip down the road from Billock.

Parlour signalled right and waited for a lime green shoppa-hoppa to whiz past before driving up the leafy driveway to the ivy-clad retreat centre. But he had barely rolled ten yards up the slope when he was stopped by a police officer in a fluorescent yellow jacket.

"Tucks?" Parlour said puzzled, rolling the window down. He recognised the constable from Billock Station.

"Good afternoon, Sir. Can't go any further, I'm afraid."

"But I have to pick my wife up!"

"Can't let you in, sorry, Sir," PC Paul Tucker apologised.

"Why on earth not?" Parlour frowned. "What's going on?"

Tucker drew up to his full height of five foot five. It was a good job the Police Force had relaxed their minimum height restrictions for police entry in recent years, or Paul Tucker would still be driving a forklift around Billock B&Q. He pulled his shoulders back:- this was the moment he'd been waiting for, it felt like all his life.

"There's been a suspicious death on the property, Sir."

"What?!" The colour drained from Parlour's face. "Who?"

"A sixty-two year old gentleman, Sir..."

"Thank God for that!" Parlour exhaled. "Sorry, I mean, my wife is in there. Sixty-two..." Parlour undertook a hasty mental process of elimination.

"It's a Commander Haynes," his constable responded impressively.

"Terence? The warden?" Parlour said incredulously.

"Dropped dead at the dinner table, Sir. Suspected poisoning."

"Poisoned? Deliberately?"

"Seems likely, Sir."

Parlour whistled. "But Terence? Who on earth would want to *poison* Terence?"

"That's what Blackman's trying to find out."

"Blackman?" Parlour frowned. "Not…"

"DI Leigh Blackman from County HQ, Sir," Tucker informed him. "She arrived a couple of hours ago."

"Yes, I know who she is, thanks," Parlour muttered irritably. Blackman! What on earth was she doing on his patch? He glanced in his rear view mirror as a horn tooted behind him. He hastily got into gear and pulled over to the left as he saw the grim face of DCI Sewell behind the wheel of a gargantuan grey Lexus. The man they all called "The Sewer" on account of his flatulence problem, motioned for Parlour to alight. Parlour quickly turned the engine off and walked round to Brian Sewell's window.

"What are you doing here, Parlour?" Sewell barked. He glared at Tucker. "I gave strict instructions not to…"

"I'm here to pick up my wife, Sir," Parlour interrupted. "She's on a church away-day here."

"I know," Sewell replied. "That's why you weren't called. Doesn't she have her own car here?"

"No, Sir. It's booked in for a…"

"Spare me the domestics," Sewell snapped. "You'll have to wait here, then. Conflict of interests, Parlour. Can't have a fellow God-squadder investigating the death of the local church warden! Especially when his wife's present at the scene of the crime! But don't worry -" the jowelly Chief Inspector added, "We've got Blackman on the case. 'Bout time she got her fangs into something."

Yeah, like me, Parlour grimaced. "But…"

He was perplexed. What on earth was going on? He groaned. Suspicious death at a church meeting - she'd enjoy that, as a fervent atheist. Typical. First decent bit of action in ages, and he was off the case! Then Parlour frowned. What a shocking attitude. A brother in Christ, albeit not a particularly close spiritual sibling, had potentially been murdered, and all he could think about was thwarted ambition and petty rivalry.

"Look, Sir. Can't I just go and get Juliet?" he asked finally.

"Your wife won't be going anywhere, Parlour," Sewell replied briskly.

"What! Surely she's not…"

"You know the protocol," Sewell interrupted curtly. "Nobody'll be let out of there till we've questioned everyone and ascertained precisely what happened."

"Can't I at least talk to her… in my marital capacity, Sir?" Parlour begged.

Sewell hesitated. He couldn't afford to stand here wasting precious time arguing with a tenacious little whippet like Parlour. He waved his hand impatiently. "Oh alright. But no snooping around. And leave Blackman to her job – God knows she's waited long enough for this."

"Thank you, Sir," Parlour replied gratefully and returned to his car. But he wasn't happy. *Blackman*, he muttered under his breath, *Damn Blackman.*

⧗⧗⧗

"Mark!" Juliet cried, breaking away from the tearful huddle of female PCC members gathered in the foyer of Zion House. She ran towards her husband. Parlour wrapped his arms around her.

"They said you wouldn't be allowed in!" Juliet said, burying her cheek in his bony chest. "They've got some woman detective on the case!"

"Blackman," Parlour muttered through gritted teeth. "Sewell let me through, so long as I don't get involved!"

"Involved?" Juliet queried, pulling her head apart. "What's there to be involved in? Terence just choked on something, didn't he?"

She searched his eyes. He hesitated, not wanting to lie to his wife.

"They're not sure, Jules. It looks more like he was poisoned."

"Poisoned!"

"Ssh – keep it under your hat!" Parlour hissed.

"What – like rat poison or something?" Juliet whispered dramatically, wide-eyed.

"Possibly," Parlour demurred.

"So it might be murder?" She put her hand to her chest, eyes wide open.

Parlour kissed her pale forehead. "Let's just wait and see, shall we?"

"That means yes, doesn't it?" Juliet said quietly, looking across to a group of men in plain clothing conversing on the far side of the foyer. "That's why that lot are here. We thought it was strange."

"I don't know anymore than you, Jules. I'm not on the case."

"Why ever not?" Juliet exclaimed indignantly, "You'd be ideal! You know – knew - Terence better than any of that lot!"

"That's the problem, darling," Parlour replied ruefully. "I'm an insider, so to speak – and you, my love, if it is murder – are a potential suspect!"

Juliet stood quietly for a moment, frowning as she tried to take it all in.

"Have they questioned you yet?"

Juliet shook her head. "They're going in alphabetical order, so I've got a while yet. They've got the Monkton-Smiths in there at the moment."

Parlour snorted. That was typical Blackman. Her methods were boring and predictable and it gave a potential culprit at the end of the alphabet plenty of time to compose themselves. He would have kept them all guessing.

Parlour frowned. These were his friends, for goodness sake! Perhaps there had been someone else on the property at the time, a caretaker or cleaner or some outside party. But Juliet dashed his hopes on that score. Apparently the vicar had been given a key as there would be no staff on site that Saturday. Beauville had locked them all in for the duration of their meeting on the instructions of the security conscious Business Manager of Zion House, who had suffered one too many unauthorised entries to the property over the years.

"So who's next up?" Parlour asked, trying to work it out in his head.

Juliet motioned to dippy librarian, Olivia Murray, across the foyer. "We were hoping Alex would come and spill the beans."

Alex Miller had presumably gone in just prior to the Monkton-Smiths. Parlour shook his head.

"They won't let anyone who's been questioned talk to you. Forewarned is forearmed and all that." Blackman was predictable in her methods, but she wasn't quite that stupid. He flashed his wife a wicked grin. "Give you a chance to work out your alibi. I could give you a few tips!"

"It's not funny, Mark," Juliet chastised him. "So they think Terence Haynes was murdered!"

"I only said maybe."

"Even so – what a thought!" Her gaze turned to her church friends just yards away. She couldn't even begin to contemplate that one of them could have killed the Commander.

"So when did Haynes die?" Parlour enquired of his wife.

"What?" she turned back to him. "Oh, after lunch…

Juliet explained that the Reverend Martin Beauville had made coffee for them all. Terence Haynes had taken one sip of his before clutching at his throat. He had then turned bright pink and fallen head-first into a plate of eclairs.

She looked at him. "We just thought he'd choked or something. Alex tried the old Häagen-Dasz manoeuvre on him –"

"Heimlich manoeuvre," Parlour corrected her, smiling inspite of himself.

"… but there was no point - he was already dead."

Parlour frowned. "Choked – on coffee? Was he eating one of the cakes with it, or something?"

"I don't think so."

"Didn't anyone else have the coffee?"

Juliet shook her head. "He brings his own, doesn't he? In that stainless steel flask he carries around everywhere."

"Interesting," Parlour mused. "Did he drink it directly from the flask?"

"No… I don't think so. No, he didn't. The vicar did the coffees in the kitchen. He brought Terence's through first, though, so not to mix it up with the others. Poor old Martin's in a real state."

"I bet he is," Parlour replied soberly. It didn't look good for the Vicar. Mind you, anyone could have tampered with that flask, if it *was* poisoning.

"How long will they keep us here?"

"Depends. Something might emerge during questioning."

"But they won't keep us here all night, will they?" Juliet checked, frowning at the thought. It was her birthday on Monday and they had planned celebrating it that weekend at a new Italian restaurant that had just opened in Deverton. She immediately reproached herself for being so callous.

"Shouldn't think so," Parlour replied. "But they'll want you for further questioning at some stage. Look, Jules, I'm going to find out when I can get you out of here."

Flashing his police badge to an unsuspecting member of Billock Police, Parlour ducked below the striped police cordon and made his way towards the conference room. He introduced himself to the unfamiliar officer guarding the door that separated Parlour from the scene of the crime. Detective Constable Dean Morrison from Foxburgh CID was under strict instructions from DCI Sewell not to admit unauthorised officers.

"Look, Dean – I just want a quick decko. I won't interfere with any suspects, I promise." He flashed Morrison his very best Crest Plus smile.

Morrison frowned. It couldn't do any harm, could it? Unaware of Parlour's status as husband to one of the suspects, Morrison cast a quick glance over to his superiors, none of whom were looking his way, before admitting the affable Detective Inspector to the conference room.

Parlour wandered over to the huddle of Scenes of Crime Officers in white overalls at the top end of the room, where Deverton Parish Church PCC had earlier created a makeshift dining area by pushing together two trestle tables. Hunched over the table, his face covered in creamy goo, was the lifeless late middle-aged figure of Falklands veteran Terence Haynes, his bald pate reflecting the bar lighting above.

"No further, please," one of the SOCOs commanded, looking up from his position at Haynes' side.

"Has the pathologist been yet?"

"On his way," one of them grunted. "Another slag's been murdered in Foxburgh – he had to go there first."

The officer was referring to the recent spate of attacks on prostitutes in the borough town .

"What was the cause of death? Poisoning?"

"Reckon," the SOCO replied. "Something in the coffee."

"Suspicious?"

"Possibly. Won't know till Hunter gets here."

"When did it happen?"

"Just after two."

Parlour looked at his wristwatch. It was four-thirty. What had he been doing at two o'clock? Strimming the front hedge, blissfully unaware that Terence Haynes was about to breathe his last.

He looked at Haynes, dressed typically in a sports jacket and chinos, his gleaming brown patent-leather shoes, a snip at £120, testimony to a career in the services. Parlour shook his head in disbelief.

He walked around the huddle surrounding the bizarre death-form at the table and stood at the back of the room, trying to picture the scene in his mind. They'd had a bring-and-share lunch, hadn't they? That's why Juliet had been making quiche at some ungodly hour last night. They'd probably just cleared up the lunch when Martin Beauville, in typical selfless fashion, had offered to do the coffees. He'd brought Terence's special decaff through first. Terence had taken one sip, turned bright pink and nosedived into the dish of eclairs. It would be comical, Parlour grimaced, had this been an episode of *Midsomer Murders,* or some other bantamweight source of televisual escapism, but not real life, with real people – his friends – involved.

It doesn't look good for Martin! Parlour thought. He had tremendous respect for the brilliant young vicar recently appointed to the new parish of Deverton. Martin Beauville was the most upstanding individual he had ever come across. He would not, could not, take the life of a fellow human being. If he had… then Parlour would lose all faith in humankind.

Behind him was a hatch to the kitchen. The doors were open and through the gap Parlour could see another couple of men in overalls taking fingerprints and searching the cupboards.

"Hey Pizza, how goes it?" He was greeted by a rotund man in a double-breasted suit whom Parlour immediately recognised as Adrian Ridings from Police HQ in Foxburgh.

"Hi, Aidy. Long time no see!"

Parlour walked round and entered the kitchen through the side door.

"Nice juicy one we got here," Ridings grinned, who was not a Sensitive New Age Guy, or *snag* as Juliet referred to this postmodern subspecies! "Seems our friend the sailor boy had a bit of a *penchant* for chocolate eclairs! Some might say he would *die* for one!"

"It's not funny, Ade – I knew the guy!" Parlour exclaimed. "Can't believe any of this bunch would do something like this."

"Try telling that to Blackman!" Ridings snickered.

Parlour frowned. He could imagine.

"It could be natural causes," he demurred.

"Yeah and I'm Posh Spice!" Ridings guffawed, his apple-shaped belly laughing with him. "Come off it, Parlour. Health-freak ex-services guy takes one sip of his coffee and keels over at the dinner table. Turns out everyone hated his guts… and that's not suspicious?"

"How do you know everyone hated his guts?" Parlour frowned.

"So you don't deny it, either!" Ridings laughed. "Robins just told me. He's been sat in the interview room with Blackman. They all start off sweet enough, but after a bit of prodding, they spill the beans. All 57 varieties!"

Parlour grimaced. Thinking the best of others was not one of Deverton Parish Church's strong points, excluding the Keltys, of course, whose naivety, in Parlour's opinion, made them a threat to society. Society, in turn, was decidedly threatening to them.

"So have you come to relieve Blackman?" Ridings enquired.

Parlour shook his head. "I've been taken off the case, Ade. My wife was at the meeting here. Conflict of interests and all that."

"Blimey! I forgot you lot were God-Squadders!" He whistled through his teeth. "So Jules is a suspect, too?"

Parlour nodded grimly. "So what's happening? How long till I can take Jules home?"

Ridings informed him that the routine questioning wasn't likely to take much longer, and that Juliet should be free to go fairly soon.

"I doubt they'll be too suspicious of your Missus," Ridings chuckled, "though it is the perfect alibi, being married to a copper!"

"Don't," Parlour groaned.

"So you must have known him quite well, then?" Ridings enquired, stuffing a Werther's Original in his mouth.

"Fairly well. I stayed out his way, to be honest. Pompous old fart. Spent most of his time telling me how to do my job, moaning about the youth of today, bring back military service, ad nauseum. Look, Aidy, gotta go." Parlour had seen Blackman emerge from a room out of the corner of his eye. Before the sergeant on the door could stop him, he had hopped over the cordon on the far side of the room to the corridor where the interviews were being conducted.

"Leigh!"

"Can't talk now, Mark," the forty something female detective replied brusquely, pushing open the door of the Ladies. Parlour followed the tall blonde woman into the toilets.

"What the…" she exclaimed.

"Leigh, listen, I can help you," Parlour hissed, grabbing her forearm. She shook him off with ease. Leigh Blackman wasn't someone you messed with. A couple of years Parlour's senior, she had kept in trim with frequent lunchtime trips to the multi-gym at Foxburgh Police HQ.

"Mark, I'm sure the Sewer's already told you - this one is mine."

"Look Leigh, you're ambitious, this is your first big case round these parts, I understand that, but my wife's on the committee, for Cripe's sake"

"And you want to protect her, Mark. It's natural. Primeval, in fact."

"Leigh, I *know* these people!" Parlour exclaimed in desperation. "They're my neighbours, friends some of them!"

"Which is exactly why it's inappropriate to involve you on the case."

"I can help you out, though!" Parlour protested. "Save you hours dicking around finding out about these people!"

But Blackman was resolute. "I'm just obeying instructions, Mark. You best leave me alone… or I'll have you arrested for loitering in the Ladies bogs!"

She slammed the cubicle door in his face.

"You want to impress the Sewer – I understand that –" Parlour persisted, leaning on the door. "I can help you on the case. I don't want the glory, I just want…"

"La La La La," DI Blackman sang at the top of her voice, relieving herself.

"To help…"

2

The Reverend Martin Beauville lay prostrate on the recently laid laminate floor of the purpose-built Deverton Vicarage. He could feel the muscles of his lower back contracting from the stress of the afternoon. He tried his usual relaxation technique, focusing on his favourite painting hung high on the facing wall. An idyllic village scene by an obscure Italian artist, it was one of the few objects, alongside his trusty leather bound Bible and a bundle of letters from his late father, that had lasted the course with Martin Charles Lucian Beauville. Generally speaking, he was no hoarder of material objects, but this painting had survived the countless moves around the country he had endured, firstly as a student, and later as a curate. Its particular value lay in its ability to soothe the nerves, which inevitably got frayed by the constant assault on his physical and mental resources by a diverse congregation of worshippers, not to mention some of the unchurched parishioners within his pastoral remit.

He focused on the ramshackle bridge and the water trickling below, but it was no good. He was unable to transcend the here and now and enter into the comforting ochre and beige world of the medieval Umbrian village. The alarming vision of Terence Haynes turning a darker shade of red just across the table from him, and the perhaps equally frightening sight of DI Blackman's eyes narrowing sceptically across another table as he gave his account of events at Zion House that day, just wouldn't fade into the background.

Beauville bent his knees and drew them to his chest. He repeated the exercise several times, and the pain in his back eased slightly. But still his mind wouldn't shut down. Later on he would try and get hold of Peter, a solicitor friend from his curacy days in the Midlands. He would be able to advise him as to the precariousness of his plight. But until then he would have to talk to a silent, but no less trusty friend.

Beauville slid his white collar out of his clerical shirt, loosened it at the neck and settled into his favourite chair. He bowed his head.

⧗ ⧗ ⧗

"Wow, I'm glad today's nearly over!" Juliet exclaimed, accepting a glass of white wine from her husband with some relief at eight-thirty that evening. She grimaced. The Frascati 2001 vintage, of which they had a caseload under the stairs, was far too sweet. She really should sample some more *adult* wines some time and donate this glorified Alcopop to the school bazaar. They had decided against the Italian Restaurant in the precinct, opting for a takeaway pizza instead. News of the death of Terence Haynes would sure to have spread like wildfire, and *La Dolce Vita* would not be a safe environment to ponder the events of the day. Besides, it didn't seem right, somehow, to be celebrating Juliet's life when that of Terence Haynes had been so recently snuffed out.

Parlour shook his head, putting some plates in the oven. "I just can't take it in."

"Oh come on! You must be used to this sort of thing in your job!" Juliet protested, sipping at her wine.

"Not in my own backyard, though! And especially not in church circles! It has that unreal feeling about it, like when you see someone you know on the TV. Cod, it's a *bona fide* whodunnit… and our friends are the suspects!"

"They're acquaintances, most of them, darling. Only Martin and Lindsay I'd call friends."

"Andrew and I got on quite well, I suppose," Parlour mused. "And you know how highly I rate Martin as a person. However…"

"However what?" Juliet queried, raising her eyebrows.

"He *will* be number one suspect, darling," Parlour informed her soberly.

"But he wouldn't…"

"He did the coffees, Jules,"

"But you don't think…" Juliet faltered, looking troubled.

"Of course I don't – but he *did* serve Terence the dodgy coffee." Parlour frowned then held his hands up. "OK, OK, I don't believe for one minute Martin did anything, at least not intentionally, I just felt I should put my objective hat on."

"But anyone could have – if it was murder – put something in his flask!" Juliet protested, refusing to entertain the idea that the dashing young vicar had been implicated in any shape or form. "We all went in the kitchen at some stage, to put our food in the fridge. Lindsay went in during the worship to get Daniel a glass of water… oh no!"

Parlour put a restraining hand on his wife's forearm. "Darling, perhaps we shouldn't get too carried away. Here's us pointing the finger, but we don't even know that it *was* murder. We won't be sure till Forensic have examined the contents of his stomach. He could've just choked or something."

"But he wasn't eating at the time," Juliet protested. "He just took a sip of his coffee then grabbed his throat and fell headfirst into the cakedish!"

Juliet laughed inspite of herself. "Oh golly, I mustn't…"

Parlour smiled wanly. "It does have comic value, it can't be denied."

They paused for a moment to compose themselves.

"He could have suffered a huge heart attack," Parlour proposed unconvincingly, not quite ready to accept the awful truth just yet.

"But he was so healthy!" Juliet exclaimed. "Only ate wholemeal bread, drank decaff coffee, walked his dog to the newsagents every morning!"

"It's not unheard of. He could've had a dodgy ticker," Parlour countered.

"He was in the navy!" Juliet protested. "He was as fit as a fiddle!"

"So? Look, maybe he was really stressed out about something – you know how he got his y-fronts in a twist about the slightest thing!"

"This isn't happening," Juliet told herself in vain. The doorbell rang. "That'll be Gianni with the pizzas."

Parlour went to the door with his wallet.

"They've upgraded you, I see!" he smiled, noting the shiny new red Piaggio moped in the driveway. He paid the teenager then returned indoors, the gnat-like droning of the scooter tailing off into the distance.

"Happy Birthday, darling," Parlour smiled, laying the two pizzas down on the table. They'd been doing a *buy one get one free,* or BOG OF!, as Juliet gleefully termed it, at the pizzeria that month. Parlour, who was not easily taken in by such commercial gimmickry, understood that a single pizza was grossly overpriced, thereby enabling them to make the second from the profits.

Parlour appeared with the pizza slice. "Tell you what – let's try and forget today or at least put it on the back burner. This was supposed to be your evening."

He topped up her wine. "Cheers!"

"Cheers," Juliet said feebly, clinking her glass against his.

"Shall I put the coffee on?" Parlour asked innocently.

Juliet shuddered, taking the pizza slice to their pepperoni and anchovy feasts.

⧗⧗⧗

Flippin' eck, what a day! Leigh Blackman exhaled, kicking off her black loafers and sinking back in her beaten brown leather sofa, laying her aching feet heavily on the scratched beech coffee table.

She checked her mobile, but no news from Forensics yet. She closed her eyes for a second and relaxed her shoulders but it was no good, her stomach was telling her it was time for action. Blackman threw her jacket on the chair and undid a few buttons on her rather tight light blue blouse. What microwavable delight awaited her tonight, if that wasn't a contradiction in terms?

The divorcee rummaged around in the freezer cabinet, in a manner befitting individuals of her recently nullified marital status and pulled out a Balti with pilau rice. That would fill a gap, for the time being at least. She had a small tub of cherry tomatoes in the fridge, they would have to do as a side salad.

Blackman poured out a German *Weissbier* and threw it eagerly towards the back of her throat. She was unlikely to be called out again tonight, in anycase, one little beer, albeit 5% alcohol content, wouldn't hurt.

It was some forty minutes later, as she was congratulating herself on correctly answering the sixty-four thousand pound question on *Millionaire*, that Blackman took a phone-call from Billock CID.

An initial investigation had been made of the dead man's body and it had emerged, somewhat surprisingly, that Terence Haynes had died of an anaphylactic shock, almost certainly brought on by the ingestion of peanuts. Traces of salted peanut had been found in his gut alongside a small amount of black filter coffee, egg and cress sandwiches and raw carrot. Samples had been taken from table remains of the latter two foodstuffs, and neither were found to contain peanut. Haynes's flask cup, on the other hand, revealed clear traces of peanut. It was probable that someone had got wind of the fact that Haynes was allergic to peanuts and had popped some in his flask as it was highly unlikely they had made their way accidentally into the receptacle.

The probability of this being murder was enhanced by the yet quirkier discovery of a tampon in the medipouch beneath Haynes's waistband which would normally house a fully functioning *Epipen®* , an instant source of adrenalin for those suffering from such potentially fatal allergies.

It seemed that the perpetrator of this evil and cynical crime had made doubly sure Haynes would meet with death through replacing his medication with a similarly shaped object, in this case a Melrose own brand applicator tampon.

Blackman shook her head in disbelief. Not a lot fazed her these days, but this really took the nut free biscuit!

⧖ ⧖ ⧖

Two pizzas, a pot of Häagen-Dazs and a bottle of replacement wine later, Parlour and his wife settled down in front of the TV with mugs of tea. Juliet had borrowed the latest Tom Hanks film from Deverton Rentals – some far-fetched romantic piffle to take their minds off the awful events of the day, which in quite a different way, were just as unbelievable. But they had only got half way through the trailers when the telephone rang.

"Can't you ignore it?" Juliet grumbled.

"No can do," Parlour said regretfully, sliding off the sofa and grabbing the cordless phone from the table. He disappeared into the kitchen with it.

"Who was that?" Juliet asked, as Parlour flopped his lanky body back down on the sofa.

"Dave Robins – Blackman's sidekick."

"And?"

"You mustn't leave the area."

"What?"

Parlour hit the pause button on the DVD player and turned to his wife. "They've examined Haynes. He was poisoned, alright."

Juliet gasped. Though they'd suspected as much, it was still awful to hear it confirmed.

"Poisoned? Was it cyanide or something?"

"You've been watching too much *Miss Marple*, darling," Parlour grimaced. "Just common old salted peanuts."

"Peanuts?" Juliet echoed rather gormlessly.

"Anaphylaxis, Jules. Turns out old Terence was allergic to peanuts. They reckon they must have been in his coffee. He took one sip and suffered a massive anaphylactic shock."

"That's why he turned mottled pink and started grabbing his throat!" Juliet exclaimed, who was aware of such allergies from her work with young people. "But couldn't it have just been in the cakes or something? Perhaps it was an accident?"

"He only had the sandwiches and carrots he brought himself, and they found no traces of peanut in either. Anyway, you just said yourself he wasn't eating at the time. He wouldn't have had a delayed reaction. There must have been traces of peanut in his coffee. Perhaps there were bits of nut in his cup to start off with," Parlour proposed. "Maybe the last people there didn't wash up properly or something."

Juliet shook her head vigorously. "No, he always drunk directly from his flask cup. I guess we just thought he was saving on washing up or something, now I suppose we know why."

"Hmm." Parlour stared at her grimly. "That would certainly point to deliberate contamination then… which would be murder."

There was a pause as both of them took it in.

Parlour described to Juliet how the pathologist, Hunter, had found traces of peanut in the contents of Haynes' stomach and that Haynes's tongue and throat had swollen up, indicating a severe anaphylactic shock. The manner of his death and the presence of peanut in his gut clearly pointed to an anaphylactic reaction to his coffee. Whatsmore, an Epipen® pouch had been found discretely concealed inside the waistband of Haynes's trousers, confirming the Commander had indeed been diagnosed with a potentially life-threatening allergy of some description. Parlour had not been informed as yet of the presence of an *ersatz* Epipen® in the pouch as his wife, or rather his wife's feminine hygiene product preference, would be under investigation along with those of the other members of Deverton PCC present at Zion House that day.

"His blasted decaff!" Juliet exclaimed, once Parlour had informed her of the pathologist's findings. "So somebody must've slipped a peanut in his flask…"

"Unless Martin put it in his flask cup after he poured the coffee into it…" Parlour said soberly.

"Mark!" Juliet exclaimed indignantly. But indignation soon turned to fear. Nothing seemed certain at the moment. Their cosy new life in the designer village of Deverton had been turned on its head by the shocking events of the day. "But wouldn't the peanut have sunk to the bottom?" she frowned.

"They would have crushed up a good number, I expect, darling, just to be on the safe side –," Parlour winced. "But if Terence was that badly allergic to the things, just the slightest whiff of one would have been enough to kill him. People with the allergy have been known to die in aircrafts without even touching a peanut, purely from the aroma of in-flight peanuts supplied by the airline. I was reading up on it just the other week in the *Observer*, after that actor chap dropped dead at the BAFTAs. Anyway, we'll find out when Forensic take a look at the lunch dishes. That'll show whether the peanuts were added to his flask, which I suppose anyone could have done, or whether they were popped into his flask cup at the last minute – which only Martin could have done."

"But surely Martin wouldn't…" Juliet began, her voice trailing off.

"Of course he wouldn't, darling," Parlour said reassuringly, ashamed that he had wavered earlier. "Martin Beauville's a top man. He would never do a thing like that. I'd bet my life on it."

Juliet shivered. "Don't say things like that."

They paused for a moment.

"So it must have been one of us," she surmised.

"Not necessarily," Parlour replied. "Somebody could have contaminated the coffee before he even got to Zion House yesterday."

Juliet shook her head. "No – that wouldn't work."

"Why not?" Parlour challenged her.

"He drank from it earlier."

"Are you sure?" Parlour frowned.

"Yes," Juliet replied, thinking hard. "We had morning coffee when we got there. He would have keeled over then, if it was in his flask."

"Yeah, he would have," Parlour agreed. "Are you sure he had decaff first thing?"

Juliet snorted. "This is Terence Haynes we're talking about! Routine is – was - his middle name!"

"Perhaps they had decaff at Zion House. Perhaps whoever did the coffees then used that. Who did the coffees first thing, anyway?"

Juliet frowned. "Lara, I think. I'm not 100% sure. We'd all just arrived and were chatting and stuff, you know. No, she wouldn't do that. She knows what he's like. Fastidious. Would only drink his posh coffee from the flask. Brings the thing to every damn PCC meeting, doesn't he?"

"I suppose so," Parlour agreed. Still, might be worth following up.

"Anyway, he'd know the difference," Juliet continued. "They always stock the cheapest stuff at these Christian places, or that nasty Nicaraguan Fair Trade muck! It wouldn't be Melrose Finest Blend!"

Parlour had to admit she had a point.

"So whoever did this knew about Terence's peanut allergy," Juliet stated.

"Yes," Parlour nodded slowly. "Did you know he was allergic?"

Juliet shook her head. "I've never heard him mention it. He doesn't wear one of those bracelets they're supposed to wear and obviously nobody would have spotted the Epipen® thingy, if he kept it down his trousers."

Parlour informed her that it was concealed just below the waistband but clearly Haynes hadn't had time to access it – an act that, unknown as yet to Parlour, would have proven futile.

"Don't only young adults and kids suffer from peanut allergy, anyway?" Juliet persisted. "I thought it was one of those modern phenomena like house dust and glutin intolerance, that older people seem immune to."

"Not necessarily," Parlour demurred, "It can onset later in life. Though it's still pretty unusual," he conceded.

"The peanuts couldn't have got into the flask or the cup by accident, then?" Juliet frowned.

"I doubt it," Parlour said, shaking his head. "You told me his coffee was ready to drink, he didn't add milk or sugar to it, so it couldn't have been peanuts in the milk jug or sugar pot, or on the teaspoon. I guess if there are traces of peanut on the worksurfaces or on other dishes, there's a chance it somehow got in his coffee. We'll just have to wait and see what Forensic come up with. But if they find traces of peanut in the flask, then it pretty much points to murder."

Juliet frowned. "I don't recall there being any peanuts on the table. Or anything nutty tasting, for that matter, either."

"You'd be surprised how many dishes do contain peanut extract," Parlour informed her, "And I guess his cup could have brushed on one of the cakes or something, those éclairs he fell into, for example. But I can't see Blackman taking that line."

"So what's she like – this Blackman woman?" Juliet asked, curling up on the easy chair opposite him with her mug of tea.

"Didn't she interview you?" Parlour frowned.

Juliet shook her head. "I had two men. A DS Sheron and a coloured chap."

"Tall with a beard?"

She nodded.

"Lerwick from Foxburgh. Doesn't mess around." Parlour settled back down on the sofa and put his feet up on the coffee table. "Leigh Blackman's a good enough cop. Lacks imagination, though. She can be quite blinkered to all the options - makes an assumption then digs like crazy to substantiate her case. Not too hot on lateral thinking. But most murders are pretty clearcut affairs, anyway. Whodunnits are just TV fodder - usually."

"I meant, what's she like generally? What does she look like? How old?"

"What starsign?" Parlour teased.

"Shut it. You know I don't read that rubbish."

"Early forties. Shoulder-length blonde hair. Bit scraggy. Could brush up well, but smokes too much – looks like Madge Bishop, definitely no Harold on the scene, though!"

"Unmarried?"

"Divorced. Husband left her – he had an affair. Said if she could have an affair with Foxburgh Police Headquarters, he could sleep with his secretary!"

"Ouch!" Juliet sympathised. As a teacher, she knew it was not always easy to get away from the job. But professional dedication was hardly justification for philandery on his part. Fortunately for Juliet, Parlour was in no position to protest at her onerous workload, frequently having to stay late to complete paperwork.

"You'll see her soon enough, anyway," Parlour grimaced. "I have no doubts she'll want to have a pop at you, if only to get at me... she'll probably meet you at the school gates on Monday!"

"Poop, I hope not," Juliet frowned, repeating her favourite *ersatz* expletive. "I've got a mountain of reports to do tomorrow night."

"Wonder if there's church tomorrow?" Parlour mused.

"Doubt it," Juliet replied. "Unless they send the curate over from St Jude's like they did when Martin went ski-ing. It would hardly be appropriate for Martin to lead the service, in the circumstances."

Parlour nodded in agreement. He wondered whether they might even take the step of closing the church for the time being. After all, if this was murder, and it was looking increasingly likely, Deverton Parish Church could well find itself the focal point of public and press interest in the unsavoury matter.

"Think I'll give it a miss," Juliet stated. "Probably need a police escort, anyway!"

"You've got one!" Parlour laughed.

"Will you – go to church?"

"Probably will, actually," Parlour nodded. "Maintain your innocence and all that!"

"Shut-up!" Juliet smacked his arm.

"Might do some subtle digging of my own, since I'm not allowed near the police station!"

"Mark!" Juliet exclaimed. "You won't, will you? I thought the Sewer made it clear he'd have your guts if you stuck your nose in!"

Parlour shrugged. "It's in everyone's interest to get whoever did this banged up asap. I've got a headstart on Blackman – she doesn't know the people or the area. Least I know a bit about the church set-up here."

"Mark – please be careful. You could lose your job over this, and then where would we be? I can't pay the mortgage on this place on my salary alone!"

"You can say that again!" Parlour laughed sardonically. It never ceased to amaze him how little Juliet earned for the hours she put in and the responsibilities she carried. As Head of Year 9, widely recognised as the most troublesome yeargroup at Billock Community School, she was in overall charge of some 180 pupils. She was also second in department in the Modern Languages section. If Billock Community School was a commercial enterprise, she'd be on 40k minimum, not the paltry twenty something she brought home now.

"Jules, I'll be careful, I promise. Tell me who was there, all in all." Parlour grabbed his Personal Digital Assistant off the table and started tapping away.

"Well - me, obviously, Martin Beauville, Terence Haynes, of course, Rose Passmore, Lindsay Briscoe, Olivia Murray, Jason Jarvis, Alex Miller, Mavis Wagstaff, Daniel and Christine Kelty, Andrew and Lara Monkton-Smith… oh, and Nicky No Knickers."

Parlour grinned at Juliet's disparaging name for the brunette twenty-something whose job it was to take minutes at meetings of the Parochial Church Council. He entered their names into his PDA. "Anyone else present – employees of Zion House, for example?"

Juliet shook her head. "Martin picked the key up on Friday afternoon, the caretaker was away today. There were no other parties booked for the weekend."

Parlour tapped some more information into one of his more useful gadgets.

"Mark – these people are our brothers and sisters in Christ!" Juliet protested in a pious manner that didn't quite become her.

"One of them is a Judas, my love," Parlour replied in part. He stood up. "And I intend to find out who's got the silver!"

3

Of course, news of Terence Haynes' suspected murder had spread like foot and mouth through the towns of Deverton and Lexington Green. However, the Vicar of St Jude's in Lexington Green, the Reverend Timothy Simmons, had only briefly alluded in his service to the sudden death of the much respected warden of Deverton Parish Church, Commander Terence Haynes, recommending the congregations of Deverton and St Jude's did not indulge in idle speculation, but instead left it to the police to conclude their investigations. His request was in vain, however, as there was only one topic of conversation on the lips of the parishioners that morning, namely:- who put peanuts in Haynes's coffee? And, perhaps more pertinently, who knew about Haynes's allergy?

Only the dazzling white Keltys refused to indulge, referring only indirectly to the events of yesterday by pointing out the amazing grace of God and His forgiveness to all who come to Him with a repentant heart.

"Our Lord himself, whilst dying on the cross, promised a murderer a place in heaven," Daniel Kelty said piously, as Rose Passmore and Lindsay Briscoe remarked on how long Beauville had taken to make the coffee. DS Robins from Police HQ in Foxburgh had telephoned all those present at Zion House yesterday, requesting not only that they remain in the area, but also that they kept details of Terence Haynes' death to themselves. Unsurprisingly, however, the horrible truth had been leaked. Parlour suspected dotty Mavis Wagstaff was responsible, or PC Tucker's somewhat talkative wife, Vicky, known at Billock Police Station as the Foxburgh Herald. Vicky Tucker was the main obstacle standing between Paul Tucker and promotion to Sergeant.

Suddenly the lanky figure of Jason Jarvis, the insurance salesman who shared a three bedroom semi with Alex Miller and Nicky Ellery on Deverton Estate, came bounding up to the little huddle of PCC members gathered outside the modern church building. Perhaps surprisingly, Foxburgh CID had elected not to close down the parish church, allowing services to proceed as normal – or as normally as could be expected in the highly unusual circumstances.

Apparently Leigh Blackman and Dave Robins had just pulled up outside the vicarage.

"Poor Martin," Parlour said soberly.

"What do you think, Mark?" Jarvis queried, turning to the detective. "You must have some inside knowledge! Did the divine Martin Beauville finally have enough of the Wind Commander bossing him around and slipped some peanuts in his coffee?"

"He was navy, not RAF," Parlour corrected him, though he had to admit, the nickname had been highly apt for Haynes with his hot-tempered rantings. "And he was a Commander, in any case."

Parlour shook his head. "If only I did know, Jase. I'm being kept well and truly in the dark on this one. Conflict of interests, and all that."

"Shame!"

"I can't imagine he did, though," Parlour added. "Martin Beauville strikes me somehow as being above such acts."

"The Archangel Beauville!" Jarvis giggled, clasping his hands together and making a soppy face heavenwards.

"I know what you mean," Rose Passmore added, ignoring the callow youth at her side. "He has something of the divine countenance about him. Surprising in a vicar," she added darkly.

"Unfortunately, that's not the attitude Blackman will take," Parlour replied wistfully.

"And hasn't, by the looks of it," Jason Jarvis added.

"Gosh, I wonder who's next in line for a home visit today?" Rose Passmore wondered.

"I have a sneaking suspicion who," Parlour muttered, and left them to their musings.

⧗⧗⧗

Ten minutes later, Parlour's fears were confirmed as he pulled into Spatchcock Drive. Leigh Blackman's dark red Vauxhall was parked up on the pavement outside his front door. Parlour frowned and kicked the back tyre of the saloon as he squeezed between car and hedge. What was wrong with pulling up against the kerb like most normal people? It felt like an act of contempt.

"Hello, darling," Parlour said, greeting Juliet with a kiss on the lips.

"Mark, the…"

"Leigh Blackman's here, I know," Parlour interrupted. "Recognised the car on the *pavement* outside."

"Good afternoon, Parlour," DI Leigh Blackman said in her husky smoker's voice, emerging from the living room and ignoring the pointed comment. "I was just going to ask your wife a few questions about yesterday. Won't you join us?"

"Is that allowed?" Parlour enquired archly.

"Routine questioning, that's all. Of all who knew Terence Haynes. We're just trying to…"

"Build up a profile of him, yes yes, I know the spiel, too," Parlour interrupted brusquely. "What have you done with Robins?"

"Sent him off to Mavis Wagstaff's."

"What's he done to annoy you?" Parlour laughed dryly. Mavis Wagstaff, hard of hearing and suffering from what was tactfully termed "confusion" these days, was not the sharpest knife in the drawer. He opted for his favourite Ikea Z-chair.

"Don't you think Jules went through enough yesterday? It is Sunday, after all!"

"Exactly! Best day for getting hold of people."

"Heathen!" Parlour muttered.

"It's OK, Mark," Juliet said quietly. "I can't stop thinking about what happened to Terence, anyway, so I might as well talk about it. Might even help."

Juliet had tossed and turned and pillow-buffed all night.

"She's alright, your wife," Blackman said gruffly, as Juliet disappeared to make some more tea.

"Hands off, she's mine," Parlour grinned, relaxing a little.

"That's what I can never work out about you, Parlour," Leigh Blackman commented. "Call yourself a God-Squadder and you can be as base as the rest of us!"

"Only Christ was without blemish," Parlour smiled.

"Oh spare me the religious rhetoric!" Blackman moaned. "I had enough from bloody Sonny and Cher yesterday!"

Parlour grinned. "So you've seen the Keltys? I'll have you know they're good friends of ours!"

"Liar!" Blackman laughed. He laughed, too.

"OK, so they're not my cup of *PG*, but they're pretty sound underneath all the fluffy bunny Jesus Loves You stuff. Can't imagine either of them bumping off old Terence!"

"Don't judge a Bible by its cover and all that," Blackman mused darkly.

"Is that why you spent the morning at Martin Beauville's?" Parlour enquired.

"How do you know?" Blackman frowned.

"You were spotted," Parlour replied. "Can't do anything round here without the old nets twitching. We have the nation's highest percentage of Neighbourhood Watch co-ordinators per capita in Deverton, you know!"

"I'll bear it in mind!" Blackman laughed throatily. Parlour looked at her side on. She wasn't beyond redemption if she would only pack in the fags and visit a good hairdresser. Cod, he was beginning to sound like one of those TV makeover bitches!

Juliet returned with a mug of tea for her husband then sank back down in the saggy easy chair.

Blackman opened her notebook and confirmed that Parlour had dropped Juliet off at Zion House at approximately 8.50 the previous morning. Juliet had then greeted those already present, namely Martin Beauville, Terence Haynes, the Monkton-Smiths, the Keltys and Mavis Wagstaff, before proceeding to the kitchen to put a cheese and cucumber quiche in the fridge.

Juliet nodded.

"And you say Terence Haynes' flask was stood on the worktop by the sink next to a few packets of biscuits?" Blackman checked.

"Yes – I remember because it always makes me laugh, how fastidious he is – was."

"Fastidious – that word keeps coming up," Blackman mused, making a note. "And then, what happened?"

Juliet explained that the remaining members of the Church Council had gradually drifted in, each stopping to put their dishes in the fridge or on the kitchen worktop. At about 9.15, Martin Beauville had banged on the table to call them to order and initiate proceedings.

"And was everyone there at that time?"

"Yes."

"Nobody was in the kitchen or out of the room?" Blackman checked.

"No – we were all there. He checked us off on his list."

"Odd, if there were so few of you!" Blackman mused.

"Oh, he did it for Nicky's sake. She's pretty new to this minute taking business. She doesn't know everyone's surnames yet, so Martin thought it was a good way of helping her out, I expect."

"This Nicky Ellery girl," Blackman frowned. "Don't get me wrong, but why would…"

"A bit of strumpet like her want to sit on the church council with a bunch of old crustaceans?" Parlour grinned.

"Oy!" Juliet pulled a face at her husband.

"She did it for a dare," Juliet explained to the slightly incredulous Inspector. She informed Leigh Blackman that Alex Miller, Jason Jarvis and Nicky Ellery had made a bet involving an unknown cash amount as to who could stand being on the committee the longest. It was a big joke between the three of them. Apparently the Keltys and Rose Passmore had kicked up a fuss about the gambling aspect of the joke, but Martin Beauville had felt it was in the church's interests to have younger views represented on the Council, and had turned a blind eye. Besides Nicky Ellery, for all her shortcomings, was a very able secretary.

Blackman made a note of this. "I see. Then what happened – after the vicar had taken the register?"

Juliet decided to rise above the sarcasm. She replied that Lara Monkton-Smith had offered to make some coffee while Daniel and Christine led the others in musical worship.

"So she made the coffee while you were all singing in the other room?" Blackman checked.

"Yes – so the coffee would be ready in time for the first session," Juliet explained.

"Session?" Blackman enquired, wondering what on earth people got up to at meetings such as this and imagining some kind of séance-like affair behind bad seventies curtains.

Juliet explained that Martin Beauville had called the meeting to impart his vision for evangelising Deverton Estate through a leaflet drop, inviting the locals to a *Cheese'n'Chardonnay* at the vicarage. He had used the first session to outline his plans, then they had split up into small groups to discuss practicalities and to pray. After that, the groups were to feedback to one another. This had lasted until 12.30, whereupon they had sung a few more songs before putting some tables together and bringing the food out of the kitchen. They had then eaten on schedule at one o'clock.

Blackman smirked to herself, taking a few more notes. "So going back to morning coffee – how long was Lara Monkton-Smith in the kitchen?"

"Oh, only about ten minutes. We only use the small kettles for PCC gatherings. There's no need to fill the urn."

"You've used that venue before, then?" Blackman enquired. This was new to her.

Juliet nodded. Zion House was the only place of its kind in the area. The Church Centre at St Jude's was always booked out on Saturdays for weddings, as was frequently the case with church halls belonging to beautiful old churches. It seemed everyone still wanted the picture postcard backdrop, even if the spiritual significance of the building and the ceremony were lost on them. Sundays were naturally out for meetings, since most members of the Council would be involved in services in some capacity.

"And who would have been to Zion House before?"

"Oh, most of us," Juliet replied. "We've had meetings there before, as Deverton PCC. I've been there when we were part of St Jude's, too, as have the Keltys and the Monkton-Smiths."

"They went to St Jude's too?" Blackman asked.

"Most of us did. Except Rose possibly, oh, and Nicky Ellery. She only became a Christian recently through *Alpha*."

"Alpha?" Blackman looked baffled. This was a whole new world to her.

Juliet looked incredulous. "Haven't you seen the posters? They're all over the place – there's one on the big roundabout as you head into Billock town centre!"

Blackman still looked blank.

"Well, anyway, it's a course run by the church to introduce people to the Christian faith. It's hoped they'll become born-again Christians through it and get integrated into the church."

"So a kind of recruitment drive by the Church of England?" Blackman enquired.

Juliet frowned. "Not quite as cynical. And it's not just the Church of England that runs the courses. There's probably one at a venue near you," she added rather wickedly for good measure.

"And you said Rose Passmore probably hadn't been to Zion House before either?" Blackman continued regardless.

"Yes. She hasn't lived in the area that long. Deverton Parish Church is a church plant, you see."

Blackman didn't see. Parlour came to the rescue this time. "A church plant is when a church gets a calling to set up a sister church nearby. Usually because it's grown too large, or there's a specific need for another church in a certain area."

"OK." Blackman was beginning to realise Parlour might indeed prove a useful ally in this particular case. "So everyone would be familiar with the layout of the building, except perhaps Rose Passmore?"

Juliet shook her head. "Jason, Alex and Nicky haven't been there before, I don't think, being new on the council."

"OK...," Blackman scribbled. "You said Lara Monkton-Smith made the coffees – nobody helped her?"

Juliet shook her head and replied that it was quite a small kitchen. It was easier just to perform such tasks alone, and besides, the others were fully engaged in worship next door.

"I gather Terence Haynes was the only one there who drank decaff?" Blackman enquired.

Juliet nodded. "And only his own decaff. Some posh brand he got on mail order. I gather he bought a lot of food and drink by post. His cleaner was always banging on about how many parcels he had delivered. Now I guess we know why - I suppose he had to be ever so careful with such a bad allergy. No wonder that flask went everywhere with him."

"Did Lara bring the flask out to him?"

Juliet shook her head and replied that Lara had poured it into his flask cup for him in the kitchen and had brought the cup itself out to him.

Blackman looked puzzled for a moment.

"Terence would have expected that," Juliet explained. "He liked his coffee served to him, that was right and proper. And preferably by a woman - he was a bit – you know – towards us. Saw us all as subservient."

"Shame I didn't have the pleasure of his company," Blackman said darkly. She would have enjoyed trading verbal blows with a bit of chauvinistic old uniform like Terence Haynes. "And did he remark on his coffee – that it was different in any way?"

Juliet shook her head. "No. But he would definitely have noticed, if it wasn't his own coffee. It had a very distinctive aroma, apparently. Jason Jarvis tried to hoodwink him once by swapping it for a different brand. You know, for a laugh, a kind of *Pepsi Challenge* to test him - but he knew straight away. I understand now why he got so cross about it. It seemed a pretty harmless scam at the time."

"So did he get his coffee brought through with the others?" Blackman enquired.

"No – Lara brought it through first while the kettle was boiling."

"I see." Blackman scribbled some more. Juliet added that Lara had brought the other hot drinks through on a tray during the worship.

"What – thirteen cups?" Blackman did some rapid calculations.

"She made two trips," Juliet explained.

"Nobody helped her?"

"Nobody went near the kitchen except Lara during the worship," Juliet confirmed.

"Did anyone go into the kitchen during the morning session?" Blackman enquired.

Juliet nodded. Practically everyone had entered the kitchen at some stage, it appeared, either to return dirty mugs or fetch glasses of water. Christine Kelty had brought a casserole with her that required a few hours in the oven, and had kept popping into the kitchen to check on its progress. Juliet herself had gone in to shut the kitchen window, as a cat had been sniffing around outside. And at lunchtime, naturally, everyone had been getting dishes out of there to put on the tables.

"So, in your view, anyone could have tampered with Haynes' flask between Lara Monkton-Smith serving morning coffee and Martin Beauville handing him the second cup at two o'clock?"

"Yes. I suppose so."

"Great!" Blackman sighed sarcastically, slamming her notebook shut.

"Look, why don't you stay for Sunday lunch, Leigh?" Juliet suggested. "We could continue this over lunch. There's plenty to go around, and I'm sure you must be hungry."

Blackman looked taken-aback, as did Parlour. Then he relaxed into a smile as Juliet winked at him. What a prize asset she was. She'd have Blackman eating out their hands, almost literally, before the day was up, enabling him to get a foot in the door of the murder inquiry. Smart move.

"We needn't talk shop the whole time," Juliet cajoled her.

"Actually, I was hoping you could tell me about Terence Haynes," Blackman said rather sheepishly.

"So you'll stay?"

"Please. The Monkton-Smiths live the next street up, don't they? It would be quite handy for me."

Parlour confirmed that they lived in Venison Row.

"Doesn't their house back onto the vicarage?" Blackman inquired.

"Not directly," Parlour replied. He explained that the vicarage was visible, all the same, from the Monkton-Smith's back garden and that the more catty members of Deverton's congregation reckoned that was the reason why Lara had persuaded Andrew to move there. His preferred option had been a traditional country cottage in Lexington Green, but Lara had argued that he would never get beyond the garden, horticulture not home *couture* being his forte. So instead they had moved to a brand new four bedroom detached, with sun terrace, in the exclusive Venison Row development.

"When was this?" Blackman asked.

"Shortly after Martin was licensed in November last year."

"Interesting…" Blackman mused.

"Red or white wine with your lamb roast?" Juliet asked, getting up.

"Nothing for me, ta," Blackman replied, waving a hand. "Need to keep a clear head for this afternoon. But I will make use of your front doorstep, if I may."

Parlour refrained from informing her there was a perfectly adequate downstairs toilet as Blackman fumbled in her bag for her cigarettes.

4

Just my luck to get stuck out in suburbia! Dave Robins groaned. He disconsolately dipped his chips in a carton of ketchup at *La Rôtisserie,* Deverton's take on the ubiquitous fast-food joint. What was wrong with bloody McDonalds, anyway, he moaned, considering the small change he had got back from a ten pound note. It had been a bad morning. Trying to elicit straight answers from dotty old ladies was not Dave Robins's idea of fun. More Sun Hill than Caulston CID, Robins could only look enviously at the hub of frenzied activity that was the Foxburgh Red Light Murders incident room. What he wouldn't give to be chasing after nasty mean-faced tarts this week, instead of pootering around bloody Volvoville interviewing a bunch of butter-wouldn't-melt God-squadders.

How come old Pizza face hadn't been marched off to Foxburgh? That's what he wanted to know. Surely he would be better getting those skinny pins of his knee-deep in sleaze than fannying around the local area, trying to solve some hopeless domestic from the 70s. For that was the task assigned to Parlour, to revisit an unsolved case nearly three decades old. The father had probably done it anyway, thought Robins. It was usually the case with these isolated farm murders, in Robins's view. Bunch of inbreds. It would be better if Parlour was well out the way, where he wouldn't stick his spotty nose in. Be a good education for him, too, Robins thought, conveniently forgetting that it had been Mark Parlour who'd handled the last murder case in Foxburgh's red light district, involving a couple of pimps and some Class A drugs.

Pulling a face as he eased three soggy slices of gherkin from his Triple-Decker Steakburger with a plastic tea stirrer, Robins flipped his notebook open with the other hand. There was nothing else to read in this glorified burger joint. The decent Sunday papers, the ones packed full of sport and babes, had long since gone walkies. Only the *Torygraph* as he called it, remained and he wasn't about to sully his hands, already greasy from burger fat, with that stuck-up cannon fodder. He supposed they had to cater for that sort in Deverton, though.

He looked over his notes. Mavis Wagstaff, it seemed, had not got off her considerable backside the whole morning, except for a brief excursion to the Ladies. Mavis, as Robins heard in great detail, found it difficult to manoeuvre herself into those tiny public conveniences, what with her hip and chronic arthritis, and as such, limited herself to just three sips of any beverage in the hope of limiting the likelihood of confronting this obstacle. He'd microwave his cat if she had anything to do with this. She appeared to sit on the Church Council merely for social interaction. There was no hint of malice nor theo-political aspirations behind that verbose exterior and gargantuan posterior.

Nicky Ellery had been an altogether more interesting proposition, and not solely on account of her physical attributes, which, to Robins' chagrin, had not been nearly so well presented on this occasion. Firmly ensconsed in the slobzone that Sunday morning in a loose-fitting sweat-top and combat trousers, there was no sign of that lift and shift thing she'd had on beneath her crop top at Zion House yesterday. She was still, nevertheless, a welcome sight after the milky tea stale wee world of Mavis Wagstaff.

Asked why she wasn't at church that Sunday morning, Ellery had replied, understandably in the circumstances, Robins thought, that she'd had an abdomen full of church life. Indeed, she'd been busy that morning drafting a letter to the Church Council, announcing her non-negotiable resignation as PCC secretary. She'd informed Robins that she wanted nothing more to do with Deverton Parish Church; it "freaked" her out to know one of these so-called Christians had murdered Terence Haynes, whom, whilst not being the most likeable man in the world, was hardly the devil incarnate. Her flatmates, or "Ali and Jase" as she referred to them, had attempted to talk her out of making such a hasty decision, and reneging on their bet, but she was not for turning. She would pay sixty quid anyway just to get away from that bunch of nerds.

It transpired that she had been becoming steadily disillusioned with church life, anyway. While the *Alpha* course she had attended had been fun and dynamic, church, or at least this local branch of the Church of England, was anything but. It seemed to Robins, however, that Deverton Parish Church was quite a happening place!

Nicky intended trying out the curiously named Wineskin Fellowship in Billock, where a couple of her colleagues worshipped on a Sunday night. Robins supposed it might be construed as suspicious, that Nicky Ellery should offer her resignation less than twenty-four hours after Haynes's murder. But not even she would be dumb enough to think she could avoid further questioning in this way.

Robins had also taken the opportunity to touch base with Alex Miller, who was nursing a cold and trying to catch up on some revision for an exam he had later that week. Altogether more level-headed than his curvaceous flatmate, he had nothing interesting to offer Robins in the way of information, and the Detective Constable had left soon after.

As he walked out the restaurant, he caught sight of a headline on the front page of last night's Foxburgh Herald, which was strewn across the pavement outside. *Red Light Killer Has Red Car* was the intriguing header. So the press had got hold of that bit of information. Forensic had found traces of red enamel paint on the clothes of the latest woman killed in Foxburgh's small but thriving red light district. It looked like they had been enticed inside a red vehicle of some description, engaging in a brief struggle before meeting their grisly fate. Their killer also appeared to be an early bird – the time of death on each occasion was put at between four and six am. Robins sighed enviously and returned to his car.

⌛⌛⌛

"Won't there be fingerprints on Terence's flask though – I mean, on the screw top inside?" Juliet enquired, as Blackman tucked into a luscious summer fruits flan Juliet had concocted during her mad cooking frenzy on Friday night. "There'll be tonnes of prints on the outer surface - it got moved around a few times, I should think. But surely the prints on the screw top'll tell you who touched it, besides Lara and Martin?"

"Probably not," Blackman replied. "There was a pair of marigolds lying in the sink. Or they could have used a teatowel."

"Can't you fingerprint the inside of the marigolds?" Juliet asked.

Blackman looked dubious. "Anyone could have put them on to wash their cup up, anyway."

Parlour wondered, given the layout of Zion House, whether it was possible somebody went to the toilet then sneaked into the kitchen from the opposite direction. Blackman conceded that it was certainly feasible. He informed his colleague that he had tried out this route on Saturday, and that it took just under two minutes to exit the meeting room, walk past the toilets, back into the main foyer and down the corridor to the kitchen. Running, the trip would take about half the time, though that was more risky, given the noise factor – unless, of course, the suspect removed their shoes.

"I gave strict instructions for you to be kept away from the scene of the murder on Saturday!" Blackman exclaimed.

"Come on, Leigh! My wife is a suspect in a murder case and you expect me to butt out!"

He had a point, Blackman conceded. "Pardon the question, Juliet, but could you hear a person in the loo? I mean, was the flush audible from the meeting room?"

Juliet laughed. "Yes, it was. It was pretty embarrassing, actually. You could hear the men doing their Niagara Falls thing quite distinctly!"

"Jules!" Parlour exclaimed, putting the wine bottle down. His wife could be rather coarse at times.

"That's why I went during the group work," Juliet continued, ignoring him. "You wouldn't hear someone tinkle while we were all discussing stuff at the tops of our voices. I mean, it's embarrassing, isn't it?"

Juliet didn't seem to be someone who was easily embarrassed, Blackman thought, a fact Parlour could corroborate.

"Who else went to the loo, as far as you can recall?"

Juliet paused for thought. "Mavis a few times. Andrew, bless him, with his prostrate trouble – we call him *Slackbladder*, you know! - he was in there at least twice. Terence – he was loud! Alex and Jason were giggling about it then went in separately afterwards to try and outdo him! Em… Olivia, I think. Oh, Martin did. After his talk."

"Cod, what are you, toilet monitor?" Parlour exclaimed, looking at his wife in surprise.

Blackman grinned. "And was anyone an abnormally long time?"

"You ask the most delicate of questions!" Parlour smirked.

Blackman ignored him as Juliet cocked her head to one side in contemplation.

"Actually, Martin was quite a while. I noticed because he was in our group."

"Could you hear him – er – weeing?"

Juliet shook her head. "But then, you wouldn't, would you – if someone was in there for ages. I mean, he was probably having a …."

"Jules!" Parlour exclaimed.

"Yes, yes, I see," Blackman said hastily, catching her drift. "Still, enough time – potentially – to run round to the front and access the kitchen from the other side."

"I suppose so," Juliet agreed unhappily.

"So you're thinking Martin could have nipped out to the loo, ran round the front, accessed the kitchen from the far end then slipped some peanuts in Terence Haynes' flask?" Parlour surmised, raising his eyebrows.

"Seems far-fetched, I know, Mark, but we have to…"

"Consider every option, I know," Parlour completed the police patter again, not without noting her more relaxed attitude towards him. This was good. Juliet had been right to invite her to stay for lunch.

"Martin Beauville would never murder anyone," Juliet said vehemently. "He's a wonderful, wonderful person."

Blackman just looked rather witheringly at her.

"But why do that, when he had the opportunity later on?" Parlour frowned.

Blackman shrugged. "Take the opportunity while everyone was otherwise engaged? He had the opportunity – two golden ones – that's all I'm saying. And so the meeting went on till when?"

Juliet replied, more calmly this time, that the morning session had finished at one o'clock at which point people had started setting up for lunch.

"Who did what?" Blackman asked. Parlour had to admire her thoroughness.

Juliet paused to think. "Jason and Alex put the tables together and Terence pulled some chairs up. Mavis went to the loo, I think, then just sat in the corner – she felt she would only get in the way, which is a fair estimation. Daniel and Christine were fiddling with some music and overhead acetates – they were going to do a few more songs after lunch. Andrew Monkton-Smith had to nip into Lexington Green to post a parcel – the Post Office shuts at one-thirty, you see."

Blackman pricked up her ears. "Monkton-Smith went out?"

Juliet nodded. Martin Beauville had given him the key to the front door, which had been locked during the meeting to stop intruders entering the property.

"So he could have sneaked in the kitchen whilst you were eating?"

"I suppose so," Juliet shrugged.

"What were the others doing?"

"Em… Martin and Rose were going through the agenda for some meeting they both had to go to – Deanery Synod, I think. The rest of us were in the kitchen dishing out the food and carrying it out to the tables. Nicky was probably adjusting her Wonderbra or something," Juliet added rather bitchily. Parlour snickered.

Blackman frowned. "The rest of you being…"

"Lindsay, Olivia and myself," Juliet elaborated.

"Were any of you alone in the kitchen during that time?"

Juliet puffed her cheeks out as she tried to picture the scene.

"Probably not, but it's difficult to say. The four of us were in and out the whole time."

"Would you say it would be possible for someone to slip some peanuts into Haynes' flask without any of you noticing? If you were in the kitchen, too, I mean?"

"Mmm… I suppose so. It was quite hectic you see. We weren't really watching what each other was doing. It was just a case of shoving stuff on plates and getting it on the table pronto."

"Terrific!" Blackman groaned. "And then you all ate lunch together?"

Juliet nodded. "Andrew Monkton-Smith arrived towards the end of it – at about quarter to two."

"And you were all eating at that time?"

"Yes."

"No-one was in the kitchen?"

"No," Juliet confirmed. "Why would Andrew want to kill Terence, though? He got on well with Haynes – 'bout the only one who did, actually. If Andrew Monkton-Smith was going to murder someone, it'd be the Vicar, not Terence!"

She blushed, aware of her indiscretion.

"I'm sorry," she apologised, looking at her husband.

"You might as well tell her, Jules," Parlour said quietly. "She'll find out sooner or later in this place."

"Tell me what?" Blackman frowned.

Juliet explained that Andrew Monkton-Smith was jealous of any man who stepped within ten feet of Lara and that the real reason he had got himself elected to the Church Council was to keep an eye on her. Though he really didn't have time for the meetings, being a successful partner in a law firm, he couldn't bear to think of her going to all those meetings with handsome younger men like Alex and Martin around, especially given the age difference between the two of them.

"So he was jealous of Martin Beauville?" Blackman surmised.

Juliet nodded. "Lara's a lovely girl, but she couldn't hide the fact that she had a dreadful crush on Martin. Andrew tried to ignore it, but sometimes it really wound him up, the way she looked at him."

Blackman furiously scribbled something in her book and underlined it vigorously.

"Returning to lunch – when was the coffee served?"

"About two," Juliet replied. "But we cleared the plates away and washed up first."

"Who cleared up?" Blackman asked. "Don't tell me, everyone was in and out of the kitchen the whole time!"

"Sorry," Juliet commiserated her. "Lindsay and I washed and dried, but everyone came in at some stage, I should imagine."

"So you were in the kitchen the whole time?" Blackman checked, seeing a glimmer of hope.

"Yes. But the sink is at the window, so I had my back to everyone. I wouldn't have seen what was going on."

"Who was last in the kitchen?"

"I was. I cleaned the sink and rinsed the cloth out, then I joined the others in the meeting room."

"It doesn't look good, Jules!" Parlour teased. She poked her tongue out and crinkled her nose at him.

"So who precisely organised the coffees?" Blackman was confused.

Juliet went pale.

"Go on, Jules," Parlour said gently.

"I asked who wanted drinks when I went into the meeting room, after finishing the washing up. So it's my fault Terence had that blasted cup of coffee!"

"Don't be a woos, Jules!" Parlour exclaimed. "It's standard to have coffee after lunch."

"But I thought the vicar did the coffees," Blackman frowned.

Juliet nodded miserably. "Martin, bless him, stood up and said the ladies had done enough, and he would do the coffees and teas. Lara offered to help him, but he said no, he'd do it himself."

"Probably wanted to escape from Lara!" Parlour chuckled.

"I think so – he looked rather horrified when she offered to help," Juliet agreed. "As did Andrew Monkton-Smith!"

"Unless he needed to be alone," Blackman said darkly.

"It *is* pokey in that kitchen," Juliet said in support of the vicar. "And you really don't need two people to make the drinks anyway."

"How long was he in there?"

"Not long. Five minutes or so. I'd already boiled the water."

"And did he bring Haynes' flask through to him first?" Blackman enquired.

"Yes, well no, not the whole flask, just the cup with coffee in it."

Blackman pricked her ears up. "So you're saying he poured it out for him first in the kitchen?"

If only he hadn't done that, Parlour groaned inwardly.

Juliet nodded. "But Terence would have expected that little courtesy. I've told you that already. That was why he left his flask in the kitchen. He liked people to serve him, he just didn't want to run the risk of contamination, I guess, from another cup."

Blackman referred to her notebook. "Another witness told me yesterday, and I quote, "Martin Beauville is a bit of a space cadet, he's a bit of a shambles at day to day level. He could no more plot a murder than organise an orgy in a brothel.""

That'll be Jason Jarvis, Parlour grinned, recognising the patter of youthful banter.

"Is he, in your opinion, *a bit of a shambles*?" Blackman continued.

"Definitely!" Juliet smiled. "Typical academic. Absolutely brilliant at public speaking and explaining things – a complete nightmare when it comes to anything practical! He got his cleaner to wire a plug for him the other week! Goodness knows how he manages in that vicarage by himself!"

"So if he was to murder someone, it'd have to be a fairly simple affair?" Blackman surmised.

"Look, Leigh," Parlour interrupted a bit more heatedly this time. "Beauville's a sound bloke. I know you don't share his – our - theology, but take it from us, he wouldn't do a thing like this. Besides, he would have to have known about Terence's peanut allergy."

"You know I can't deal in abstracts like faith and morality, Mark," Blackman replied calmly. "I have to deal with the facts as I see it, and so it's a question of who had the opportunity to fiddle with Haynes's coffee. The drink must have been contaminated after Lara Smith served Terence Haynes' first coffee at approximately 9.20 and before coffee no.2 was handed to Terence Haynes at just after two pm. Given the risk factor of slipping peanuts into Terence's flask while the others were milling around, it's likely it was done by someone alone in the kitchen. At the moment, Martin Beauville had the greatest opportunity to do this, as he disappeared for a considerable amount of time mid-morning on the pretext of going to the loo, and he volunteered to make the after-lunch coffee which resulted in Haynes's death. Andrew Monkton-Smith also had the opportunity to tamper with Haynes' coffee whilst everyone was having lunch. His wife could have slipped peanuts in the flask after serving Haynes his first coffee, while she was waiting for the kettle to boil for the others."

"Lara?" Juliet questioned in surprise. "Didn't you interview her yesterday?"

"No, Lerwick did. I'm off to see her this afternoon, actually. You don't think Lara could have done it?"

"Oh, Lara's lovely. She'd never do a thing like that. You'll see."

"It would be rather odd," Blackman conceded. "She had ample opportunity to contaminate coffee number one. And surely, feeling the way she does about Beauville, she would've tried harder to prevent him from making the coffee after lunch, if she already knew she'd tampered with it. And she certainly wouldn't have volunteered to help him."

"That's right," Juliet agreed.

"Anyway, plenty of other people were alone in the kitchen at various points during the morning - I shall have to check out all their stories. But you have to admit, Beauville has to be number one suspect at the moment."

"But what motive would a thoroughly decent bloke, running a successful parish, have for murdering his church warden?" Parlour asked. Personal loyalties aside, Parlour had a hard time picturing Martin Beauville putting weedkiller in the vicarage flowerbeds, let alone slipping killer peanuts in Terence Haynes' coffee!

"That's what I intend to find out," Blackman replied curtly.

Parlour pushed his chair back from the table, looking troubled. "Would you excuse me?"

⏳⏳⏳

I can't believe we're just sitting around, discussing this murder like it's some blinking whodunnit off the telly, Parlour thought, adopting his favourite thinking pose in front of the bathroom mirror. He wrinkled his nose. There was a peach of a spot brewing on his right nostril. Best give it a day or two til it had a nice juicy head on it – then it'd be really worth having a stab at.

Parlour wandered into his study and sat back in his black club chair. He put his fingers together and made a steeple out of them, frowning as he contemplated the events of the last twenty-four hours. One of their church friends was going through the motions of being a disciple of Christ. It was an abomination. Now, that was a word he hadn't heard in a long time, Parlour thought. He said it aloud this time. *A veritable abomination!* That was a phrase much used by the Reverend Alfred Surley-Jones at the hell, fire and brimstone Baptist church his father had dragged him along to during his childhood in Wales. But this was more than a minor misdemeanour; this was murder, the ultimate sin. One of the fourteen present at Zion House yesterday had sat in their front rooms plotting this atrocious assault on the life of a fellow church member. It beggared belief.

Parlour closed his eyes and exhaled. When he opened his eyes again, they were drawn to a big red cross on his wall calendar, marking Monday 27 May. It was Juliet's birthday tomorrow. *Great!* Parlour groaned. He couldn't imagine anything he felt less like doing than celebrating Juliet's 39th –

55

not that Juliet herself was inclined to make a big deal of the milestone it foreshadowed. Still, he supposed he ought to make an effort. Try and take her mind off the awful events of Saturday afternoon, at least. He'd pop into the florists tomorrow and get a big bunch of orchids delivered to the school. That should bring a smile to her face… perhaps get them brought to her in the middle of one of her lessons or something. Give the kids a laugh, too!

Parlour rose to his feet decisively. Time for some retail therapy, well, window shopping, anyway. Audi TTs didn't come cheap! Best not tell Juliet. She wouldn't approve, not on the Sabbath. Even moseying around the local showroom encouraged staff to work on a Sunday, in her eyes. She was far more idealistic, some would say legalistic, than him. But he was the steadier of the two when it came to matters of faith. He didn't seem to experience the highs and lows that Juliet did. This was, in Parlour's view, because he didn't set the bar so high, wasn't so hard on himself. He thought, not for the first time, what a blessing a happy and secure childhood was. It did make you more level-headed, more confident in your own worth. Juliet was still inclined to be all over the place at times, probably due to the constant criticism she had suffered as a child, and later as an adolescent, stuck at home with parents who denied her many of the basic freedoms and rights to self-expression teenagers require to develop into confident young adults.

"Just going out for some fresh air," Parlour yelled, slipping past the dining room, where he could make out the two blonde heads of Blackman and Juliet through the frosted glass door. He shut the front door behind him and marched purposefully down Spatchcock Drive.

5

"So tell me about Terence Haynes," Blackman commanded Juliet, leaning back in her chair with a cup of coffee in her hand. There was still another half hour to kill before she was due at the Monkton-Smiths.

"Well," Juliet began hesitantly. She felt a little guilty at the earlier ease with which she had imparted information about her church friends to this officer who was, essentially, a stranger. She wished Mark was still here. His facial expressions served as goalposts, indicating whether she had fired wide of the mark or hit the target.

"We've known him about nine years – since we moved to Billock in 1992. There were no decent churches in Billock, so we started going to St Jude's in Lexington Green. Terence Haynes was a church warden there, too, so everyone knew him. He was also on the Church Council with me there. We've always had a fairly civil relationship with him. He did tend to rant on about young hoodlums and tell Mark and I how to do our jobs, but you learnt not to take it personally. You know what these ex officer types are like, had his head right up his own backside. Thought he could control everyone and everything with systems and routines. Ran a tight ship, pardon the pun, as PCC secretary, but that wasn't a bad thing."

"Oh no?" Blackman raised her eyebrows.

"St Jude's has a high percentage of academics and professional people," Juliet explained. "In short, everyone thinks he or she knows best – you can imagine a PCC meeting could drag on for hours with everyone trying to have their pound coin's worth. He was good at cutting across people, reaching consensus and getting things actioned. Ideal in the circumstances, though he did wind an awful lot of people up."

"I can imagine," Blackman nodded, thinking of her superior at Foxburgh Police HQ, who spared no sentiment in his pursuit of efficiency.

"We didn't really get to know Terence well till we started going to Deverton, though. He expressed a desire to join the church plant team, and Timothy Simmons, the vicar of St Jude's, was only too encouraging – Haynes trod on his toes a fair bit, you see."

"When was this – when did you start going to the new church plant?"

"As soon as the new church building was commissioned and Martin was licensed last November. Terence got himself elected warden – nobody dared oppose him – and I was elected to the PCC."

"So you see a lot of him." Blackman concluded.

"Yes. We have PCC meetings once a month, but I see him most Sundays, too," Juliet replied.

"Was he, in general, an unpopular figure in the church?"

Juliet cocked her head to one side. "I suppose that would be a fair comment. He was respected, though. He was a bit of a hero in the Falklands, you see. Escaped from HMS Coventry, you know. Though he was quite badly injured, he hung around and helped a load of junior ratings onto life rafts. Only just got airlifted out himself. Retired in a blaze of glory when the war ended. Received a personal letter from Margaret Thatcher which he had framed on his wall. A real true blue Tory, our Terence. Couldn't bear what he called wet liberalism which he saw as being all pervasive in our society. Campaigned vigorously against women priests and the repeal of Section 28. Wanted a return to what he called family values."

"What about his family? His wife, I believe, died two years ago?"

"Yes, that was very sad," Juliet nodded. "Bowel cancer. She deteriorated pretty rapidly – it was horrible to see. We thought he might mellow after that, but if anything, he got worse. Shut up shop, feelings wise, and got more and more militant about issues he felt strongly about."

"Children?"

Juliet shook her head. "They couldn't have any. Davinia had something wrong with her ovaries, I think."

"Didn't have much going for her, did she?" Blackman commented rather callously. "Did anyone in particular incur his wrath at Deverton PC?"

She was enjoying this. It was proving to be an intriguing case, and Juliet was interesting to talk to.

"Ooh, lots of people!" Juliet exclaimed. "He was that sort – got wound up pretty easily. He had a spat with Rose just the other week."

"Rose Passmore, the other warden? I think I interviewed her yesterday." Blackman grimaced. "Social worker… ugly bitch."

Juliet raised her eyebrows at Blackman, who flushed, suddenly self-conscious. Juliet Parlour had that effect on her, with her polished Never Say A Bad Word About Anyone veneer. But a veneer it was. In private, with just Mark for company, she was as capable as the next person of a healthy dose of vitriol, despite her most valiant efforts to think the best of everyone.

"Sorry," Blackman apologised, "Do-goody types really get up my nose - blaming everyone's problems on that mysterious void called society. We all have responsibilities, and we all need to compromise from time to time, bit of give and take and all that. Can't all be standing up for our individual rights and getting our own way the whole time, if we want the world to go round."

Juliet smiled warmly at her this time. "I couldn't agree with you more."

Blackman smiled back. There was a brief lull in the conversation.

"So tell me about Haynes and Passmore," the Detective Inspector continued, settling back in her chair. Things were going well. Things were a bit more relaxed now Parlour had left them to it.

"Terence Haynes threw his weight around, as you may have gathered," Juliet began. "As the other church warden, Rose Passmore felt she had equal say in how things were done, but he wasn't having any of it. He wound her up a fair bit. Called her a humbug humanist heathen with no respect for the Word of God."

"I take it she didn't share his views on female priests and Section 28?" Blackman surmised, remembering Parlour's comments from earlier on. They were not issues with which she herself was particularly *au fait*.

"Too right she didn't," Juliet nodded. "The problem with Rose is, she has the intellectual armour to put the likes of Terence in his place, but she gets all stressed out and hormonal and ends up looking a fool. I can't say I share her viewpoints – she's a martyr for political correctness - but neither do I subscribe to the bullying tactics employed by Terence. We called him the Wind Commander, you know, though he wasn't really one, a Wing Commander that is. He really was full of hot air at times!"

"Was there any particular incident which might lead Rose Passmore to want him dead?" Blackman asked.

Juliet looked uncomfortable.

"Come on, I'll find out from someone less tactful than you, otherwise…" Blackman cajoled her.

Juliet hesitated, idly stirring her coffee. "Rose wanted to set up a women's discussion forum," she offered eventually. "Terence was opposed to the idea. Said he didn't want her left-wing socialist nonsense infiltrating Deverton Parish Church – everything was couched in military speak, you see. Didn't want the women of Deverton corrupted with her feminist rantings, accused her of trying to break up perfectly decent families, etcetera etcetera. It was pretty ridiculous. I think the idea was quite harmless."

"When was this?" Blackman asked.

"Last month."

"Did anyone support her idea?"

Juliet shook her head. "No, that was the funny thing. Most of us were either too busy to even contemplate going to such a thing or, frankly, didn't see the point of it."

"Do you like Rose Passmore?"

Juliet shrugged. "She's not my cup of tea, I must admit. Too intense, too – well – social workery. I find people like that are often reacting to situations in their past. Trying, with the best will, to create a better, fairer world as a way of somehow getting over the pain in their own lives. Only thing is, as Christians, we have the hope of the Gospel. Rose Passmore, I feel, never quite got a handle on her salvation. Didn't realise she was saved as a believer, or didn't feel she deserved it. I sometimes wonder what kept her coming to church."

"Interesting," Blackman murmured, though not quite sure she understood the psychoanalysis on first hearing. "In your opinion, would Rose Passmore be capable of murder?"

Juliet chewed her lip. "She certainly lacks self-control at times. But I can't imagine her doing anything premeditated, which this murder must have been, unless she carried peanuts around in her handbag just in case someone allergic to them crossed her!"

"Was she alone in the kitchen at any time, as far as you can recall?"

"Not that I can recall," Juliet replied, shaking her head, "She's not very mumsy or domesticated, she wouldn't think of helping out with food and stuff, well, not without being asked. But I couldn't say for sure – as I said, everyone was going in and out. Anyway, Rose Passmore would have killed him straightaway, if she was going to. Her behaviour pattern is:- blow up, spend a week having a good bitch about the person in question, let it simmer till someone or something else incurs her wrath. I think a very cool and calculated person must have done this, and Rose Passmore is neither."

"Fair enough," Blackman said. "What about Haynes and Reverend Bovril?"

"Beauville," Juliet corrected her, grinning. "Terence made it quite clear he saw Martin as a young upstart who needed keeping in order, lest he get too big for his boots. It was quite odd, really, the way Martin acted around Terence – Mark and I were discussing this just the other night. You've met Martin Beauville – how did he strike you?"

"Clever... confident... composed. Yes, very composed," Blackman replied. "He was a bit rattled yesterday, as you might expect. But today he was quite serene. What did he say again? Oh yes, said he'd committed the dark events of yesterday to the Lord and was at peace with himself once again."

Juliet smiled. "Sounds like Martin!"

"You said he acted strangely around Terence – what did you mean?" Blackman challenged her.

Juliet cocked her head to one side. "Not strangely exactly, just a little out of character. I mean, Martin is such a self-confident kind of bloke. Bags of self-esteem. Yet, for some reason, he allowed Terence Haynes to dictate to him. Went all subservient when Terence was around. Yet he'd never let anyone else boss him about. Not that he's ever rude to anyone, you understand, but he has what you call good leadership skills – manages to please everyone whilst getting what he wants. I guess that's why he's a vicar at forty-four," she concluded.

"Can you give me an example?" Blackman frowned.

"Hmmm..." Juliet racked her brains, then suddenly clicked her fingers. "Communion. Martin usually takes communion informally in a semi-circle at the front of the church. He goes round with the bread then comes back round with the wine. Terence Haynes always made sure he was standing on the end, on the far right, so he got to go first. It was a kind of status thing. For some reason, Martin always started on the left, Haynes' right, so that Haynes *was* first. If I was him, I'd alternate it, just to keep Haynes guessing, take him down a few pegs. But Martin never did. It struck us as odd."

"Hmm. You've told me already you don't believe he would kill, but are you aware of any grudges he had against Terence Haynes?"

Juliet shook her head. "It irked him, I expect, that Terence looked down on him, but the Bishop thinks the sun shines out his backside, Martin's I mean, so it was neither here nor there what Terence Haynes thought of him."

"Is this Bishop Shadwell who appointed him?" Blackman asked.

"He was on the panel, yes," Juliet replied. "They say Allbright's lining him up for St Jude's when Simmons retires. He's not quite there yet, old Timmy boy, so Beauville's learning his trade at Deverton. It's a piece of pee for someone of Beauville's calibre. Got the highest grades ever at Bible College, you know. Has a first from Cambridge, too."

"My cousin's got a first from Cambridge," Blackman scoffed. "Can't tell his left from his right. It's no indication of intelligence."

"Martin Beauville *is* intelligent," Juliet said firmly.

"Ambitious?"

"Yes. Undoubtedly," Juliet replied. "But not unhealthily so."

"So he'd have no reason to bump Haynes off, as far as you can see?"

"No, and he wouldn't," Juliet said strongly.

"Even if severely provoked?" Blackman persisted.

"He's a man of God."

Blackman could see she wasn't going to get any further with that line of enquiry. "I keep hearing that Terence Haynes was fastidious. Could you shed some light on that for me?"

Juliet smiled. "Oh, you know. Got up at seven every morning, probably had a cold shower, too. Had his eggy soldiers then marched down to the corner shop with his dog at eight o'clock on the dot. We saw him go past every morning. A creature of habit, was our Terence, like many ex-servicemen."

"As a matter of interest, did you see him this Saturday morning?" Blackman asked.

Juliet nodded. "I got up early to sort some stuff out for school, I knew I wouldn't get the chance later. I saw him from the kitchen window." She got up and Blackman followed her to the window. "If you turn right out of our road and keep going for half a mile or so, you'll come to a triangle. There's a newsagents, a mini-mart and a launderette-cum-ironing service. He walked past the end of our road at just after eight every morning to fetch his paper."

"Daily Mail?" Blackman hazarded a guess.

"Telegraph," Juliet replied. "He had some standards."

"He lived in King Edward Mews?" Blackman checked her pocketbook.

"Yes. No 8. Big house. He had the downstairs converted into a purpose-built flat – for his late wife, you know."

"Did you ever go inside?"

"Only once, to discuss some PCC business," Juliet replied. "He tended to keep his private life separate, as a rule. He was paranoid about getting burgled – what with all his medals. Didn't want people looking in. Got a ruddy big burglar alarm the size of a satellite disk on his gable wall."

"So a pretty substantial place?"

Juliet shrugged. "At least four bedrooms, I'd say."

"How does he manage alone – with the cleaning and stuff? Or is that just another task he applies himself too?" Blackman enquired.

"He probably could manage," Juliet replied, "but he considered that women's work. Had a cleaner – a Mrs Fosthlewaite. I believe she does the Monkton-Smith's and the Keltys, too."

"Fossilwaite," Blackman repeated, misspelling it in her book. She snapped it shut then got up and stretched. "Well, thanks for some smashing grub, Juliet. I better pay the Monkton-Smiths a visit. What have they got Mark doing this week, now he's off the case?"

Juliet grinned. "They've got him investigating some unsolved murder from twenty years ago, to keep him out of mischief!"

Blackman chortled, she could guess what case they'd put him on, they'd kept trying to fob her off with that one but she'd had none of it. "Well, wish him luck for me!"

Juliet just laughed. Luck was no more than a mythical concept in her eyes, but now was probably not a good time to discuss it. "Give my regards to Andrew and Lara."

"Will do," Blackman promised with no intention of doing so. She grabbed her car-keys and mobile telephone from the worktop and bid Juliet goodbye.

6

"DI Leigh Blackman, Foxburgh Police," Blackman announced, as a pretty blonde lady in floral print slacks and a white linen blouse opened her diamond-paned front door to her.

"Good afternoon, Inspector Blackman," Lara Monkton-Smith smiled brightly. "Won't you come in – I was just hanging some curtains I've made."

"Very pretty," Blackman murmured, following her into the living room and looking blandly at the pale yellow floral material ensconcing the bay window. "Sets off your carpet beautifully."

She had been watching some of those home makeover programmes in a vague attempt to appear informed on interior décor. Her last appraisal had thrown up a number of areas in which Blackman's performance was rated less than satisfactory and the whole area of social skills was one of those areas she needed to put some effort into. Not that an in-depth knowledge of window drapes and floor coverings was a necessary pre-requisite to successful police work, but it was slowly dawning on Blackman that twenty years of dedication to the job had left her somewhat depleted of even a basic appreciation of how most women lived these days and what values they held dear. And she was rapidly coming to the conclusion that the shallow and the chic were most women's currency in the decade known in Sunday Supplement world as the Noughties, a term perhaps indicative of the zero content between the majority's ears.

Lara smiled politely at the police inspector, neglecting to inform Blackman that they were having the drab brown carpet that had come with the house replaced by a corn yellow design next week.

"So what can I do for you?" she asked, sitting pertly on the edge of her wicker sofa. She beamed at the female inspector.

God, does she ever stop smiling? Blackman wondered. It was like sitting opposite Carol Bloody Smillie. "I need to ask you a few questions, Mrs Monkton-Smith. I believe you talked to DI Lerwick yesterday at Zion House?"

"Yes, that's right," the younger woman confirmed.

"Well, I'm the investigating officer for this case, and I just wanted to track back, make sure we haven't missed any details that may prove vital to our investigations."

Checking up on him, you mean, Lara thought. DI Lerwick had seemed pretty thorough to her.

"Very sensible, Inspector," she smiled instead. She cocked her head coyly at her husband, who had entered the room and was standing behind the sofa, stroking her hair affectionately. "Hello, darling."

It was a picture of marital bliss.

"Hello again – Inspector Blackman, wasn't it?" Andrew Monkton-Smith smiled. He walked over to where Blackman was sitting and extended a long, pale hand. *Now there's a man who doesn't get his hands too dirty!* Leigh thought to herself, noting the expensive gardening gloves he had removed and laid down on the window sill on entering the room. *The kind of guy who'd rather slip some nuts in someone's drink than strangle them with his bare hands...*

"That's right," Blackman said, forcing out a smile. She explained once more that she was interviewing all those questioned by DI Lerwick the previous day.

"So you won't want to see me, then," Monkton-Smith smiled. Blackman herself had interviewed him yesterday at Zion House.

"Actually, there are a few minor points I need to check out later, if that's alright," Blackman informed him. "Perhaps I could talk to you in a little while, when I've finished with your wife?"

Did she imagine it, or did he look slightly taken-aback?

"Of course. I'll be in the garden." He nodded courteously at her, then left the room, squeezing his wife's hand on the way out.

Blackman turned her attention back to Lara.

"Are you aware how Terence Haynes, died, Mrs Monkton-Smith?"

"Peanut poisoning, wasn't it? They reckon one of us popped some nuts in his coffee and he had some kind of allergic fit. Sounds a pretty strange way of murdering someone, if you ask me!" Lara laughed.

"Strange but true," Blackman replied dryly, opening her pocket book and unfolding Lerwick's notes that she had printed off late last night. She read aloud Lara Monkton-Smith's statement to her, that she had arrived at Zion House at around a quarter to nine yesterday morning. She had then proceeded to put a waldorf salad and Melrose (premium) cheese and bacon puffs in the fridge and some colourant free Fondant Fancies on the worktop, before chatting to the other members of the Council already there.

"Then at around 9.15 you offered to make coffee for everyone."

"Mm."

"Why did you offer, if that's not a stupid question?" Blackman asked.

Lara Monkton-Smith laughed, revealing perfect white teeth. "My motives weren't purely altruistic, I must confess! To be honest, Inspector, I was gagging for one. I couldn't very well go into the kitchen and help myself, like I would at home."

Blackman smiled blandly, making a note in her book. "So you put the kettle on and while you were waiting, poured Terence Haynes a coffee from his flask, which was on the worktop."

"That's right. Terence was a frightful coffee snob, by his own admission. They're on the increase, you know! Had to be his own fancy decaff stuff – that's why he took that flask around with him everywhere. I poured some into his flask cup and carried it through to him. That's what he would have expected – the full service."

Blackman nodded. That tallied with Juliet Parlour's comment.

"Surprising he didn't carry his own bone china cup around with him, too," she commented dryly.

Lara Monkton-Smith smiled. "He used to, actually, kept it wrapped in a little sandwich bag, we all thought it was a bit *poncey* to be honest, but he sat on it once by mistake and cut himself in rather a delicate area, so that was the end of that!"

"I bet you enjoyed that!" Blackman chuckled, inspite of herself.

"Oh, I managed to conceal my amusement, but Jarvis and Miller, our resident double-act, thought it was the funniest thing since Monty Python – said it lent a whole new meaning to bum crack!"

Lara Monkton-Smith guffawed poshly and Blackman smiled faintly. Though she berated herself for feeling this way, such women always made her feel grubby, dowdy, somehow inferior. It was that same uncomfortable feeling she always experienced on making one of her seasonal visits to London to take her elderly mother to see the Christmas lights. Though Blackman knew such women were by no means representative of society as a whole, there was something about the array of chicly dressed ladies and trendily kitted out teenagers that never failed to arouse in her a profound feeling of inadequacy and self- loathing.

Blackman proceeded with the routine questions she had earlier addressed to Juliet Parlour.

Lara Monkton-Smith confirmed that she had resealed the flask immediately after pouring Haynes's coffee that morning and agreed that anyone seeking to put peanuts in the flask would therefore have had to unscrew the lid first. She had not, at any other point that day, had recourse to unscrew Haynes's flask. Neither had she seen anyone else tamper with the flask, though obviously Martin Beauville must have unscrewed it while they were singing in the other room. In her opinion, it would have been fairly simple, albeit somewhat risky, to have nipped out of the room and slipped something in the flask at some point that morning, under the pretext of going to the bathroom or fetching a glass of water.

No, she had not herself gone to the toilet that morning, though her husband had along with a number of others. Lara avoided using public lavatories if she could help it, a vanity aided by a particularly robust bladder control reflex. On the question of whether anyone had spent an abnormally long time in the WC, Lara Monkton-Smith recalled Martin Beauville taking quite a long time in the bathroom after his talk. She remembered as she had been waiting to ask him something about his evangelism plans for Deverton but he had dashed off to the loo immediately after the opening session. She had hung around for a while, hoping to grab him before he joined his discussion group, but had given up after a few minutes. Lara added that she had been rather concerned about him, as he appeared rather pale.

Blackman enquired whether she had heard him in the toilet, as by all accounts, the "sound-proofing" in the Gents was rather ineffective. It was rather a delicate question, but it had to be asked. Lara Monkton-Smith replied that she hadn't, adding that she hadn't really been listening out for sound-effects. She looked faintly bemused.

"Your husband left at one o'clock to go to the post office in Lexington Green," Blackman stated, sensing a change of tack was in order.

"That's right." Lara looked a little uncomfortable.

"He had a parcel to post, I believe?"

"Yes. It had to go that day to get there for Tuesday. It was a car manual for his cousin in Scotland. He's just bought an old VW Golf. We used to have one, so he sent him his old Haynes manual – oh, what a coincidence. It was no use to us anymore."

"My constable timed the drive from Zion House to the post office in Lexington Green there and back. It only takes about thirty minutes, yet your husband took forty-five."

Lara Monkton-Smith shrugged. "Perhaps there was a queue in the post office."

"There wasn't – we checked with the postmistress this morning. She remembers him – he was in and out in a minute."

"Perhaps he nipped into a shop, or filled up with petrol or something, you'll have to ask him. That road can be busy on a Saturday."

If Lara Monkton-Smith was rattled, she certainly wasn't showing it.

"I intend to," Blackman said coolly. Two could play at that game. "When Martin Beauville volunteered to make the coffee after lunch, you offered to help him. Why did you do that?"

Lara shrugged. "Just to help him out. He's not the most practical of people, as I'm sure you'll find out. Besides, I never got a chance to talk to him about the evangelism drive at lunch. He was having a tête-à-tête with Rose Passmore about something. She rather monopolised him over lunch."

Much to your annoyance, Blackman thought. "Did he often volunteer to make the coffee at church, or at church meetings?"

Lara Monkton-Smith nodded. "Yes. He believes in setting an example of servanthood. He's wonderful like that. He quite often does the drinks – not after church, because he always gets cornered by everyone, but at PCC meetings and other church meetings. He's a brick like that."

She chuckled suddenly. "Only problem is, he makes a foul cup of coffee. But nobody's got the heart to tell him. I thought I might save the day yesterday, but it wasn't to be…"

Her voice trailed off as she realised the significance of her comment.

"So you could say people might have expected Martin Beauville to have made the coffee yesterday?" Blackman persisted.

"Yes – I suppose so," Lara Monkton-Smith agreed.

"Why do you think he turned you down?" Blackman asked. Did she imagine it, or did Lara Monkton-Smith jump slightly?

"Pardon?"

"I mean, why did he say no to your offer of help?"

"Oh, I expect he thought I'd get in the way. You couldn't swing a kitten in the kitchen at Zion House!"

Or secretly slip some peanuts in a cup of coffee! Blackman thought to herself grimly. "There's a hatch leading through to the meeting room from the kitchen. Did you, or anyone else, see Martin Beauville pour out Terence Haynes' coffee?"

Lara Monkton-Smith shook her head and pointed out that most of them would have had their backs to the hatch at that time. The hatch was pretty small and high-up on the wall, in any case, allowing only someone's heads and shoulders to be visible through it, and not their hands.

Blackman made a mental note to check this out. "How well did you know Martin Beauville?"

"About as well as everyone else, I should think," Lara shrugged. "I made the move from St Jude's to Deverton with most of the gang in November, when he arrived from the Midlands."

"Had you met him before he became vicar of Deverton Parish Church?"

"No. Why?" Lara asked smoothly. If she felt uncomfortable, she didn't betray it.

"It seems, from what various suspects have said, that you harbour quite strong feelings for Mr Beauville." Blackman looked her straight in the eye, but she didn't flinch an inch.

"I think an awful lot of Martin, that's true," Lara conceded. "I suppose I did have a bit of a thing for him at the start. Andrew and I were going through rather a rocky patch in our marriage – I'm sure you know all too well – you are married, aren't you?"

"Divorced," Blackman grunted.

"Well, you do know, then. Not communicating too well and all that. Well, Martin arrived on the scene, young, good-looking, around through the day like me. It was difficult not to find him attractive. And he's so brilliant. One doesn't come across people like him too often. I could talk to him forever! But I came to my senses, realised what I had with Andrew – "

"Did anything happen between Beauville and yourself?" Blackman interrupted, not interested in a *Woman's Weekly* style insight into the Monkton-Smith's marriage.

"Oh no!" Lara exclaimed. "There was just a mutual attraction, that's all. But he's far too good to do anything about his feelings! He would certainly never run off with a married woman, and I would never do anything to hurt my darling Andrew. It was just a passing fancy. Problem is, mud sticks. I suppose I wasn't discreet about my attraction to him – he's very wary of being seen alone with me, because of what people will think, you know."

"I see," Blackman said. She would need to check this out with Beauville and see if he had returned her affections in any way. "In your opinion, could Martin Beauville have killed Terence Haynes?"

"Absolutely not! He would never do a thing like that. Martin Beauville's a good man, Inspector."

"I'm not in the business of making moral judgements, Mrs Monkton-Smith," Blackman informed her, looking her in the eye. "I'm just after the facts."

Lara Monkton-Smith met her stare, then hesitated a second.

"He had the opportunity," she replied finally, "therefore I suppose in theory he could have, but I see no reason why Martin should wish Terence dead."

"Have you ever seen Martin Beauville lose his temper?"

"Dear me, you had got it in for poor Martin, haven't you!" Lara Monkton-Smith laughed ironically. She cocked her head to one side in contemplation. Finally she shook her head. "No.

He had exemplary self-control, even when Terence talked down at him in front of people."

"Talked down at him?"

"Oh you know," Lara replied breezily, gesticulating, "patronised him a bit, called him wet behind the ears, that sort of thing."

"Where did Martin stand politically?" Blackman asked.

Lara frowned. "What do you mean?"

"Excuse me, I'm not terribly *au fait* with ecclesiastical jargon. From what people have said, Terence Haynes was pretty right-wing, views he carried into church with him. Is Martin Beauville a liberal, or a traditionalist? Did they see eye to eye about church issues, or were they frequently at loggerheads?"

"Oh, Martin's pretty conservative, with a small c," Lara replied. "Bishop Shadwell wouldn't have taken him on, otherwise. He's real old school, is Shadwell Allbright. No, Martin is officially against female priests, gay vicars, same-sex marriages, doggie burials, etcetera etcetera. But he manages to be against things *lovingly*, if you know what I mean, and his arguments against are always plausible and well-informed. Terence always had to be so bombastic, so hard about everything!"

Blackman made some notes in her book. "Can you think of anyone there on Saturday who might have had a grudge against Terence Haynes and wished him dead?"

Lara Monkton-Smith inclined her head to one side again as she considered the question. "To be honest, everyone there found him downright annoying, but kill him? This is the Church of England, not *Gunfight at the O.K. Corral!* I know Rose Passmore had a bit of a barney with him a few weeks ago about some women's group she wanted to set up in the church centre – but I don't know if she'd quite want him dead! Alex and Jason couldn't stand him and liked to play tricks on him…"

"Tricks?" Blackman queried.

"Oh, you know, practical jokes. Spiked his Pimms with laxatives at the Parlours' barbie last summer! Poor old Terence left pretty sharpish, I can tell you!"

"Really?" Blackman enquired, pricking her ears up.

"But they wouldn't have done *this* to Terence – not if they'd known about his peanut allergy thing. Alex is a nurse, you know. He would have been aware of the possible consequences."

"Perhaps somebody wanted to frame one or both of them?" Blackman suggested.

"It's possible," Lara conceded, tipping her head to one side again. It really was quite an annoying habit, Blackman thought. Did she imagine it, or was it directly lifted from the Bashir Diana interview? Lara Monkton-Smith struck her as a Dianaphile, that brand of pleasant yet essentially shallow woman who poured through Royal supplements and celebrity magazines.

"And did you like Terence Haynes?" Blackman enquired.

Lara frowned. "Church life isn't about liking one another – though it's a bonus if you do. It's about loving one another, irrespective of whether we would naturally choose to spend time with that person. We've all received the calling to attend Deverton Parish Church, so we all pull rank together – bar a few practical jokes."

"I see," Blackman said, but she didn't really. Nothing would induce her to sacrifice her free time for frightful old bores like Terence Haynes, no matter how worthy the cause.

"But I didn't dislike Terence," Lara added. "He annoyed me at times, but to be honest, things ran more smoothly because of the way he was. Though he was bumptious, people didn't tend to faff around so much when he was around. Most people just got on with things he asked them to do - they were too scared to oppose him. Take the new church building, for example…"

"I'm getting the picture," Blackman interjected hastily before she embarked on a lengthy slice of church life. Lara Monkton-Smith's view of Haynes concurred with that of Juliet Parlour. She made a few notes, then looked up again. "Would you mind if I asked you a few personal questions? Lerwick concentrated on the events of Saturday afternoon – I don't actually know much about *you*."

"Fire away!" Lara Monkton-Smith smiled genially. A more shrewd observer might have noticed a slight paling of the Max-Factored cheeks.

"You've lived in Deverton how long?"

"We moved here just before Christmas - as soon as the house we wanted was built. HomeFromHomes bought our last house in Lexington Green from us – you lose some money, but it's less upheaval that way."

"You've clearly invested a lot of loving care into this place, Mrs Monkton-Smith – are you at home through the day?"

"Yes, I have time on my hands, which I suppose is what you're driving at."

"I hear the church secretary is very overworked – you didn't fancy helping her out a few hours a week?" Blackman enquired rather slyly.

"Oh no!" Lara laughed. "They do everything electronically these days. I wouldn't know where to begin! I can just about switch Andrew's computer on!"

"So how do you spend your days – I believe you employ a Mrs Fosthlewaite to do the cleaning?"

"Yes – arduous task! We can afford it – Andrew makes a mint – so I gladly hand over the marigolds to Mrs F! No, I do a lot of church work. Parish visiting, taking the communion to the old folks… I sit on various committees, like the PCC – all voluntary work."

"Very commendable," Leigh Blackman murmured. She couldn't imagine doing anything unpleasant for free, at least not above and beyond the endless unpaid overtime she put in as a police officer. "If you don't mind me saying, you appear to be considerably younger than your husband – "

"Eighteen years, yes. I'll be thirty-three in June," she replied. "I was twenty-one when we married. I met Andrew at a legal function. My cousin, who was a legal assistant at that time, didn't have a date, so he took me along. Andrew actually spilt some red wine down my cream cocktail dress. He couldn't apologise enough – drove me home to get changed then took me out for a meal locally, as the party was miles away. We got talking and it turned out he was a church-goer, too. I knew straightaway he was the one for me – a very spiritual man, which is important to me, but not penny-pinching or wet like a lot of Christian men can be!"

Like Daniel Kelty, she wanted to add, but thought better of it.

"Surprising he hadn't been snapped up," Blackman commented dryly. "I hear the Church of England is awash with desperate spinsters!"

"He was divorced, actually. His first wife left him. Petra couldn't deal with his faith – he was born-again in his twenties, you see. He wasn't the man she married. He has two children by her, Shaun and Louise. They're both in Scotland, so he doesn't see them often."

"Andrew is Scottish?" Blackman hadn't realised when they'd talked yesterday.

"Yes, from Livingston, just outside of Edinburgh. But you can hardly tell, he's been down South that long."

"I see." Blackman stood up and closed her notebook. "Thank you, you've been very helpful. I just need to have a few words with your husband, clarify a few things. He said he'd be in the garden?"

"Yes, he's tidying up the lawn. Lindsay Briscoe brought her kids round the other day and I'm afraid they ruined the edges by the beds. Andrew's frightfully fussy about these things. I was supposed to supervise them – got a real dressing down from him when he came home!”

Blackman followed her out the patio doors into the garden, which was even more impressive than the front room.

“Andrew!” Lara called. “The Inspector wants to talk to you now!”

Andrew Monkton-Smith appeared from behind a yew hedge and beckoned Blackman over.

“Just a few little things, Mr Monkton-Smith,” Blackman said, joining him on a bench beneath a green stained wooden pergola.

“Please – call me Andrew!”

“Andrew.” Blackman said uncomfortably. “You told me yesterday you left Zion House at one o’clock to nip to the post office at Lexington Green.”

“That’s right,” Monkton-Smith confirmed. She could just about detect a clipped Scottish accent now.

“Yet you didn’t return to Zion House until one forty-five.” She informed him that her officer had timed the round-trip at just half an hour, allowing a generous three minutes in the Post Office. “How do you account for the other fifteen minutes or so?

Monkton-Smith smiled wryly. “My, you do have a suspicious mind, don’t you, Inspector!”

“Prerequisite for the job, Sir.”

“Well, if you must know, I sat in my car and prayed when I got back. It was deserted outside, and nobody saw me, so I don’t expect you’ll be able to prove it. But that’s where I was.”

“Prayed?” Blackman looked dubious. Praying was something you did in church, wasn’t it, not in your car in broad daylight?

“Yes, Inspector. Are you a believer?”

“No. I have a very tiny mind, Sir,” Blackman replied dryly. “I can only cope with things I can see and touch.”

“What about electricity?” Monkton-Smith asked smoothly.

"What about peanuts, Mr Monkton-Smith?" Blackman asked rather brutally. *Condescending idiot!*

Monkton-Smith's expression changed from benevolent father-figure to hardened lawyer in a split second. "I didn't sneak into the kitchen while the others were having lunch, if that's what you're driving at. I did go to the toilet a couple of times in the morning, though. The old prostrate's giving me gip these days. But I didn't break into Terence Haynes' thermos flask!"

"Why did you sit in your car and pray?" Blackman persevered. "I mean, why not wait till you got home that afternoon?"

"I wish I had now!" Andrew Monkton-Smith laughed ironically. "Might have saved myself all this grief!"

Blackman watched in silence as he sobered up again.

"I needed some time out, Inspector. Needed to hand my feelings over to God, as they say. Lara says she's got over Beauville, but she spent the whole morning trying to catch his eye. Hanging onto every word he said, trying to get his attention. It's painful for a man to watch his wife act like that around another chap – especially the blasted vicar! I wish he had never come here!"

Blackman could see he regretted that statement the moment it flew from his lips.

"It must have been hard for you," she said, attempting to put into action some empathic skills she'd learnt at the last police training day, and failing dismally.

"Look – Inspector, I don't mean to be rude, but isn't there any way I can talk to Parlour? He knows me. There are some things I don't feel comfortable talking about in front of strangers. You'll pardon me for saying, but you're neither a believer nor a married man, and I don't see how you can possibly understand."

"Try me," Blackman said hardly, but regretted it immediately. He certainly wasn't going to open up if she responded like that.

"Look, Mr Monkton-Smith – Andrew," she continued, more genially this time. "Parlour's off the case. As a lawyer, you'll understand there's a clear conflict of interests where Mark Parlour is concerned. Anyway, even if I did let you talk to him, he would be morally and ethically obliged to pass on any relevant information to me, so you may as well cut out the middleman."

"I suppose so," Monkton-Smith muttered. Blackman watched as he removed his gardening gloves and examined his well-manicured fingernails for dirt. He was but a titillator of this outdoor empire, mirroring his wife's efforts indoors. Andrew Monkton-Smith would no more tackle the compost bin than his wife would clean the toilet. He squinted up at the sky, which was streaked golden white from the late-afternoon sun.

"I don't know if anyone's said anything to you, but Lara had a bit of a crush on Beauville, when he first arrived. Of course, she didn't do anything about it – she's far too sweet and loyal – but it was pretty clear how she felt about him. I don't know if he felt the same way, he certainly didn't let it show if he did. Stupid fool that I am, I got all silly and jealous, had a bit of a scene with Lara about it. I guess, Inspector, I've never quite been able to believe my luck, finding Lara like I did. I never expected to get a second bite of the cherry, threw myself into my work instead. So when she came along, young, pretty, laughed at all my old jokes, I decided to snap her up before I could talk myself out of it! I suppose deep down I've always feared she'd meet someone younger, more attractive."

"Has she ever had an affair?" Blackman asked.

Andrew shook his head. Apparently there had been a few male friends who had got too close to comfort, but nothing serious. "Lara's a good woman, Inspector."

"It seems Deverton is full of good women and good men, Mr Monkton-Smith," Blackman said dryly in a moment of Inspector Goole-sque insight, "yet one of these good people murdered Terence Haynes."

"Unbelievable, isn't it?" Andrew Monkton-Smith looked up at the heavens. There was a brief pause before he turned back to Blackman. "Divorced, are you?"

"Is it that obvious?" Blackman grinned.

"Working on a Sunday!" Monkton-Smith laughed. "Kids in McDonalds with Dad, are they?"

"We didn't have any," Blackman replied quietly, uncomfortable with the brief digression into her private life. "And this is a murder enquiry, anyway, Mr Monkton-Smith. Speed is of the essence."

There was a pause before Andrew Monkton-Smith rose to his feet and stretched.

"Will that be all, Inspector Blackman? I really must get on…"

"For now," Blackman replied, standing up. "Think I might call it a day, myself. Thank you for your time, Mr Monkton-Smith."

He's hiding something, she thought, as he returned to his lawn manicure. *Praying in the car, my arse!*

7

What the fuchsia! Parlour exclaimed, peering through the glass of the Incident Room at Billock Police Station at eight-thirty that Monday morning.

Attached to the giant white-board were blown-up photographs of the entire Deverton Church Council, including a shot of his own wife taken at the Church Christmas party. Clearly Blackman's team had paid a visit to the church office. Underneath were various anecdotes in black marker scrawl. Parlour squinted, but he couldn't quite make out what the inscriptions said.

"Can I help you?" a voice said dryly behind him. Parlour turned round and came face to face with Leigh Blackman.

"Oh good morning, Leigh. I was just wondering what you'd written about my dear wife."

"You know the lads are calling her Joyce? Present at the scene of the crime like old Tom Barnaby's wife!" Blackman grinned sardonically, referring to the popular ITV crime series.

Parlour frowned, his sense of humour distinctly lacking as his wife's beloved visage stared back at him from the white boar

Blackman slapped his back. "Don't worry, Parlour – she's on odds of 120-1 at the moment. An outside runner with Mavis Wagstaff."

"You what?" Parlour shook his head in disbelief. Like some kind of sub-branch of William Hill's, Blackman had betting odds up for each suspect!

"Dave's idea," Blackman informed him. "He's got one of the DCs running a book. The odds will be revised each day. Beauville's hot favourite at 5-1, assuming we can find a nice fat juicy motive. Andrew Monkton-Smith's close behind at 10-1. Reckons he was in the car *praying* for ten minutes after his little jaunt to Lexington Green Post Office. And I'm Claudia Schiffer. We'll need to get that prostrate gland checked out too

– made a few too many trips to the bog, if you ask me! Third favourite at 20-1 is old Loopy Leftie, Rose Passmore."

"Is this ethical?" Parlour frowned.

"No – but it adds a bit of incentive!" Blackman grinned, slotting some coins into the coffee machine.

"I don't think the Sewer will be too impressed," Parlour said soberly.

"Oh come off your high horse, Mark!" Blackman exclaimed, selecting a black coffee. "Lerwick's been dragged off to handle some politically sensitive sex crime in Foxburgh and I'm on my todd here. If it takes a bit of bribery and corruption to nail the bugger who did this, I'm not complaining!"

"Sewell will be, though, when you get taken to the court of appeal for a false conviction. Pressurising staff to guarantee results leads to bully-boy tactics and slipshod police work."

"Lecture over?" Blackman enquired archly, turning to face him, coffee in hand. Parlour was such a prig sometimes, and something else along those lines, too!

"Just trying to help, Leigh," Parlour said seriously, furrowing his brow.

"Look, Parlour," Blackman snapped, "You're not even supposed to be up here. Why don't you just piss off and find out who murdered Joe Telfer's dog, or whatever it is Sewell's got you doing!"

"It was his daughter who was killed," Parlour informed her quietly. "Blow to the back of the head. With a Woolworth's spade." He turned to leave, pausing briefly to look behind at his colleague.

"Oh, and Leigh… it'd be a shame if the team found about you and the Sewer aboard the *Oriana* last summer!"

Blackman flushed. "That was pure coincidence we ended up on the same bloody cruise liner, and you know it!"

Parlour grinned and walked off whistling.

Blackman slammed the coffee machine with her hand. "Mark?"

He turned around.

"Meet me at the Waggoner's at twelve?"

"Make it one," Parlour grinned, then punched the air in front of him in a rather twee Henmanesque fashion.

⧗⧗⧗

Just time to nip into the florists, Parlour thought, glancing at his watch as he left Bywater Farm, where he'd been checking out some geographical details in the historical case he'd been assigned.

Ten minutes later, he arrived outside *Ring'O'Roses*, the little flower shop Juliet had favoured during their time in Billock. Though there were no customers in the shop, the florist took a while to appear from the back room.

"Hello there!" the lady Juliet knew as "Naz" finally greeted him. "Juliet's husband, isn't it? We met at Deverton Church a couple of months back – I did the flowers for the Fat Geek Wedding! You opened up for me, remember?"

Parlour grinned, recalling the rather unsavoury alliance that had been officially forged at his parish church earlier that year.

Juliet's husband! That makes a change! Usually it was Juliet complaining at being referred to as "Parlour's wife" or "That Detective's Missus".

"That's right," Juliet's husband smiled. He explained that they had left the area and hence not frequented the florists as often.

"Sorry to take so long. Someone just came in and spent over three hundred pounds on flowers for South America! Had to make a few phone calls, check out the local florist's details! Course, I don't speak a word of Spanish! Took a while. But I think it's sorted, now."

"Wasn't Elton John was it?" Parlour grinned.

Naz chuckled. "Just a local. Some bit of Laura Ashley skirt from up your way! So, what can I do for you?"

Parlour explained his plan and let the florist select some voluptious white orchids for his wife.

"Been busy?" he enquired, as she processed his credit transaction.

Naz made a face. "Not half. Run-up to Easter, then we have that prossy's funeral next week. "

Of course, Parlour thought. That was the big news around here. He didn't expect anyone was even talking about the tinpot murder of Terence Haynes in Billock.

"You wouldn't believe what her family are like!" Naz continued, getting Parlour to sign on the line. "Loaded! Spent over a grand on roses alone. Wonder what made her go on the game?"

"Oh you know, sex mad some people!" Parlour commented flippantly. He returned to his car.

⧗⧗⧗

The Waggoner's Arms was a family pub on the far side of Lexington Green, on the Foxburgh road. It was not the best venue for working lunches, as it was pretty expensive with a limited bar snack menu. This, Parlour knew, was to try and entice customers into the seated restaurant area, where they could enjoy an overpriced processed meal in an atmosphere just a tiny step up from the local burger restaurant. At least at The Waggoners, infant diners were provided with wet wipes with their *Kidz Mealz* to clean their hands and faces afterwards. Though in Parlour's view, this commodity should also be available to subsequent adult diners, for the removal of ketchup stains from the chairs and table. This should be accompanied by a mini dustpan and brush set for the sweeping away of stray peas, cold chips and the broken crayons supplied to the infant diners.

85

Bah humbug! Parlour grinned to himself, knowing he would probably feel quite differently in a couple of years' time, should they be blessed with the offspring they so eagerly desired.

The Waggoners was, however, ideal for clandestine meetings, tucked back as it was some hundred yards from the main road down a leafy lane. He couldn't afford to be spotted here with the Investigating Officer of the Haynes' case, they would both be in hot water.

"Blimey – spot the secretaries!" Blackman scoffed, as they made their way to the bar. The place was awash with greying men in suits accompanied by young women in cheap chainstore garb.

"Grim, isn't it?" Parlour frowned, consulting the beers on tap. He shot Blackman a sidelong glance. Her old man had dumped her for his secretary, hadn't he?

Five minutes later, they were ensconced in a booth at the far side of the bar area, well out of earshot of the nearest customers.

"To what do I owe the pleasure of your company then, Leigh?" Parlour enquired, taking a swig of the local bitter.

"I realised yesterday, after visiting the Monkton-Smiths, that I may have been a little hasty in my decision to shut you out of the investigation."

"You were only obeying orders," Parlour replied, smiling.

"Yeah well, orders schmorders – what the Sewer don't know won't hurt him. You'll keep stumm if I - er – consult with you on certain matters?"

"Of course," Parlour replied, his heart beating faster below the cool exterior. *Yes!* "I just want this matter sorted out – for the sake of our church. It's not about personal gain, I can assure you."

"I'll believe you," Blackman grinned.

"So what have you found out so far?" Parlour asked, settling back in his chair to listen.

Blackman groaned. "Not a lot. It appears everyone had some reason for disliking Terence Haynes. He was a right-wing, full-on, insensitive old warhorse. The kind of person you might jokingly say you could murder. That aside, nobody appears to have a strong enough reason to kill him."

Martin Beauville, Blackman continued, had ample opportunity *and* he had handed Haynes the contaminated coffee, but overall consensus was he was squeaky clean and would never stoop so low. He was also, as yet, motiveless, though Blackman conceded she hadn't really put him through the paces yet. Another person with several opportunities to murder Haynes was Andrew Monkton-Smith, though again, there was no clear motive. Rose Passmore passionately disliked him and had a possible motive, but claimed not to have visited the toilet the whole day and hadn't been seen in the kitchen at any point. Lindsay Briscoe did have the opportunity, having spent a lot of time in the kitchen but Blackman felt she wasn't the type. With two young children whom she patently adored, it was questionable why she should wish to get herself locked up for life. Olivia Murray was more of a dark horse and did have the opportunity, but was again without a clear motive. DI Lerwick had found her very frustrating to interview, digressing at a tangent at the slightest opportunity.

Parlour grinned. "That's Olly for you. I don't think I've ever heard her string a complete sentence together. But I can't imagine her murdering someone. Far too esoteric."

"Which brings me onto the Keltys," Blackman continued. They hadn't been in the kitchen much, having been occupied with the music side of things. Both appeared to be snow-white on the surface without the authority or brains of a Martin Beauville. Again there was no clear motive. There had been a few minor set-tos with Terence Haynes about worship styles and rotas, etcetera, but nothing significant. Blackman felt Mavis Wagstaff couldn't be totally ruled out, as it was not beyond the realms of possibility she had popped some peanuts in Haynes's flask, however it was unlikely. Haynes didn't appear to bother her as much as the others, largely, by her own admission, because she was as deaf as a post, and thus much of his ranting passed her by. Alex Miller and Jason Jarvis enjoyed poking fun at Haynes and both expressed a dislike for him. They had even put laxatives in his drink on a previous occasion for a laugh, but didn't appear to have any desire to see him off permanently.

"Prank gone wrong?" Parlour suggested.

"Miller's a nurse, isn't he?" Blackman replied. "If he did know about Haynes' allergy, he'd never have put peanuts in his coffee. If he didn't know, why put them in? It's not as if they have any embarrassing side effects."

"True. More likely somebody wanted to frame them, given their past history," Parlour remarked.

"Exactly," Blackman nodded. "Then we have Lara Monkton-Smith."

Lara Monkton-Smith, she summarised, wasn't overly fond of Haynes, but viewed him as a valuable asset to the church who was good at keeping affairs in order. She did indeed have the opportunity to kill him, but would hardly, in Blackman's view, incriminate herself by spending ten minutes alone in the kitchen first thing making coffee, and why volunteer to help Martin Beauville later and risk implicating herself again?

Parlour looked at Blackman. "So, in short, anyone could have done it, but nobody has a motive."

"Dire, isn't it?" Blackman groaned, taking a hefty swig of her lager. "Andrew Monkton-Smith has a possible motive, but it's a long-shot."

"Oh yes?" Parlour enquired, sobering up.

Blackman informed him of Monkton-Smith's admission the previous day that he was jealous of Beauville and Lara's feelings for him, and that was why he had sat in his car praying for ten minutes on returning from Lexington Green. "He actually told me that he wished Martin Beauville had never been appointed vicar of Deverton."

"So?" Parlour shrugged. It was a perfectly natural reaction from a red-blooded male.

"Then Lara told me the vicar often offered to make the coffee – that you could generally assume he would do so at some point during the day."

"What are you driving at?" Parlour frowned.

"What if Andrew Monkton-Smith set up Martin Beauville, to get Beauville locked up?"

Parlour went to open his mouth, then shut it again. He leaned back in his chair and nursed his pint glass. He had to get beyond seeing the likes of Andrew Monkton-Smith as friends and put his objective detective cap on.

"It's possible, I suppose, but why not simply mow down Martin Beauville on his bicycle? Why get poor old Terence bumped off to achieve the goal?"

"To deflect suspicion from himself?" Blackman argued weakly.

"Well, it hasn't worked, has it?" Parlour commented dryly.

"But it would incriminate Beauville without throwing suspicion on himself, as he, I mean Andrew, has no motive to kill Haynes. Haynes' life did not matter to him."

"It's pretty far-fetched, Leigh, and far too risky. Nobody could guarantee Martin would offer to make the coffee."

"But what if Monkton-Smith popped out at lunchtime to buy some peanuts?" Blackman persevered. "Beauville got up his nose so much that morning, he decided it was a good time to frame him. He would have had time to dash into the kitchen and pop the nuts in Haynes' flask while the others were having lunch."

"Those would be the actions of a cruel and callous man, with no respect for human life," Parlour replied with feeling. "And Andrew Monkton-Smith does not strike me as being that kind of person. I know he can be a bit patronising, but he's sound.

Takes his faith seriously, whereas with Lara, you sometimes get the feeling it's all for show. A lifestyle choice, like what magazines you have on the coffee table –"

"What pattern you have on your curtains," Blackman intervened.

"Lovely house, isn't it?" Parlour smiled.

"Bit show-home for me," Blackman grinned, who preferred the lived-in look.

"Jules and I can never quite work Lara out," Parlour commented. "She says all the right things, has the right Christian paperbacks on her shelf, listens to the right sort of music, is a pillar of the community… but at the centre, always, this void. She's very easy to talk to at a superficial level, but try getting serious about anything… Jules has decided there simply is no deep side to her! I'm not so sure."

"Me, neither," Blackman agreed. "I liked her – on the surface. The Anthea Turner smile was a bit off-putting at first, but she came across well. Her husband, I thought, had something to hide. He wasn't at ease with me, like Lara was."

"Andrew's a man's man," Parlour stated, as if that somehow explained everything.

"Well, anyway, he seemed a bit sus to me," Blackman replied. There was a pause as their sandwiches arrived.

"Look, Leigh," Parlour said, as soon as the waitress was out of earshot, "I don't think the murderer/murderess *cared* who did the coffees after lunch. The damage was already done. Whoever put the peanuts in Haynes' flask knew someone would make coffee after lunch, and that was all that mattered."

"Or Beauville put them directly in Haynes' cup and that's why he offered to make the coffees," Blackman replied.

"That would be far too obvious," Parlour said.

"Perhaps he was relying on his reputation – assumed nobody would believe it was him."

"Far too risky," Parlour replied, "and where's his motive?"

Blackman looked deflated.

"You won't get anything on Beauville," Parlour insisted, shaking his head. "I'd bet my last dollar on it – were I a betting man. He might have a few mini-skeletons in his closet, but you can be sure he would have never got past the Bishop if there were the slightest blemish on his character. Shadwell Allbright is a real puritan."

"Not if something happened after he was appointed vicar."

"Well, one of us would know about that. Deverton is a small place and Terence Haynes had a big mouth."

"We'll see," Blackman said darkly. "So what are your thoughts?"

"What are my thoughts?" Parlour drummed his fingers on the arms of his chair. "I think you need to concentrate on the peanut aspect. Who might have known about Terence's allergy? Whoever did this was fairly well informed on anaphylaxis. Who might have detailed knowledge of peanut allergy and its potentially lethal consequences? Have any Church Council people worked in the health sector, or are any of them related to doctors or nurses or health workers? Get some of your men onto that. Ring around the local surgeries. Find out if there's been any requests about peanut allergy. How about contacting local dietitions and nutritional experts. Is there an allergy control centre in the vicinity? That kind of thing."

Blackman met his stare. "Well, Alex Miller has a medical background, of course. But he wouldn't have been Terence's GP or anything – he's only a nurse."

"Yes, but Terence might have sought his advice on his allergy," Parlour replied.

"You think Miller might have let it slip?"

"Unethical, but possible. It's hardly an embarrassing problem, say, like Monkton-Smith's prostrate trouble, or – "

"Rose Passmore's hairy chin!" Blackman grinned.

"I'm glad *you* said that," Parlour smiled. "Talk to Miller – see if he knew about Haynes's allergy, and if so, did he tell anyone. Then what about the peanuts? Somewhere the wrapper for them is floating about. Have the grounds of Zion House searched. Perhaps someone brought them in loose in their pocket. Get clothes worn that day – and car interiors - searched for traces of peanut. Where were they purchased? It's a long shot, but the supermarket or corner shop might remember someone coming in specifically for peanuts that day or that week. Perhaps check till receipts, both in people's homes or at retail outlets."

Blackman groaned. "Christ Almighty! That'll be a nightmare to organise!"

Parlour winced as Blackman blasphemed. Industrial language he could cope with; indeed, he wasn't averse to letting slip the odd *bloody* or *bugger* himself. And goodness knows, he came across enough of it in his job. But someone taking the Lord's name in vain still had a profoundly unsettling effect on him. However, he said nothing. It was like water off a duck's back to the likes of Blackman. Years ago, as an eager young copper, he'd have made his voice heard, but not now. It rarely had any effect, other than to incite ridicule. All he could do was set an example by finding slip-off-the-tongue alternatives.

Parlour shrugged in reponse to Blackman's apprehension. "It's the nature of the beast. Whoever did this was clever, very clever. Which means you're either going to have to be a genius, or very painstaking, to catch up with them." Parlour suspected it would be the latter. "Have you ruled out someone popping it in his cup at the table?"

"Not entirely but it seems far too risky, and nobody spotted anyone lean over Terence's cup. He kept his plate and cup very close to his body," Blackman replied. "Had we known the cause of death at the time of initial questioning, we could have taken samples from the suspects' fingernails. Of course, we'll look for traces of peanut in pockets and bags, but I guess it'll be too late anyway. Anyone with half a brain would have got rid of the evidence by now."

She sighed, propping her head on her hands. "I suppose you think I'm pretty green at this stuff."

"It's hardly a routine case," Parlour said generously. "And you've been left in the lurch by Lerwick. Take heart – it's less than forty-eight hours since Haynes was murdered. Have you searched his house yet?"

Blackman shook her head and replied that she was waiting for Robins to find some time in his busy schedule as she didn't wish to search Haynes's flat alone. The serial killer in Foxburgh was taking up most of the available manpower.

"I asked the Sewer for more staff, but it's no go. Reckons the Foxburgh case has priority. There was a similar case in Bowhampton last month – they think they may be linked."

"We certainly don't appear to have a serial killer on our hands here in Deverton," Parlour agreed. "When an opinionated old so-and-so like Terence Haynes gets murdered, it does stink of personal retribution of some kind."

"Hopefully we'll get round there tonight," Blackman said without much conviction.

Parlour drummed his bitten fingernails on the table. He didn't want to hand it all to Blackman on a plate, as he was planning a few subtle undercover investigations of his own. But it was perhaps unethical not to point her in another obvious direction, especially if it prevented another murder from occurring.

"What is it?" Blackman frowned, sensing his hesitation.

"Leigh, have you thought about his will? A regimented old so-and-so like Terence Haynes is… was… bound to have made such arrangements. His wife is dead, isn't she, and there are no children."

"What are you driving at?" Blackman looked puzzled.

"Think about it… would someone have stood to have gained from his death? It's not going to be the usual suspects, they're either already dead or non-existent. Perhaps he left everything to the sister-in-law in New Zealand or to his god-daughter in the Midlands.   Or perhaps to some charity or military organisation. Some people in his situation leave everything to friends or people who have cared for them in some capacity in their widowhood."

Blackman clicked her fingers. "The cleaner!"

Parlour contorted his mouth and tilted his head from side to side dubiously. "It's an option. Personally I think he was far too devoted to his ex-wife to consider favouring another woman in any way. And this would be a pretty major favour to bestow on someone."

"Not if they were having an affair!" Blackman exclaimed. "It adds up… someone popped in his house first thing, the only person who knew the burglar alarm was the cleaner, Mary Fosthlewaite. Perhaps she popped something in his coffee and tampered with his medipouch!"

"Tampered with his whattalotta?" Parlour frowned. Blackman tutted at her own indiscretion and was forced to enlighten Parlour concerning the medical pouch and tampon insertion. Parlour failed miserably to suppress a grin.

There was a pause as he gathered his thoughts again. Blackman took a swig of her drink.

"The coffee in the flask idea doesn't work," Parlour said finally.   "Or he would have snuffed it after the first cup he drank from it, which Lara Monkton-Smith served him."

Blackman acceded glumly that he had a point.

"But check out the will thing, Leigh, it may just point to your killer. Someone must stand to gain from his death, after all. Unless we have a psychopath in our midst at Deverton PCC, and I think we would have unearthed them by now!"

Blackman wasn't so sure.   The sleepy old Church of England had taken on a whole new light in the last few days, a light that was decidedly stained.

Parlour got up. "Another drink?"

Blackman laughed hollowly. "You can ask the barman if he's sold many nuts, while you're at it!"

⧗⧗⧗

Dave Robins let out a loud whistle as a blown up photo of the latest Foxburgh murder victim appeared in the fax out-tray next to his desk at Billock Station. It couldn't be, could it? He held the fax up for closer inspection. It was. Better get hold of Blackman.

8

Unaware that her mobile phone was out of charge, Leigh Blackman decided to knock on a few doors on the Deverton Estate before returning to the incident room at Billock station.

Much to her annoyance, Forensic still hadn't finished testing the food and dishes taken from Zion House on Saturday. What was the hold-up? There hadn't been any more murders in the red light district of Foxburgh since Saturday, as far as she knew.

Blackman frowned as she took the turn off for Deverton. She had been like a bloody nodding dog in the pub there with Parlour, she should park her arse on the parcel shelf of that slinky silver car of his. She loathed the way she turned all subservient around more experienced colleagues. So Parlour had intimate local knowledge of the boring residents of a tinpot little housing estate – didn't make him an effing authority on policing methods, did it?

Blackman pulled over into a bus layby to consult her A-Z. Number 21 Battenberg Close, the two bedroom semi shared by nurse, Alex Miller, and insurance consultant, Jason Jarvis, was located at the far end of the estate where the smaller, less upmarket houses were found.

It's like bloody Toytown here! Blackman grumbled to herself, driving very slowly and incurring the wrath of the driver behind as she attempted to get her bearings. The little streets of red brick houses looked more or less the same, having had no time to noticably deteriorate as yet. The age of the car in the driveway was sole testimony to the prosperity or lifestyle of their occupants.

At last! She exhaled in relief, finding the cul-de-suc. But there was no car in the driveway of number 21. Blackman pulled up on the pavement and got out, but nobody came to the door when she rang the bell. She could see a pile of post on the floor through the glazed front door. Cursing, she fumbled in her pocket for a business card and shoved it through the door.

Returning to her car, Blackman sighed. What next? She ran through the names on her list. Perhaps she ought to pay Olivia Murray and Lindsay Briscoe a visit. They weren't out of the running, though Parlour and Lerwick had both expressed doubts at their likely culpability.

It made sense to visit Briscoe first, as she also lived on Deverton Estate. Blackman consulted her notebook again. Maris Piper Way – that was easy enough. It was on the far side of Deverton, near the cricket pavilion.

Five minutes later, Blackman was ringing on the door of number nine.

A tall lady with a neat black bobbed haircut appeared from the side gate, balancing a chubby toddler on broad Conference pear hips.

"Hi there – Inspector Blackman, wasn't it?"

"Yes. We talked on Saturday."

"Who could forget?" Lindsay Briscoe laughed. "Won't you follow me?"

Blackman followed her down some red flagstones, shutting the gate behind her.

"Thomas, don't do that!" Briscoe commanded, as an older child with the same dark hair and dark eyes dug up mud from the flowerbeds with a stick. "I'm afraid it'll be rather difficult to talk, Inspector," she apologised, leading Blackman into the kitchen.

"Can't be helped," Blackman said gruffly, who didn't find small children in the slightest bit interesting.

"Tea? One doesn't like to offer coffee!" Lindsay Briscoe gave an embarrassed laugh.

"No thanks. I've had my daily quota."

"Health conscious?" Briscoe enquired, putting the younger child in its playpen.

"No – it's just a pain stopping off for the loo all the time when you're out and about!"

"I can imagine!" Briscoe laughed, pouring herself a glass of chilled water. "Thomas! Come inside and play, darling!"

Thomas waddled in and Briscoe murmured something in his ear. He obediently disappeared into a room and fetched some colouring books.

"You've got 'em well-trained!" Blackman laughed politely. She could do this small-talk malarky.

"Yes – well – it's hard work, but if you're consistent and fair, you get there with them in the end. Do you have kids?"

Blackman shook her head. "Never had the time, to be honest."

"Nor the inclination?" Briscoe laughed, her eyes twinkling.

"Something like that," Blackman muttered, opening her notebook. "Now, down to business. As I'm sure you already know, Terence Haynes suffered an anaphylactic shock brought on by peanuts. Not an innocent victim, though, I'm afraid. We haven't had our reports through from Forensic yet, but it's almost certain the peanuts were deliberately placed in his coffee."

"Yes, well, it doesn't take a genius to work that one out," Briscoe smiled wanly. "He was fine till Martin Beauville handed him that cup of decaff."

Blackman read Briscoe's statement to her, that she had been in and out of the kitchen at Zion House a number of times, though mainly first thing that morning and during the lunch preparations. Briscoe had not touched Terence Haynes's flask at all between arriving at 8.55 and the time of his death.

Lindsay Briscoe confirmed that this was correct.

"There are three obvious scenarios, as I'm sure you've already worked out -" Blackman informed her.

"Either the peanuts were in the flask, or Martin Beauville popped one in Terence Haynes's coffee while he was in the kitchen, or someone popped one in his drink at the table,"

Lindsay Briscoe said quickly. The conundrum surrounding the church warden's death had been the subject of much dinner table debate on Deverton Estate.

There's no flies on her, Blackman thought. She could see why Briscoe would be Juliet Parlour's natural ally at Deverton Parish Church. It was interesting how they all tended to refer to one another by their full names now, as if the events of Saturday afternoon had somehow created a distance between them all. Neither was anyone referring to Martin Beauville as Reverend Beauville now.

"Correct. If it's the former, anyone could have done it. We know that Haynes had a "clean" cup of coffee, so to speak, during the morning worship, served to him by Lara Monkton-Smith. The third scenario is highly risky as you were all sat so close together and Haynes was not the type to overlook someone popping something in his cup. If his flask was tampered with, then this must have taken place some time between 9.20 and 2pm. Given the risk of doing such a thing while people were preparing lunch in the kitchen, it's probable it was done during the morning session, perhaps during a trip to the toilet or to fetch a glass of water. Did you leave the meeting room for any reason during this time?"

"I went into the kitchen shortly after Lara made the coffee for everyone. Poor old Daniel had a bit of a coughing fit while leading worship. I went to fetch him a glass of water. But that's all I did!"

"What about trips to the toilet?" Blackman pressed her.

"I was coming to that. I went once, during Martin's talk. I would've waited, but Lara made the coffee so strong! Trying to drop an unsubtle hint to Martin, I daresay. That man makes the weediest cup of coffee you ever tasted, but being thoroughly English, none of us have the guts to ask him to put more powder in! I think quite a lot of people had the same problem, the toilet was much frequented!"

"But –"

"But I didn't go on a magic mystery tour via the kitchen, no," Lindsay Briscoe smiled.

"Are you aware of any reason Martin Beauville might have for wishing Terence Haynes dead?" Blackman carried on.

"You don't seriously suspect Martin, do you?" Lindsay Briscoe looked genuinely shocked. "Surely he was just in the wrong place at the wrong time?"

"Or he assumed we'd think that?" Blackman suggested.

Lindsay Briscoe shook her head definitively. "I'm sure he didn't do it. Besides, he has no reason to. Haynes bossed him around something rotten, but there was no bad blood between them - at least, not that I know of."

"What about Andrew Monkton-Smith? He disappeared to the loo a few times, and left the building for forty-five minutes at lunchtime."

"Andrew?" Lindsay Briscoe echoed. "Oh yes, he shot off to the post office, didn't he? I must say, that was rather odd! I'm sure it could have waited! Not that I'm saying he's lying or anything," she added hastily.

"Oh, he wasn't lying," Blackman replied. "He went to the post office all right. Just took rather a long time over it. Says he prayed in his car for fifteen minutes when he got back, which sounds decidedly fishy to my heathen ears."

"Andrew is a very spiritual man," Lindsay Briscoe agreed. "But you'd think he'd come and get his lunch, wouldn't you? He was probably cross with Lara about something – needed to cool down."

"Did he seem agitated in any way, either before or after he went out?" Blackman asked.

"He did look a little upset about something before lunch," Lindsay Briscoe nodded. "He whispered something in Lara's ear before he went out – he didn't look too pleased."

"What did she do?"

"Oh you know Lara," Lindsay laughed dryly, "just smiled serenely and nodded her head. At a guess, he was annoyed with her about Martin. She was batting the old lashes at him a bit that morning. She has a bit of a thing for him, you know."

"Yes, I did know."

"I don't think she can help the way she feels about Martin, really," Lindsay Briscoe continued. "He's much closer in age to her, after all."

"He's a lot older than her, isn't he – I mean, Monkton-Smith," Blackman commented.

Lindsay nodded. "Mmm… Jules and I have often wondered what drew her to him. I mean he's in pretty good shape for his age, successful, spirtually mature, but the likes of Lara Monkton-Smith could have her pick of the crop – why not go for a younger model?"

"Perhaps it was, as you lot would make out, God's will," Blackman suggested. But she wasn't convinced, either.

"We reckon she was after a father figure," Lindsay confided in Blackman. "Her dad dropped dead from a heart attack when she was sixteen – I don't think she ever really got over it. Andrew was – is – a replacement. That's how she acts around him. There's a lot of affection, but not much spark, if you know what I mean."

Blackman nodded. She had thought the very same thing when she had interviewed them both on Sunday. It was a bit like one of those American films where they need a heavyweight star, so they draft in Michael Douglas to partner their latest Hollywood starlet. There was a comparable lack of chemistry on the set of Lara and Andrew Monkton-Smith's showhome property.

"Not that she'd ever do anything to hurt dear old Andrew," Lindsay added quickly. "She patently adores him."

But does she? Blackman wondered, thinking back to a comment Juliet Parlour had made to her over lunch that Sunday. Juliet had a theory that you could spot whether a couple were really in love, "organically" in love, as she had phrased it, by what they called one another. Couples who referred to one another solely by their real names most decidedly were not. But many couples put on a public front, Blackman thought, not without bitterness. You never really knew what went on behind closed doors. Being formal around one another did not preclude love from the equation. But Juliet Parlour was convinced Lara had married Andrew Monkton-Smith for respectability and security, she was "no way" in love with the greying solicitor.

"What about your husband, Mrs Briscoe?" Blackman enquired. "He's not on the Church Council?"

Lindsay Briscoe snorted. "Charles? Heavens, no. he works in the city. Doesn't get home till nine most evenings."

"He's not a church-goer, then?"

"What makes you say that?" Lindsay enquired, amused. "Because he's a stockbroker?"

"I thought money was the root of all evil," Blackman grinned.

"No, *love* of money is the root of all evil," Lindsay corrected her, attending briefly to Thomas, who had been remarkably undemanding that past ten minutes.

"A stock-broker who doesn't love money?" Blackman laughed, surveying their comfortable surroundings. She felt at ease around Lindsay Briscoe. Despite being a full-time mother, she was interesting and articulate to talk to - much to the surprise of Blackman, who liked to package people in neat little boxes from which they rarely escaped. For Blackman, full-time middle-class Yummy Mummies like Lindsay Briscoe were not generally an interesting subspecies of the human race with their endless debates on child psychology and the evils of chicken nuggets.

She felt briefly uncomfortable as she watched the dark haired woman dab at her young son's nose with a piece of floral kitchen roll. Had she been too forthcoming with details pertaining to the murder enquiry? In her relief at finding someone intelligent to talk to, who had spare time to boot, she had perhaps been a little free-flowing with what could be classed as confidential information. Blackman frowned to herself, feeling suddenly insecure as she had done on leaving the Waggoners. Damn cocky old carrothead Parlour. He wouldn't be in this quandary.

"My husband doesn't love money really," Lindsay protested. "Charles believes Christians should make their presence felt in all echelons of society, not confine themselves to the caring professions – but I won't deny the money doesn't come in useful!"

"Must be hard for you, though," Blackman commented. "You can't get much of a break."

"I don't get out much, no, though Charles does take the kids off my hands at the weekend. That's why I was able to go to the PCC thing last Saturday."

There was a lull in the conversation. Lindsay looked out the window.

"I can't believe one of us would do such an abominable thing, I really can't. It doesn't seem quite real, somehow. I keep thinking this is a tv drama, and there'll be a commercial break any minute!"

"If only," Blackman smiled wryly. "If you had to say one of the PCC members was guilty, who would it be?"

"Oh really, Inspector – you can't expect me to answer that!" Lindsay protested. "I feel I've gossiped enough about my church friends to you already – I'd really rather not indulge in idle speculation, if you don't mind."

"Fair enough," Blackman smiled. "But I would remind you this is a murder inquiry, and what you may classify as gossip or speculation may prove vital to our investigations."

"I suppose so." Lindsay Briscoe looked dubious.

Blackman stood up. "I'll be in touch. And thanks for all your help."

"Only too happy to help," Lindsay smiled. She shook Blackman's hand.

"Oh, Inspector!" she called out, as Blackman let herself out the side gate. "This sounds trivial, but do you know when I'll get my cake tin back? Thomas has a birthday party next week and I don't want to buy another one, if I can help it."

"You should have it back in the next couple of days," Blackman replied, rather non-plussed by the question, then bleeped her car door open.

⧖⧖⧖

Olivia Murray had just got home from work when Blackman arrived at her ramshackle end of terrace cottage in Lexington Green.

"Welcome to my humble abode," Olivia said in her breathy, high-pitched voice, throwing her Danimac loosely over the banister. She stooped to pick up a pile of post which had evidently been hurled through the letter box at high velocity, as if the postman was privvy to the chaotic state of her hallway and had adjudged it appropriate behaviour in the circumstances.

Humble hovel, more like, Blackman thought to herself, surveying the untidy clutter of the hallway. That American bitch from the *Housedoctor* programme would make mincemeat of Olivia Murray!

"Clear yourself a space," Olivia called out, rushing through to the kitchen to feed two of what Blackman, who was allergic to cats, termed sneezes on legs. Blackman helplessly surveyed her surroundings. Every available space was covered with pages of *The Guardian* and library books.

Counselling Theory; The Idiot's Guide to Psychoanalysis; Rogerian Models, Blackman read. So Olivia Murray was one of those feely-touchy group therapy types. A Rose Passmore without the politics. The only thing Olivia Murray had probably burnt in her life was josticks. Blackman laughed at her own joke, then wandered through to the kitchen.

"Mind if I smoke?" she asked. The house was such a tip, she couldn't see it'd make a difference.

"Oh – sure – yes – why not?" Olivia said, looking mildly confused. This appeared to be her natural facial expression. Blackman pulled out a Rigolo paper from her tin and rolled up a cigarette. At least it should help block out the appalling waft of oniony body odour and rotten cat meat that pervaded the cluttered cottage.

"Was it the library you worked?" she enquired, exhaling pleasurably and blowing a smoke ring above her head.

"That's right – yes – the library – yes – at Foxburgh, you know – yes," Olivia mumbled, putting the fork she'd just used to mash up the catfood back in the cutlery drawer. Blackman nearly heaved.

"But you're training to be a counsellor, right?"

"A counsellor – yes – group therapy – mm – you saw my books – yes, that's ri... now where did I put the back door key?" Olivia Murray looked anxiously around, running her hands through her long honey frizz of split ends.

"In the door," Blackman said dryly.

"Oh yes – there it is – right – where was I – cats done – gosh – oh yes, cup of tea, Const.. er.. "

"Inspector," Blackman informed her. *"Detective* Inspector."

"Right – right – Detective Constable – cup of tea coming up – "

"Don't worry about me, Miss Murray, I'm fine, just see to yourself." It was easier in the circumstances.

"See to me – right – OK."

Blackman wandered back through to the living room to escape the horrors of the kitchen. Environmental Health could prosecute, even if she couldn't!

She tilted her head to read the spines of the books untidily "arranged" on some cheap off-white MFI shelves. More counselling textbooks, some dog-eared Virago paperbacks, Origami for Beginners, but no guide to popular allergies!

Blackman swept a mound of paper off what she adjudged to be a sofa, wrinkling her nose up in disgust as a small brown pellet sized object bounced across the floor. She selected an easy chair instead, this time cursing as she got tangled up in a throw. Why did some people persist in putting those things on their furniture? They just looked so untidy and were a pain in the neck to sit on. And then there was all the time-consuming rearranging of the stupid things afterwards. Why not just buy a decent design of suite in the first place?

Olivia Murray came through five minutes later with a buttered crumpet that looked as if it would bounce, and a pint glass of grey tea.

"Right – oh there you are – fine – good – I expect you want to ask me some questions – yes?"

"That's right, Miss Murray," Blackman confirmed, adopting the tone of voice one would use on a small child. She reminded Olivia of her statement that she had arrived at Zion House at 9.10 on Saturday and had entered the kitchen a number of times, but had not touched Haynes's flask.

"Yes – that sounds about right – mm."

Blackman enquired whether she had been eating peanuts, or had nuts in her possession on Saturday.

Olivia Murray shook her head slowly, looking totally dazed. Blackman sighed. She had neither the time nor the patience to make her run through it all again. Olivia Murray couldn't put a ham sandwich together, let alone carry out a premeditated murder requiring cunning and dexterity!

"Could I just ask if you were aware of anyone who may have a grudge against Terence Haynes?"

"Terence – grudge – oh no – why?"

"He did throw his weight about a bit, Miss Murray," Blackman pointed out dryly.

"Weight about – yes, I suppose he did somewhat – mm – authority figure – yes – mm – clearly had control issues – can't think of anyone wanting to – gosh – mm – murder him – haven't given it much thought, really, Inspector!" Olivia Murray looked up from her crumpet.

"An acquaintance of yours has been murdered yards away from you and you haven't given it much thought?" Blackman asked incredulously.

"It's been awfully busy in the library," Olivia replied, looking apologetic.

"No more questions," Blackman said dryly and stood up, feeling a sneeze building up in the bridge of her nose. She was wasting her time here.

⌛⌛⌛

It was quarter past ten when DS Robins finally arrived back at Billock Station clutching a bag of fish and chips.

"Robins – where the flying fudgecake have you been?" Blackman exclaimed, slapping her desk in relief and standing up to greet her sidekick. "Been sat her all on my jacksy waiting for you!"

"I could ask you the same question myself!" Robins retorted. "Charged your mobile recently, boss?"

"What?" Blackman fumbled in her pocket for her mobile. She groaned as it refused to respond. "Sorry, Dave. Been trying to get hold of me?"

"Thought you might like to see this." He handed her a crumpled copy of the fax he'd stumbled upon earlier that afternoon.

"Oh my God!" Blackman gasped. "It's.."

"Nicky Nockers Ellery!" Robins grinned.

She sat down heavily, studying the smudged mascara-ed face of the latest victim of the Foxburgh Red Light Killer.

Nicola Ellery had been strangled, by the looks of it, doubtlessly following a sexual attack.

Blackman looked back up at Robins, mouth still open. "Don't tell me she was…"

"On the game?" Robins grinned. "You'd love that, wouldn't you, boss? Add a bit of spice to proceedings! Unfortunately not."

Apparently Nicky Ellery had met up with some friends in Foxburgh on Sunday night, after which they'd gone on to a club on the corner of the notorious Arches Alley, where the majority of the county capital's "women of the night" hung out. In an attempt to blot out the horrors of the weekend, Ellery had consumed rather a large quantity of alcohol and had fallen asleep under a table in the corner of the *Armadillo* night-club. Thrown out on the street when she was discovered by the club's owners some time after 3 am, and with no money for a taxi, Ellery decided to call her housemate, Alex Miller, on her mobile. Suffering from a heavy cold, it was with some degree of annoyance that Miller agreed to drive to Foxburgh in the early hours of the morning. But when he finally arrived outside the Armadillo club just after 4 am, there was no sign of Nicky Ellery. Eight hours later, in a disused warehouse on some wasteland near Foxburgh Station, a homeless youth with canine companion, seeking shelter from the elements, had stumbled upon the semi-naked body of Nicola Louise Ellery and had alerted the local police.

"Good God, I guess Alex Miller's in a bit of a state!" Blackman exclaimed.

Robins nodded. "Blaming himself, of course. Said he was pissed off with Nicky for getting him out of bed and hadn't exactly shifted his arse to get to Foxburgh."

"But our Red Van man was probably had his eye on her as soon as they chucked her out that club," Blackman protested. "It's the clubowner, if anyone, who's to blame."

"That's what we told him," Robins informed her.

"And it's definitely the work of the Red Light killer?" Blackman checked.

Robins nodded. "Same marks on her body, evidence of sexual assault, death by strangulation. Oh, and red paint under a couple of fingernails."

"No link to Haynes's murder, of course," Blackman stated. "Just an appalling coincidence. Better let the Church know, I guess."

"I think old Motormouth Jason Jarvis has already seen to that, boss," Robins smiled wryly. "So where've you been all day? Lerwick was trying to get the low-down on Nicky Ellery from you."

Blackman snorted. "Bloody Poxville, where else? Gawd, give me some hardened prostitute over Olivia Bloody Murray any day!" She grabbed a handful of Robins's soggy chips. "Dozy bitch!"

"Been interviewing all day?" Robins asked through a mouthful of cod in batter.

"Home visits," Blackman grunted. "Forensic still haven't touched the stuff from Zion House. At least they've sent Haynes' keys on, as requested."

"They were starting on it this afternoon, I think," Robins informed her.

"Well, they didn't bloody tell me," Blackman complained.

"Beauville still our chief suspect?"

Blackman made a face. "Yes, though everyone reckons Beauville's whiter than white."

"You want it to be him, don't you?" Robins asked, polishing off the chips.

"It would be a great scoop, you have to admit," Blackman grinned. "Mr Perfect Vicar bumps off nasty Church Warden."

"Is this a personal vendetta against the Church of England or can anyone join in?"

"They get up my nose, that's all, bloody Christians," Blackman snorted.

"I'll tell Parlour to stay away from the coffee machine!"

"Oh, Pizza's OK. It's the rest of them. Praying in the carpark, my arse! If one more person tells me Andrew Monkton-Smith is a "very spiritual man," I'll clock 'em one!"

"So what's the crack? We're going to raid Terence Haynes' drawers tonight?" Robins grinned.

"You betcha. As yet we've no clear motive for anyone to kill him. Hopefully we'll find something incriminating amongst his stuff."

Robins wiped his hands on his suit trousers and grabbed his keys. "What are we waiting for, then?"

⧗⧗⧗

It was dark in King Edward Mews at ten forty that Monday night. With the majority of the residents being professionals facing an early start, most of the houses stood in darkness, with only the odd muted light in the upstairs rooms.

"Come on, Mulder," Blackman grinned.

"Got your swag bag?" Robins chuckled. A security light came on as they approached the front door of the large red brick property that had been home to the late Terence Haynes.

Blackman turned the key in the lock and beckoned Robins inside. She turned the hall light on then retrieved some items of post from the wire basket attached to the inside of the door. She paused to leaf through the letters. There was nothing of interest, just a couple of bills and the ubiquitous car insurance junk mail.

"Shit Shit Shit!" Blackman suddenly yelled as a burglar alarm started to shriek like an air-raid warning. "Why didn't I think of that? Idiot!"

Robins froze for a second, before spotting the flashing panel above the front door. "What's his date of birth?"

Blackman hastily leafed through her pocket book. "Twentieth of April, nineteen forty. Try 20440."

She clicked her tongue nervously as lights in the houses opposite began to flicker on.   As Robins fumbled unsuccessfully with various combinations, a steady trickle of bleary-eyed residents appeared on the pavement outside. It was no good, she would need to radio for assistance.

Blackman strode outside, assuming the required air of brazen confidence, and addressed the small posse in dressing-gowns. Fortunately for them, it was a warm evening. She held up her police badge. "Detective Inspector Blackman, Foxburgh Police. We have a warrant to search Terence Haynes' house. Does anyone know the combination for this bloody thing?"

Doh! As if. Unsurprisingly, Haynes had put Fort Knox to shame with his complicated security device and nobody could offer any assistance.

"Not having much luck here, boss!" Robins moaned, having exhausted all the logical combinations based on Haynes' date of birth plus a few relevant dates in modern warfare history.

A familiar figure pulled up outside in a silver SLK five minutes later.

"Leigh – what the hell's going on?"

"Mark!" Blackman exclaimed. "What are you doing here?"

"You can hear that blinking alarm for miles! Thought I'd better come and investigate!"

"You don't know the number for Haynes' burglar alarm, do you?"

"No idea, sorry," Parlour apologised, then looked in his rear view mirror. "Here comes the cavalry!"

Blackman groaned, as a cavalcade of police cars, blue lights flashing, screamed into King Edward Mews, adding to the commotion. "Who rang the bloody station?"

"It's probably linked to a security firm," Parlour bellowed at her through the deafening wail of the alarm. "It would alert the police automatically. Nice one!"

Parlour grinned unhelpfully as he leant against his car. "Gordon Brown, that burglar alarm cannot be legal!"

Robins joined them outside. "I've tried every combination I can think of, boss!"

"Got any ideas, before I take an axe to it?" Blackman asked Parlour desperately.

"I tell you what you could do," Parlour replied, suddenly having a brainwave. "Ring the Monkton-Smiths. They use the same cleaner as Terence Haynes did. Get her number from them – she'd know the combination."

"God, I'll be popular!" Blackman moaned, glancing at her wristwatch. It was just before eleven.

Five minutes and several phone calls later, the alarm was successfully turned off.

"OK OK, show's over," Blackman yelled, waving her arms at the huddle of angry neighbours and disgruntled police officers.

She stopped Parlour in his tracks as he followed her up the driveway. "Sorry, Mark. I can't let you in on this."

Parlour hesitated a moment, then sighed in resignation, returning to his car.

Blackman shut the door behind her and took the first room on her left. It appeared to be the late Mrs Haynes's sitting room, as a collapsed wheelchair leant against the wall, and some dusty embroidery lay on the coffee table. It was a pretty poignant scene. Clearly Terence Haynes had not felt able to discard her belongings. *So the man was human,* she thought. But before Blackman could proceed further with her investigations, Robins called down from the landing.

"Boss – come up here! He's got a study!"

Blackman ran upstairs. Robins emerged from a back bedroom. "Looks like this is the nerve centre."

Blackman followed him into the small box room that Haynes had converted into an office.

"Right – get searching," Blackman commanded. One side contained wall to wall shelves, jammed full of military books and journals and expensive, leather-bound photo albums.

Blackman leafed through them but they all seemed to contain pictures of naval vessels with the odd group photo. The last album, clearly a personal collection that Haynes, true to character, had kept separate from his professional photos, contained a number of shots of his beloved wife. Blackman, who could not stand to think about death and disease, snapped the album shut as Davinia Haynes began to visibly decay before her.

"Hello hello, what's this?" Robins murmured. Blackman turned round. Robins was unzipping an A4 leather wallet next to a smart black *Dell* computer. Suddenly he drew in his breath.

"Here – have a decko at this!" He handed a sheet of paper to her. It was high quality cream writing paper, which Haynes had clearly had professionally designed for him with his name, title and address emblazoned across the top. On it was typed a letter, dated Friday 24 May 2002.

Dear Bishop Shadwell, Blackman read to herself, *I feel I cannot hide my dissatisfaction any longer at the appointment of Martin Beauville to the position of Priest in Charge at Deverton Parish Church. As I have mentioned to you on several occasions recently, I deem him wholly unsuitable for the post for reasons I now wish to make known to you in person. This is a delicate matter that I would not wish to discuss by letter or by telephone, therefore I am requesting a private meeting with you at your convenience. I await your prompt response, yours in Christ, Cdr Terence Haynes, Church Warden, Deverton Parish Church.*

"Yes!" Blackman yelled triumphantly. "Got him!"

"You think Beauville got wind of this?" Robins asked.

"You bet I do!"

"Wonder what the naughty bugger's been up to!" Robins chuckled. "Want me to put a call through to the station to arrest Beauville?"

"No – not yet," Blackman replied. "We'll get an officer on the house, check he stays put, then we'll pay him a visit tomorrow morning with some reinforcements. Let's search the rest of the house first."

But there was nothing else of interest, aside from a very impressive collection of medals and the much-touted letter from the former Prime Minister.

"Need to set the alarm again," Robins reminded Blackman as they headed towards the front door. "The cleaner said it was the same number, plus *away*."

"Blimey – what's that?" Blackman asked as a number of green and orange lights came on and a message flashed up. *"Display log?"* she read.

Robins pressed the enter key and a number of lines appeared on the LCD panel.

"That's pretty hi-tech!" Robins commented, peering at the screen. "It tells you what time people last entered and exited the house. Pretty smart bit of kit – wonder what the old boy paid for that?"

"Here – gis a look!" Blackman shoved him out the way. "What's this H and A before each time?"

"Home and Away," Robins warbled, *"with you each day! Let me be the one –"*

"Dave!" Blackman interrupted him. She whistled. "That's interesting!"

"What?"

"Haynes went out three times on Saturday morning. He went out at 8.00, returning two minutes later. Then he went out again at 8.15, returning at 8.21, before leaving for Zion House shortly after."

"Perhaps he forgot his wallet or something," Robins said, thinking nothing of it.

"He wasn't the forgetful type, by all accounts," Blackman replied, staring at the panel, thinking hard. "He couldn't have, anyway. Juliet Parlour saw him walk past her house just after eight."

"Could have been 8.15," Robins commented. "That's just after eight, isn't it?"

"By Robins Mean Time, yes," Blackman replied. "By normal people's standards, that means about five or ten past. Otherwise you'd say quarter past eight, wouldn't you? Anyway, it takes about five minutes to get from his house to hers, so it would've been 8.20, so there's no way he could have gone to the newsagents and come back by 8.21! It's a good twenty-five minute walk, there and back."

"How do you know he went to the paper shop?" Robins, who wanted to get home, frowned.

"Christ, Dave!" Blackman blasphemed. "Don't you ready any of my notes? He took the dog out at eight on the dot every morning. Anyone in Deverton can tell you that."

"Where *is* the dog?"

"Mrs Fosthlewaite's looking after it. She came to collect it Saturday night when she heard of Haynes' death. That's the 18.32 entry on the screen."

"So what are you saying?" Robins frowned.

"I'm wondering whether someone was in the house while he was out his walk," Blackman replied. "Waited to see him go out at eight, then sneaked in, leaving at 8.15 in good time for him returning from the newsagents."

"Could have just been what's her name, Mrs Fossilthingy, the cleaner."

"I think she would take a little longer than twenty minutes to clean the house!"

"I was operating on *Robins Clean Time*!"

"Ha ha."

"She might have come in, seen there wasn't much to be done, and just quickly tidied up for him," Robins suggested.

"I suppose she could have. We'll need to check up on that. Or she could have left something there by mistake and came to pick it up," Blackman reasoned. "He wasn't in, so she let herself in with the key."

"But if she knew his routine, she'd know he was out. Why not come round when he was in?"

"Perhaps she was in a hurry?" Blackman suggested. "Or she disliked him as much as everyone else, didn't want to be there while he was at home? She's the obvious candidate, as she would have a key in any case – though I suppose someone could have copied Haynes's key from her collection of the things. She seems to clean half the houses in Deverton. I can't imagine for one minute Terence Haynes ever left his keys lying about. Not if he was so security mad that he had a system like this installed!"

"Whoever it was would have to have known how to turn off this bloody air raid siren, anyway," Robins stated. "Either Mrs Fossil or –"

"It's Fosthlewaite-"

"- or a friend, or a member of his family."

"He didn't have any close friends, by all accounts, and he didn't have any family. His wife couldn't have children and both sets of parents are long since dead."

"Siblings?" Robins suggested.

"Haynes was an only child. His late wife has a sister in New Zealand. I should think it's rather unlikely she turned up, though I suppose we ought to check up on it."

"I reckon either Mrs Fosthlewaite popped round for something, or Haynes forgot something and Parlour's wife got the time wrong."

"Still couldn't have gone to the newsagents and back in six minutes," Blackman said, shaking her head. "However, he could have gone somewhere else. We'll never know, I suppose."

"We could check with Mrs F, see if she did come round on Saturday morning," Robins shrugged.

"And check with Juliet Parlour that she did see him at just after eight as she said," Blackman added, "oh, and ask the neighbours if they saw him."

"Can we go now?" Robins begged. "My dinner's already in the girlfriend – it would be nice if I could get back for a bedtime story."

"Is that what they call it these days?" Blackman muttered, watching him set the alarm. Switching the lights off, they locked the door of 8 King Edward Mews and returned to their vehicles.

<h1 style="text-align:center">9</h1>

"Could I have a bit of hush, pur-lease!" Blackman bellowed, entering the incident room at Billock Police Station at nine o'clock that Tuesday morning.

The debate on last night's Premiership soccer match died down.

"OK. Robins and I have some news for you-"

"Wey-hey!" the shout went up.

"Very funny. But first I want to hear your news. Denton – you managed to get hold of our resident double act, I believe?"

"Jarvis and Miller, yes," DC Sean Denton replied, nodding. Both had been in a state of shock about the death of their housemate, Nicky Ellery, but had managed to talk to the Detective Constable in the end. Jarvis had admitted to playing a few tricks on Haynes in the past, but none recently. Apparently Andrew Monkton-Smith had given them a ticking off after the last escapade involving some laxative pills, accusing them of un-Christ like behaviour, and they had decided to give Haynes a break. Neither Jarvis nor Miller had gone near the silver flask all morning, and neither had they popped crushed peanuts into the flask cup at the table nor seen anyone else acting suspiciously.

"What about Haynes?" Blackman barked impatiently. "Did he consult Alex Miller about his allergy?"

Denton shook his head. "Miller said the first he'd heard of any allergy was when Haynes died on Saturday. Said Haynes had never mentioned anything about it, and wouldn't have, anyway. They didn't have a respectful relationship. Apparently Haynes felt nursing was a woman's job – told Miller on several occasions he ought to pack it in and get a real man's job."

Blackman snorted. "Sounds like our Terence. What about Jarvis?"

"I got hold of Jarvis at work. He hadn't been near the flask, either. To be honest, boss, neither of them struck me as being the murdering type, especially given how cut-up they were about Nicky Ellery's death. They might like a laugh from time to time, but they seemed pretty clean-scrubbed and decent below the jokey exterior. Can't imagine they did it."

"Well, let's not rule them out just yet," Blackman warned them. "What about the peanuts – Preece, you were on that, weren't you?"

DC Karen Preece nodded. According to the Store Manager at Melrose Supermarket, hundreds, even thousands of people bought peanuts from their store every week and they could not possibly remember faces. Due to Data Protection laws, they had been unable to access a list of loyalty card owners who had purchased peanuts at that branch, despite Preece's best efforts. The young Detective Constable had had enquired in the local shops as well, but without any joy.

"To be honest, Ma'am, it seems like a bit of a wild goose chase, as peanuts are the kind of thing you keep knocking around in your drinks cabinet for months."

"Point taken, Preece," Blackman sighed. "What about surgeries or the Allergy Control Centre?"

Preece had contacted all the dieticians, nutritionists and GPs in the area, as well as the biomedical sciences department at Bowhampton Institute and the National Allergy Control Centre, but apparently there had been no pertinent requests for information. However, in Preece's opinion, the murderer could easily have found that kind of information on the Internet, in any case.

Blackman groaned. "The World-Wide Bloody Web's got a lot to answer for. Who was interviewing the Keltys?"

"Me," DC Darren Keough replied. "Daniel Kelty admitted under duress that he'd had a minor set to Haynes two weeks ago. Haynes wanted more traditional hymns in the worship, but Kelty told him traditional hymns didn't bring young people into the church. However, they thrashed out a compromise, so it didn't really come to anything. Other than that, Kelty said they had a perfectly civil, if not exactly close, relationship. Christine Kelty ditto. She said she was rather afraid of Haynes and tended to stay out his way. Both denied touching the flask, and neither appear to have any motive to want Haynes dead."

"Well, I revisited Lindsay Briscoe and Olivia Murray yesterday," Blackman informed them. "Briscoe was in and out the kitchen quite a lot, by her own admission, but said she never touched the flask. Haynes didn't bother her particularly and, frankly, I can't see her doing it, unless there's some massive skeleton in her closet. She's got two lovely kids, her husband earns a packet in the City, why would she want to get herself banged up for life? Besides, she's very pally with Parlour's wife, which isn't in itself a character reference, but I can't imagine Juliet Parlour hanging around with anyone dodgy. Olivia Murray is completely dippy – could hardly get her brain in gear to answer a few simple questions, so can't imagine her planning a crime like this. Ditto Mavis Wagstaff."

"A fax arrived from Forensic half an hour ago," Robins continued. "They haven't checked everything, but they've checked Haynes's flask for prints. As predicted, there are just three sets of prints on the screw top – those of Haynes himself, Lara Monkton-Smith and Martin Beauville. But, as we know, anyone could have unscrewed the top using a teatowel or wearing marigolds, so that doesn't tell us much. As far as peanuts are concerned, there are clear traces of salted peanut in Terence Haynes' coffee cup *and* the flask itself, which would seem to rule out the insertion of peanuts in the cup at the table. It would also seem to weaken the case against Martin Beauville, however..."

Blackman had decided to allow Robins the moment of glory, as finder of the incriminating letter.

"We found this in Haynes's study when we searched the house last night."

Robins clicked the overhead projector on. He had made a transparency of the letter. A few whistles were let out as the murder inquiry team read its contents.

"Robins and I are going to pay Beauville a visit this morning," Blackman informed her team. "We'll take some constables with us just in case he makes a confession or anything like that. However, I need one of you to contact the Bishop, to ask if he had an inkling what Haynes was so mad about. We need someone with tact and diplomacy to do this – the Bishop is a very powerful man in these parts. I thought you, Karen."

Karen Preece nodded, visibly pleased. Blackman did not hand out praise readily.

"Also, as some of you may have heard, Robins and I had a fight with a burglar alarm last night. Haynes has got some super-duper space-age security system that tells you what time people entered and left the house. It looks like someone entered the house while he walked the dog down to the newsagents on Saturday morning. The only person with the key and knowledge of the security system, as far as we know, is a Mrs Mary Fosthlewaite, his cleaner. Firstly, could one of you find out whether she popped round there Saturday morning and if not, whether she gave the key or details of the burglar alarm system to a third party. We also need Haynes's PC examined – Sean, could you organise that for me as well?"

Denton met her eye and nodded.

"Also, Sean, if it wasn't the cleaner who entered the house, and if she didn't either lend someone else the key or leave it knocking about, someone must have made a sneaky copy of it. Can you get a uniformed officer to check out all the local locksmiths, and outlets providing keycutting services? Ta."

Blackman took a deep breath.

"OK everyone, report back here at 5 o'clock sharp! Robins - tell Tucks and Singh to follow us in a marked car, I'll meet you in the carpark."

The vicarage was a split-level detached a hundred yards down the road from Deverton Parish Church. On first appearances it seemed rather large for a single man with limited material possessions to his name. Yet somehow Martin Beauville seemed to fill it with his sheer presence.

"Come in – the door's open!" beckoned a voice from the front room, as Blackman and Robins knocked on the door at five to ten that sunny spring morning.

"Bit of a security risk, isn't it, Vicar?" Blackman asked dryly, entering the front room, where the Reverend Martin Beauville was elegantly arranged in a winged armchair opposite a figure in purple, whom Blackman guessed to be the Bishop of Foxburgh, the Right Reverend Shadwell Allbright.

"I work on the theory that if some poor soul needs my belongings so badly, he resorts to burglary, he's welcome to them! What are possessions but mere hay and stubble?"

"All the same," Blackman added somewhat acerbically and a mite ironically, "I would be a little more careful, with a murderer on the rampage!"

"Anyway," Beauville waved his hand, standing up, "You're just in time to meet the Bishop! He's just come back from a four week retreat in the Swiss Alps. Some would call it an extended jolly, of course, but I shall give him the benefit of the doubt!"

Clearly Beauville was on very pally terms with the Bishop. Blackman smiled politely, shooting Robins a sidelong glance. Good job they'd told PCs Tucker and Singh to wait round the corner in the marked car. She murmured a good morning to the rather gangly man before her, not sure whether she should curtsey or something.

"I'm Detective Inspector Leigh Blackman of Foxburgh Police, and this is my colleague, Detective Sergeant David Robins. We're investigating the murder of Terence Haynes."

"Yes, yes, awful business," Shadwell Allbright nodded gravely. "I was shocked to hear the news when I got back from Heathrow late last night. Of course, I took the first opportunity to come down and see Martin."

"Do sit down," Beauville smiled at the two detectives. "We've just had a cup of tea – can I get you two something?"

Blackman shook her head, still looking at the Bishop. "No thanks. We actually came to ask Mr Beauville a few questions, but we do need to speak to you too, er, Bishop. One of my officers was going to contact you today – but perhaps we could speak to you after we've spoken to Mr Beauville?"

The Bishop shook his head. "Regrettably I have a service to attend at St Jude's, hence the full regalia. However, I shall be free around midday. Perhaps I could pop by the station in Foxburgh?"

"The incident room's at Billock Police Station, actually."

"Oh well, I'll come to Billock! Have car, will travel!"

"That would be most helpful, Bishop," Blackman replied. *You might be grinning the other side of your face by the time I've finished with you,* she thought to herself. "I'll ensure DS Preece is available to talk to you."

"Well, it was nice meeting you," the Bishop smiled, then turned to Beauville. "Chin up, Martin. You'll come through this. Let's just hope the police can sort this sorry mess out before word gets any further."

The Bishop gave him a comforting pat on the back as Beauville saw him to the door.

"So what can I do for you?" Beauville smiled, returning to his floral easy chair, leaning his elbows on the rests. He ran a slender hand through his silky, jet-black hair. Pianist's hands, Blackman thought, and right enough, there was an upright piano to one side of the room. Did she imagine it, or did he look vaguely nervous below the polished veneer?

"As you are doubtless aware, Terence Haynes died of an anaphylactic shock on Saturday afternoon, and forensic reports indicate this was caused by the insertion of peanuts in his Thermos flask, sometime between the end of morning coffee and the serving of afternoon coffee."

"I didn't put anything in his coffee," Beauville said calmly, "but do carry on."

"Thank you. We have reason to believe Terence Haynes had some objections to your appointment as Vicar of Deverton Parish Church."

"Oh yes?" Martin Beauville queried calmly.

"You don't seem very surprised, Mr Beauville," Blackman commented. Beauville looked her straight in the eye.

"Terence Haynes was a difficult man to please, Inspector, as I am sure you're already aware. It doesn't surprise me in the least that he should object to me in some shape or form. I'm only a humble parish vicar, after all, and certainly not beyond contempt!"

"That's not the impression we've gleaned from others," Blackman said dryly. "Excuse the industrial language, but people round here seem to think the sun shines out your backside."

Beauville laughed, a faint flush rising up his sculptured features. "There's no accounting for taste, Inspector!"

"Are you aware of any reason why Terence Haynes should dislike you, or object to your recent appointment as parish priest?"

"No good reason, no," Beauville replied. "I think he felt I was too young to occupy such a position, but there was no brawl in the vestry, if that's what you're inferring."

"Had you met Terence Haynes before you arrived at Deverton Parish Church last November?" Robins chipped in, bored of spectating.

"I never made his acquaintance before arriving at Deverton, no," Beauville replied, shaking his head. "He introduced himself at the licensing and informed me he was likely to be voted in as church warden, which duly took place."

"Some of your parishioners have commented that you appeared oddly deferential to Haynes, in a way that you didn't appear to be with, say, Rose Passmore, the other church warden," Robins stated. "How do you account for this?"

Beauville raised his eyebrows at Robins. "He's a senior member of our congregation. He was also much decorated in the Falklands War, which I should say commands one's utmost respect, irrespective of status within the church, wouldn't you, Inspector? As parish priest, I have to set an example of love and humility, as was modelled by our Lord Jesus Christ. I do not see it as my place to react to, shall we say, a little self-importance on the part of parishioners."

"Even if he threatened to report you to the Bishop?" Blackman said bluntly, delivering the killer blow. Beauville frowned, his dark eyebrows almost meeting in the middle.

"Report me to the Bishop? Whatever for?"

He's a good actor, Blackman thought, *I'll grant him that.*

"We have evidence that Terence Haynes requested a private meeting with the Bishop to discuss your appointment," Blackman informed him, trying not to sound too smug.

"Well, the Bishop didn't say anything about it just now," Beauville replied, looking somewhat bemused.

"Haynes never got round to asking him."

"Look, what evidence is this?" Beauville enquired, his tone suddenly changing. "I don't lay much store by tittle-tattle."

Blackman coolly handed him a photocopy of the letter. He scanned it quickly.

"Oh dear!" Beauville exclaimed, looking mildly shocked. "He wrote this Friday – the day before he died," he stated, looking up and meeting Blackman's narrow eyes.

"Yes," she said, meeting his gaze and holding it. Suddenly Beauville put two and two together.

"Oh I see. You think I killed Haynes because he wanted to vent his disapproval of me to Bishop Shadwell! Scraping the proverbial barrel a bit, aren't we, Inspector?"

Robins studied his face. He seemed genuine enough.

"Seems rather an extreme step on the part of Terence Haynes, don't you think, Mr Beauville, writing to the Bishop, just because he felt you were a little wet behind the ears?" Blackman enquired smoothly.

"Indeed," Beauville replied. "Perhaps he had something else against me, but I cannot think of a single thing I have done to incur his wrath since I've been here. He certainly never informed me of anything I had done to annoy him over the course of the last few months."

"Some ideological or theological differences, maybe?" Blackman proposed.

"No, nothing like that," Beauville replied, shaking his head, glancing at the letter again. "In fact, Terence and I agreed on most things. Neither of shared the liberal views of, say, Rose Passmore or Olivia Murray. I would say we had a very good working relationship. Of course, we weren't bosom buddies, but it doesn't do to get too pally with one's parishioners, anyway. That's when misunderstandings arise."

He's referring to Lara Monkton-Smith, Blackman guessed. She'd get round to her in a minute.

"Really," Beauville continued, "I can say hand on heart, I am not aware of anything I have done since my arrival here in November that would incur the wrath of Terence Haynes."

"It's all very odd, Mr Beauville, wouldn't you agree?" Blackman said, with the tone of silken sarcasm she had perfected over the years and reserved for her juiciest suspects.

"A veritable mystery," Beauville responded equally smoothly, handing her back the letter. "You'll have to ask the

Bishop – and perhaps you'd be good enough to let me know if you find out why."

"Naturally," Blackman replied. Time for bullet number two.

"What are your feelings for Mrs Monkton-Smith, Mr Beauville?" she enquired.

"Pardon?" Beauville asked, looking non-plussed.

"I have it on good authority that Lara Monkton-Smith carried a torch for you."

"Dear me, the church gossips have been exercising their tongues, haven't they?" Beauville chuckled, but his eyes weren't smiling.

"Actually, it was Mrs Monkton-Smith who told us herself. She had some reason to believe the feeling was mutual."

Beauville sobered up. "I'm aware she's – um – attracted to me. But nothing has ever happened between us, and never would. She's devoted to Andrew, and I, Inspector, am devoted to my job. If I gave the slightest impression of feeling anything for her beyond pastoral concern, it was certainly never intentional."

He looked at her very hard with his piercing blue eyes.

"Perhaps Terence Haynes was aware of Mrs Monkton-Smith's feelings and, seeing you together, arrived at a false conclusion?" Blackman proposed.

Beauville shrugged. "It can't be ruled out, I suppose, but I was careful not to be seen alone with her for that very reason. As a vicar, and a single man, I have to protect my image."

"Do you intend to marry, Reverend Beauville?" Blackman enquired.

"Gosh – that's rather a personal question. If you must know, I believe I've been called to celibacy."

I'm celibate, Robins smirked to himself, remembering a Jane Horrocks line from *Absolutely Fabulous*. But in this instance, the claimant was neither fat nor ugly, and almost certainly not short of offers.

"I see," Blackman replied dubiously.

"If you're inferring that Terence saw Lara and me together and I killed him to stop him blabbing, you'd be exceedingly wide of the mark, Inspector," Beauville informed her, an edge to his voice this time.

"So why *would* you kill him, then?" Blackman asked, taking a gamble she'd catch him on the hop. Robins took a sharp intake of breath.

"I did not murder Terence Haynes, Inspector," Beauville stated firmly.

There was a lull in the conversation. Blackman looked around the room. "Don't have much stuff, do you, Reverend?"

"What do you mean?" Beauville enquired, bemused.

"Well most people, even your age, have acquired a fair amount of paraphernalia by now, yet you have very little in the way of possessions."

"Must be all those burglars that pass through," Beauville smiled, referring to their opening exchange. Robins smirked. "Actually, Inspector, I try not to accumulate too many material possessions. Can't take them upstairs with you."

"Quite," Blackman responded, not wishing to enter into a debate on the afterlife at that delicate juncture.

"Mind if we have a quick look round?" she asked. Robins frowned at her. But Beauville just smiled serenely and extended a welcome hand.

"Be my guest, Inspector. I have nothing to hide."

"Is this really necessary?" Robins hissed in Blackman's ear as Beauville went to answer a ringing phone.

"Oh come on, Robins!" Blackman hissed back. "The guy's obviously hiding something. You read that letter – there's no smoke without fire. Besides, don't you think it's weird he's got this huge house that's practically empty bar a piano and a few paperback books?"

"He's a single man, for God sake," Robins replied. "It's women that fill their houses up with fluffy bunnies and nicknacks. I think it looks better this way."

"Don't give me all that sexist crap!" Blackman hissed. "The man's either made one almighty trip to the Household Refuse Site or he's run away from somewhere. I've seen it before – people who move to another town and completely reinvent themselves. Sell their possessions, make a whole new life for themselves."

"You'll be telling me next he's Elvis!" Robins exclaimed. "The Sewer won't approve of this, you know," he added. "You haven't a shred of evidence he's any more guilty than the next man – or woman."

"Beauville gave his permission, didn't he?" Blackman challenged him. Robins couldn't argue with that. "Now get looking."

"You might like to see my office," Beauville smiled, re-entering the room. "I believe you will find a higher density of material possessions there."

"Smartarse!" Blackman cursed under her breath as they followed in his wake.

"Here's my filing cabinet – do feel free. I would request, however, that you do not reveal any material of a confidential nature to parishioners on your suspect list. These are just reference books on the shelf. The bedroom's next door, when you've finished here. I'll be downstairs if you want me – I've just joined the local light operatic society and have a piece I need to practise."

"Satisfied?" Robins asked Blackman. "The guy's as clean as a whistle, I'm telling you."

"Don't bet on it," Blackman replied darkly, searching through the green hanging files in the metal cabinet. *Church Expenditure, Church Insurance, Deanery Synod, Diocesan Grants,* she read, briefly rattling through the contents. There was nothing of interest here. Blackman double-checked, but it all seemed in order.

But hold on, what was that covered over with a dark cloth? Blackman pulled it up and found a spanking new AppleMac computer underneath.

"Robins!"

Her colleague appeared from the bedroom next door.

"He's got a computer!" she went to switch it on, but Robins put a restraining hand on her arm.

"Boss, I think you should ask his permission first. He's been up front with us."

"Has he?" Blackman challenged him. But it wouldn't do to incur the wrath of Sewell, should Beauville decide to report her for unlawful entry to a computer system.

She went downstairs where the vicar was belting out a Gilbert and Sullivan number.

"Mr Beauville –"

"Yes, Inspector?" he smiled, coming to a halt.

"You have a computer upstairs."

"Yes – ugly thing, isn't it? And they say it's cutting edge technology. Looks like a bubble! That's why I keep it covered up. The vicarage came equipped with it. It's got email and the dreaded Internet on it, but to be honest, I hardly touch it. Someone showed me how to use the email thing, but frankly, it's not my style. The art of conversation is dying quickly enough without this *bête-noir*, don't you think?"

"It has its uses," Blackman replied neutrally, who was herself something of a technophobe.

"Oh, I dare say it has. I've used the word processing package a couple of times, to type letters and things, but frankly I don't see the point. That's what we pay a secretary for."

Philistine! Blackman thought to herself.

"Do you mind if we take a look?" she enquired.

Beauville looked slightly taken-aback. He shrugged. "I don't see why not – but you won't find anything much on it.

As I said, I rarely use the thing. But you'll need a password to open my emails. Hold on."

He went into the hallway and fished a slimline electronic organiser from the pocket of his sports jacket.

"This is about the limit of my technical knowledge!" Beauville smiled, tapping on a few keys. "It's supposed to increase my street-cred as a vicar! Here we go, my password. I can never remember the stupid thing."

Could just be for show, Blackman told herself, *to give us the impression he never uses the computer.*

He passed Blackman the organiser and she noted the combination of digits and letters down in her notepad.

"Thank you."

"I should say, however, I do have half a dozen young mums coming round in ten minutes. Would it be at all possible to come back another time to look at the computer?"

That's convenient, Blackman thought cynically. "Perhaps we could take it with us?" she suggested.

"Gosh... that seems a little extreme, Inspector," Beauville replied, raising his considerable eyebrows at her. "But I don't see why not. As long as you put it back together again for me – because I wouldn't have a clue!"

"Naturally," Blackman said curtly. She got her walkie-talkie out her coat pocket and radioed her police constable. Tucker, evidently bored, responded immediately.

"I see you came with reinforcements!" Beauville commented dryly, as the marked car slunk up outside two minutes later.

"We have to be prepared for every eventuality," Blackman said functionally, as Tucker joined Robins upstairs.

"Sorry I couldn't oblige with a nice confession!" Beauville smiled.

Blackman just smiled blandly and waited for her men to return downstairs with the vicar's computer.

10

Alex Miller glanced up from his nursing textbook to the clock on the kitchen wall. *Any moment now you're going to walk through that door, fling that silly little rucksack of yours across the table and demand a cup of tea!* But it was no good. Nicky wasn't coming back, not today, not ever.

He closed his green eyes and backcombed his dry black hair with large, knuckly fingers. A dead-ringer for the former Olympic sprinter, Allan Wells, Alex Miller had the well-bred, well-fed physique of a rugby-playing doctor's son. Unable to take up a place on a Medicine degree course, having squandered the educational opportunities afforded him by the local tertiary college in favour of the 25 watt allure of Billock's nightlife, Miller had settled for the next best thing in his view, a career in nursing. This was a view not shared by his father, who was much of Terence Haynes's opinion when it came to male nurses. But Alex didn't care. He'd always been fascinated by the hospital environment, which, allied with a caring personality, made nursing an ideal vocation. Besides, he didn't want to sit around for a year taking resits in the vague hope he might scrape onto a medical degree course. Life was too short. In any case, the starting pay in nursing was reasonable at the moment, with the Labour government desperate to train up more nurses to cover the national shortage. He'd have to take the long hours on the chin, though.

Alex had cared a great deal for Nicky Ellery, though his feelings ran somewhat beyond a concern for her physical wellbeing. He wandered into the living room in the considerable soles of his white sports socks and picked up, not for the first time since the shocking news of Nicky's murder had come through, a framed photo of the three of them at Jason's birthday party just last month. He put it down again, sighing. They'd had fun, the three of them, in the relatively short time they'd spent as housemates. Who knows what could've happened between Nicky and himself, had her future, their future, not been so cruelly snuffed out? Nothing, he smiled ruefully, if Terence Haynes had had anything to do with it. Terence had not approved of their houseshare on Deverton Estate. For Haynes, it was tantamount to living in sin, Nicky sharing the house in Battenberg Close with two unmarried men. Despite their protestations that it was a purely practical arrangement between friends, that made financial sense, and was hardly a menage-a-trois, Terence would not back down. Nicky, perhaps naturally, given society's unfair onus on women to uphold moral standards, had borne the brunt of Haynes's ire, and had, in turn, reacted the most vehemently of the three, reminding Haynes that they were in the 21st century now and this was suburban Britain, not Army Boot Camp. Jason, on the other hand, had found it something of an accolade to be publicly branded a stud, but Alex, as the more spiritually mature of the two young men, had felt the slight on his reputation more keenly.

Alex had no intention, though, of mentioning the dispute to that ballsy female inspector, or to Mark Parlour, either, for that matter. He might be a brother in Christ and all that, but Miller didn't believe for one minute that Parlour would hesitate to keep a choice bit of ammunition like that to himself. And Alex certainly wouldn't be letting on that Nicky had been aware of Haynes's peanut allergy, either. She'd only revealed that over lunch on Sunday. Apparently the last standing committee meeting of the Church Council, involving Beauville, Haynes, Rose Passmore and Nicky, had taken place in the function room of the *Yorkshire Pudding* public house, as the Church meeting room was booked. Nicky had bought a round of drinks and Haynes had gone to the bar to assist her. She'd asked him if he cared for any nuts or crisps, to which he'd expressed a preference for crisps, as nuts didn't agree with him. He hadn't mentioned a potentially fatal allergy as such, but it was enough to heap suspicion on Nicky, were she to admit this knowledge to Blackman and co. It wasn't as if anyone had overheard their conversation, anyway.

Miller wasn't usually overly sensitive when it came to speaking ill of the dead – he couldn't afford to be in his job – but Nicky was a different matter. He was convinced his sweet-natured, fun-loving housemate had had nothing to do with the dramatic events at Zion House last Saturday. She'd become number one suspect, if he let on about her argument with Terence and recent discovery of his intolerance to peanuts. And then they'd be sure to start poking around in her pre-Christian past. Miller didn't want her memory tarnished with revelations about past exploits before her sins had been forgiven and her slate wiped clean through her faith in Christ. A faith that had been severely dented by recent events. If only Haynes hadn't been murdered, Miller thought to himself, packing the room.   Then Nicky wouldn't have been in Foxburgh that fateful Sunday evening, seeking an escape from the whole unpleasant business. Oh the irony of it, he grimaced. Hopefully the pathologist had finished poking around in her insides now, and Nicky could rest in peace. At least she had given her heart to the Redeemer before surrendering her body to the Devil, Miller thought.

Why, oh why, had he dilly-dallied so much in picking her up from that stupid nightclub? If only he could turn back the clock. He'd been nursing a broken heart along with a heavy cold and had been feeling bitter and antagonistic towards Nicky on the night in question. But now it all seemed so pathetic and trivial, now that she was dead, never to return to the house they shared.

⧗ ⧗ ⧗

"You're barking up the wrong tree, Leigh," Parlour stated, sweeping into Blackman's temporary office at Billock Police Station at seven o'clock that evening.

"Do come in, won't you, Parlour," a bespectacled Blackman said dryly, looking up from her reports. He leant against the filing cabinet.

"I just saw Martin Beauville in the carpark at Melrose. Told me you'd called round and searched his house. The guy's pretty upset."

"Look, shut the door, will you, Parlour? I'll catch it in the neck if anyone hears you discussing this with me."

Parlour obliged, taking the seat opposite her this time.

"Didn't look too upset to me," Blackman said mildly. "Smooth as a baby's bum, in fact."

"Well he wouldn't look rattled in front of you!" Parlour exclaimed. "But I can tell you, he's hating all of this!"

"Did he tell you about the letter?" Blackman asked, taking her glasses off and massaging the bridge of her nose.

"Letter? What letter?"

Blackman handed him the original, enclosed in a transparent pocket. Parlour read it, frowning.

"Where did you get this?"

"It was next to Haynes' computer in his study. We found it last night. Look, Mark, the man's obviously got some serious skeletons in his closet - and Haynes knew what they were."

"Oh come on, Leigh!" Parlour exclaimed. "I must admit, this letter's pretty inflammatory and I don't know why Beauville didn't mention it, but Haynes was that kind of person. If he hadn't died of peanut poisoning, he would've died of a heart attack sooner or later. He got too wound up about silly things of no ultimate consequence. Beauville probably parked in his space at church or something silly like that. I think you're letting your cynicism of the church cloud your judgement."

"And I think your bias towards the church is hampering yours," Blackman retorted. "A man has been murdered. We find a letter in his house suggesting he had some kind of disagreement with the vicar. The self-same vicar hands him a cup of coffee that kills him. If that doesn't make him our chief suspect, what does?"

"It's all circumstantial, Leigh! Anyone could have put nuts in that flask, we've already ascertained that. Lara Monkton-Smith could have shoved them in his flask after giving him his first cup of coffee, and I don't see you hounding her. Anyway, have you spoken to the Bishop? He might be able to shed some light on this."

Blackman informed him that Karen Preece had interviewed Bishop Shadwell Allbright after lunch. Apparently Haynes had voiced some reservations to the Bishop about Beauville's age and relative inexperience on several occasions, but Allbright had taken no notice. In the Bishop's opinion, Beauville was an exceptionally talented young priest with a bright future, and he had no reason to doubt him. Allbright had no idea why Haynes should have suddenly requested a private meeting with him.

"Well, there you are then," Parlour replied.

"Oh come on, Mark, even you must admit he's too good to be true! He needs oiling, he squeaks that much! In my experience, people like that are always hiding something!"

"My, what a cynical little world you live in!" Parlour laughed. "Putting my church hat aside, I still don't think he did it. It's just too simple. No-one, not even the naivest of people, would incriminate themselves so obviously."

"Unless he was double-bluffing -" Blackman countered.

"That's far too risky," Parlour replied, shaking his head. "He would never have done it, I'm telling you."

"It's all very well you telling me how thoroughly saintly all these people are," Blackman frowned. "Don't forget – one of them murdered Terence Haynes."

There was a pause as both caught their breath.

"Point taken," Parlour replied finally. He stood up and stretched. "Did you find anything else in Haynes's house last night?"

Blackman told him about the burglar alarm and the conundrum of the electronic logbook.

"Hmm," Parlour pondered, digesting the information. "Haynes could have forgotten something, I suppose… no, that wouldn't work, would it? Why wait till 8.15 to go out again? Anyway, Julès saw him walk past at his usual time, just after eight."

"Could she have been mistaken?" Blackman asked.

"I doubt it," Parlour replied, "but I'll check with her."

"Do you think it's significant?" Blackman wondered.

Parlour shrugged. "It could be. Obviously we can't ask Haynes, but we can try his neighbours. What about the cleaner?"

Blackman informed him that Mary Fosthlewaite had been out all day and therefore unavailable for questioning. However, none of Terence Haynes's neighbours had reported seeing anything untowards, though one of Blackman's team had discovered the existence of a lane running behind the houses on Haynes's side of the road, along which anyone could slip unnoticed and sneak into the late Warden's house.

"They'd have to know the alarm combination though," Parlour said.

"Yes."

"Wonder if Mrs Fosthlewaite told anyone," he mused.

"But why would she do that?" Blackman asked.

"Because they asked her?" Parlour suggested. "Sorry to be simplistic, and all that. Because they needed access to Haynes's house?"

"It's more likely she popped in to pick up something – we'll soon find out."

"Have you had the alarm dusted for prints?" Parlour asked.

"Not yet," Blackman conceded. "They'd have worn gloves, anyway, I expect."

"True. What about the key – did anyone else have a copy?"

"Not as far as we know," Blackman replied. "Denton's got some uniformed officers trawling the local keycutting services."

"Any other leads on anyone else?"

Blackman shook her head. "We've more or less eliminated Olivia Murray and Mavis Wagstaff on the grounds of diminished responsibility –"

Parlour chuckled. "I'd have to agree with you there."

"Nicky Ellery was pretty new to the scene, had precious little chuch history. Can't see her being involved, and I don't suppose we'll ever know for sure now."

Parlour nodded sadly. Juliet had taken the murder of the recently elected Church Council secretary particularly badly, troubled by a guilty conscience over some of the less edifying comments she had made about Ellery recently.

"Lindsay Briscoe seems disgustingly happy, and disgustingly motive-less," Blackman continued, "though I suppose she could be having some kind of affair that Haynes found out about – her husband does work long hours, after all –"

"He is also, to continue a theme, disgustingly good-looking and filthy rich!" Parlour laughed wryly. "The competition would have to be fairly awesome."

"Martin Beauville?" Blackman suggested.

"The salary's crap!" Parlour grinned. "Somehow I don't think Martin Beauville's very interested in marriage," he continued soberly. "Not casting aspersions in any particular direction – I just get the impression he's 101% sold out to the Church."

"That's the impression he gave us," Blackman nodded. "He told us he was celibate, actually."

"My, we did get personal, didn't we!"

"I've got Richardson checking out the Keltys," Blackman continued. "They seem too wet, on the surface, but it could all be a façade. Your wife appears to have absolutely no motive, unless you can enlighten me on that score, and Jason Jarvis and Alex Miller likewise. Miller had no idea about Haynes's allergy, by the way, and I guess we have to take his word for it."

"Shame –" Parlour commented. "What about the peanuts? Did anyone have any about their person? Could it have been an accident?"

Blackman shook her head. "We've double-checked with all the suspects. Nobody brought any into the building, and nobody had eaten any recently or would be likely to have traces of them on their hands or clothes."

Parlour grimaced. "Not getting very far, are we? Someone, somewhere, must have had serious grounds for wanting Haynes dead, though."

Seemingly on cue, Robins rushed into Blackman's office.

"Boss – come with me!"

"And I think we're just about to find out," Blackman said, and followed her colleague out into the corridor.

⧖⧖⧖

"You're not going to believe this!" Robins said excitedly, shutting the door of the incident room behind them to keep Parlour out of earshot.

"Try me!"

"Sit down here," he commanded, pulling a second chair up in front of the computer they had earlier confiscated from the vicarage. Blackman sat down beside him. She watched as Robins clicked on the icon of Beauville's internet service provider. He keyed in Beauville's password from his notebook then waited for the homepage to come up. He clicked on another icon on the menu bar.

"What are you doing?" Blackman frowned, who was relatively new to the world-wide web.

"This would list the most recent websites he looked at, boss," Robins explained quickly, impatient to move on. Blackman, who had rushed out without her glasses, peered at the screen.

"What am I looking at?"

Robins pointed to an oblong box on the toolbar.

Blackman squinted again. "There's nothing there, Dave."

Her colleague grinned triumphantly. "Exactly. Odd, isn't it? I don't care how technophobic he claims to be - who has internet access and never looks up any websites, *like* ever?"

"What's your point?" Blackman frowned, shaking her head.

"Beauville's tried to wipe the evidence, boss! His PC would keep a record of all websites visited, but if you know how to, you can delete this "history" as it's called from the screen. But our resident super-nerds in IT were able to find out what sites he'd been looking at on the hard drive of his computer. Beauville had stored the web files in a special directory on his PC, then obviously wiped them once he realised we'd be on his back – pardon the pun!"

"What files, what evidence?" Blackman enquired, a little trickle of hope entering her voice. Evidence was a commodity that had proved thin on the ground thusfar and at that point in time, assumed a property akin to golddust.

"When Millbank examined the hard drive on Beauville's computer, he found that these websites had been entered and these images saved on his PC."

Robins extracted some sheets from a folder next to the computer and handed his superior the saved HTML files pulled from Beauville's computer.

"*Sex'n'pecs*," she read, "*Greek Island Boyz, Men in Uniform*… bloody hell, Robins, he's a…"

"Willy woofter!" Robins grinned, political correctness going out the window in the heat of the moment, had it ever been present in the first place.

Blackman whistled as she leafed through grainy colour photographs of teenage boys in an assortment of poses *au naturel*.

"Ready for the real meat?" Robins laughed crudely, barely able to contain his excitement. He pulled some more bits of paper from the cardboard folder on the desk. "We found these saved on Haynes's PC this time – the boys found a shortcut from the Desktop to some saved HTML files."

"I'll take your word for it, Dave," Blackman grinned, for it was all gobbledygook to her.

Robins handed Blackman a small wad of sheets stapled together.

"These are printouts from a website Haynes had obviously looked at, boss."

"Camping Out?" Blackman frowned.

"It's a militant gay website, boss," Robins explained eagerly, "edited by gay political activists intent on "outing" homosexuals in the Forces. They're allowing gays in now, of course, but there's still some pressure to remain in the closet."

Blackman whistled as she scanned through the document, which contained a mixture of propaganda and topical articles relating to gays in the military.

"Look at this," Robins said impatiently, snatching the printout from her hand and turning to the penultimate page. "They've stuck quotes from various news articles on the website as well."

He tapped his finger on some paragraphs highlighted with a yellow fluorescent marker. The first was an extract from an article that had appeared in the *Southern Regional Informer* back in 1980.

"Court Martial discharges naval officer for sexual misconduct," Blackman read. *"Midshipman Martin Charles Lucian Beauville, 22, of Milton Feltbury, Wiltshire, was yesterday found guilty of homosexual offences at a General Court Martial hearing in London. The charges pertain to three*

Blackman rubbed her eyes. "So Beauville was ex-Forces."

"This one's even better," Robins sniggered salaciously, pointing to another extract, from a tabloid newspaper this time.

"Seamen Spills: Court Martial declares You're Out! Blackman read. She hastily scanned her eyes down the sensationalist piece. It was a classic piece of tabloid journalism laden with saucy double-entendres.

She sat back and looked at Robins. "*Haynes* was in the Forces."

"Exactly."

"But Beauville said he'd never seen him before…"

"No he didn't," Robins replied eagerly. "I've been thinking back to what his actual words were - he said he'd never *made the acquaintance of* Terence Haynes, i.e. he might have seen him, but they'd never been formally introduced. We also asked if he had any reason to suppose Haynes had something against him, to which he answered he had no reason to think he'd done anything to anger Haynes *over the last few months*. So he might have done something to annoy him *before* he moved to Deverton. He was very clever. Managed to avoid telling lies, like a good Christian."

Blackman frowned. "Let me think – so Haynes knew of Beauville, and vice-versa, but they'd never actually talked to one another face to face."

Robins nodded enthusiastically. "It's my guess Haynes was present at the Court Martial – on the panel, or whatever they call it. Beauville turns up in Deverton, having retrained as a vicar, bumps into Haynes at the licensing service. He probably wouldn't have recognised Haynes, but Haynes immediately recognises Beauville. He keeps stumm at the time but later warns Beauville he's onto him. It's my guess Bishop Shadwell had no idea of all this – Beauville's presumably glossed over the years he was in the Forces – and Haynes threatened to grass him up. Hence…"

"Beauville had to silence him – for good!" Blackman exclaimed. She stood up and turned to Robins.

"My God, we've got him!"

"Male hooker, line and sinker!" Robins laughed.

"Who would have thought?" Blackman chuckled. "Told you he was too good to be true!"

She slapped the wall in delight, the adrenalin pumping now, then turned back to Robins.

"Round up two squad cars. We'll go in mine. Quick!"

⏳⏳⏳

They screeched up outside the vicarage fifteen minutes later.

"Looks like he's having a bit of a shindig!" Blackman laughed, seeing Daniel Kelty playing the guitar in the lamplight through the window.

"The Keltys are there, Andrew Monkton-Smith, the Briscoe woman, and Pizza's missus!" Robins exclaimed, excitement mounting as they prepared to confront Martin Beauville. Tucker and Singh had pulled up just ahead and PC Rossi and WPC Fullerton were just behind. The select gathering in the front room of the vicarage remained oblivious to events outside.

Blackman banged on the door, but there was no answer.

"Can't hear us for the singing!" she commented.

"Is that what they call it?" Robins scoffed. He tried the door. "It's open."

They gave the thumbs up signal to the possy outside and walked down the hallway. Daniel Kelty stopped singing as the two detectives entered the room and the others came to a gradual halt. There was a deadly silence as Martin Beauville met the steely gaze of Leigh Blackman, the colour draining from his handsome face.

"Martin Beauville, I arrest you on suspicion of the murder of Terence Haynes on Saturday 25 May 2002. You do not have to say anything. But it may harm your defence if you do not mention when questioned something which you later rely on in court. Anything you do say may be given in evidence."

Tucker and Singh ran in with Rossi and Fullerton in pursuit, but Beauville did not struggle, merely looked up to the heavens in a silent plea for help as he was handcuffed and led out to the police car.

There was a stunned silence before Juliet Parlour turned on Blackman.

"This is all wrong," she said fiercely to Blackman. "All wrong."

"I'm sorry, Juliet," Blackman said blandly, before turning on her heels and returning to her car, leaving them all to stare at each other in shock.

⧗⧗⧗

A monogrammed canteen of cutlery, Mary Fosthlewaite said aloud, leafing through the *Goulds of Galston* catalogue that had come with this week's *Radio Times*. *That'll do me nicely!* She wrote the reference number on the order form below the eight digit figure she had already entered for a set of Beatrix Potter porcelain plates, limited edition of course. She could get used to this, she thought, dunking a finger of Walker's shortbread in her mug of filter coffee. And why on earth shouldn't she continue to enjoy herself, she wondered smugly. After all, there was no conclusive proof that all good things had to, by some invisible law of nature, come to an end.

⧗⧗⧗

"Mark – something awful's happened!" Juliet exclaimed when Parlour finally returned home at 9.30 that evening.

"I know, Jules, I was there when they brought him in."

"Please say it's all a horrible mistake!" she begged, sinking down on the sofa.

"I wish I could, darling," Parlour sighed, raking a tired hand through his Brylcreamed ginger hair. "I hear you were at the vicarage when they came for him."

"Yes – Martin wanted some of us, those he could trust, to pray with him. Daniel brought his guitar. He'd just started playing a few songs when they came for poor Martin. It was horrible!"

"I can imagine, darling," Parlour replied, taking off his shoes. He turned and faced his wife. "They found gay porn on his computer, Jules."

Juliet gasped.

"But that's not all – there was some web article on Haynes's PC from the *Southern Regional Informer*. Turns out Martin was in the navy for a while and was Court Martialed in 1980 for homosexual offences."

"No!" Juliet exclaimed.

"Guess who was on the committee that found him guilty?"

Juliet blanched. "Terence Haynes?" she whispered.

Parlour nodded dismally.

"Holy shoot," Juliet exhaled. Then she frowned. "They don't think Martin…"

"Murdered Haynes? I'm afraid it gives him a pretty meaty motive, my love. The Bishop had no idea whom he was appointing – he's down there, now. They've pulled him in for questioning, too."

There was a pause as Juliet attempted to digest the shocking news.

"Leigh Blackman must be loving this," she said finally.

"She's got the motive she was after," Parlour commented.

"What'll happen to Martin?"

"Nothing, unless they can prove it," Parlour replied. "But it's not looking too good. And I don't think he'll be able to remain vicar in Deverton when word gets around."

"But you don't think he did it, do you?"

"I want to say no," Parlour answered slowly, "but it seems we don't know Martin Beauville as well as we all believed."

Juliet shuddered. It was a horrible thought, not that Martin Beauville may have had homosexual experiences, though that in itself, if true, was somewhat of a revelation, but that he did have a motive to murder Terence Haynes, and as such, could not be ruled out of the picture.

"So what will they do with him?"

"Keep him in overnight, make him sweat, try and force a confession out of him tomorrow. They can't keep him there beyond twenty-four hours, unless they come up with some concrete evidence."

"Did you talk to the Bishop?" Juliet asked.

"I grabbed him in the carpark," Parlour replied. "Have to keep my head down at the station."

"And?"

"And he said Beauville didn't even mention the navy at his interview. But the Bishop doesn't believe Martin murdered Terence Haynes, and said he'll stick by him. He wanted to speak to Martin, but they wouldn't let him yet."

"Gosh!" Juliet exclaimed. "I would have thought the Bishop would have a hernia if he found out Martin was gay!"

"We don't know that Martin's gay," Parlour frowned. "He may or may not have had a homosexual encounter twenty odd years ago, not that it would bother me anyway. But even if he did, it doesn't make him a practising homosexual now, does it?"

"Is that the line the Bish is taking?" Juliet asked.

"The Bish says he'll reserve judgement till he's spoken to Martin."

"Bravo for Bishop Shadwell," Juliet commented. "He's a real old fuddy-duddy, but at least he's fair."

Parlour stood up and paced the room.

"It's so damn frustrating, being left in the cold!" he exploded. "Blackman's a sound cop, but with all due respect, she's out of her depth on this one. She doesn't know these people! She doesn't know how church circles work!"

"Do we anymore?" Juliet asked, looking troubled. Parlour turned and faced his wife.

"I suppose that's a very good point."

11

It was just after ten o'clock the next morning when WPC Fullerton knocked on Parlour's door at Billock Police Station.

"Man in a purple frock to see you!"

"Show the good man in, Lisa," Parlour said soberly. He straightened his tie and stood up to greet Shadwell Allbright. Fullerton shut the door behind her.

"Good morning, Bishop."

"Good morning, Mark," the Bishop said gravely, taking the seat offered him.

"What can I do for you?" Parlour asked, sitting down and resisting the temptation to finish off the spot about to burst on his chin.

"Is it all right to discuss Beauville with you?" the Bishop enquired. "I hear you're not on the case."

"Yes – my officers are officially nil by mouth on the subject of Terence Haynes's murder. But DI Blackman's pretty much keeping me informed, so long as I don't let on to the Chief Inspector."

"Aah, good. You see I've just talked to Martin Beauville. This really is a terrible business. The man looks awful. You'd think they'd at least provide him with a razor and clean clothes!"

"What did he have to say for himself?" Parlour interrupted, not particularly interested in the finer aspects of Beauville's *couture* that morning.

Martin Beauville had confessed to the Bishop that he had indeed been in the navy for three years, however the allegations of homosexual activity made against him were entirely false. Apparently he had refused to succumb to a more senior officer's advances, and the other man had decided to set him up, his word against Beauville's. A secret camera located below deck had filmed Beauville laying hands on several young officers requiring prayer for various physical ailments.

The officers had all been briefed beforehand by Beauville's aggressor to position themselves around Beauville in such a way that corroborating evidence of a homosexual act could be provided. This photographic evidence allied with Beauville's rather dashing appearance, plus the absence of a female love interest back home, had enabled the prosecution to build up a convincing case against Beauville. Faced with photographs and accounts of the midshipman in close physical contact with young officers, the Court Martial had no reason to doubt that Martin Beauville was a closet homosexual and he had been duly discharged. It had been a total set-up to protect the senior officer, popular among his peers and feared by his juniors.

Unsure as to whether the Bishop was a believer in the presence of smoke without fire, Beauville had decided not to mention his three years in the navy at his interview for the post at Deverton, for fear the Bishop chose to accept the navy's version of events. Allbright was not renowned for his liberal views on homosexuality, though he was not a hard man in other respects. Neither had Beauville mentioned his ill-fated career in the Forces at his interview for Bible College, claiming he had been travelling, which was not, in itself, an out-and-out lie.

With regard to the pornographic images found on his home computer, Beauville had again pleaded his innocence to the Bishop, claiming he only used his computer once a week at the most, and then only to write letters. Beauville believed he had once again been set up, that someone had gained illicit access to his computer with the prime purpose of framing him. It was probably the same person who guessed he would volunteer to make the coffee that Saturday and had put peanuts in Terence Haynes's flask to deliberately incriminate him.

"And do you believe him?" Parlour asked, once the Bishop had finished.

"Yes I do," the Bishop replied. "I don't think Martin Beauville's the murdering sort, do you?"

"I didn't think any of our friends on Deverton PCC were the murdering sort until Saturday," Parlour said dryly. "But I must agree, I can't imagine for one minute Martin murdered Haynes. It is possible somebody planted those articles on his PC, then deleted them knowing it would look as if Beauville had wiped his PC. But whoever did that presumably knew about his past and wanted to make damn sure we all knew, too. Has Martin any ideas who that person might be?"

The Bishop shook his head. "He's as clueless as we are, which is where you come in."

"Me?" Parlour said in surprise.

"Beauville wants you to embark on a little investigation of your own – behind the scenes, of course. Doesn't think much of this Blackman character."

"I can't withhold any information from the official murder inquiry team, he does realise that, doesn't he?" Parlour frowned.

"But you'll do it?" the Bishop asked eagerly, leaning forward.

"I have been sniffing around myself, already, to be honest," Parlour smiled. "I am, at least officially, investigating a historical murder up at Bywater Farm, but it's a complete wild goose chase. They're just trying to keep me occupied so that Blackman can get on with the job without me chipping my two pence worth in every five seconds. I could engage in a bit of – shall we say – extra-curricular activity!"

"Good man!" Shadwell Allbright exclaimed. "That should cheer Beauville up."

"Yes, well, keep it under your mitre, or I'll be seconded to the Highlands Branch!"

"Now – I had some piece of information to pass onto you from Beauville."

The Bishop leaned forward again. It seemed Beauville had lost his electronic diary a few weeks ago. It had eventually turned up in the Lost Property box at church a couple of days later. A free gift from an ecclesiastical publication to which he had recently subscribed, Beauville used the PDA to store his pin numbers and passwords amongst other things, confessing he did not have a head for figures. The electronic diary itself had a password, Deverton, which – regrettably in light of recent events – he had made known to other members of the church council, lest he forgot that as well! Beauville was of the opinion that whoever had tampered with his computer had found the password to his PC in the PDA.

"It's certainly possible," Parlour nodded slowly. "Has he told Blackman all this?"

The Bishop waved his hand impatiently. "Yes, yes, but she's not having any of it. Thinks he's cooked it up as a cover."

"Well, she doesn't know Martin after all," Parlour said in defence of his colleague, "and the evidence *is* overwhelmingly against him."

"Any fool can see the man is as straight as a die!" Allbright exclaimed.

"Well, Blackman can't," Parlour said firmly, thinking what a shame it was the Court Martial hadn't shared the Bishop's viewpoint all those years ago. "So I shall have my work cut out."

⧗⧗⧗

"SHURRUUPPPPP!" Leigh Blackman bellowed at ten past five that afternoon as she entered the noisy incident room at Billock Police Station.

Her officers immediately stopped their chatter and turned their chairs round to face the front.

"Here's the latest. Martin Beauville still maintains he did not kill Terence Haynes – the guy's as slippery as Parlour's head –"

There was muted laughter at this reference to Mark Parlour's Brylcreamed ginger locks.

"- so it looks like we're going to have to release him tonight. We could keep him in for downloading child porn, which he incidentally also denies doing, but the Sewer won't approve without hard evidence – ha ha - and I don't want him, as well as the Almighty, coming down on me like a tonne of bricks!"

Blackman paused for breath.

"Beauville remains our prime suspect, however. Sean, did you manage to get in touch with Haynes's cleaner?"

Sean Denton nodded. Mary Fosthlewaite had stated with some degree of indignation that she had never and would never breathe a word about Haynes's burglar alarm system to anyone and hadn't gone near his house the previous Saturday morning, either, having taken a bus to Lowden Market with her sister. Denton had been unable to reach Fostlewaite's sister by telephone to check out this version of events, but the bus driver from Foxburgh Regional Transport had confirmed that two women fitting their description had boarded the bus to Lowden on the 25th of May. Neither had Mary Fosthlewaite leant her keys to anyone or left them lying around to the best of her knowledge. As far as she knew, nobody else had a copy of Haynes's front door key, he was neither the type to lock himself out nor to rely on neighbours for anything. Uniform had not come back with any keycutting leads, which surprised nobody:- it was a task akin to searching for a small embroidery needle in a ginormous haystack, given the plethora of local outlets providing this service in the Deverton/ Billock/Foxburgh conurbation, and the standard size of the key.

Sean Denton had also been assigned the task of unearthing Terence Haynes's will and had duly consulted Haynes's solicitor in Lexington Green. No provision had been made for any individuals, family or otherwise, Haynes had left his entire estate to the Foxburgh Veteran's Association for retired military personnel.

"Good work, Sean. How was the Bishop, Karen?"

DC Preece frowned. "He had no idea Beauville had been in the Forces. Can't believe he murdered Haynes – fine morally upstanding young man ad nauseum."

"Any hint of a conspiracy against Haynes?"

Preece shook her head. The Bishop had known that Haynes was not overly enamoured with his appointment of Martin Beauville, but had no inkling why and appeared to have little contact with Deverton PCC as a rule, spending the majority of his time in Foxburgh.

"Can we dig up some background on our good friend the Bishop?" Blackman requested. "He could be protecting Beauville."

Preece nodded.

"What about Forensic? Have they found anything else of interest?"

DC Keough shook his head. Apparently the other dishes and foodstuffs in the vicinity of Haynes's chair had been clear of peanut or peanut extract and besides, no traces of these foodstuffs had been found in the Commander's stomach.

"OK. This is the plan," Blackman informed the incident room. "I want you to try and dig up old navy or school friends of Martin Beauville. He's got a sister somewhere, too. Find out what he got up to between the sheets. Also, did he have a vindictive side to him? Beauville reckons he didn't go out on Saturday morning before leaving for Zion House, but it's just possible he called round to see Terence Haynes."

Blackman took a deep breath then grinned. "Any progress on the tampon trail?"

A few snickers. Shy junior constable Ian Jenkins had been mischievously assigned the task of enquiring after the sanitary requirements of the female members of Deverton PCC.

Jenkins coughed and opened his notebook, blushing furiously. He had that patchy red skin often associated with very fair haired men.

"It seems Ma'am that only Lindsay Briscoe and the late Nicky Ellery used Melrose own brand applicator tampons. Juliet Parlour was of the opinion that only the anally retentive refused to … er… perform digitally, so to speak, by which I deduce that…"

"She uses non-applicator, Ian, I snooped about in their bathroom cabinet last Sunday," Blackman smiled, enjoying his obvious discomfort.

"Mavis Wagstaff is obviously past it, Ma'am, and Olivia Murray uses sanitary towels."

And probably recycles them on the radiator alongside her teabags, Blackman grinned to herself. "Rose Passmore?"

"Ditto, Ms Passmore thinks tampons are pandering to male expectations of the female body,"

"Oh for f*** sake!" His senior cursed. "And what about Lara Monkton-Smith?"

"Mrs Monkton-Smith uses the winged variety, Ma'am," Jenkins replied.

A communal guffaw greeted this revelation from the junior constable. Jenkins' report had provided a welcome stress reliever from the tension that had built up in the incident room with the entry of Leigh Blackman.

"Why does that not surprise me?" Blackman groaned, though her eyes were twinkling. Like Martin Beauville, there was something angelic about Andrew Monkton-Smith's honey-toned wife.

"Of course, anyone, male or female, could have purchased the aforementioned brand of er.. feminine hygiene product from Melrose," Jenkins countered.

He added that he had met with the same problems as DC Preece with regard to the customer loyalty scheme, with Melrose again unable to divulge personal information concerning its customers under the Data Protection Act. As Blackman conceded, such information proved little anyway.

Blackman enquired whether a tampon machine was located in the ladies toilets at either Deverton Parish Church or Zion House, but there was no such facility at either property.

"Any further questions?" Blackman surveyed her officers. Silence.

"No? Right, step to it! I'll be downstairs with the Irrelevent, if anyone wants me!"

⧗⧗⧗

"So it's Parlour undercover?" Juliet chuckled as they discussed the day's events across the supper table that evening.

"Cool, isn't it?" Parlour laughed. "Can't wait to get my teeth into this, to be honest, Jules. It's not going to be easy, though. I don't really know where to start. If Beauville didn't do it, who did, and why? Nobody was a great fan of Terence Haynes, but I can't see why any of us would want him dead."

"You know what I think?" Juliet said slowly, chewing on a piece of raw carrot from the salad bowl.

"What?"

"I think you should start with his computer, since Blackman's drawn a blank with the peanut thing. If he was framed, then whoever did it is firstly, computer literate and secondly, has access to a computer themselves with internet connection. I can't imagine they surfed the net and just happened to come across those webpages while they were at the vicarage! They'll also be a frequent visitor to the vicarage who knows when Martin is out and knows where he keeps his computer."

"*Oooh,* clever Jules!" Parlour grinned, patting his wife fondly on the head. He sobered up again.

"Access to the vicarage is easy," Parlour surmised. "He leaves the front door open half the time!"

"He keeps the spare key Ducktaped to the underside of the kitchen window sill," Juliet added.

155

“How do you know?” Parlour enquired.

“I heard him tell Christine Kelty in front of everyone at church a few weeks back. She wanted to use his piano while her organ was in the repair shop.”

“Who else was there?” Parlour asked.

“Who wasn’t there!” Juliet laughed. “Most of the church, I think! Haynes told him off for being so lax with security, but Beauville read him that passage from Acts where the disciples shared their possessions and had everything in common! Alex Miller asked whether that gave us licence to have an almighty party there next time Martin went off on one of his skiing trips!”

“Great!” Parlour groaned. “Anyway, returning to computers, let’s think about this. Mavis Wagstaff doesn’t own one, I presume!”

“She doesn’t,” Juliet confirmed, who had been to most of their houses at some time or other. Neither did Olivia Murray nor the Keltys. “Daniel Kelty thinks they’re a tool of Satan designed to put people out of jobs and reduce communities to solitary enclaves.”

“How much time have you been spending with the Keltys recently?” Parlour enquired, eyes twinkling.

“Andrew Monkton-Smith has one in his study, but I don’t know if it has a modem attached. I expect so. He doesn’t seem the emailing sort - too old school! As for Lara, I don’t think she’d know what one was if it fell from the sky and hit her on the head! Charles Briscoe has a PC, which I believe Lindsay uses from time to time to type letters to friends. I expect he has email – but I don’t think for one minute Lindsay had anything to do with this. I don’t know about Jason or Alex. I expect they do have one. They would have access to one at work, presumably, anyway. Nicky was obviously comupter literate, since she typed up the minutes – but I can’t imagine she had anything to do with this. Though admittedly we don’t know her as well as the others.”

Parlour nodded. "If this hasn't all been a terrible accident, and I refuse to rule the possibility out, then it's someone with a bit of church history, who knows about computers. Mind you, I suppose someone could always go to one of those cybercafés to surf the net. There's one in Foxburgh."

"Or use the computers in the library," Juliet proposed.

They looked at one another.

"Olivia Murray!"

Then both shook their heads in unison.

"I'll eat my Brylcream if she did it!" Parlour chuckled, then sobered up. "I think you might be onto something here, Jules. I'll check out that cybercafé place in the city, and the library. They must have a list of registered users. I'll get Martin's computer and spare key checked for prints, too."

"How are you going to do that?" Juliet frowned. "I thought you were working undercover?"

"I'll get Stuart Beattie to help me. He won't split on me."

Beattie was part of the Forensic team at Foxburgh Police HQ and an old college friend of Parlour's.

"What about Andrew?" Juliet asked quietly.

"It's funny how his name keeps cropping up, isn't it?" Parlour commented soberly. "But I still don't think he would do a thing like that. But I need to keep an open mind. That goes for your friend, Lindsay, too."

"Want me to do some subtle investigations of my own?" Juliet enquired. "Lins and I are pretty close. It could be she lets someone from church use the computer through the day or something."

"Mm, it's possible," Parlour nodded.

"You forgot us!" Juliet laughed suddenly. "We have a computer!"

"Yep, but I still haven't got round to loading that CD-Rom BT sent us!"

"Mark!" Juliet exclaimed in horror. "I told you I had to have internet access by the start of the summer term to plan the school exchange – I really can't afford to wait any longer!"

"Keep your hair on! Let's not have a marital – my brain hurts and I need some TLC."

"You've got to be joking!" Juliet scoffed. "I have twenty-seven reports to write by tomorrow morning, not to mention four lessons to plan!"

"Who'd be a teacher?" Parlour wondered. "All you've done is moved the other side of the desk. Still have blasted homework every night."

"You're hardly Mr 9 to 5, so shut it!" she swatted her husband with the salad tongs as she cleared up the remains of the first course.

"Got any more theories, Poirot?" Parlour called through to the kitchen, as Juliet scooped out some ice-cream.

"There is one thing that crossed my mind," Juliet said slowly, resuming her place opposite him.

"What's that?"

"Well, assuming Martin didn't plop peanuts into Haynes's cup at the last minute, someone must have bunged them in Haynes's flask, right?"

"Ye-es," Parlour frowned.

"But don't you think it's incredibly risky doing that? I mean, Terence might have kept his flask at his side all day. How did anyone know he would put it in the kitchen alongside the food?"

"Did he do that, though?" Parlour asked. "Or did someone else do it for him?"

"No – I saw him bang it down next to the kettle."

"You're thinking nobody could have guaranteed they'd have an opportunity to do it?" Parlour asked his wife.

She nodded. "That's right. And even if they knew he would probably put the flask down in the kitchen, how could they be sure they'd have the time or opportunity to put the nuts in it?

Even if you sneaked in there during the morning session, you couldn't guarantee someone wouldn't come in at the same time, would you? I don't think I would want to take that risk, if I was the murderer."

"Perhaps they weren't in a hurry to kill Haynes," Parlour mused. "It just seemed like a good opportunity on Saturday, so they took some nuts along with them in case they got the chance."

"But murders like that are always planned, aren't they?" Juliet said. "It's far too risky, otherwise."

"True," Parlour nodded. He yawned. "I've got a headache. Some serious vegging is in order, I think."

He ambled over to the sofa and flicked the TV on with the remote control, squeezing her buttocks as he walked past.

"Leave the dishes, Jules. I'll do them later."

"Thanks, darling," Juliet sighed in relief, contemplating her evening's workload as Parlour found some fuzzy football on Channel 5.

12

The county town of Foxburgh was eminently more attractive than its larger neighbour, Billock, with its listed buildings dating back to mediaeval times and its tasteful shop façades. Unlike Billock, a hideous new town built in the seventies to serve the commuter population, Foxburgh was full of character, its diverse range of shops, public amenities and business services linked by a network of narrow, cobbled side streets and quirky arched passageways. The County Library, though recently refurbished, did not let Foxburgh down, its white wall exterior kept pristine by a zealous community integration scheme, aimed at keeping disaffected youth recently released from the Young Offenders Institute well occupied during the waking hours.

The only uncontrolled commodity in Foxburgh was the weather. Parlour grimaced as he made a dash for it from the carpark to the library, pulling his suede jacket over his head.

The Reference section, which housed fifteen computers arranged in an *n* shape, was located on the lower level of the building. It was a popular burrowing hole for the more dedicated of students from Foxburgh College, as a strict no talking rule was enforced throughout the Reference Library.

Fortunately, Parlour thought, Olivia Murray worked in the lending library, so there was no danger of running into her while he did a bit of informal sleuthing.

Removing his notebook and pen from his pilot case – he ought to do a little bit of research on the Bywater Farm murder while he was here – Parlour found an empty study booth near the computer workstations. He got up and wandered around, finally finding what he was looking for – namely, information on computing facilities. He noted that workstations were available for private study until 6.45 pm weekdays, and from 9 till 5 on a Saturday. The library was closed on a Sunday. *It's about the only thing that is, these days,* Parlour thought to himself. Juliet had been right - all the computers were connected to the Internet, though one had to register with the library to take advantage of this facility. Parlour looked around, but there did not appear to be a list of users anywhere in sight. Time for a bit of badge-waving!

"Excuse me," Parlour murmured quietly, approaching the information desk opposite. A petite lady with short dark hair looked up from some books she was inserting in plastic sleeves and smiled at the thin ginger-haired man before her.

"Yes?"

Parlour got his badge out and said quietly. "Detective Inspector Mark Parlour, Billock Police. I'm trying to trace someone who's been downloading information from the Internet. We think this person doesn't have a PC at home, hence would be likely to use public workstations. Do you have a list of registered users I could consult?"

The petite librarian checked his credentials, then smiled. "Yes of course."

She tapped a few details into her computer then turned the monitor round to face Parlour.

"Here you go – it's a couple of pages long. Just use the arrows to scroll up and down."

"Thanks."

The librarian returned to her books.

Adams, Albiston, Ansell, Parlour scrolled down. Nothing of interest... hold on, what was that? He scrolled up again. *Bingo!* Who would have thought?

He beckoned to the librarian, who came back over to him. He pointed to the relevant line on the database. "This Kelty person – can I access their full details?"

"Of course," the librarian replied. She highlighted the name with the arrow and hit return.

"Is that who you were looking for?" she asked, as Christine Kelty's details came up on the screen.

"It might be," Parlour replied, scanning the information. "So she first registered with you on 23 February?"

"That's right," the librarian replied, looking at the record on the database. Parlour frowned, doing some quick mathematics. "February 23 – that would have been a Saturday."

"Yes. We find most of our casual users come in on a Saturday."

"Casual?" Parlour queried.

"Yes – occasional browsers. People who like to use a computer now and again, but don't want the expense of running a PC at home. Teachers, for example, like your Mrs Kelty, who wouldn't have a lot of time through the week often come in on a Saturday."

"I see from this record that Christine Kelty had registered to use the Internet," Parlour remarked. "Is there any way of knowing which webpages she accessed?"

The librarian looked perplexed. "That I couldn't tell you. But I could get our IT chap to speak to you, if you like," she offered.

Parlour smiled at her. "That would be most helpful, thank you."

Two minutes later the librarian returned with a tall man with frizzy hair and glasses who couldn't look any more like a computer bod if he tried! The bespectacled man introduced himself as Kevin Murphy, IT co-ordinator for Foxburgh Library.

Parlour shook a clammy hand and explained the situation to Murphy, who nodded vigorously as Parlour outlined his requirements.

It transpired that Foxburgh Library, like most large organisations, used specific software to track every site viewed by its users. The information was held by a web server and was vital in preventing the downloading of child pornography amongst other things. So Murphy would indeed be able to track the websites visited by Christine Kelty. Unfortunately, essential maintenance to the library's computer system that week meant that Murphy would be unable to provide Parlour with the requisite information for at least two days.

Damn! Parlour cursed, returning to his study booth. Still, he'd found something out at least, namely that Christine Kelty did not share her husband's aversion to all things computronic! Parlour drummed his pen on the desk. He had the faintest sensation he was neglecting something obvious. But the vague notion wouldn't form a recognisable shape at the front of his brain.

☷☷☷

"Look, don't you think I've seen enough of you the last forty-eight hours?" Martin Beauville asked wearily, opening the door to DS Robins at two-thirty that afternoon. He had been released at eight thirty the previous evening, exactly twenty-four hours after his dramatic arrest at the vicarage. During his time at Billock Police Station, he had been a model of calm self-control, firmly asserting his innocence without jumping to the bait alternately dangled before him by Blackman and Robins. But this was too much.

"Just be grateful Blackman's not with me," Robins said dryly, squeezing past him in the hallway and inviting himself into the front room.

"There is that," Beauville acknowledged. "Gone to put some other poor soul under the cosh for something they didn't do?"

Beauville, though still drained and off-colour, had cleaned himself up, and was classically dressed in a royal blue cotton shirt and pressed grey lambswool slacks. He returned to his favourite chair.

"She's paying your surviving church warden a visit," Robins replied, getting his notebook out of his trenchcoat pocket.

"Rose?" Beauville frowned. "Oh, give me strength! Rose Passmore would never do a thing like that! She has a social conscience that puts most of us to shame - murdering senior citizens is hardly her style!"

"So who did do it, in your opinion, Vicar?" Robins asked mildly.

"Probably someone from outside the church with a very old grudge against Terence sneaked into the kitchen whilst we were all eating our lunch," Beauville said tiredly.

"Yes, that must be a soothing thought for you, Reverend Beauville," Robins replied smoothly. "Unfortunately Andrew Monkton-Smith locked the front entrance when he went out, and unless someone the size of a marmoset squeezed through the kitchen window with a bag of peanuts in their paw, your theory is entirely out of the question!"

Beauville looked too tired to even care.

"Nice chrysanths," Robins commented, his eyes catching a large vase of yellow flowers on top of the piano.

"Yes," Beauville reponded abstractly. "Christine Kelty brought them round this afternoon on the way home from school. Sympathy flowers, I think! How very *snag* of you to notice, Sergeant," he added dryly.

"Snag?" Robins frowned.

"Ask your Mother Superior," Beauville replied. "So what do you want from me now?" He swept his floppy black hair back from his eyes, a weary gesture.

Robins explained that they had reason to believe somebody had entered Haynes's property while he had been walking his dog on the Saturday morning.

"And let me guess – you think that person was me!" Beauville said sarcastically. His impeccable manners were slowly disintegrating as he lost all patience with Blackman and co.

"Did you enter Terence Haynes's house at 8.02 a.m. on Saturday 25 May 2002, leaving the property at 8.15 a.m.?" Robins asked functionally.

"No, I did not enter Terence Haynes's house at 8.02 am on Saturday 25 May in the 2002nd year since our Lord's birth," Beauville replied acerbically. "I was, in fact, doing the Times crossword and drinking a mug of tea."

He rooted in the wastepaper bin next to his chair. "And here – as if by magic – the Times from Saturday, complete with almost finished crossword. I struggled with eighteen down, if I remember rightly."

He threw the curled up newspaper at Robins.

"With respect, Vicar, you could have done that at any time on Saturday," Robins said dryly.

"With respect, *Sergeant*, I wasn't in the mood for doing the crossword when I got back on Saturday evening, or on Sunday, for that matter," Beauville replied archly. "Anyway, it was probably his cleaner that was in there Saturday morning, the one half the church use."

"How well do you know Mary Fosthlewaite?" Robins asked.

"Haynes's cleaner?" Beauville frowned. "Never spoken to her in my life."

Robins stared him out. It was impossible to tell whether he was telling the truth or not, but decided that asserting more pressure, as Blackman would in his position, would serve no purpose. He returned to some questions in his notebook which Blackman had earlier dictated to him.

"What do you think suddenly prompted Haynes to write his letter to the Bishop?"

"There was no Stand Down or I'll Out You threat, if that's what you're after, Sergeant," Beauville laughed dryly. "As I told you at the station, we never had words, although Haynes's, shall we say, misdirected homophobic prejudice against me had been simmering under the surface since November. At a guess, my recent decision to open a Scout Troop in the Church Centre prompted this decision to contact the Bishop. That would be the sort of thing, I expect, that would send his blood pressure sky-high."

"When did you inform Haynes of this decision?" Robins asked, making a few notes in his book.

"Last Tuesday, I believe," Beauville replied. "We have a warden's meeting fortnightly here at the vicarage."

Robins stood up suddenly and rushed over to the window.

"Whatever's wrong?" Beauville frowned, rising from his chair.

"I thought I heard someone outside!" Robins ran to the front door and dashed outside, but there was nobody to be seen.

"It was probably just cats or something," Beauville dismissed him, following him round the back of the vicarage garden. "Can't move for the blasted things in Deverton!"

"I heard a scuffle – like someone trying to beat a hasty retreat," Robins insisted, inspecting the soil and driveway for muddy footprints. But there was no evidence to substantiate his claims. "Must have been cats, like you said."

He looked around. "Nice houses, these."

"I think so," Beauville agreed, the gentle spring breeze calming his rather frayed nerves. "Some people say Deverton lacks character, but I can think of a lot worse places to live! Now you should see where I did my curacy -"

"Whose is that big house with the pergola up there?" Robins interrupted, putting his hands above his eyes to peer at a large property a couple of streets up from the vicarage.

"That's the Monkton-Smiths' house," Beauville replied genially, rediscovering his normally calm demeanour. "We're just about in waving distance. And that -" he said, pointing to a pretty ivy clad link detached house a hundred yards in the other direction, "is Mark Parlour's place."

"Nice," Robins whistled, comparing it with the pokey two bedroomed flat he shared with his girlfriend in Foxburgh. They obviously got paid too much in Billock.

"Was there anything else, Sergeant?" Beauville enquired, "I'm really rather tired. I could do with a nap."

"No, that'll be all for now," Robins replied, rummaging in his pockets for his car-keys. "But we'll be in touch."

"Whatever," Beauville replied diffidently, and returned to the sanctity of Deverton Vicarage.

⧗⧗⧗

"I hear you released Beauville," Parlour said to Leigh Blackman, intercepting her in the corridor at half past five that evening.

"No need to crow," Blackman replied glumly. "We can't get anything on him. It's like trying to get blood from a precious stone! We haven't found one single person with dirt on him."

"That's because he's innocent," Parlour replied. He hastily pulled her into a vacant office off the corridor as a couple of colleagues approached. "Discussing rotas, if anyone asks."

"So what's your theory, then, smartypants?" Blackman growled, shaking her arm free. "Cos from where I'm standing, he's the only one with any reason to want Haynes dead."

"I don't have one - yet," Parlour conceded, "Doesn't make Beauville guilty, though. Did you get hold of any navy guys?"

Blackman nodded. "They won't squeal. Not allowed, are they? A fellow naval officer at that time did think Beauville was a bit odd. Not one of the lads. That's all he'd say."

"What about family?"

"All incredibly distraught, Martin's such a decent chap, no hint of bum-banditry, etcetera etcetera."

"You have the most delicate turn of phrase, Leigh. Any fingerprints?"

"No foreign prints on the computer, and none on Haynes's burglar alarm or front door. Just Haynes's, mine, Robins' and the cleaner's."

"Have you spoken to Mary Fosthlewaite?" Parlour enquired.

"Yeah – eventually! She was murder to get hold of!" Blackman laughed ironically. "Seems she cleans half of Deverton!"

"That I can believe!" Parlour said wryly. There was no shortage of well-off professionals residing on Deverton Estate, DINKYS with neither the time nor the inclination to hoover their staircase. "She's seen a business opportunity and seized it by the broom handle! And good luck to her! She lives in Lexington Green, you know. Gets the first bus into Deverton every day to tidy up after the yuppy idiots!"

"May I remind you of your own upwardly-mobile, dual income status?" Blackman commented dryly.

"We're planning kids next year, and in any case, we're not young!" Parlour laughed. "So what did Mrs F have to say?"

Blackman confirmed Mary Fosthlewaite's whereabouts. "Is she an honest type, in your opinion – the cleaner, I mean?"

"Have you not met her?" Parlour frowned.

"No – Sean Denton interviewed her. What's she like?"

"Tall lady, mid-fifties. Spinster. Husband passed away last year – left her up to her ears in debt. Squandered all their savings on beer and the gee-gees. She had to move to a little flat in Lexington Green, take up numerous cleaning jobs. Jules and I felt sorry for her."

"No pension or life insurance?" Blackman enquired. Parlour shook his head.

"Neither of them took out any insurance and he never stuck a job long enough to have built up any kind of pension - I gather he took his drink problem to work with him."

"Liver?"

"Yep."

"Reckon Mansfield's going that way," Blackman grimaced, referring to her much hated boss at County Police HQ. "Old tyrant. Can't say I'll be too gutted when he finally snuffs it."

Parlour shrugged non-committedly, not wishing to speak ill of a man who'd always been civil to him.

"So going back to the Fosthlewaite lady – does she strike you as the gossiping type?"

"Type to reveal Haynes's burglar alarm combination in passing, you mean?" Parlour asked. "Not really – but I don't know her that well. I can't see it would be in her best interests to blab out details of people's security arrangements to all and sundry - if she wants to remain Deverton's Supermop!"

"True," Blackman conceded.

"Why – what were you thinking?"

"That she gave it to Beauville," Blackman replied, "and he was Terence Haynes's visitor on Saturday morning. I know his prints weren't on anything, but he could've worn gloves –"

"But why would Beauville want to sneak into Haynes's house on Saturday morning when he was going to see him at Zion House later that day?" Parlour frowned.

"Perhaps he got wind that Haynes was writing a letter of complaint – wanted to see it for himself before having words with him? To avoid revealing unnecessarily that *he* knew that Terence knew about his past?"

"It's possible," Parlour shrugged, "but it sounds a bit lame."

"Or perhaps he popped round and Haynes bumped into him in the street and invited him back for a few minutes to talk, to avoid arguing in public?"

"That's also feasible," Parlour replied, "I must admit – the thought didn't occur to me that Haynes might have popped back indoors with someone. But it still wouldn't have left him time to go to the newsagents, and Juliet saw him just after eight, anyway. Also, Beauville must have lied about not having had words with Haynes, and Haynes never struck me as the type to avoid a public confrontation! Got any other ideas who it could've been?"

Blackman shook her head. "Went to see Rose Passmore again today. She's the only one we know for sure had a fall-out with Haynes. But she maintains she never went near his flask. Tried to crack her, but she just got all HRT on me. Can't see her doing it, myself. Unfortunately – I hate that misguided do-goodyness she practises. It's types like her - letting kids run riot in the name of self-expression - that's ruining this country!"

"Yes, Miss Widdicombe!" Parlour grinned. "What about the peanuts – got any further with that?"

Blackman shook her head again dolefully. There had been no traces of peanut on anybody's clothing or car upholstery and she had decided it was a waste of time tracking down sales of peanuts in retail outlets. Not only could the murderer have purchased them anywhere in the country, they were also the sort of perishable item people kept in the house for months.

Parlour enquired about Haynes's will. Blackman informed him that this had potentially promising theory had soon died in the water.

Parlour frowned. "So what will you do, if you can't trace the nuts and the burglar alarm lead comes to nothing?"

"Keep trying to track down friends and family of Beauville," Blackman replied. "And see if anyone heard Beauville and Haynes having a ding-dong prior to the meeting at Zion House."

"I'd try and keep an open mind, Leigh," Parlour said soberly. "I agree Beauville has a fat juicy motive, but it's well possible he was set up. I can't say I've ever seen him use the computer, and Jules said she's never ever received anything word-processed from him. On the contrary, he tends to scribble everyone notes with that awful smudgy fountain-pen of his."

"It's our only lead at the moment," Blackman replied firmly. "And I intend to follow it through."

Parlour grimaced as she left the room. Looked like poor old Beauville wasn't off the leash, yet. He looked up at the ceiling. Something was bugging him. He'd had that sensation earlier on that morning at Foxburgh Library. The feeling that he was missing some obvious link. Suddenly it came to him, much in the manner of some inconsequential name that had been on the tip of one's tongue for days.

He picked up the phone and punched some numbers in.

"Hello, Christine? Mark Parlour here."

⧖⧖⧖

Fortunately Daniel Kelty had popped out to the DIY warehouse to get some value magnolia when Parlour arrived at their little two up two down in Battenberg Close, just three doors up from the property shared by Jason Jarvis and Alex Miller.

"This is all very mysterious," Christine Kelty giggled, leading Parlour into the kitchen, where she was marking some schoolbooks. Like Juliet, Christine was a teacher in Billock. Unlike Juliet, she taught primary school children, a vocation nevertheless arduous, given the difficult catchment area from which her pupils were taken.

Parlour sat down at the table, wishing she'd turn off that awful reedy meditation music they always had on in the background. He knew where he'd like to shove those blinking panpipes!

"Cup of tea?" she asked in the honeyed tone that got on both the Parlours' nerves.

"Thanks," Parlour smiled.

"Juliet not home yet?"

"She has a parents' evening tonight," Parlour replied. "She won't be back till nine or so."

"Poor thing!" Christine sympathised. "It's no fun staying on after school like that. Feel like you haven't got away the next day!"

"Yes, she doesn't look forward to them," Parlour nodded, gratefully accepting the mug of tea she had just poured from the teapot.

"So what can I do for you?" Christine asked a little nervously, sitting opposite him.

"It's rather delicate, actually, Christine," Parlour said seriously. "Can you keep a secret?"

"Ooh, of course," she replied, then frowned. "What about Daniel?"

"You might want to keep it from him, anyway," Parlour replied soberly. She looked perturbed at this suggestion.

"As you know," he began, "I'm not heading the inquiry into the murder of Terence, due to Juliet's involvement, so to speak. However, the Bishop is not happy with the line DI Blackman is taking –"

"You mean interrogating poor old Martin?" Christine frowned.

"Exactly. So he's asked me to carry out a little investigation of my own into Terence Haynes's death. This is where I need you to keep stumm – I'll be in big trouble if the Chief Inspector finds out, OK?"

Christine nodded slowly. "But –"

"But how does that affect you?" Parlour interrupted. "Well, as I'm sure you know, they found some material of a sexual nature on Martin's computer. They think he downloaded it, but he believes he was framed – and I must say, it looks that way to me. So it stands to reason that whoever set him up like that got access to his computer. Now, whoever used his computer must have firstly known his password, and secondly how to use the Internet. It's likely then that the person either had their own PC or regular access to one."

Christine Kelty began to look visibly nervous.

"So, I thought I would try and find out who might have had access to Martin Beauville's PC and which of us, among those present at Zion House, are *au fait* with the Internet."

"I see," Christine mumbled.

"Christine – knowing how Daniel feels about computers, I immediately crossed your name off my list. However, as part of my investigations, I paid a visit to Foxburgh Library this morning, where I found your name on the list of registered PC users."

His deep blue eyes bore into her watery green ones. She looked down at the farmhouse table, sighed, then met his stare.

"You're right. I have been using the computers at the library. It all began after I'd been on a training course at school – you know – basic computing and introduction to the Internet. I didn't tell Daniel, but I really enjoyed it, and I was surprisingly rather good at it. I decided, since he's so dead set against getting one, that I'd go to the library and use their computers there. It's a brilliant source of information for us teachers, you know, but you can never get near the workstations at school unless you hang around for hours after school. And you know how Daniel likes his dinner on the table at five."

She looked at him rather balefully - like a cow ripe for the slaughterhouse, Parlour thought. She was a sweet lady, but so ill-treated by her husband's malappropriation of Scripture. Still, she had a mind of her own, didn't she? She had demonstrated that by her little act of Saturday subterfuge at Foxburgh Library. Perhaps she would egg herself onto greater acts of courage and begin to assert her God-given right to use her gifts and talents for the benefit of those around her.

"But I never looked at any X-rated websites or anything," Christine added. She got up and started routing around her pile of stuff on the table. She handed him some A4 sheets.

"Look – here's some information about Elizabeth 1 I found on there. And here –" she rustled some more papers, "- here's some stuff about the penguins at Chuddington Zoo. I'm organising a class trip there in July, you know."

Parlour looked at the sheets handed him. Of course, there was nothing to say she hadn't looked at less wholesome material on a private computer somewhere and jotted down the web addresses, but she seemed too sweet and innocent.

"Oh please don't tell Daniel, will you?" she pleaded. "He wouldn't understand, and I do so want to continue using the computers at the library!"

"It's really up to you to tell Daniel, don't you think?" Parlour said gently.

"Yes – yes, I suppose it is," Christine Kelty replied, looking confused and flustered. "You must think we're awfully strange."

Parlour's lips twitched. Juliet would have launched into an assault on Daniel's sexist interpretation of Scripture and branded Christine a dishcloth for not standing up to him. He was not Juliet.

"We all have our principles," he smiled tactfully instead.

"So is that all?" Christine asked nervously.

"Just one more thing," Parlour replied. "I gather you've been using Martin's piano this past few weeks."

"That's right. I had to take my organ to the workshop. Some strange foreign part needs replacing. It's taking longer than I thought. But it should be ready tomorrow." She frowned, then suddenly grasped what Parlour was driving at. "Oh – I see – I've had access to Martin's house – to his computer! Oh dear! It doesn't look to good for me, does it?"

Parlour smiled reassuringly. "I'm sure it's purely circumstantial, Christine. So long as you're straight with me, it shouldn't be a problem."

"Oh please, ask away!" Christine implored him. She didn't have the face of a Natural Born Killer, Parlour thought, trying hard not to smile. If ever there was a less likely candidate…

but experience taught him that they were often the ones with dark secrets.

"Did you at any time over the last few weeks turn on Martin Beauville's computer?"

"No," Christine replied firmly. "I went there to practise the piano, and that's all I ever did while I was there. I may have helped myself to the odd glass of water, but I never laid a finger on any of his stuff otherwise."

"Are you aware that Martin Beauville uses a personal organiser?" Parlour enquired, taking a sip of his tea. It was Beauville's one little foray into the 21st century.

"A personal what? Oh, you mean a Filofax?"

Parlour shook his head. "I meant an electronic organiser. Little black thing – slimline – bit like a calculator."

"Oh, you mean that thing he gets out every time you ask him if he's free one evening?"

Parlour nodded. "We have reason to believe it went missing for a few days recently. Did you know anything about that?"

Christine Kelty shook her head, looking bewildered, a facial expression that came naturally to her. "No, can't say I did. Did he find it?"

Parlour informed her that it had turned up in the lost property box at church.

She shrugged. "Sorry. Can't help you there. I don't understand…"

Parlour hesitated. There wasn't any harm in her knowing, was there? "It contained his password for the computer – well, for accessing the Web."

"Right… oh, I see. You think someone got their hands on it and that person might have been the one who used his computer?"

"Yes." Parlour stared keenly at her. She held his gaze this time. If she was lying, she was doing a very professional job.

"Did you know the combination for Terence Haynes's burglar alarm?" he asked. It was worth a shot.

Christine shook her head. "None of us did, did we? He was frightfully uptight about security – mind you, it's understandable, with all those medals of his on display."

Parlour nodded. "Thinking back to Saturday morning now, did you pop round to Terence's house before making your way to Zion House?"

"No. Why should I?" Christine looked genuinely perplexed.

"We're just wondering if anyone had words with him on the morning of his death," Parlour replied. It was a half-truth, or half-lie, whatever way you wanted to look at it.

Christine frowned. "Not guilty. I never crossed swords with him, so to speak. I admit I didn't find him the easiest person in the world to talk to, but we never argued as such. Daniel had a bit of a quarrel with him about the worship the other week, but it was all settled amicably."

"Mary Fosthlewaite's your cleaner, too, isn't she?" Parlour enquired.

"Yes… though she only does an hour a fortnight for us. Daniel thinks even that's a bit of a luxury. But the house gets so messy otherwise, with us both working, which annoys Daniel even more."

My, what a charmed life you lead, Parlour thought to himself, pitying Christine Kelty her petty-minded husband.

"Did she at any time give you details of Haynes's burglar alarm?"

Christine shook her head. "No – why would she have? Terence would've sacked her on the spot if he found out she'd revealed that number to anyone."

"It seems unlikely, I know," Parlour agreed. "But we have to ask. We're pretty sure someone entered his house while he went for his paper on Saturday, and it wasn't Mrs Fosthlewaite."

Christine's eyes opened wide. "Gosh! Did they steal anything?"

"No. But we'd still like to trace whoever it was. It may have something to do with his death."

"Of course," Christine replied anxiously. Parlour stood up.

"Look – I must be making tracks. I have a pile of work I should've been doing whilst acting as the Bishop's private investigator! Christine –"

"Yes?"

"It would be an enormous help both to me, and to Martin Beauville, if you kept details of this conversation to yourself – and I mean only you, at present. OK?"

Christine Kelty nodded meekly and saw him to the door. She couldn't help but feel a little flutter of excitement as she watched Parlour depart. She could get used to keeping secrets from Daniel, it made her feel nicely jittery inside. And it was the first time in a long while she had experienced such internal pleasure.

13

"I've now officially come to a dead end," Leigh Blackman informed Chief Inspector Sewell gloomily that Thursday morning. "Everyone disliked Terence Haynes, but nobody hated him enough to want him dead. Beauville has a nice meaty motive but denies everything we throw at him and the evidence is all circumstantial. They all deny touching his flask and we have a cat in hell's chance of tracing the peanuts. Furthermore, none of those present at Zion House reckon they popped round to pay Haynes a visit at two minutes past eight on Saturday 25 May so who knows how that bloody tampon got in his pouch thing."

"You think Beauville is telling the truth now?" Sewell frowned, taking a hefty swig of his black coffee, oblivious to Blackman's unfortunate turn of phrase.

"I don't know," Blackman replied honestly, "but until we can find something to firmly link him with the crime, I guess we have to consider he might have been set up, like at that Court Martial of his, and proceed accordingly."

"I agree," Sewell nodded, who had taken a keen interest in the case, despite his involvement in the Foxburgh Red Light murders. "Shame, though. He does seem the most likely candidate, I have to admit. Have you exhausted the list of contacts?"

"Yes, Sir," Blackman replied. "They're calling Keough "Titchmarsh", he's been digging that much dirt! But nothing to nail him. To be honest, Sir, it's neither here nor there whether Beauville played *Hello Sailor* in the navy, anyway. It's his relationship with Haynes that matters."

Sewell nodded. "Have you taken into account Haynes's death might have been a conspiracy?"

"What, like *Murder on the Orient Express*, Sir?" Blackman grinned.

"Seems far-fetched, I know, Blackman, but you know what those church types are like. Stick together like glue, relying on their wholesome reputation to save face."

"I did think a number of them might have been involved, yes," Blackman admitted, "but having met them all at least once, it seems unlikely. It pains me to say it, Sir, but they all seem pretty decent. Beauville and Andrew Monkton-Smith seem to have had the most opportunity, but Parlour's dead set against either of them being involved – and he does know them better than most, Sir."

"Yes, well, he would be, wouldn't he?" Sewell replied sarcastically, sharing Blackman's antipathy towards the Christian faith and those who practised it. "What does Robins think?"

"Robins? He thinks Beauville is a real smartarse. Reckons, on the balance of things, he's telling the truth, but it wouldn't surprise him if he's hiding something, either."

"Hmm," Sewell exhaled. "It's a tricky one. Shame I'm committed to the Foxburgh Tarts – I'd like to have a pop at our silky smooth vicar friend. I suppose the next step, assuming Beauville *was* set up, would be to ascertain who might have had access to the vicarage computer."

"And which of those present at Zion House are computer literate," Blackman added. "Can't imagine for one minute that the likes of Mavis Wagstaff downloaded some naughty websites!"

"Quite," Sewell replied. "You might want to search all their houses – look at their PCs, and look out for peanuts, while you're at it. I'd be prepared to request a search warrant in the circumstances."

"Thank you, Sir."

He got up. "Keep your pecker up, Leigh. You're doing a good job. Keep Beauville under surveillance but, as I said, might be an idea to cast your net wider."

"That's what Parlour reckons," Blackman admitted gloomily.

"Parlour?" Sewell enquired, frowning. "Has he been badgering you for information?"

"No," Blackman lied, "but he couldn't help but notice we'd arrested Beauville. Wasn't too happy about it."

"Yes, well, he's one of his cronies, isn't he?" Sewell said dryly, manoeuvring his considerable frame into a grey trenchcoat. "Exactly why we need someone like you on the case, Leigh."

"Thank you, Sir," Blackman smiled politely, realising it was more of a slight on Parlour's personal beliefs than an acknowledgement of her abilities.

⧗⧗⧗

"Blooming 'eck, not you as well!" Jason Jarvis exclaimed as DS Robins and a younger officer drove up to his kiosk at Counter Claim, the innovative new drive-thru insurance quote centre where Jarvis had worked for just over a year.

"Why, who else has been here?" Robins asked suspiciously.

"Technical Support," Jarvis replied hastily, remembering he'd promised Parlour he'd keep his mouth shut. "Wanted to take my computer apart – routine maintenance they say! But how the heck am I supposed to do my job without a PC, I ask you?"

"This won't take a minute," Robins said dryly. "We just want to look at your email and internet – you do have internet access, don't you?"

"Naturally," Jarvis replied. He proposed they parked at the back of the building and joined him inside the building.

"This is Sergeant Millbank, he's an IT specialist," Robins explained, once they were stood behind Jarvis's desk. "We just need to check out a few things with your line manager."

"They found loads of dodgy sites on the vicar's PC, didn't they?" Jarvis grinned matily once Millbank had left to consult his superior. "Well, wasn't me, gov!"

He'd cheered up a bit since last time he'd seen him, shortly after Nicky Ellery's murder, Robins thought to himself.

"Got a PC at home, too?" Robins asked.

"Nope. But Alex has."

"Would he be in later?"

"He's in now. Cramming for an exam. Might not be too chuffed if you lot pile round. Man, I've never seen him so stressed!"

"We'd only need a few minutes," Robins replied. "Who else has got a PC at home, of those present at Zion House on Saturday?"

Jarvis bit his lip, thinking. "Lins has got one – but it belongs to her old man. She wouldn't have done it, though. Squeakier than chalk on a blackboard!"

"Spare me the character analysis," Robins said sarcastically. "Who else?"

"Well, Juliet Parlour, of course, with internet access, I believe! Ho ho, that would make a good story!" Jarvis chuckled, then sobered up. "Actually, this isn't very funny, is it?"

Robins just rose his eyebrows at him.

"Rose Passmore might have one," Jarvis continued. "Mavis wouldn't, of course, though I suppose she could be a closet *surfy*! Olivia Murray hasn't. They wouldn't give her a job in the Reference Library cos she was such a ninny with computers – that's why she's stuck in Grannyville in the Large Print section! Andrew Monkeybreath's definitely got one… Lara thinks PC stands for Photocopier, though, so I doubt she's your man, so to speak. Is that everyone? Oh no, I forgot the Keltys. Easily done. Daniel hates the things, refuses to go within ten feet of one. Christine, I suspect, likewise. They say she sold the rights to her own opinion to Daniel as part of the marriage contract, you know!"

"I gathered as much," Robins acknowledged, watching his officer at work through a glass partition.

"Nothing suspect," Steve Millbank informed him a minute later. "We've checked his user profile and there's nothing incriminating. The software would have flagged it up in any case."

Robins turned back to Jarvis. "You say Alex Miller is at home this morning?"

"Yep."

"We'll pay him a visit."

"Bye then," Jarvis called after their retreating backs. He picked up the phone as they left the building.

⧗⧗⧗

"Any joy?" Robins enquired hopefully, as Blackman crossed the bar of the Waggoners, mineral water in hand. His senior shook her head despondently, joining him at a little round table by the window.

Blackman informed him that Rose Passmore didn't own a home computer and that all client information had to remain in the office in any case for reasons of confidentiality. Passmore's boss at Foxburgh District Social Services had created a real stink when Blackman had enquired whether her assistant could examine Rose's computer, but was finally allowed access. Again, nothing suspicious had been found.

As anticipated, Mavis Wagstaff did not own a PC at all. Pleased to have some company, she had kept WPC Fullerton there for over an hour!

Blackman enquired how her colleague had got on.

"Went to see Jason Jarvis at work," Robins replied. "His PC was clear, but he pointed us in the direction of his flatmate, the male nurse."

"Alex Miller?"

"That's the one. Poor guy has an exam tomorrow – he was up to his ears in medical textbooks! His PC appeared clear at first. However –"

"Yes?" Blackman leant forward eagerly, sensing Robins had found something of note.

"It was suspiciously clear, if you know what I mean, like Beauville's was. The guy has email, yet there were no messages on there and he had no bookmarks listed on the Internet package."

"You reckon he got tipped off by Jarvis?" Blackman frowned.

Robins nodded. "He wiped the files off his computer pretty pronto this morning, at a guess. But when Millbank examined the cached images stored on the hard disk, he found several porn sites had been accessed recently. *But...*"

Robins held his hand up to curb Blackman's rising excitement.

"... it was all standard girly porn stuff. Much like you'd find on the average bloke's PC."

"I wouldn't know," Blackman commented dryly.

"I hate to disappoint you, boss," Robins continued, "But he just seemed like such a nice guy – totally the wrong type! He's still pretty cut-up about that Nicky Ellery business, too. If you ask me, that cheeky git Jarvis would've been much more likely to have been playing silly buggers with Martin Beauville's computer. It's not necessarily the case that whoever downloaded all that stuff onto his PC killed Terence Haynes. Could've just been doing it for a laugh."

"It's in very poor taste, then," Blackman commented. "Jason Jarvis may like a bit of fun, but I don't think he would set the vicar up like that just for kicks. Somebody malicious who presumably knew about the Court Martial was the likely perpetrator of this."

"Any ideas who that might be?"

Blackman shook her head. "That's the problem. Everyone thinks the goddamn sun shines out of Martin Beauville's arse. It's very difficult to see who would want to do the dirty on him like that."

"What about that Kelty woman?" Robins asked. "She was in and out of the vicarage tinkling the old ivory, wasn't she?"

Blackman snapped her fingers. "Yes! She was, wasn't she! But she's another fully paid up member of the Martin Beauville fan club."

"Could just be for show," Robins countered. "Mind you, she *did* buy the vicar a mighty big bunch of yellow chrysanthemums to welcome him home! Perhaps they were having an affair! Haynes found out and threatened to blow the whistle on them. Beauville plots Haynes's murder, then frames himself on the computer with some gay porn to make it look like a set up!"

"Bit drastic, isn't it?" Blackman frowned. "If I'd been falsely accused of homosexual activity, I wouldn't want anyone thinking for a minute I really was a lezzer!"

"Exactly!" Robins exclaimed, on a roll now. "Beauville was banking on us assuming he was framed. After all, nobody would voluntarily let on they were batting for the other side! Remember how casual he was about us inspecting his computer! Almost like he wanted us to."

"Perhaps it was just the confidence of an innocent man," Blackman replied. "Aren't you forgetting something, though?"

"What?"

"If Beauville was bonking other men during his time in the navy, why on earth would he be having an affair with Christine Kelty?"

"Bisexual?" Robins shrugged. "Or perhaps he was innocent of the charges and he's as straight as you or me. He just needed Haynes out the picture."

Blackman drummed her forefingers on the table.

"Come on," Robins cajoled, "isn't it worth a shot?"

Blackman sighed then slapped her hand decisively on the table. "OK, eager beaver. You can tackle Christine Kelty. I'll work my feminine charms on our friend the vicar. But remember the Kelty woman won't be back from school until fourish."

"Shall I carry on with the computer stuff till then?" Robins asked. It was only half past one.

"I'll see if I can get anything out of Beauville first," Blackman replied. "Why don't you go back to the station and see if the boys have any more leads. Oh, and can you radio Sean and ask him to meet me outside the vicarage. Probably best not to visit strange men alone, even if he is a vicar!"

"Will do," Robins replied, adrenaline pumping once more.

⧗⧗⧗

"Mark – what a pleasant surprise," Andrew Monkton-Smith said genially, opening his front door to the thin ginger detective that Thursday afternoon. "Won't you join me – I've just made a pot of tea. Lara's off at one of her committee meetings and I'm working from home today."

"Yes – I saw the car outside and thought I'd drop by." Parlour followed him down the hallway to the picture perfect kitchen at the back of the spacious four-bedroomed house.

"Nice day, isn't it?" Monkton-Smith commented, setting two mugs out on the large oak table. "Makes a change. It's been a bit of a washout so far this week!"

"Yes, it has," Parlour nodded, folding his overcoat over the back of the chair and loosening his tie. He sat down and stretched his long, thin legs.

"So what can I do for you – or is this just a social visit?"

"Not really," Parlour replied honestly, gratefully accepting his tea. He outlined his commission from the Bishop.

Monkton-Smith laughed. "So the Bish has hired a private investigator! Must be desperate to clear Beauville's name – and save face himself, I don't doubt."

"He is," Parlour nodded, sipping his tea. "Doesn't believe for a minute Beauville is guilty."

"And do you?" Monkton-Smith frowned, his considerable grey eyebrows almost meeting in the middle.

"No," Parlour replied. "Of course I don't. But I have to put my personal loyalties aside and consider all the possibilities."

"Of course."

"Which is why you won't mind if I ask you a few questions…"

"Fire away!" Monkton-Smith laughed, reclining in his chair and folding his arms behind his head. But it was a slightly nervous laugh.

"I gather you will have heard by now that the police found a load of pornographic pictures on Martin's computer-"

"And some article on Haynes's computer saying he'd been buggering men in the forces, I hear," Monkton-Smith frowned.

"To put it bluntly. Whether he did or didn't is irrelevant for the purposes of our enquiry," Parlour continued. "However, if he was set up, as he believes, then someone must've known about his past, or about the allegations, at least. And that someone would also need to be computer literate to have accessed that information on him. My guess is they just downloaded the pictures of teenage boys onto his PC as a finishing touch."

"Good grief, Mark," Monkton-Smith interrupted, leaning forward in his seat, "you don't think I –"

"No, no," Parlour replied hastily. He didn't really believe his friend was involved, but he couldn't be 100% sure. It was certainly worth having a snoop at his computer. "But it's possible someone used your computer to surf the web – to avoid leaving traces of the relevant websites on their own PCs.

Can you think of anyone who might've had access to your computer? You often have church meetings here.."

"Yes, but the computer is in my study, and I usually lock the door."

"Mind if I take a look –" Parlour asked. Monkton-Smith frowned, then stood up.

"I don't see why not, Mark, but you'll only find endless letters and reports."

"It's your email and Internet package I'm interested in," Parlour replied. "I only want to see if anyone's tampered with your machine."

"Well, you can certainly look, but I really can't see how anyone could've gained access to it."

Parlour followed him down the corridor to his study at the side of the house. Was it his imagination, or was Monkton-Smith more than a little defensive?

"Just come out of that," Monkton-Smith instructed him as Parlour sat down before a letter on the screen. "I saved it when you rang the bell."

"Do you have a password?" Parlour enquired, clicking on the relevant icon for access.

"It's entered automatically," Monkton-Smith replied. Parlour drummed his fingers on the mousemat as the computer crackled away. Once the homepage had come up, Parlour clicked on the Favourites icon. But there were no incriminating sites listed under Favourites, nor on the list of recently viewed sites. Parlour clicked on the mail icon which brought up Monkton-Smith's email messages.

"These are all letters from clients and colleagues," the lawyer informed Parlour. "I delete all the junk mail immediately. You're welcome to read any of them, though I would ask you kept the contents to yourself."

"Naturally," Parlour murmured, bringing up the messages one by one, including those in the delete box. Then he came out and looked in the recycle bin, but there was nothing suspect.

He clicked on Monkton-Smith's address book; it was empty save two names he recognised to be partners in the firm. It seemed Monkton-Smith was pretty limited in his forays into cyberspace. Suspiciously so? Parlour wanted to think the best of his friend and neighbour, but his PC did seem oddly free of the usual eclectic electro-paraphernalia. Had he wiped half the stuff on his machine as a precaution?

"What are you doing now?" Monkton-Smith frowned, as Parlour clicked on a special utility programme on the computer.

"The information may have been deleted on the screen but may still be stored somewhere on the hard drive," Parlour explained. But he found nothing of note.

"What about Lara – does she ever use your computer?" Parlour asked. It was worth a shot.

"Lara! Good heavens, no! Wouldn't let her touch the thing with a barge pole! She can't even programme the blasted video recorder, though goodness knows, I've explained it to her enough times."

Thank heavens for Jules, Parlour thought not for the first time. If there was one thing he couldn't bear, it was technophobes. You couldn't prevent progress, so why resist it? In his view, all good things were sent from heaven above, and computers came into that category. The difference they had made to police work alone justified their existence. Parlour enquired whether Monkton-Smith had modified the computer in any way since purchasing it, perhaps changing his internet service provider, but Monkton-Smith hadn't.

"And you say you lock the door when there are people in the house?" Parlour checked.

"Yes. Always. I have a great deal of confidential information stored in here, you know." He tapped the cardboard box files on the shelves above the PC. "And many of my clients are locals. I can't afford to be lax with security."

"Of course," Parlour nodded. He rose to his feet. "Well, that's all I wanted to know.

He followed Monkton-Smith back to the kitchen.

"You will let me know if there's anything else I can do to help, won't you?" the lawyer stated, as Parlour put his coat on.

"Of course. And thanks for your assistance," Parlour smiled broadly, masking the malaise that lay beneath.

⧖⧖⧖

Juliet was watching out the front window as Parlour strode up the driveway at twenty to six that evening.

"Mark – thank goodness you're back!" Juliet exclaimed, as he stooped to kiss his petite wife on the forehead. "Daniel Kelty's just been on the phone!"

"Daniel?" Parlour frowned, hanging his coat over the banister.

"They've taken Christine down the station for questioning!" Juliet burst out.

"Christine? Whatever for? She wouldn't hurt a fly!"

"Daniel came back from work and heard Dave Robins having a go at her in the kitchen. Reckons she was having an affair with Beauville and Haynes found out!"

"But that's ridiculous!" Parlour exclaimed, hands on hips, "Daniel might take his ideals to extremes, but Christine is devoted to him! I only spoke to her yesterday…"

"Did you?" Juliet asked, furrowing her brow. "You never said…"

"I forgot – you got back late and were telling me about school and it slipped my mind," Parlour apologised.

"Supper's ready," Juliet informed him as he followed her into the kitchen.

"It's a bit early, isn't it?" Parlour frowned, sifting through the day's post.

"I have aerobics tonight, don't I?" Juliet reminded him. "Hence the pasta salad."

"Makes a change," Parlour said. "I've eaten that much junk this week."

"Thanks!"

"I meant at work," he explained himself, washing his hands and joining her at the table. He held his plate up as she dished out some tuna pasta with a serving spoon.

"I think Daniel would appreciate a call," Juliet informed him.

"I'll call him when I've had my dinner," Parlour replied. "I need to talk to you while you're here."

"Oh yes?" Juliet raised her eyebrows.

"You said you'd ring Lindsay, ask about her computer."

Juliet confirmed that she had indeed rung Lindsay Briscoe. It seemed Charles was very protective of his PC and wouldn't let anyone bar Lindsay touch it. He had installed some expensive financial software on the computer that he didn't want accessed by amateurs. Lindsay was under strict instructions not to let the children or anyone else near it.

"Sounds much like Andrew Monkton-Smith," Parlour nodded, crunching on a celery stick.

"Did Stu Beattie check Beauville's computer for prints?" Juliet enquired.

Parlour inclined his head. "It's clean, apart from police fingerprints all over it! Doesn't mean much though. Anyone with half a brain would've worn gloves to set Martin up like that."

"Must be pretty difficult to type with gloves on, though," Juliet frowned.

"Not if you wore surgical gloves," Parlour replied, shaking his head.

"So what's Leigh Blackman up to, apart from arresting Christine Kelty?"

“Taken in for questioning, not arrested,” Parlour corrected her.

“Same thing, isn’t it?”

Parlour shook his head. “Not necessarily. They probably needed some privacy. Can you imagine Daniel letting Christine speak for herself, if they questioned her at home?”

“Not really,” Juliet conceded.

“Leigh’s still got her head up her backside, thinks Martin is definitely involved. I gather the Sewer told her to widen the net, though. Thank goodness.”

“He doesn’t reckon Martin did it?” Juliet asked, hope in her voice.

“On the contrary, the Chief agrees with Leigh that Beauville is up to his neck in it. But they haven’t come up with any concrete evidence linking Beauville to the crime, so they have to consider other options.”

“Such as?”

“Well, last I heard, they’ve been looking at people’s computers,” Parlour replied smugly, forgetting that it had been his wife’s idea and not his in the first place. It gave him no small degree of pleasure to note he was one step ahead of the official investigation team, with all the manpower and resources they had at their disposal.

The phone rang.

“That’ll be Daniel again,” Juliet informed her husband.

Parlour grabbed the portable handset from the worktop. It was indeed Daniel Kelty.

12

"Phew, am I glad to see you!" Daniel Kelty exhaled, opening the door of his pokey semi-detached to Parlour an hour later.

"Best welcome I've had all week!" Parlour grinned, but Kelty was in no mood for banter.

"They think Christine's been having an affair with Martin! It's ridiculous!"

"Nothing would surprise me, the way this investigation is going," Parlour said dryly. "They'll be saying Haynes and Beauville had a lover's tiff next!"

"Ooh, don't," Daniel Kelty shuddered, who liked to keep his sensitive mind clear of salacious imagery.

"So what were they saying to Christine?" Parlour enquired. Presumably Blackman and co had done their homework and traced her name on the list of Internet users at Foxburgh Library, too.

How can they live like this? Parlour wondered, flopping down on Keltys' hand-me-down sofa. The Keltys, or at least Daniel Kelty, did not believe in spending money unnecessarily, hence the house was a characterless affair, drably kitted out with the basics for day to day living. It didn't say in the Bible that it was wrong to have nice things, Parlour grimaced, just that one shouldn't honour the material above the spiritual.

Kelty frowned. "They reckon she was spending a suspicious amount of time at the vicarage – even bought him flowers or something!"

He looked thoroughly baffled.

"It was just a welcome home gesture," Parlour explained, sticking up for Christine. "Women do nice things like that."

"Not Christine!" Kelty replied. "I mean, she wouldn't waste a couple of pounds on some flowers for the vicar!"

"I think you'll find they cost a bit more than two quid, Daniel," Parlour informed him mischievously. "More like a fiver – maybe even a tenner!"

"What?" Kelty exclaimed, horrified.

"Daniel – Christine is entitled to spend her own money, you know," Parlour stated. "She is earning, after all!"

"I know, I know," Daniel mumbled, in the resigned tone of one who had heard the same argument many times, "but it's the principle. Why scrimp and save to give your ten per cent to the church then blow good money on stupid flowers for the vicar!"

"Giving to the church should be done cheerfully," Parlour replied, "and anyway, giving Martin some chrysanths to cheer him up *is* giving to the church. We all benefit if the vicar feels cared for. "

"I suppose," Daniel mumbled, too distraught to argue. "But what a ridiculous idea – Christine and Martin! She'd never look at another man!"

"But they might look at her," Parlour said quietly. "She's an attractive woman, Daniel, or hadn't you noticed lately?"

Daniel looked up, colour rising in his cheeks. "Mark, I asked you around because I thought you might be able to shed some light on the matter. If I'd wanted Marriage Guidance, the number's in the book."

Parlour looked him straight in the eye. "Look, Daniel, I'll be honest with you. I don't think for one minute Christine would look at another man, either – but one thing this whole business has brought home to me is we can't take one another for granted. Someone we know well, perhaps even intimately, has carried out an atrocious assault on another person's life. That beggars belief in itself."

"But Christine would never-" Daniel began angrily, struggling to get his mouth around the awful words, "have an affair – least of all with the leader of our church!"

"What do you think she does on a Saturday morning, then?" Parlour asked, aware he was stirring. But it was intentional.

Christine could easily make up an excuse for her weekly trip to Foxburgh if she needed to, but meanwhile he might help rejuvenate a stale marriage between two good people by removing the blinkers of misguided piety from Daniel Kelty's eyes.

"She goes to the library in Foxburgh, of course," Daniel frowned. So she had told him that much, Parlour thought with relief. "Why – you're not suggesting –" he faltered.

"I'm not suggesting anything," Parlour replied firmly. "I'm just saying, we all think we know one another intimately, but how much do we really know? You assume Christine faithfully trots off to Foxburgh Library every Saturday morning, because she tells you so. I assume Juliet is at aerobics right now, because that's what she told me. So maybe we shouldn't take one another for granted."

"It's called trust, Mark," Daniel Kelty frowned at him. "What are you saying – I should keep Christine under 24 hour surveillance?"

"I don't know, what do you think?" Parlour enquired absent-mindedly as something he'd just said suddenly struck him as really rather significant.

"I think it's an appalling idea!" Kelty exclaimed. "Christine is free to make her own choices about what she does in her spare time!"

"I couldn't agree more," Parlour smiled, turning his attention back to a baffled Kelty. Hopefully he'd remember this conversation when Christine got back from Billock Station. They wouldn't get anything on Christine. They were simply trying to eliminate her from the enquiry. Any moment now, Daniel would get a call to pick her up.

⧗⧗⧗

But just for once, Parlour was wrong. Like Parlour, they had found Christine Kelty's name on the list of users registered to log onto Foxburgh Library's public workstations.   Unlike Parlour, they were not inclined to believe her little spiel about downloading information for school, and even less inclined to view Daniel Kelty as some kind of Scroogesque technophobe.

"Come off it, Mark!" Blackman exclaimed five minutes after he'd come hurtling into her office at eight o'clock that evening demanding why she'd seen fit to bring Christine Kelty in for questioning. "Why make a thirty mile round trip to Foxburgh every Saturday morning to use a computer when she could use one of several at her own blinking school?   She probably registered there to cover her back and is hanging out at some dodgy backstreet cyber café surfing the net for God knows what!"

"You are *so* bloody cynical!" Parlour exclaimed. "Why shouldn't she use Foxburgh Library to do her schoolwork? You certainly don't get any time or space at school - Jules'll tell you that. The weekend's the only time you get to do some decent preparation!"

"She could have done it after school," Blackman snapped back. "If her husband's as tight as she makes out, she'd never drive to Foxburgh every Saturday if she didn't have to! I bet the miserable sod gives her a fuel allowance!"

"So what's your theory now, then?" Parlour enquired acerbically. "Terence finds out Beauville and Christine Kelty are at it hammer and *tongue* and threatens to spill the beans to the Bish? In defence of Beauville's honour, Christine poisons Terence at the PCC Away Day. Horrified, Beauville dumps Christine for bumping off Tell-Tale-Tit-Terence, but she then turns nasty and decides to frame Martin with some lewd gay piccies, relying on her whiter-than-white Anchor-Wouldn't-Melt-In-My-Mouth reputation to provide an alibi for herself. Hell hath no fury like a woman scorned, and all that-"

"It's possible," Blackman countered. Parlour's theory was even better than Robins's.

"It's pants!" Parlour exclaimed. He took a deep breath to compose himself, hands on hips, then looked at Blackman across her desk.

"I never said we'd worked the whole story out," Blackman defended herself feebly.

"Said the DI to the judge," Parlour said sarcastically.

"Anyway, that's only one theory."

"And what's the other?" Parlour enquired. "Beauville and the Bish?"

"Robins reckons Beauville might have killed Terence because he threatened to split on his affair with Christine," Blackman replied, attempting composure, though she felt her temperature rising. "Beauville then framed himself to make it look like a set up."

"And I thought they took *Jackanory* off air years ago," Parlour snorted, shaking his head.

"Well I think I prefer my hypothetical theory to your non-existent one!" Blackman retorted. Parlour slammed the table, more Rusedski than Henman this time.

"Leigh – these people you're haranguing with your kwik-fit ideas are my friends! You can't expect me just to stand back and watch you cast all sorts of aspersions on the morals of perfectly innocent people! I do wish you'd at least consult me before dragging in the likes of Christine Kelty for questioning! Gordon Brown, the woman would no more cheat on her husband than fly the world in a hot-air balloon!"

"Mark, you're not seeing things from my point of view!" Blackman replied in frustration. "No, I don't know these people as you do, but it's a bloody good thing, too! You can't get past what they mean to *you* – but I'm trying to work out what they had against Haynes! I don't give a fuchsia that you think the sun shines out of Martin Beauville's backside and Christine Kelty's halo glows in the dark – I wish you'd just butt out and let me get on with my job! You've already cocked things up for me the last few days, badgering suspects about their PCs. Now they all have advance warning to clear their computers of any suspicious material!”

“I’m sorry about that,” Parlour said honestly, “But you were so obsessed with Beauville, you were missing the obvious leads. Someone had to check people’s PCs before it was too late.”

“And that someone just had to be you,” Blackman said bitterly. “God, you’re arrogant!”

“And you’re burying your head in the sand!” Parlour fired back.

“Will you two shut up?” Chief Inspector Sewell exploded, bursting into the room. “Parlour – take a hike.”

Parlour grabbed his coat in frustration and slammed the door behind him.

“Now then, Leigh,” Sewell said acidly, sitting on the corner of Blackman’s desk, “perhaps you’d like to tell me what you were doing discussing the Haynes murder case with DI Parlour?”

⧗⧗⧗

“That was Leigh Blackman,” Parlour said gloomily, flopping down on the sofa opposite Juliet later that evening. He threw the phone down on the table, narrowly missing his mug of tea.

“Bad news?” Juliet enquired, flicking the volume down on the late evening news.

“She’s refusing to collaborate anymore. Says the Sewer gave her a right old dressing down about leaking information to enemy forces.”

“He said that?” Juliet frowned.

“Not in so many words, but he’s on Leigh’s side on this one,” Parlour replied, screwing a leaflet up in frustration and aiming it at a cheap figurine on the bookshelf. “Reckons I’m

197

too biased to be of any use – told Leigh to give me a wide berth and keep her findings to herself.”

“I take it our friend Sewell found out you’d been moonlighting…”

“Robins guessed I’d been to see Jason Jarvis at work – Jason said something about the whole world wanting to look at the company’s PC. I should’ve been more careful.”

“Trust Jase!” Juliet remarked. “That guy should shut his mouth once in a while – he could catch flies for England! So what are you going to do now?”

“I won’t be giving up on this, don’t you worry,” Parlour replied grimly. “So long as they keep dragging in the likes of Christine Kelty for questioning, I’ll keep at it. Something’s got to give. There’s some vital piece of information I’m missing that holds this thing together, I know it. It’s not some urban killing that anyone could’ve carried out. One person did this, I’m sure, and it must be possible to work out whom – I just need a motive.”

“Want to pick my brains?” Juliet offered. “I was going to go upstairs and read for a while – but I can stay here with you, if you want.”

“Thanks, Jules,” Parlour smiled at her fondly, “but I need to be alone. A couple of things have been bugging me all day – need to sit in my cave and ponder!”

“Well, I’ll leave you to it,” Juliet smiled, picking up their dirty mugs from the coffee table. “Don’t be too late.”

She was used to Parlour staying up late to “brood”, as she termed it. Unlike Juliet, who was a morning person, Parlour was often at his sharpest late at night, and many a conundrum had been solved in the wee small hours over a glass of his favourite white port.

The murder of Terence Haynes, however, was more than an interesting riddle. A much respected, if rather cantankerous, elder statesman of the church had lost his life, and what’s more, one of Parlour's friends had almost certainly carried out the evil deed.

Putting his feet up on the table, now that Juliet was not there to rebuke him, Parlour opened his notebook. A bit of clarity was what he needed, a beam of light to cut through the fug of ideas circulating in his brain. It was an obvious starting point, and Parlour hated orthodoxy as a rule, but it made sense to jot down on paper the name of those present at Zion House last Saturday.

Parlour wrote his header in bold caps, underscoring it with an admirably unshaky hand. To avoid any bias of rank or any form of favouritism, Parlour paused before proceeding in alphabetical order.

MEMBERS OF DEVERTON PAROCHIAL CHURCH COUNCIL IN ATTENDANCE AT ZION HOUSE, SAT 25 MAY 2002

1. Beauville, Martin – Vicar & Chairperson
2. Briscoe, Lindsay - Treasurer
3. Ellery, Nicky – Secretary to the PCC [deceased]
4. Haynes, Terence – Church Warden [deceased]
5. Jarvis, Jason
6. Kelty, Christine – Musical Worship Leader
7. Kelty, Daniel – Musical Worship Leader & Co-ordinator
8. Miller, Alex
9. Monkton-Smith, Andrew
10. Monkton-Smith, Lara
11. Murray, Olivia
12. Parlour, Juliet – Electoral Role Officer
13. Passmore, Rose – Church Warden & Deanery Synod Representative
14. Wagstaff, Mavis

"Hmm, that's odd," Parlour thought to himself as he finished his list. He meandered through to the kitchen and double-checked it against the list of PCC members with telephone numbers on their kitchen pinboard. They had had full attendance at Zion House that day. Usually at least one person cried off with a heavy cold or an unavoidable family crisis. Parlour cast it to the back of his mind for the time being. A couple of other things had struck him that day and he needed to commit them to paper before they slipped his mind again.

But first of all, he flipped back a page to some questions he had jotted down earlier that week. Most of them had now been answered, without providing any new leads, much to the frustration of all involved in the murder enquiry. Mary Fosthlewaite was now out of the picture, given her confirmed trip to Lowden Market. There was no way she could have paid a visit to Haynes's house in Deverton to tamper with his belongings and got back in time to board the bus from Lexington Green, where she lived. Neither had she been in the vicinity of Zion House to fiddle with the flask.

Kevin Murphy, the IT specialist from Foxburgh Library, had confirmed that Christine Kelty had not attempted to download any information of a sexual or military nature or indeed anything suspicious whatsoever. This, of course, did not preclude her from doing so on another PC, but that went for all members of Deverton Parochial Council – there was no way a search could be made of every computer within a thirty mile circumference of Deverton.

With regard to Beauville's personal organiser, the only fingerprints found on the electronic gadget aside from the vicar's belonged to the church administrator, Sandra Neale, who had hand-delivered the organiser to Beauville when it had suddenly appeared in the Lost Property Box at church. Blackman had already interviewed her – she had not seen anyone place it in the box that was kept in the photocopying room. Although only Beauville, the wardens and Daniel Kelty had a key to the room, the door was frequently left on the latch as people dashed in and out to fetch multifarious church items also housed in the room. Parlour scored that lead out, too.

Returning to the mysterious intruder, nobody had seen anyone enter Haynes house on Saturday morning. A young mother up early with a baby had told Blackman she had seen the postman at around quarter to eight and had heard Haynes's dog bark at around eight o'clock, but she hadn't been looking out her window at that time, and had not seen Haynes or anyone else enter or exit the house in King Edward Mews. Parlour had himself taken a walk along the lane that ran behind the even numbered houses and had ascertained that it would indeed be possible to enter Haynes's property through the back gate. However, this lane was accessed from the main road, and therefore those living on the other side of the close would not be able to see anyone enter the properties from the rear. Those with properties on Haynes's side of the road would have had to have been looking out their back windows at that time, but PC Tucker's wife had already informed Juliet that Tucks had questioned all the neighbours of the even numbered houses and none of them had seen anyone enter his property through the back gate on Saturday morning. Parlour would have to check up on that, but Vicky Tucker, for all her indiscretions, could generally be relied on to provide up-to-the-minute, accurate information.

Parlour turned to a fresh page in his spiral-bound notepad. First of all, he wrote down the name of Jason Jarvis. He had got the feeling that Jarvis had been hiding something from him when he'd gone to see him that morning. Perhaps he would pay Alex Miller a visit, too. Miller was more up front, as a rule, than Jarvis, who was generally the mastermind behind their good-natured pranks. Whilst Parlour did not think for one minute either Jarvis or Miller would deliberately murder Terence Haynes, it could have been the result of a practical joke gone wrong. Pop some nuts into the Commander's precious flask of decaff just to wind him up – he could see them doing that. They weren't to know that he was allergic to peanuts with potential fatal consequences. Mind you, as a nurse, you would think Alex Miller would only be too aware of the possible dangers of such a prank… maybe this was Jason's work, then.

Next he penned in the name of Lara Monkton-Smith, followed by a hyphen and Mary Fosthlewaite. Something had been bugging him earlier on in the library and now it had come to him. The Monkton-Smiths also employed the widowed cleaner, alongside the Keltys and the late Terence Haynes. Though Lara was more or less in the clear, given her feelings for Martin Beauville and her technical inadequacies, it was nevertheless possible she had inadvertently passed on information on how to operate Haynes's burglar alarm to a third party. Mary Fosthlewaite needed pressing some more – though she denied having told anyone the combination for the alarm, it was just possible she was shielding someone.

Finally, Parlour printed Zion House in bold capitals. He had a feeling that the Christian Centre where Terence Haynes had died somehow held some clue to the appalling crime. Blackman's team had found no foreign items in the kitchen or anywhere on the grounds to give a clue as to the logistics behind Haynes's murder. He would go there some time this week. His research into the Bywater Farm Murder would take him to the fields just behind Zion House; it shouldn't be too difficult to find an excuse to enter the property, which had long since been given the all clear by Forensic and had been reopened for conference activity.

Parlour snapped his book shut and put his hands behind his head. Something was still bugging him. He stared at the wall opposite, desperately willing the grey cells to bring the relevant information to the forefront of his mind. But it was no use – it wouldn't come to him.

15

Parlour shook his head in confusion as he emerged from a bizarre dream sequence involving Julia Roberts and the local postman at twenty to eight the following morning.

"What time did you come up last night?" Juliet frowned, as she entered the bedroom to deliver a goodbye kiss.

"Just after midnight," Parlour replied sleepily, returning her embrace.

"Poo, you smell like a brewery!" she exclaimed, pulling away and straightening her hair.

"That's an improvement, then!"

"The postman's been. You've got a letter from your brother," Juliet informed him.

"I just dreamt about him," Parlour frowned, rubbing his temples.

"Allan?" Juliet enquired.

"No, the postman!" Parlour laughed. "He was chasing Julia Roberts along a beach!"

"Definitely too much port," Juliet commented wryly.

"I should write them down, my dreams," Parlour yawned. "Could have a best-seller there – you never know. You can make money out of any old twaddle these days!"

"Only if you're a TV chef or gardener, though, my dear," Juliet replied, opening the curtains. Parlour winced.

"Anyway, he's early," Parlour remarked, referring to the postman. "It's been at least nine o'clock the last few days!"

The tall, blonde youth who delivered the post to the Parlour's property in Spatchcock Drive and the neighbouring streets was decidedly erratic in his timekeeping.

"I wouldn't know," his wife replied dryly, who was rarely at home after eight am. "See you tonight."

"Yep. Have a nice day!" Parlour chorused languidly, before rolling back over and burying his pimply chin in the limp blue pillow.

⧗⧗⧗

"Holy shoot!" Martin Beauville exclaimed with wide-eyed disbelief, coming to a standstill before the newsstand at the local petrol station that Friday morning.

"Gay Vicar took me below deck!" The headline of the Foxburgh Herald screamed at him. *"This was the astounding claim made by barman Christopher Wilkes from his home in Taddleworth yesterday. Wilkes, 39, told the Foxburgh Herald of his torrid night of passion between standard issue sheets with the vicar at the centre of the so-called "Death by Peanuts" affair in Foxburgh, the Reverend Martin Beauville. Wilkes first met Beauville, 44, at a local gay haunt in Portsmouth, where, Wilkes claims, Beauville seduced him and took him back to his naval base for a night of gay passion."*

Martin Beauville felt sick to his stomach. Setting his jaw grimly, he walked into the service station and silently paid the girl behind the counter. Then he got back in his Audi Estate and headed toward the county town - and the headquarters of the Foxburgh Herald.

⧗⧗⧗

"Alex! What are you doing here?" Parlour exclaimed, as a familiar black Corsa parked up alongside him outside Billock Police Station just after ten that morning.

"Come to pick Jason up," Miller replied, locking his car door. "That female inspector brought him in for questioning at the crack of dawn."

"Whatever for?" Parlour enquired, feigning innocence, though he had imagined it was just a matter of time until Blackman got her claws into the over-confident insurance salesman.

204

"Something they found on our computer at home, that Jason had tried to wipe off," Miller answered uneasily. "They wanted to know what other computers he had access to, reckoned he might've had something to do with all that stuff that was on the vicar's PC."

"And did he?" Parlour asked, trying to sound casual as they approached the main entrance to the station together.

"Incriminate Martin?" Miller asked, turning to look at Parlour. "No way! He had no idea – none of us did – what happened to him in the navy."

"So why both deleting a load of stuff from your computer?" Parlour asked, though he had a fairly good idea.

Miller flushed and looked away. He came to a halt outside the entrance and turned to Parlour. He opened his mouth to speak, then looked away.

"Is this a man thing?" Parlour asked gently.

Miller nodded, embarrassed. "Jase had downloaded some stupid pictures of tarts and that from the Internet. Silly tit – pardon the pun!"

"He suspected the police would start sniffing around people's PCs and didn't want anyone in church to find out, right?" Parlour surmised.

"Yeah," Miller smiled wryly. "He's never done it before, though, Mark." He looked anxiously at Parlour.

"Hey, you're not his mother!" Parlour exclaimed. "Look, I can't say I haven't been tempted myself from time to time. It's pretty harmless, compared to say –"

"Murder," Miller interjected brutally. Parlour inclined his head in agreement.

"Alex, the only people who get hurt from a bit of porn are the poor women who can't meet Jason's ideals. Popping crushed peanuts in Terence Haynes's coffee and slandering an innocent man, however, are a completely different matter."

"Spose," Miller nodded. "Hey, I hear they had Christine Kelty up here, too!"

"They just wanted to ask her a few questions," Parlour replied shortly. "She's got nothing to do with it."

Miller looked at him, but he was revealing nothing.

"I'll see you later, Alex," Parlour said, as they got to reception. "Duty calls."

He took the lift up to his office on the Fourth Floor. Parlour cursed as the doors opened almost immediately on Level Two.

"Packed in the fitness regime, have we?" he enquired of Leigh Blackman as she entered the lift to go up one level.

"Ditched the *Biactol*?" Blackman retorted, considering Parlour's pimply complexion that morning. "Heard the latest about Beauville?"

"I thought you were officially nil by mouth on the subject," Parlour replied archly.

"Yeah, well, it's splashed across the front pages of the Foxburgh Herald, so it's hardly top secret!"

"*What's* splashed across the front of the Foxburgh Herald?" Parlour asked, mildly exasperated with Blackman's supercilious sneer.

"Some local barman reckons The Irreverent Martin Beauville rogered him senseless in Pompey twenty odd years ago!"

"*What?*" Parlour exploded.

"Read all about it!" Blackman laughed, and thrust a tatty copy of the regional "news" at his chest as she exited the lift. Parlour's pale blue eyes opened wide as he read the sensational lead story. *This has got to be a wind-up!* He grimaced and stepped out at his floor.

⌛⌛⌛

I could do without this! Juliet Parlour frowned, dashing out to the carpark at Billock Community School at twelve-thirty that lunchtime. Having only had its MOT last weekend, her car was playing up again, practically dying on her when she pulled up at the lights. Hopefully it wasn't the fuel tank again – that cheap petrol she'd bought at the local supermarket had proved very costly indeed.

Fortunately Juliet was known at the garage to be the wife of a "copper", and the mechanic promised to look at it as soon as he'd changed the tyre on a blue Punto. Juliet sat down, sipping at a paper cone of water pumped from one of those spring water machines. Bored, she meandered out into the showroom, where a callow salesman was busy enthusing to a well-dressed lady in a camel coat with her back to Juliet.

Don't do it! Juliet thought to herself, grimacing, then gasped in surprise as the well-groomed lady turned to admire another model. What on earth had Mary Fosthlewaite done to herself? Juliet hastily turned away as Terence Haynes's cleaner looked in her direction. Just wait until she told Mark! Had she won the lottery or something?

⧗ ⧗ ⧗

"If Billock Police operated a loyalty card system for visits to their premises, I'd have won a canteen of cutlery by now," Martin Beauville said dryly to Parlour, who had poked his head round the Interview Room door, having spotted the vicar's black Audi Estate in the station carpark.

"I wish I was in Florida," Parlour replied, nodding towards the window. The rain was hammering down outside, beating its incessant message of doom against the grubby station windows.

"Me too," Beauville sighed.

"Hear some low-life's been cashing in on your misfortune," Parlour sympathised. "Saw the Herald this morning."

"Never set eyes on the guy in my life!" Beauville exclaimed. "Just thought he'd make some money out of this whole sorry mess. Makes me sick."

"But let me guess – Blackman's viewing it as evidence against you," Parlour grinned.

"It's not funny, Mark," Beauville groaned. "I would have thought it was obvious to anyone that he's just after a quick buck. Like I could have smuggled some chap back to the base anyway!"

"It may not be that simple," Parlour replied more seriously this time.

"What do you mean?" Beauville frowned.

"Well, what if whoever tried to frame you with the computer stuff put him up to it?"

Beauville looked at him. "Do you really think so?"

Parlour shrugged. "It's plausible."

"Then maybe they can get him to say who it was!" Beauville exclaimed excitedly.

Parlour put his hand up. "Woah! Slow down. It was only an idea. Thinking about it, it would be a pretty risky thing for the murderer to do. The majority of accessories to murder squeal under duress. I should say it's still far more likely this is just some guy after some easy money."

"Yes… yes, I agree," Beauville sighed.

"Look, I must run – I'm not supposed to be down here. Give us a call at home if you need to talk," Parlour said, patting his shoulder comfortingly.

"Thanks, Mark," Beauville replied dully.

It's really beginning to get to him, Parlour thought, as he took the staircase to avoid any further encounters in the lift with Blackman.

"Hey, Marky!" came a familiar voice from above. Parlour looked up to see his good friend and colleague, Stuart Beattie.

"Stu! What are you doing here?" Parlour ran up to the third floor, his gangly legs making light work of three flights of stairs.

"Training," Beattie replied. "How's it going?"

Parlour made a face. "Still stuck out in Hicksville!"

"Not that old chestnut!" Beattie laughed. "Found out anything new?"

"Nah," Parlour shook his head. "Need to get stuck into it this afternoon – got a progress report to do for tomorrow. How about you?"

"Been stuck down at Foxburgh most of the week – they found some other call-girl lying in a pool of blood in Siloh Street."

"Yeah, I heard," Parlour nodded, visibly perturbed. "She was just a kid, this time, wasn't she?"

"Seventeen," Beattie replied. He leaned conspiratorially towards Parlour. "How are you getting on with the Haynes case?"

Parlour pulled a face.

"It's not going well," he conceded. "Blackman still reckons Beauville did it, especially given the front page of the Herald this morning. But I reckon it's all too easy. He believes he's been framed, and I agree. But there's nobody, besides Beauville, who would want Haynes dead. He was a patronising old sod, that's for sure, but I can't see why anyone should want to murder him."

"Mm," Beattie nodded. "You know what struck me, when I was at Zion House last Saturday?"

"What?"

"The way he died. He took a sip of his coffee, turned beetroot, then fell headlong into a dish of eclairs conveniently placed on the table in front of him."

"I'm not with you," Parlour said, shaking his head.

"Well, think about it. Pretty dramatic, huh? Strikes me our murderer was a bit of a showman. They could have chosen any time to plop crushed peanuts into Haynes's food or drink – why risk doing it there, so publicly? Why risk being found out? Why not, say, sneak into his garden and stick them in his mug while he's mowing the lawn? Why bother with the blasted peanuts anyway – why not run him down on the Lexington

Green Road or whack him with a baseball bat when he was walking his dog?”

“What are you saying, Stuart?” Parlour frowned.

“I’m saying our killer *wanted* everyone to see Haynes die. He wanted to see him publicly humiliated. It’s almost as if Haynes’s death was more important than his own life – that to see Haynes die like that was worth the risk of getting caught.”

“Hmm.” Parlour furrowed his brow to consider his friend’s theory. “So we should find out who put those cakes on the table?”

“It’s just a thought, Mark,” Beattie shrugged.

“You know, I think I might pay Zion House another visit,” Parlour said. “Revisit the scene of the crime. I had an inkling the place might give me some clues.”

“Good idea,” Beattie nodded. “Look, Mark, must fly. See you around.”

“Yeah,” Parlour replied vaguely, deep in thought.

⧗⧗⧗

One Hundred and One Damnations! Leigh Blackman cursed, as WPC Fullerton handed her a telephone message. DS Denton had called while she’d been interviewing Martin Beauville. Christopher Wilkes had admitted fabricating the allegations against the vicar for financial gain, much to the fury of the Foxburgh Herald News Team, who were now being threatened with a hefty libel claim from lawyers representing the Church of England. Wilkes hadn’t been tipped off or coerced into contacting the Herald by a third party, which didn’t support Beauville’s argument that he was framed. However, neither did it provide Blackman and co with any new leads.

“You’d have thought the Foxburgh Herald would check out he was kosher before printing such stuff!” Blackman moaned to Robins, who was sitting opposite her.

210

"You know how it is," Robins replied dryly. "One sniff of religious scandal and people go into overdrive."

He cast a sly look at his superior. In his opinion, Blackman was increasingly barking up the wrong tree, concentrating on Beauville as she was. Whilst he didn't share Parlour's view that the vicar was beyond reproach, there wasn't a shred of hard evidence against him. Not of the kind that would stand up in court. As far as Robins could see, Blackman was more interested in getting one over on Mark Parlour than finding the real killer of Terence Haynes. And that was not a healthy state of affairs.

⧗⧗⧗

Home sweet home, Parlour sighed pleasurably, pulling up outside his house at just after half past five that evening. He felt a sense of fulfilment, having finished his progress report on the Bywater Farm murders that afternoon. It had been difficult to juggle his research into the historical case with his subterfuge investigations into Terence Haynes' death. But the work he'd completed this afternoon should get the Sewer off his back, leaving the next few days clear to probe further into the mysterious murder of the church warden.

Hello, where was Juliet's car? Parlour frowned. He had been looking forward to catching up with his wife and sharing the day's news. It had been a hectic week.

Gone swimming with Kate. Back 6.30.

Parlour screwed up the note and hung his jacket over the chair. He was just about to go upstairs when the weirdest feeling took hold of him. He felt light-headed, then elated, as several strands of thought came together to form an image, if not the complete picture. Raking a hand through his short ginger hair, he sat down at the table and unscrewed the note. That was it! That was what had been bugging him for days!

211

Who would have thought that a Julia Roberts film could hold the key?

16

"Are you feeling alright, Mark?" Juliet enquired as Parlour leapt out of bed at seven o'clock that Saturday morning.

"Got an appointment in Billock at eight," Parlour replied. "Tell you tonight."

He dashed into their en-suite shower. Juliet shook her head. Nothing her husband did surprised her these days. And he had been quirkier than usual this week, since the death of Terence Haynes. What on earth could he be up to in Billock at eight o'clock in the morning? But she couldn't worry about that now. It was Saturday, her one and only chance to lie in, as Sunday was Church which meant dashing around fetching old ladies for the 9.30 Communion Service. As she snuggled back into her pillow, it occurred to her that she had forgotten to tell Mark last night about Mary Fosthlewaite at the Fiat Garage. Never mind. It could wait.

⏳⏳⏳

"DI Mark Parlour, Billock Police," Parlour introduced himself to the Delivery Manager at Billock Main Delivery Office. "Thanks for meeting me at this ungodly hour on a Saturday!"

"Mid-morning to me, Inspector!" Richard Bruton grinned, shaking his hand. "How can I help you?"

"I'm investigating the death of Terence Haynes, the church warden who was murdered in Lexington Green last weekend. In an unofficial capacity – I've been assigned another case. DI Leigh Blackman is actually heading the official enquiry. I'm just taking a personal interest, so to speak."

"Understood," Bruton smiled, winking conspiratorially. "Was he a friend of yours?"

"A church acquaintance," Parlour replied. "My wife was actually present at the scene of the crime."

Bruton whistled. "They say someone spiked his coffee with nuts. Is that right?"

Parlour inclined his head. "He died of an anaphylactic shock induced by peanuts, yes."

"So where do we fit in?" Bruton enquired, leading him into his office and shutting the door behind them. Parlour averted his gaze as he was immediately confronted by an X-Certificate wall calendar. It was a bit early in the morning for such crass visual stimulation.

"A neighbour of Commander Haynes, a Mrs Cranfield, claims she saw one of your men delivering post on Deverton Estate at around quarter to eight on the day of the murder, 25 May – that's last Saturday. I believe she shares the same postman as me - a young, blonde chap. Long hair, bit gormless looking."

Bruton grinned. "That'll be our Wayne. Does the posh end of Deverton Estate. The police have already questioned him, actually."

"I gathered as much," Parlour replied. "But I wanted to ask you a few things, too, if that's OK."

"Feel free!" Bruton laughed. "Though I doubt I'll have anything much of interest to say."

"How long has Wayne been working your patch?" Parlour asked.

Bruton frowned. "Let me see... about a year? Started off alright, but he's been a bit unreliable of late."

"Yes, he is a bit hit and miss, to be honest with you," Parlour nodded. "Sometimes you get the post nice and early at breakfast, other times you'll be lucky to see him before noon."

Bruton sighed. "That's Wayne, alright. We've had words with him a couple of times. Some old biddy in Zucchini Avenue keeps ringing up to complain – it's costing our

Customer Services Division a fortune in complimentary stamps!"

"Well it doesn't seem to have worked," Parlour remarked dryly.

"Look here, Chief Inspector," Bruton began rather tetchily, "You haven't just come here to complain about Wayne Shaughnessy, have you? Because if you have, you'll have to take your place in the queue like everyone else - I'm a busy man."

"No, of course not," Parlour replied hastily. It wouldn't do, given his status – or lack of – in this enquiry, to be reported to Billock Police Complaints Desk!

"Between you and me," Bruton replied, more genially this time, "Wayne Shaughnessy's inches away from being fired. He's juggling his shift with some nightclub job – hence the terrible timekeeping. The lad's still half-cut most mornings, not to mention drugged up to the eyeballs."

"That figures," Parlour replied, considering the young postman's bedraggled appearance. "But returning to last Saturday, can you tell me what time his round was?"

Bruton looked dubious. "I can certainly tell you what time he left the Delivery Office, but what time he eventually got to Deverton Estate, I couldn't tell you. He has a rough time schedule to follow, but knowing our Wayne, he probably stopped for a fag or fell asleep behind a hedge for half an hour! Regular Little Boy Blue, is Wayne."

"Could you tell me when he left here, then, at least?" Parlour enquired a little impatiently. What a grubby little man Richard Bruton was, with his nasty office décor and supercilious air.

"Give me a few minutes." Bruton left the room, to return five minutes later. "According to our records, Wayne left here at six thirty-five on Saturday 25th. . He would have taken the Billock Hoppa to Deverton Estate and began his round on Maris Piper Way. What time he arrived on the Estate, I couldn't say. The bus ride is around twenty minutes, so at a guess, around seven o'clock."

Maris Piper Way, Parlour thought to himself. *The Briscoes live in Maris Piper Way. I could check up on that.*

"And what route would he take from there?" Parlour enquired.

"That's Upper Deverton Estate, so…" Bruton reached over and pulled a map from the wall. He reeled off a list of streets on the east side of Deverton Estate where Parlour himeslf lived.

"So say he arrived on Deverton Estate at seven, about what time would he have reached King Edward Mews?"

Bruton made some rapid calculations. "Maris Piper Way takes a good fifteen minutes 'cos of all the flats, Guava Gardens about five, Zucchini Avenue say ten, Upper Foxburgh Road about fifteen – he'd have got to King Edward Mews around seven forty-five, I'd say."

Parlour nodded. "So our neighbour was probably right, then? She said she saw him at about quarter to eight."

"I should say so," Bruton agreed. "But you surely don't think Wayne had anything to do with this, do you?"

"Oh no, of course not," Parlour reassured him, debating how much to say. Some information was common knowledge, other bits were more sensitive. "It's just that someone entered the deceased's property on the morning of the murder and we don't know who that was. It's possible Wayne saw this person."

"He didn't," Bruton informed Parlour. "He's already told the police that. He never saw a thing."

"I'd still like to talk to him anyway," Parlour replied. "He may have forgotten something."

Bruton sighed. He looked at his watch. "He'll still be in Deverton."

"That's alright," Parlour smiled. "I'm heading back home for breakfast. I'll catch him on his round. Thanks for your help."

"My pleasure," Bruton replied, not looking particularly happy about it, though. He shook Parlour's hand.

Dirty git, Parlour thought rather uncharitably, returning to his car. He would pay Haynes's neighbour a visit, too, he decided. He had a theory concerning the mysterious visitor to 8 King Edward Mews.

⧗⧗⧗

As predicted, Wayne Shaughnessy was still completing his round at the top end of Deverton Estate. Parlour found him leaning against the street sign for Spatchcock Drive, dragging on a cigarette. He looked away when Parlour rolled his window down and flashed his police badge.

"I've told your lot already. I didn't see no-one in King Eddie Mews last Saturday," he said in a languid manner befitting his appearance.

"What time were you there, Wayne?" Parlour asked.

He shrugged. "Dunno. Just before eight, I think. Can't remember."

"About quarter to?"

"Could have been," he replied distractedly. "Who cares?"

"It could be important, Wayne," Parlour said soberly.

"I reckon it was just before eight. More than that, I can't say," Shaughnessy growled, turning to face Parlour this time. He exhaled a curl of smoke in the direction of his open window. Parlour hastily wound his window back up before continuing along Spatchcock Drive to his own house.

She's still in bed, lazy moo! Parlour grinned, spotting the bedroom curtains were still shut as he rolled up the driveway and turned the engine off. He let himself in. Shaughnessy evidently hadn't got as far as their house yet as there was no post stuffed carelessly in the letterbox. He quietly went upstairs to check on his wife. Yep, still dead to the world. He padded back down then set about preparing a breakfast fit for a king. Zion House would be his next port of call that Saturday morning. Perhaps some little detail would give him a clue as to who murdered Terence Haynes. But first of all he needed to revisit Leigh Blackman's notes.

He had a feeling the postman may have rung twice last Saturday morning.

⌛⌛⌛

I don't believe it! Parlour exclaimed an hour later, as he turned the bend just before Zion House to meet with a blue POLICE SLOW sign on the road. For the second Saturday in succession, he was stopped by a member of his own force as he signalled right to turn into the Christian Retreat Centre.

"Morning, Lisa," he greeted WPC Fullerton. "What's on the menu today, then?"

"Nasty RTA a couple of hundred yards away. We're closing the road. Victim is a middle-aged lady in a red Punto. Unidentified as yet. The other party scarpered, callous bastard. Can't let you past, I'm afraid."

Parlour frowned. "Fatal?"

Fullerton nodded. "Been dead at least eight to ten hours, Hunter reckons."

"Does the deceased have a name?"

"Not yet," the WPC shook her head.

"Probably some idiot kids on crack," Parlour muttered. "Better check out any stolen cars."

"Rossi's onto it, Sir," Fullerton said respectfully, thinking how patronising he could be at times.

"Can I go up to Zion House?" Parlour enquired. "I thought I'd go for a walk in the gardens."

"And I'm an Egg McMuffin, Sir," Fullerton grinned. She winked at him. "Go on then."

"Thanks, Lisa," Parlour smiled, swinging the big SLK up the hill to the building owned by Lexington Green Priory. He

218

parked in the forecourt under some trees then entered through the front doors. There was nobody at reception, so he wandered down the corridor to the function room where last Saturday's fateful meeting had taken place. Through the glass square on the door he could see that the room was now restored to its former state, all evidence of police presence carefully removed. He tried the adjoining kitchen door, but it was locked. Parlour clicked his tongue in frustration.

"Can I help you?"

Parlour turned and found himself face to face with a gaunt figure in grey suit trousers and a burgundy V-neck sweater.

"Jeremy Waugh, Business Manager, Zion House."

"Mark Parlour, Billock Police," Parlour replied, fumbling in his pocket for his badge. He showed it to the thin gentleman some ten years his senior.

"What are you doing here, Inspector? I thought DI Blackman had finished her investigations here."

"She has," Parlour confirmed, deciding honesty was probably the best policy in the circumstances. He could never bring himself to bend the truth for fellow believers – which he assumed Waugh was, as an employee of the Priory. He certainly looked the part.

"I'm here on behalf of Bishop Shadwell Allbright," Parlour explained. "Terence Haynes was an acquaintance of mine at Deverton Parish Church and my wife, Juliet, is a member of the PCC that met here on the day he died. The Bishop isn't altogether satisfied with the direction the official enquiry is taking and has asked me to carry out some private investigations of my own."

Waugh frowned. "Do you mind if I just confirm that with the Bishop's office? I am under instructions not to let any unauthorised persons into the building."

"By all means," he smiled. "But you probably need to try him at home on a Saturday. His secretary won't be available."

He scribbled down the Bishop's number from his mobile phone and handed it to Waugh.

"I'll be right back," Waugh said, then padded back down the corridor as noiselessly as he arrived. Parlour peered through the glass pane on the door to the meeting room, trying to picture how Haynes met with his dramatic death.

Waugh was as good as his word, reappearing almost immediately with the keys to the kitchen door.

"That's fine," he said more genially this time. "Come and find me when you've finished, or if you need anything – I'm just down the corridor to the left."

"Thanks," Parlour replied and shut himself in the kitchen. He opened each cupboard door and rooted around in the drawers, but there was nothing irregular to report. Parlour was just about to search the conference room when he spotted a typed list on the wall, yellowed at the corners.

That could be useful, Parlour thought. It was an inventory of kitchenware owned by the Retreat Centre and stored in this very kitchen.

Parlour began to systematically check off each item in the assortment of base and wall units against the list. There appeared to be a couple of coffee mugs embossed with the Lexington Green Priory crest missing. They were probably broken and hadn't been replaced, or gathering mould in Jeremy Waugh's office, Parlour thought. He didn't bother checking the cutlery. There seemed little point. In fact, there seemed little point to this exercise *per se*, as Blackman's team had already made an extensive search of the property and grounds in search of alien objects, but Parlour somehow felt it was relevant. He wandered into the meeting room and surveyed the hatch to the kitchen. You would only be able to see someone from the forearms up through it, unless you happened to be standing right by it.

Parlour returned to the kitchen. He had a sudden desire to open the big cupboard again, where the pots and pans and bulkier kitchen items were kept. As he stared at the four white coffee butlers on the right hand side, he was struck by the appearance of one of them. Was it his imagination, or did one of them look decidedly newer than the others?

Parlour removed the four butlers from the cupboard and lined them up on the worktop. He glanced across at the Zion House inventory. Yes, there were meant to be four. Parlour looked at the base of the spouted flasks frequently used at conference venues. They were all the same brand, manufactured, as one might expect, in Italy, the home of the coffee house. He unscrewed the tops. The one that seemed newer boasted far fewer brown stains on the interior than the remaining three. Perhaps one broke and this is a recent replacement, Parlour reasoned. Unless… *no!*

Parlour spun out of the kitchen and rushed down the corridor to Jeremy Waugh's office.

"Mr Waugh?" he called, not waiting to be invited inside. Waugh looked up at him warily. "Do you have a more recent copy of the kitchen inventory, or is the one on the wall up to date?"

"Gracious, no!" Waugh chuckled. Parlour took a sharp intake of breath, feeling his heart pound as the Business Manager of Zion House clicked his mouse a few times to bring up a file on the computer sat on his desk.

"Here you go. Inventory for Zion House, updated December 1st 2001. Want a print-out?"

"Please," Parlour replied.

"What's it for?" Waugh enquired, frowning as he activated the printer.

"Just need to check a small detail," Parlour murmured. After what seemed like an age, Waugh handed him the hard copy. He tutted in disapproval as the detective snatched it from him.

Parlour scanned his eyes down the inventory, hand shaking. He inhaled deeply. *Three white coffee butlers!*

"Only three butlers?" he asked, looking up at Waugh.

"Yes. Our cleaner broke one a couple of weeks back."

"It wasn't replaced?" Parlour enquired.

Waugh shook his head. "We're waiting till we have a bulk order for our catering suppliers."

"So it definitely hasn't been replaced in the last few weeks?" Parlour checked.

"No," Waugh replied firmly. "Do you mind me asking what's so fascinating about the contents of ..?"

But Parlour had already left the room. Shutting the kitchen door behind him, Parlour leant on the worktop and took a few deep breaths. *Let's think this through.* Yes, it worked. He now knew the logistics of how Terence Haynes had been killed. But what, on God's earth, was their motive?

17

Shocked by the implications of his discovery at Zion House, Parlour had forgotten all about the commotion outside. But his attention was soon drawn back to the accident as the wreckage of a red car dangled in the air like a gigantic tin fly on the end of a large vehicle recovery hoist. In the cheery early June sunshine, the scene seemed all the more incongruous.

"Good grief!" he exclaimed, seeing the extent of the damage to the small car. He rolled the window down as WPC Fullerton ambled over to him.

"A write-off on both counts, I see," he remarked soberly to his subordinate from Billock Station. No-one could possibly have survived that wreckage.

"She was way over the limit," Fullerton informed Parlour. "Whisky. Smelt like a brewery in there. They reckon she might've hit someone who swerved out the way and kept going. You can just about make out traces of black paint on the back bumper. Forensic are taking it down the lab now for investigations. The SOCOs are investigating the tyre marks on the road for evidence."

"Why scarper if it wasn't your fault?" Parlour frowned.

Fullerton shrugged.

"Did you find out her identity – the victim?" Parlour enquired.

"It was a Mary Fosthlewaite of Lexington Green," Fullerton replied.

Parlour blinked. "Fosthlewaite, you say?"

"That's right, Sir."

"She was Terence Haynes's cleaner, Lisa," Parlour informed her.

"I thought the name rang a bell!" Fullerton exclaimed.

"Doesn't that strike you as strange?" he enquired.

Fullerton shrugged. "She took her new car out for a spin, had a bit too much to drink and crashed it. It's just a coincidence."

"But where would a cleaner get the money for a spanking new Fiat Punto?" Parlour asked. "And who in their right mind stops off for a double whisky when they take their new car out for a spin – so to speak."

"I don't know – you're the detective!" Fullerton replied.

But Parlour's mind was already elsewhere. He wound his electric window back up and headed for home. At the traffic lights ten minutes later, he called Stuart Beattie.

He informed his colleague of the RTA on the Lexington Road and of its possible link to the Haynes case, and requested Beattie let him know of Forensic's findings, once the wreckage of the red Punto had arrived at the lab.

Parlour grimaced as he pulled into Deverton Estate. He had a feeling foul play was involved again – foul play that good policing could have prevented. It seemed pretty obvious to him that Mary Fosthlewaite must have bleated some information concerning Terence Haynes to a third party.

The curtains were open this time and he could see the mop-haired head of his recently arisen wife busying herself in the downstairs kitchen as he walked briskly up the driveway.

"Morning darling!" Juliet Parlour smiled, pouring herself a drink. "Fancy a coffee?"

"Please," Parlour called back, throwing his jacket on the sofa. He sat down and put his head in his hands. His cosy existence in Deverton was being challenged in the most cynical way by the events of the past seven days.

"What's happened, Mark?" Juliet frowned, entering the room with her arms folded.

He looked up. "Mary Fosthlewaite was killed in a car crash last night," he replied dully. "I just saw the carnage on the Lexington Green Road. The car was a complete write off."

Juliet grasped. "Mary Fos dead? But I only saw her yesterday!"

"The bizarre thing was," Parlour continued, "she was driving. I didn't even know she had a licence. A brand new car, a.."

"Fiat Punto," Juliet interrupted, sitting down heavily on the coffee table. "Oh my goodness!"

"What?"

"I forgot to tell you last night – I saw her yesterday in the Fiat Garage, when I took the car in to get the fuel tank checked out. She was all dolled up, chatting to one of their salesmen. She must have been picking up a new car! She looked so different – you would hardly have recognised her. All dolled up, *Ladies Who Lunch* style. I meant to tell you, but it slipped my mind with all that happened in school yesterday."

Juliet had had to deal with a child who had reacted badly to a bee sting in one of her classes the previous day. Fortunately, on that occasion, a fully-functioning Epipen® had been available to provide immediate relief.

Parlour groaned, standing up and massaging his temples.

"Was it important?" Juliet asked fearfully.

"No.. yes.. it might have been," Parlour replied, not wishing to lie to his wife, but not wanting to lay a guilt trip on her either.

"I don't understand," she began, bewildered.

"Think about it, Jules!" Parlour exclaimed, stress levels rising as the horrible reality dawned on him, piece by piece. "Someone hatched a cunning plan to murder Terence Haynes. That person needed information about him and possibly access to his home. He was a very private man. Who might be the only person with access to that information?"

"Mary Fosthlewaite," Juliet replied slowly.

"Who has suddenly come into money, by the looks of it," Parlour stated.

"Oh my goodness!" Juliet exclaimed, the awful truth dawning on her. "You think she blackmailed someone!"

"Unless she won the lottery – which is easy enough to check out – how else could Mary Fosthlewaite suddenly afford a brand new car?"

Juliet shook her head.

"What time did you see her yesterday? After school?"

"No, I went to the Fiat dealers in my lunch hour," Juliet replied. "It must have been about one."

"She was killed late last night, they reckon," Parlour said. He informed her that the road had been immediately closed for Forensic to carry out some initial investigations, but that they had taken ages to get there due to yet another murder in Foxburgh.

"But if she was over the limit…" Juliet began.

Parlour explained that in all probability, erratic driving on Mary Fosthlewaite's part had caused the accident. However, it could not be ruled out that someone had rammed into her on purpose. Apparently traces of black paint had been found on her car.

"Black paint?" Juliet echoed, the colour visibly draining from her cheeks. "Martin…"

"… has a black Audi, I know," Parlour finished her sentence grimly.

"But…"

"He wouldn't harm anyone, I know… but two people have died now and all the signs point to Beauville. Perhaps it's time we took a reality check, Jules." Parlour looked soberly at his wife.

Juliet drew her palms down her cheeks, her fingers meeting and steepling beneath her chin. "It's all my fault, isn't it, Mark? If I'd told you about seeing Mary yesterday, you could've prevented this happening."

"I have no authority to prevent anything," Parlour said bitterly. "But you mustn't blame yourself. It was probably just an accident. Don't beat yourself up about it, Jules, please!"

"How could I be so dim, though?" Juliet moaned, thumping her fist against the wall. "I wondered why she looked so flash all of a sudden. I don't expect she's a very pretty sight now, though."

"Don't." Parlour said quietly. "I'm going upstairs, Jules. I need to think."

"Do you know who…" Juliet began.

Parlour raised a hand. "I don't want to talk about it – not now."

"But you *do* have an idea?" Juliet exclaimed, looking up at him.

"I have an idea who *could* have done it, but I have absolutely no motive, so it's a dead duck until I have."

"Who then?" Juliet persisted.

"I don't want to talk about it, Jules," Parlour said more firmly this time, his eyes warning her against pressing him further at this juncture.

⧖⧖⧖

The phone call from Stuart Beattie did not come until eleven o'clock that evening.

"What did you find out?" Parlour asked, keeping one eye on the football highlights.

"It was manslaughter at least," Beattie replied. "She was bundled off the road at high speed, hence the state of the car. Ploughed into the barrier on the bend – died instantly."

"That's one small mercy," Parlour commented as Michael Owen skipped past the keeper and coolly slotted the ball in the back of the net. He had calmed down since earlier in the day and now had his cool, rational head on.

"The black paint found on the taillights and bumper of the Punto is similar to that used by German car manufacturers – Mercs, VWs, Audis."

"Audis?" Parlour's ears pricked up.

"Amongst others."

"Has the report gone to Blackman yet?" Parlour enquired.

"Not yet – they're just clearing up a few details."

Parlour heaved a sigh of relief. "Did they find anything else?"

"Yes – this is pretty interesting, actually – pathology pumped her stomach. Found no traces of alcohol."

"But.." Parlour began.

"She stunk of booze?" Beattie pre-empted him. "The killer stopped to check she was dead, by the looks of it. Poured some whisky in her open mouth to make it look like drink driving, then made their getaway."

"But wasn't there anyone else on the road?" Parlour queried, puzzled. "Didn't anyone see or hear this take place?"

"It was about one in the morning, Mark," Beattie informed him. "The fuel tank on the Punto was practically empty and the tyres were slightly worn for a brand new car. Looks like some kind of car chase through the lanes took place."

"Cape Cod!" Parlour exclaimed, adopting his favourite expression. "The plot thickens."

"Glad I don't have to untangle it," Beattie chuckled.

"Is Blackman on duty?" Parlour asked.

"Are Saints going down?" Beattie chuckled, hearing the football commentary in the background.

"Stupid question," Parlour groaned. Blackman was well-known for working round the clock, even at weekends. "Thanks for ringing, Stu."

He put the phone down then picked it up immediately. He was just about to ring the vicarage when he thought better of it. It wouldn't look too good if Blackman had already got round there.

"Just nipping out for a bit," he informed Juliet, who was still preparing material for school on their computer, having lost all track of time. She grunted, not looking up from the screen.

There was no sign of Blackman's Vauxhall outside the vicarage. Parlour cautiously approached the front door. He could see a crack of dim light between the curtains and the melancholy sound of classical music mourning in the background. Parlour rapped the knocker a few times. It somehow felt too harsh to ring the doorbell, and not solely due to the lateness of the hour.

There was no answer at first, so Parlour tried again, this time a little louder. He heard footsteps in the hallway.

"Who is it?" Martin Beauville asked cautiously. *Now there speaks the voice of a hunted man*, Parlour thought.

"It's Mark. I'm alone."

Beauville opened the door with a countenance to match his beleaguered tone.

"It's a bit late for visitors, isn't it?" he queried.

"I know how you love to burn the midnight oil," Parlour replied, following him down the hallway to his sitting room.

"What can I do for you?" Beauville enquired listlessly, resuming his position in his favourite armchair.

"Well, I hate to be the bearer of bad news, but I thought I'd warn you Blackman will be round here any minute now."

Beauville raised his dark eyebrows as if nothing would surprise him anymore.

"They ought to sort out a little room for me at the station," he remarked dryly. "Or camp out here. Goodness knows, I have the space."

"I wouldn't fancy facing Leigh Blackman over the breakfast table, though, would you?" Parlour grinned, trying to lift his spirits but failing.

"You may have a point there," Beauville replied without smiling. "What do they want this time? Don't tell me – some penniless student is claiming to be a lover from a past life!"

"It's a bit more serious than that, Martin," Parlour replied soberly. "Mary Fosthlewaite died in a car crash in the early hours of this morning. They reckon she was deliberately targeted."

"And don't tell me, they think I was behind the wheel!" Beauville laughed hollowly. It was all getting too preposterous for words. He couldn't even muster up any sympathy for the dead woman.

"They did find traces of black paint on her car – Forensic reckon it's paint from a German car."

"Gracious, I am in the poo again, aren't I?" Beauville sneered, a tone Parlour would never have previously associated with the vicar. "I went to bed pretty late as usual, but I never ventured outside. They won't find any dents on the Audi. And before you ask, I never blackmailed Mary Fosthlewaite for info on Haynes, either – I expect that's the motive, isn't it? She threatened to grass up the murderer to the police?"

Parlour nodded. Beauville was no fool. The telephone rang.

"Look, that's probably the Wicked Witch of Billock," Beauville said. "You better get out of here. I don't think she'll be too pleased to see you here."

"Mind if I slip out the back?" Parlour asked. "She's probably calling you from outside."

"Be my guest," Beauville shrugged. "It's open."

He went to answer the phone, and Parlour gathered from the resigned tone of his voice that it was indeed Leigh Blackman.

Hiding in the bushes, he watched as Blackman and Robins stepped out of Blackman's car and marched purposefully up the driveway. He heard their low voices then the squeal of the garage door opening. He saw Beauville's thin, dark silhouette as the dim garage light was switched on. Then he heard Beauville utter a shout of disbelief as the Chief Inspector and her sidekick discovered signs of impact on the front wing.

I don't believe it! Parlour muttered à la Victor Meldrew as he heard Beauville protesting his innocence in vain. His attention was suddenly diverted from the posse in the garage by a light coming on in the distance. He looked behind him. It seemed to be coming from the Monkton-Smith's house. But almost as quickly as it came on, it was switched off again. *Probably just went in the room to get something*, Parlour thought and turned back to the drama in the garage.

"I'll have to get Forensic here to look at the car," he heard Blackman inform a stupefied Beauville.

He groaned and hid in the bushes until he could bid a safe retreat.

⧗⧗⧗

One of Juliet's fluorescent orange Post-it notes awaited Parlour when he returned home some fifteen minutes later.

No nooky till you connect us to the Web, Juliet's bold capitals shouted at him. Ah, you couldn't beat a bit of sexual blackmail, he grinned, looking in the fridge for something to nibble on. Slicing himself a generous wedge of Irish cheddar, Parlour wandered up to their office and rummaged around in his domestic in-tray until he found the free Internet trial CD he'd picked up in the foyer of Melrose a couple of months back.

Half an hour and a phone-call later, the Parlours were floating in cyberspace. It had been a piece of pee, really, Parlour thought to himself, debating the curious physical conundrum this expression posed as he located a well-known search engine. Perhaps Eskimos had invented the expression. Maybe their pee froze before hitting the pan up on the Arctic Circle.

But something had been bugging Parlour ever since the "revelations" about Martin Beauville's past had come to light, and it wasn't the nature of urine in Greenland. He entered the words "Beauville" into the query box and waited for some relevant websites to magic their way to him across cyberspace. Parlour scrolled down numerous real-estate websites featuring properties in the French town of Beauville before being briefly distracted by the Chevrolet Beauville G20 Sportvan.

But there was no listing for a Martin Charles Lucian Beauville and no Court Martial involving the aforementioned. Parlour tried multiple combinations of Beauville's name and various titles, but with no joy.

Parlour's lips twitched and his heart beat a little faster. He returned to the search engine and entered "Southern Regional Informer" in the query box. Once the homepage of the online version of the newspaper had appeared on the screen, Parlour clicked on the heading "archive" and waited a second. He frowned as he skimread the new page with its red header. Apparently you could only access articles from the last seven days free of charge. Only the header and first sentence of archive articles were given on the screen - you had to subscribe for the whole story. That would take time. But wait a minute, what was this? The database only contained articles dating back to 1985... the newspaper article found on Haynes's computer was from 1980.

And what was the name of the host website that had contained archive extracts from the Southern Regional Informer and the Billock Courier? Some gay website, wasn't it, which existed for the pure purpose of outing military men and women? Parlour couldn't imagine for one minute it was kosher. It would never be allowed, surely? He retrieved his notebook from his back pocket and leafed through to some notes he had made earlier that week with the help of some illicit inside information. *Camping Out* was the not so ingenious title of the website in question. Parlour entered the title in his search engine and waited for the necessary information to wing its way back to him through cyberspace.

He scrolled down numerous articles on outdoor holidays and camping materials before finding what he was looking for. Feeling decidedly queasy, Parlour ran his mouse over the header:- *Come On Out if You Think You're Hard Enough!* and was directed to URL *www.camping_out.co.uk.*

But hello, what was this? All the link brought up was a page from an Internet Service Provider called *Speedsurf,* noting that the web address had been registered by another user but the domain was unavailable at that present time. But the website had clearly been up and running when Haynes stumbled upon it on his computer.

Parlour sat back in his chair and drummed his fingers on the table. He would hazard a guess that whoever was responsible for the "revelations" against Beauville had created this website on a webpage design package, manufacturing part or all of the information contained within int. They had then set up their own domain on a temporary basis, removing it from the World Wide Web once the damage had been done – in this case, once the incriminating evidence had been successfully planted on Terence Haynes's computer. A simple phonecall to the Southern Regional Informer and the Billock Courier should confirm whether the articles concerning Beauville were authentic or not. And a further call to the ISP under which the *Camping Out* domain was registered may reveal the identity of its author, if he could get round data protection laws, though that would be tricky given the unofficial nature of his investigations.

The killer was smart, but fortunately for him and for Beauville, not smart enough. It was as he suspected. Martin Beauville had been well and truly framed. And his job was to prevent him being strung up for a crime he hadn't committed.

Parlour now had a clearer idea of the psychological profile of the killer, too. This person was devious and clever, yet at the same time, rather inexperienced and arrogant, as they had overestimated their own skills of duplicity. It was probably their first attempt at murder. It was Parlour's guess that the novice killer was also responsible for running Mary Fosthlewaite off the road. This act had been a panic response to an unforeseen spanner in the works, namely an approach for silence money from the cleaner. It was therefore likely that the killer would have had precious little time to prepare a watertight alibi for the second murder. This should unlock the case nicely.

Parlour's heart started to thump against his prominent ribcage. He sensed he was on the way to unmasking the murderer!

<h1 style="text-align:center">18</h1>

Parlour put the phone down the following morning. It was a colleague from the station, who had agreed to keep Parlour up to speed on events behind Blackman and Sewell's back.

Beauville was being held at the station for further questioning, it transpired. Leigh Blackman, smelling blood now, was relentlessly attempting to grind down Martin Beauville and force a confession from him.

Parlour's PC was not the only item in the house to have been turned on and transported afar last night, and emerging tousle-haired from the bedroom, Juliet caught up with the latest on the Haynes/Fostlewaite murder case across the breakfast table.

She shook her unruly head and neatly pushed some Spanish omelette onto her fork.

"It's out of order, bang out of order."

Parlour nodded. "It is, I agree. But let's stay positive. If Martin didn't do it, as he says, Forensic'll be able to find out from his car. He probably just pranged it on a post and didn't notice."

"They'll make sure he looks guilty," Juliet muttered, who was growing increasingly cynical of Blackman's attempts at criminal justice.

"She can't do that," Parlour replied and picked up the copy of *The Observer* they had delivered to the door each Sunday.

"Are we going to church?" Juliet enquired.

"Is the curate doing the service again?" Parlour asked.

"Mm."

"Then I'll give it a miss," Parlour replied. "I've had my eight hours already, thanks."

"Mark!" Juliet reproached him. While it couldn't be denied that Miles Fakenham hardly set the soul on fire with his fluffy feel-good homilies, he was by no means the most bland or soporific that the diocese of Foxburgh had in the way of licensed clergy.

"Seriously, I have some paperwork to do, Jules. I know it's Sunday, but there's something I want to check out in Leigh's original notes."

Retiring to the living room with his mug of coffee, Parlour pulled out a sheaf of photocopied notes from his pilot case. He was looking for the responses of each suspect to Blackman's questions relating to their actions on the morning of the murder. Somebody was not telling the truth about their whereabouts between a quarter to eight and twenty past on Saturday 25 May.

Here we go, Parlour thought, finding the relevant batch of notes. At least he'd managed to acquire these before Sewell warned him away from the enquiry. Could he rule out those who didn't live on the Estate? Not really – it was feasible they drove to Zion House via Deverton. But it was more likely to be someone who lived in Deverton, who knew his routine and knew the area - which implicated Lindsay Briscoe, Daniel & Christine Kelty, Andrew & Lara Monkton-Smith, Jason Jarvis, Alex Miller, the late Nicky Ellery and, of course, Martin Beauville. He had an alibi for Juliet, Parlour grinned, recalling how he had lured her back to bed once her quiche was safely in the oven!

Lindsay had been giving the babies breakfast between half seven and quarter past eight last Saturday. Then she handed them over to Charles and took a quick shower before leaving for Zion House. Parlour could not imagine it would be very easy for Lindsay to nip round to Terence's in the circumstances, and neither did he believe for one minute she had done so. Daniel and Christine had also been having breakfast at that time, leaving the house at twenty past eight to get to Zion House early enough to set up the music. They had breakfasted together, and no, neither of them had left the house during the period in question. Jason Jarvis had, typically, slept through his alarm, only waking up at eight-thirty. He had immediately woken up Alex Miller and Nicky Ellery, who had been relying on a wake-up call, and they had hastily shoved some toast down before getting dressed and driving to Zion House, swearing much in the manner of Hugh Grant in the opening scenes from *Four Weddings*. It was possible, Parlour admitted, that one of them was lying and had nipped out without the others knowing, but unlikely. He couldn't imagine any of them having the guile to carry out a murder, let alone the energy to be at Terence Hayne's house at the crack of dawn, and Nicky Ellery was new to the area and therefore unfamiliar with Haynes's routine. Still, it was feasible one of them was covering for the other – had Blackman checked their story out? He rummaged around amongst his papers. Yes, she had. She was thorough, if a little predictable and plodding in her methodology.

It seemed that Jarvis, Miller and Ellery had corroborated each other's accounts in separate interviews. Furthermore, the next door neighbour to the right had got up early to paint the eves of their house, since it was a nice day, and had seen nobody leave the house during the period in question.

Who was next? Martin Beauville. Parlour skimmed through the interview to the relevant part. *You might think you're a hard nut, Leigh,* he thought, *but you haven't half got girly handwriting!* She all but fell short of circling the tops of her i's!

Beauville had eaten an early breakfast at seven then had sat in his living room reading over his talk and praying, before tackling the *Times* crossword. Then he had nipped out to Melrose, which like many of its rivals, had started operating round the clock. This was at twenty to eight, in order to buy some eclairs for the Bring and Share lunch. Beauville had then headed for Zion House, arriving there just after half past eight, in order to open up for Daniel and Christine. Blackman had checked out his story to see if his times tallied, but none of his neighbours had noticed him leaving the vicarage at any point. However, a till receipt from the supermarket showed that Beauville had indeed purchased twelve eclairs from the

Patisserie section at eight-o-three am. It would have been difficult, yet not impossible, for Beauville to have popped in at Terence Haynes's house prior to driving to Zion House, had he driven like a maniac and spent just a minute or two at Haynes's abode. Hence Blackman had circled his response and annotated it with a question mark.

Last of all, he came to the Monkton-Smiths. Andrew, he noted, had only got up at twenty-five past eight, having had a few whiskies the night before. He had dashed in the shower and grabbed a bowl of cereal before leaving for Zion House with Lara at a quarter to nine. His wife had been downstairs working out until eight twenty, having had an early breakfast at seven fifteen. She had jumped in the shower after her husband and had dried her hair quickly while he was wolfing his breakfast down. Their stories matched up from the separate interviews. Blackman had evidently found nothing untowards in all of this and taken their word for it.

Parlour reread the accounts of all the suspects' actions and sat in silence for a moment. Then he took a sharp intake of breath. It wouldn't do to get too excited. But it seemed the theory that had come together in his head the previous day was plausible. He tapped his pen thoughtfully on the arm of the sofa, then ran upstairs.

"Jules – do me a favour," he called out, wandering into the bedroom where she was getting dressed.

"Not now darling, I've just had a shower!"

"Ha ha. Could you just stay up here a minute – I need to test something out. Don't leave the bedroom."

"What?"

"Please!"

"OK," Juliet sighed, used to Parlour's idiosyncrasies. Anything for a quiet life. She sat down at her dressing table and massaged some mousse into her thick ash blonde hair.

Parlour reappeared upstairs two minutes. "What was I doing?"

"What is this?" Juliet frowned. "Guess the sound? Watching TV of course."

"What makes you think that?" Parlour challenged her.

"I could hear you!" Juliet snapped. "Look, Mark, I've lots to do today…"

"OK OK!" Parlour halted her midstream, "You've answered my question!"

He bounded back downstairs, leaving a puzzled Juliet staring at her own reflection in the mirror.

⏳⏳⏳

"You've just missed him actually," Juliet informed a crestfallen Martin Beauville at midday that Sunday. "But why don't you come in anyway?"

"Thank you," Beauville smiled wanly, crossing the threshold. "I could do with seeing a friendly face."

"Mark said Leigh Blackman paid you another visit last night," Juliet nodded, leading him into the kitchen.

"Just for a change," Beauville muttered.

"Did they give you a hard time last night?" Juliet sympathised, handing him a glass of apple juice and joining him at the table.

"At first. Just typical I should have a car similar to the one that mowed down poor Mary Fosthlewaite. But Forensic have now eliminated me, well my Audi, at least. Goodness knows how I managed to get those scratches all over it, but they were the wrong kind of scratches, apparently."

"Mark said that Mary's new car was mashed to a pulp," Juliet commented. "The moron who drove into her must have done so with some force. I can't believe whoever shunted her into that crash barrier got away with a few scratches on their paintwork."

"No," Beauville agreed. "Hopefully they'll leave me alone for a while. Goodness, that Blackman woman is enough to scare anyone off murdering for life!"

"I get on alright with her," Juliet admitted. "But from what I've heard, she *is* pretty tenacious."

"She's certainly got her teeth into me," Beauville remarked, "and I can't seem to shake her off."

"I wouldn't lose all hope yet, Martin. Mark's keeping his cards pretty close to that skinny little chest of his, but I reckon he knows more than he's letting on. I don't want to build your hopes up too much, but this morning he just had that crazed look in his eyes – like he was onto something."

"Really?" Beauville asked, sounded vaguely hopeful. "I know Bishop Shadwell said he'd been burning the midnight oil to clear my name."

"He has," Juliet confirmed. "But like I said, don't get too excited just yet."

"I'll try not to," Beauville said, standing up. "It's times like this that you just have to pray and rely on God to protect you."

"Well, you have our support, too," Juliet smiled.

"It's very much appreciated," Beauville smiled warmly. "Will you tell Mark I called when he gets back?"

Juliet nodded, seeing him to the door.

⧗ ⧗ ⧗

"Aah, Parlour, I was wondering when you were going to get in touch!" Shadwell Allbright beamed at the ginger detective on his doorstep.

"I had to use the police library at County Headquarters – "

"Working on a Sunday, tut tut!" the Bishop laughed, ambling down the hallway in his civvies, which consisted of a baggy Fairisle cardigan and shapeless flannel slacks, which true to their name, were decidedly loose around the buttocks where he lacked natural padding.

"Need's must," Parlour replied soberly. "I have my normal workload alongside trying to clear Martin Beauville's name."

"Of course, of course," the Bishop muttered hastily, taking a seat on a large floral sofa, kindly left behind by the wife of the previous incumbent of the Diocesan property in Foxburgh.

"However, I thought I would drop by while I was in town and give you a progress report on the Haynes case."

"Splendid – do take a pew," the Bishop smiled and Parlour obliged, his bony knees cracking as he lowered his lanky frame into an armchair in the corner.

"I actually need you to do me a favour, Bishop Shadwell," Parlour began, "and I think you'll understand why, once I've explained the stage I've got to in my investigations."

"Oh?" the Bishop queried, raising his thin white eyebrows as Parlour leaned forward to outline his theory.

19

"I'm not sure I can do this," Shadwell Allbright murmured nervously as they pulled up just around the corner from Andrew Monkton-Smith's generous four-bedroomed detached in Venison Row.

"Just think of it as aiding the course of justice," Parlour grinned. "It'll all be worth it if it helps clear Beauville's name."

"OK, OK," the Bishop backed down, none too convinced. "Just tell me what I have to do again."

Parlour explained that he would alight here and slip into Andrew Monkton-Smith's back garden. He could see already that a few of the ground floor back windows were open – it shouldn't be too difficult to sneak inside. The Bishop was to drive up to his door, as it would look odd otherwise. Allbright's task was then to keep Monkton-Smith talking as long as possible, which was to be achieved by consulting him on a legal matter. Hopefully this conversation would take place out of the way in Monkton-Smith's study, where Parlour knew he usually conducted such conversations, not being overly fond of the rather frame-absorbing pastel suite Lara had chosen for the living room. However, it wouldn't be too problematic, were he to invite the Bishop into the lounge, since it was mainly upstairs Parlour needed to investigate in any case.

"How do you know Lara isn't there?" the Bishop frowned.

"She's at our house," Parlour grinned, explaining that Juliet had invited her to their house for afternoon tea. He reckoned he needed at least twenty minutes to rummage through the Monkton-Smiths' personal effects, and arranged to telephone the Bishop later on to report on his findings, rather than hang around outside looking suspicious.

"OK, OK, Parlour," the Bishop frowned, "but why does it have to be me who acts as decoy? I do have a reputation to keep up, you know!"

"Precisely!" Parlour laughed. "He won't suspect a thing. I can't use any of my men, can I, and I couldn't possibly ask anyone from church!"

"True," the Bishop conceded.

"Besides," Parlour continued, "you're probably about the only person he'd agree to see on a Sunday, at least to discuss work with. It's not the done thing, among us lay folk, to say no to the Bishop."

"I suppose not," Allbright sighed. He consulted his watch. "It's nearly four o'clock. Let's get this over with."

"OK, oh and Bishop -" Parlour said as an afterthought.

"Yes?"

"You might like to ask him while you're at it whether they were out late last night..."

Shadwell Allbright frowned. "Really, Mark..."

But Parlour had already got out of Allbright's car. Trying to look as natural as possible, he proceeded at a leisurely pace, to any watching eyes, a man much like any other man walking off a heavy Sunday lunch by taking a gentle stroll around the block.

Parlour watched as the Bishop turned into Venison Row and rolled his car slowly up the Monkton-Smiths' driveway. He retreated into a hedge as he saw Andrew Monkton-Smith shake the Bishop's hand and cordially invite him indoors with only the merest hint of a frown on his forehead. He waited a minute and surveyed the neighbouring houses. There didn't appear to be anyone about – probably all enjoying the beautiful spring weather in a local beer garden or park or in the comfort of their own back gardens. It was just a risk he would have to take – hopefully he would find the evidence he required to justify his actions, anyway.

He disappeared into the hedgerow and scuttled around the back of the large red brick house. Getting down on his haunches, he edged along, back to the wall, below window level until he got to Monkton-Smith's study. Yes, he could hear the Bishop explaining his daughter's rent dispute to the middle-aged lawyer.

Parlour backtracked on himself and hauled himself through a narrow side window. Not for the first time, his lanky frame came in useful. Taking his shoes off, Parlour crept upstairs in his stocking soles.

The upstairs bathroom was at the top left of the stairs, that much he knew. Next to that was the guestroom. Parlour tentatively entered the room, but it was empty, its picture perfect appearance suggesting it had not been slept in recently. He tried a few cupboards and drawers, but they contained nothing but spare linen and towels. The wardrobe contained some spare suits of Andrew's and a dozen or so empty hangers. Parlour got down on the floor and looked under the bed, but there was nothing to be seen but a few dustballs that had escaped the hoover attachment.

Next to the guestroom was a separate toilet with no storage space. Then there was another room which evidently served as some kind of studio for Lara's home décor ambitions, as rolls of fabric were stacked in one corner, and a sewing machine stood on a large brown table with a tailor's rule embedded in it. Parlour rooted around in the various cupboards and among the box files on the shelves, but they contained nothing more exciting then patterns and various samples of material.

Next door was another guestroom, this time more lived in. By the clothes draped across the back of the chair and the dirty cups on the bedside cabinet, Parlour gathered it had been used recently. Or perhaps it was the "air-raid shelter" as Juliet called their guestroom, a haven to escape to when Parlour's snoring went off the Richter scale!

Parlour decided to return to it in a minute. Time was of the essence, and he hadn't even looked in the master bedroom yet, the most likely source of incriminating information.

Gordon Brown! He whistled, entering the enormous room to the front of the house with its leaded glass windows. It must have been at least twice the size of his bedroom at home, and theirs was by no means the smallest four bedroom semi on the estate. As per the rest of the house, it was like something from a TV makeover programme, with its luxurious colours and chunky dado rails. The kingsize bed was covered with an intricate patchwork quilt and the ceiling almost collapsed under the weight of a splendid eight-legged chandelier that cocooned the room in a web of light when Parlour switched it on.

He glanced at his watch. He'd already been in there ten minutes, with nothing to show for his efforts. Time to stop admiring the scenery and get down to business.

It was difficult to know where to start, with some fifteen feet of wall to wall hanging space, but Parlour went for the obvious places first. Being careful to tiptoe less the noise arouse Monkton-Smith's suspicions, he opened the mirrored wardrobes and rooted around in the bottom. But all he found were boxes of accessories – hats and shoes and matching scarves, and unopened silk tie and golf ball sets in Andrew's side of the wardrobe. Not one solitary box of postcards or other private memorabilia.

Parlour turned his attentions to the ornate bedside cabinets either side of the quilt bedecked bed, which sat plum in the centre of the room like a giant fondant fancy – colourants very much included on this occasion.

Hello, who was this? Parlour picked up a seven by five photograph of a handsome young man with blonde hair in a frame on what was patently Lara's side of the bed. An old flame? No – there was no way a possessive man like Andrew would allow his wife to keep mementoes of past lovers in so intimate a location, no matter how platonic their relationship was these days. Frowning, Parlour took the photo out of the frame, but there was no inscription on the back, just a date:- Feb 1982. Shaking his head, he returned the photo to its rightful place and started on Lara's personal effects in the three drawer cabinet. Parlour felt distinctly awkward rooting around among Lara's best silk lingerie, but it had to be done. Again, though, no joy. Soap, bath salts, endless trinkets with earrings in them, tissues, facial creams, a travel guide to Tuscany, but no revealing letters, nothing to link the Monkton-Smiths to Martin Beauville or Terence Haynes.

Parlour bent down and looked under the bed. That was where he always slid the case notes he didn't want Juliet to see, the ones that were too confidential or simply too grisly for innocent eyes. But Mary Fosthlewaite had done her job well, he grimaced, for the carpet below was spotless.

Shucks! He exclaimed under his breath. Where next? Parlour felt under the pillows and below the mattress, but found nothing but a few old tissues. He scratched his temple. Perhaps they had a bureau or something downstairs. That would be more tricky to investigate. But who on earth hid things in a bureau? If he had something he didn't want Juliet to see, he put it in his bedside cabinet among the pyjamas he never wore, not in his office, which would be sure to be the first place she'd look. Or he'd leave it at work, or in the boot of his car... Parlour clicked his fingers.

He padded down the stairs, then softly down the hallway. Parlour could still hear Andrew Monkton-Smith and the Bishop talking in the study. It was risky... but worth a try. He slipped into the kitchen and removed a bunch of keys from the keyholder on the wall, as he had seen Andrew do before. Fortunately the car was around the side of the house, with its boot rear facing, so it should be possible to sneak out the kitchen and open the boot without the neighbours catching sight of him. Praying under his breath that Monkton-Smith and the Bishop did not choose that precise moment to conclude their discussion and emerge from the study, Parlour sneaked out the back door and opened the boot of Andrew's red E-series Mercedes. A tetra-can, a toolbox, the obligatory tartan rug, several empty bottles of mineral water, a first aid kit, distilled water and some Castrol GTX. Parlour checked out the toolbox and first aid kit, but there was nothing to be found. He lifted up the boot upholstery and rooted around the spare tyre, but no joy there either. The interior of the car revealed nothing but parking tickets and a receipt from the Post Office in Lexington Green for a parcel. Must have been the Haynes manual he sent to his brother on the day of the murder, Parlour thought, noting the by now familiar date on the receipt. He paused for a second, feeling that odd sensation again that he was missing something, but it wouldn't come to him.

Time for a sharp exit, Parlour thought wistfully, and locked the car. He sneaked back in the kitchen to replace the key then slipped back out the back door and through the garden.

Well that was a dead loss, he frowned, trying to look as natural as possible as he emerged from the hedge onto the pavement outside the house. The Bishop's car was still outside, he noted. He could have searched downstairs, but it would have been pretty risky, given Monkton-Smith could have emerged from his study at any moment and he, Parlour, would have absolutely no excuse for being in the house.

Parlour turned out of Venison Row and walked towards his own house in Spatchcock Drive.

⧗ ⧗ ⧗

"Hi Jules, hello Lara," he smiled politely to the tall, blonde wife of Andrew Monkton-Smith as he entered the house through the conservatory, where the two women were conversing.

"Hi Mark – how's life?" Lara smiled radiantly.

"Hectic," Parlour replied, smiling blandly back at her.

"Terrible about Mary, isn't it?" Lara remarked, looking suitably sorrowful. "They say she was drink driving – who would've believed it?"

"Are they now?" Parlour enquired mildly, shooting Juliet a *Please Say You Didn't Tell Her the Truth* look. Juliet, out of Lara's line of vision, gave a brief shake of her head.

"I didn't even know she had a car!" Lara continued.

"There's lots of things we don't know about one another," Parlour replied cryptically and walked through to the kitchen. Juliet appeared moments later.

"Well – what did you find out?" Juliet hissed. Parlour had felt obliged to admit his plans to search the Monkton-Smiths' house to his wife, in order to justify his request that Juliet entertain Lara for the afternoon. Whilst the two women got on fine at surface level, Lara was by no means a natural companion for Parlour's altogether quirkier wife.

"You know I can't tell you anything, Jules," Parlour frowned, taking a hefty swig from a glass of water.

"Oh come on, Mark, what's the big deal? I'm hardly going to get on the phone to Blackman and grass you up!"

Parlour turned around and faced her, leaning back on the sink. "I didn't find anything, darling, if you must know. I might have to face up to the fact that I'm barking up entirely the wrong tree. I'm loathe to tell you anything and jeopardise your friendships with people from church who may well be perfectly innocent. Can you understand that, Jules?"

Juliet made a face. "So long as you tell me as soon as you know something for sure."

"I promise," Parlour nodded. "Now, if you'll excuse me, I need to go upstairs and put my thinking cap on."

But it was impossible to focus his mind on the mysterious motive behind Terence Haynes' death with Lara Monkton-Smith's well-bred guffaw and Juliet's infectious giggle punctuating his thought processes at regular intervals. He couldn't really complain – after all, he had asked Juliet to invite Lara round, but he needed to get a handle on this case before someone else met with a tragic fate.

Parlour stood up and stretched.   Perhaps some country air would clear the fuzz in his head.

20

Parlour glanced at his watch the next morning as he stood in the front room of their house in Spatchcock Drive.

Lara Monkton-Smith had a committee meeting in Lexington Green at 10 o'clock, she'd told Juliet as much yesterday afternoon.

Nine thirty. If Lara Monkton-Smith was getting a lift to this meeting, her benefactor should turn up soon. He pointed the binoculars left by his late father-in-law towards "Larcombe", number 7 Venison Row. He'd consulted the bus timetable – there was a nine twenty-five and a nine fifty-five to Lexington Green, so if she was taking the Hoppa to her meeting, she would have left the house by now. Lara Monkton-Smith, unusually for a woman of her station in life, did not drive a car. Apparently she detested driving, despite having a valid driver's licence.

But hello, what was this? The blonde head of Lara Monkton-Smith suddenly appeared from the front door. Parlour frowned in puzzlement as she walked down the driveway and out of Venison Row. Perhaps she had missed the bus… but if so, why leave so early to catch the next one?

Lest he miss her altogether, Parlour put the binoculars down and grabbed his keys. He got in his car and crawled slowly to the end of Spatchcock Drive. He saw her emerge on Lower Deverton Road a minute later. Parking behind some flats, he watched as she walked briskly down the main road. Suddenly she turned off to the left a couple of yards down the road beyond him. Parlour frowned. Why would she be heading towards the industrial estate? He had presumed she was walking to someone's house to get her lift, or had decided to pop to the shop before getting the next bus to Lexington Green. He decided to park up and go by foot. He might lose her otherwise, as it would take a good five minutes to drive the long way round.

He followed her down a makeshift path through the bracken to the small industrial estate, which housed a few small factories and repair workshops. Parlour skirted around the back of the metal hangar type constructions and watched her proceed past all the factories to a concrete area to the far end.

Wishing he had brought his binoculars with him, Parlour scurried around the perimeter of the estate until he was behind the concreted area. Now he could see that this was not only a turning circle for lorries, but also home to a dozen or so lock-ups, presumably for private rental. Parlour felt himself physically bubble with excitement as Lara Monkton-Smith opened the last garage on the block. The up-and-over door grated as she pushed it up, second time lucky. He hastily hid behind the building as she looked around furtively to check nobody was around. Clearly the lock-up boasted neither power nor light, for he could see a yellow circle of torchlight bobbing about in the darkness. Parlour bit his lip. He wanted to see what she was up to, but there was no way he could get any closer without risking her seeing him.

Parlour shrank back against the back wall as he heard the garage door creak shut, then watched as Lara Monkton-Smith reemerged from the dark lock-up and headed for the footpath leading back onto the main road.

Committee meeting, my bottom! Parlour grimaced. Poor old Andrew. What else did she get up to in the name of altruism?

Waiting until she was safely out of sight, Parlour peered through the window of the last lock-up again. Had he imagined it, or had he heard the slam of a boot being shut? But it was too dark to make out anything, and the natural light was obscured by foliage. He could have a bash at breaking into the garage, but it was perhaps better to come back later with a torch and lock-picking device. As a truck approached the concreted area, Parlour decided in favour of a return visit. It wouldn't do to be caught breaking into private property, especially given the decidedly unofficial nature of his investigations.

Returning to his car, Parlour was just in time to see Lara Monkton-Smith's blonde head disappear into a Billock Shoppa Hoppa en route to Lexington Green. He decided to follow the bus – goodness knew what, or whom, was on the morning's agenda.

Anticipating she would alight at the townsquare, the final stop, Parlour pulled into the free two hour carpark behind the market. Rushing through the stalls, he watched her enter Roberts the Baker's and head upstairs to the teashop. From his position on the pavement below, he saw her greet four other women with kisses and smiles. One of them appeared to be handing out some papers. So the committee meeting wasn't a complete fabrication. He looked at his watch. Half-past ten. She had just lied about the time to Juliet, that was all.

Feeling suddenly peckish, Parlour wandered into the supermarket and headed for the confectionary aisle.

"There are Christians who believe chocolate bars are tools of the devil," came a familiar voice as Parlour debated which was the lesser of two evils – a Snickers or an Aero.

"And I'm a liberal backslider," Parlour grinned, turning to face Shadwell Allbright, who was incongruously dressed in his purple frock and carrying a basket of groceries. "Good morning, Bishop."

"Good morning, Detective Inspector," Allbright grinned. "What brings you to Lexington Green this fine spring morning?"

"Oh, this and that," Parlour replied aerily. You never could tell who was in the next aisle. "How about you?"

"I took the early morning communion service at the Priory this morning," the Bishop replied. "Thought I'd do a bit of shopping on the way home. Sounds rather anti-social of me, but I always seem to get waylaid in my local shop by well-meaning parishioners asking my views on the world and its wife. A simple trip to the corner shop for a pint of milk can take anything up to an hour!"

"Yes, it's a bit like that when I nip into the local pub," Parlour agreed. "You've heard of those "Grill a Christian" events? Well I get "Grill a Copper", only I'm usually well-roasted by the end of it!"

The Bishop chuckled.

"Thanks for helping me out yesterday," Parlour smiled, guiltily remembering he had forgotten to phone Allbright last night as promised.

"Don't mention it," the Bishop waved his hand. "Only too glad to be of assistance. Had quite an interesting chat with Monkton-Smith, anyway. It seems rental agreements can be a legal minefield!"

"I didn't find what I was after, unfortunately," Parlour conceded. He looked around. There was nobody within earshot of them. "However, I saw something this morning which leads me to believe I'm not barking up the wrong tree, after all."

"Oh yes?" the Bishop enquired, raising his eyebrows and his tone of voice in unison, an exaggerated mannerism much ridiculed by Deverton PC's resident double act, Jarvis and Miller.

"I can't say more than that at present," Parlour replied, shaking his head regretfully, "but hopefully I'll have some news for you very soon."

"Hadn't you better tell that lady detective if you think you know who the murderer is?" the Bishop remarked. "They could kill again."

"Ssh!" Parlour hissed. It was neither the time nor the place for such discussions. "Blackman wouldn't listen," Parlour replied quietly. "That's why I have to be sure. She's that convinced Beauville is involved, I'd have to have a pretty watertight case to persuade her otherwise. Plus, it could jeopardise my investigations if I laid my cards on the table too early. If Blackman dragged a suspect in for questioning without achieving a conviction, it'd give them a chance to cover their tracks, and then I'd never prove anything."

"Mm, I see what you mean," the Bishop replied thoughtfully. He slapped Parlour on the back. "Now don't go putting your life in danger, will you?"

"I'll try not to," Parlour smiled. He watched Shadwell Allbright continue down the aisle in his purple cassock, much to the amusement of the other shoppers in the supermarket that morning.

⧗⧗⧗

Having followed Lara Monkton-Smith back home to Venison Row just before nooon, Parlour decided he really ought to plod on with the Bywater Farm murder case. He was well behind in the second phase of his research programme and had neglected to call some potentially useful sources of fresh information.

He grabbed himself a sandwich and a cup of tea, then spread his notes on the coffee table. Parlour had elected to work downstairs and not in his rear-facing office upstairs so that he could keep a regular track of movements at the Monkton-Smith's through his trusty binoculars.

⧗⧗⧗

"It's alright for some," Juliet exclaimed, walking into the living room at five o'clock that afternoon and finding her husband prostrate on the sofa.

Parlour rubbed his eyes and pulled himself to an upright position.

"Must've dozed off. This historical murder is enough to send anyone to sleep!"

254

"Perhaps you should work at the station then, where you don't have the option," Juliet remarked dryly.

"It's nice to see you, too," Parlour said, feigning hurt. "Actually, I had to work from home."

"So I see," Juliet remarked, noting the binoculars mounted on a tripod by the window. "Giving James Stewart a run for his money?"

She peered through the lenses. "Ah-haah! Keeping the Monkton-Smiths under surveillance, are we?"

"Something like that," Parlour mumbled, trying to edge her out of the way to check up on the latest state of play at the house in Venison Row. Hopefully Lara hadn't disappeared off anywhere whilst he had been asleep.

"No you don't!" Juliet pushed him back as she gazed with fascination at the nearby property through the glasses. "Looks like they're having a little *soiree* – very nice! Why weren't we invited?"

"Let me look," Parlour commanded, jostling her out of the way. "Looks like some of Andrew's work colleagues. The guy in the grey suit is his partner in the firm."

He noted to his relief that Lara was very much present, ladling out what appeared to be some kind of punch from a large glass bowl.

"You might as well tell me your theory now, Mark," Juliet commented, throwing herself down on the sofa and picking up the day's mail. "It's pretty obvious you think Andrew is involved in some way, or you wouldn't have got the Bishop in to sidetrack him yesterday while you went sniffing around in his drawers!"

"Later – I promise," Parlour replied, tidying up his papers. "There's something I need to check out first. At the moment my theory is pure supposition. I have too much respect for Andrew, or for any of our friends, for that matter, to blacken their names unnecessarily."

"Mark – I'm your wife!" Juliet exclaimed indignantly. "And if Andrew Monkton-Smith is the killer – and I can't believe for a minute he is – I'd like to know about it before I get shunted off the Lexington Green Road, too!"

"There's no danger of that, Jules," Parlour replied fondly, planting a kiss on her blonde head.

"Huh!" Juliet grunted and trudged upstairs. Parlour returned to his binoculars and followed Lara Monkton-Smith across the patio. She was doubtlessly ingratiating herself with some of Andrew's lawyer friends, he grinned, watching her bob her head flirtatiously as she spoke. Her husband, meanwhile, was marshalling the stream of expensive cars drawing up to the property, suggesting the night had just begun.

Good. The little party on the front lawn should see Lara occupied for the best part of the evening, keeping the coast clear for him to break into the lock-up. Best wait until the traffic died down about half six or seven. It was probably less risky to go in daylight and be as discreet and natural as possible, than to start poking around in the dark with a torchlight and risk getting taken unawares, there was a murderer on the loose after all. It should be deserted down there by then. Of course, the lock-ups could well be patrolled by a security firm and he might have to resort to badge-flashing. Hopefully the result would justify the means, though, and he could find what he was looking for without incurring a professional misconduct charge.

⧗⧗⧗

Leigh Blackman nervously swallowed a lump in her throat as Brian Sewell's whisky-beaten face appeared in the checkered glass square on her office door. She had been dreading their progress meeting scheduled for five-thirty that afternoon.

"Hello, Leigh, how are you?" the Superintendent enquired, shutting the door behind him and pulling up a chair at her desk.

"I've seen better days," Blackman replied, removing her reading glasses to meet Sewell's gaze.

"Like my Merc," Sewell chuckled, peeling open a tube of mints and popping one in his mouth without offering Blackman one. "She's not been the same since I took her down to the South of France last August."

"Wish I was in the bloody South of France," Blackman moaned.

"By the absence of communication, I gather you've come to a bit of a standstill," Sewell remarked.

Blackman sighed. "Sorry Sir. All roads still point to Beauville but we can't get a damn thing on him."

"I gather his car was clear?"

"Had a few scrapes on it, but no signs of impact," Blackman confirmed.

"Did Keough's enquiries throw up any possible leads?" Sewell enquired. Darren Keough had been assigned the task of tracing black cars taken to bodyshops or found abandoned in the area.

"Oh, he found plenty smashed up black cars, alright," Blackman replied, "but none with the right *type* of damage to the bodywork, apparently."

"What about ones that have been repaired?"

Blackman informed him that DC Keough had checked garage records and had still drawn a blank. Neither had the local scrapyard reported any recent arrivals of black cars with signs of front and side impact. In fact, not one single car, stolen, abandoned or otherwise, had been found matching the vehicle spec of the one that shunted Mary Fosthlewaite off the road.

"What about Beauville? Any blasts from the past come forward, pardon the pun?" Sewell asked.

Blackman shook her head disconsolately. "Just that phoney guy from the Herald."

"And you're sure Mary Fosthlewaite's death wasn't just a coincidence?"

"Clear case of shutting up the witness for good, wouldn't you say?" Blackman replied.

"It certainly looks like we have a double murder on our hands," Sewell agreed. "Were any of our beloved PCC members out road-racing in the early hours?"

Blackman shook her head. "They've all got alibis as watertight as a bleedin' *Tena* pantyliner!"

"Well, don't make any assumptions, that's all I'm saying," Sewell warned her. "It wouldn't be the first time you've tried to make events fit the theory."

"No, Sir, I'll try not to," Blackman said meekly.

"Has Parlour given you any trouble since I had a word?" Sewell enquired.

"I've hardly set eyes on him," she replied, shaking her head. "Course, he could be sticking his spotty little nose into matters that don't concern him, but I've not seen hide nor hair of him."

"Good stuff," Sewell nodded. "So where next, Leigh?"

"I wish I knew, Sir," Blackman replied gloomily.

21

Parlour looked out the window at six twenty that evening, as Juliet busied herself in the kitchen preparing a cheese sauce for the macaroni. He didn't need binoculars to see that the party was in full swing at the Monkton-Smiths'. A throng about a dozen strong were gathered in the front room while other members of the party could be seen milling in the garden, which was illuminated by an array of strategically placed night-lights and candles on poles. Parlour believed he could make out the elegant figure of Lara Monkton-Smith chatting in the front room, but decided he'd better make sure.

Yep, Parlour said aloud, peering through his binoculars, it was her alright, dressed for the occasion now in a little black number. Feeling his heart beat a little faster, Parlour went out to the hallway, where his torch and "toolbox" of lock-picking devices were waiting on the telephone table. Now was as good a time as any, with Andrew and Lara clearly occupied at home for the night.

Parlour slipped on a dark jacket and baseball cap to coneal his distinctive ginger crop and placed the implements in the large inside pocket. He slapped his right hand side – yep, he had his mobile. Better switch it on incase he had to make a call in a hurry.

"Jules, I'm just nipping out for a bit," Parlour called out.

"Well don't be long, dinner will be ready in…"

But Parlour did not stay to hear the rest of the sentence, shutting the door behind him and leaping into his car. Though the lock-up was just ten minutes walk from his house in Spatchcock Drive, it provided some degree of protection from unleashed guard-dogs and besides, he may need it to follow something up.

He reversed deftly out of the driveway and headed towards the main road. He would have to take the long way round by car, which meant driving through the industrial estate.

However, there wasn't a soul to be seen, and there didn't appear to be a security guard in residence, either. But to be on the safe side, Parlour slowed down until he was barely crawling along to avoid too much crackling on the gravel. *This is easier than I anticipated*, Parlour thought to himself, sliding his car under some conveniently located overhanging trees next to the block of garages.

He uttered a quick prayer then got out the car. Trying to look as inconspicuous as possible, Parlour set about picking the garage lock. This bit wasn't so easy. Despite their rather tatty appearance, the locks on the doors were of a fairly robust design and it took Parlour a good ten minutes to manipulate the mechanism. Finally the metal handle turned, and he gently rolled the up and over door towards the ceiling, as noiselessly as possible.

Bingo! Parlour exclaimed inwardly as his eyes immediately rested on a bulky shape housed beneath a green canvas cover. He lifted the sheet gingerly, hardly daring to believe he had hit upon the truth.

But there it was before him, in all its efficient, German glory. An old Y-reg, pristinely maintained black VW Golf GTI Mark 1. That is, aside from the large dent in the side wing and smashed headlight. Parlour tried the passenger door, but it was locked. But he could have this baby open in seconds – car doors were his speciality, testimony to a misspent youth.

Parlour clambered into the front seat. It was like stepping back in time, with the selection of late 70s/early 80s music on the tape holder stuck to the dashboard. *The Police, Rainbow, Blondie, Rush*, Parlour noted. He opened the glove compartment, making sure his own hands were covered. There he found a copy of the *Sun*, dated January 1982, yellowed at the edges. Why hadn't she cleared the car of all this rubbish?

Finding no further clues, Parlour turned his attentions to the boot. Again he had to manipulate the lock – central locking hadn't even made it to Germany in the early 80s.

Gotcha! Parlour exclaimed, aloud this time, as he found a pair of navy shorts and baseball cap, and a pale blue shirt. He rummaged around some more until he found a slim black plastic box that he recognised immediately to be a laptop computer. That could come with him. There was no time for playing at Guess the Password now. Parlour threw it in the back of his car then returned to the VW Golf.

It just gets better, he grinned, shining his torch on a half empty bottle of Jack Daniels and a glossy paperback entitled *Web Design for Beginners*. So this was the killer's treasure trove of incriminating evidence – the boot of an old VW Golf.

Hello, what's this? He pulled out a crumpled brown envelope which contained a grubby handwritten letter on spiral bound notepaper. Holding his torch up with one hand, Parlour began to decipher the scrawly blue ink. Realising he was in the throes of discovering the missing link of the puzzle, Parlour sat on the lip of the boot and took in the contents of the letter.

It appeared to be an eye-witness account from a naval officer who had survived the attack on HMS Coventry that torrid Saturday in May 1982. The officer, signed James Mallinson, described how a character referred to only as Jonathan had been left for dead in the water as all around him fellow officers were airlifted to safety... presided over by one *Commander Terence Haynes*.

Parlour stood up very suddenly. The picture, at last, was clear. All the pieces slotted into space. He turned back to the book. "Jonathan" had met his tragic death on May 25th 1982!

Parlour stuffed the letter in his coat pocket. Halting for five seconds to jot down the registration on the back of his hand, Parlour neither heard nor saw a tall figure in a hooded top emerge from the foliage and scale along the side of the lock-up.

There was a groan and the crackle of gravel as Mark Parlour hit the ground.

Retrieving the laptop from the back seat of the SLK, and the letter from Parlour's coat pocket, his assailant reversed the worse for wear black VW out of the lock-up. Pausing only to drag Parlour's limp body into the garage and to lock the door, the hooded figure got back behind the wheel of the Golf and screeched out of the industrial estate.

⧗⧗⧗

Juliet Parlour frowned, looking up at the clock on her computer screen. Seven forty-five. Mark had been out well over an hour. She was used to his impromptu ventures outdoors, but he usually came back within the hour, unless warning her to the contrary, and certainly did not miss dinner, especially not his favourite home-made macaroni cheese. She'd give him another half hour. Perhaps he had popped round to see how Martin Beauville was doing and felt he couldn't leave in a hurry.

But eight fifteen came and went without any sign of her husband. Juliet tried his mobile, but it just rang without a response. She opened the study door. It wasn't ringing anywhere in the house – he must've taken it with him. Perhaps he was driving and couldn't answer it. It didn't usually stop him, though.

Feeling rather foolish, she dialled the vicarage. But there was no answer and she left a message on the ansaphone, requesting Martin give her a call. Where else might he have got to? It wasn't late, she acknowledged, and goodness knows, they weren't tied to routine in their respective professions, couldn't afford to be, but Juliet could not shake off the feeling of malaise inside. It was *not* like Mark to miss his evening meal, and why hadn't he called her if he had got delayed somewhere? He was by no means perfect, but he was not a thoughtless man.

262

Next she tried Billock Police but the Desk Seargent hadn't seen nor heard anything of Parlour all evening. He might have decided to gatecrash the party at the Monkton-Smiths, Juliet thought, though unlikely. She punched in Andrew's number, who answered the phone after a considerable time.

"Hi, Andrew. Juliet Parlour here. I don't suppose you've seen Mark tonight? He disappeared out the front door nearly two hours ago and I have no idea where he is!"

"Have you tried his mobile?" Andrew Monkton-Smith enquired in the kindly, yet rather patronising tone he reserved for female members of the race.

"Yes – it's just ringing with no reply. I rang the vicarage, but there's no reply there, either."

"Perhaps Mark took the vicar out for a stiff drink to calm his nerves!" Andrew laughed.

"I don't think so," Juliet replied. "Mark likes to keep a clear head through the week… generally."

Her thoughts briefly flashed back to Parlour's foray into the drinks cabinet the other night.

"Very sensible," Andrew chuckled. "Wish I could say the same. Look, why don't I go and ask Lara?"

"Thanks," Juliet mumbled, doodling on the phone pad as she awaited his return. In the midst of her concern for her missing husband, it hadn't occurred to her that phoning the Monkton-Smiths might not have been an altogether wise move, given Parlour's suspicions. Whilst he had not downloaded his exact thought patterns to her concerning the couple in question, it was clear to Juliet that he knew they were implicated in some way in the murder of Terence Haynes and possibly Mary Fosthlewaite.

"Funny, I can't find Lara anywhere, either!" Andrew replied eventually, sounding out of breath. "I assumed she was still entertaining our guests in the garden. I've been stuck in a beastly game of bridge in the kitchen for the past hour! I have an awful hand - quite glad you rang, actually!"

"So you haven't seen Mark?" Juliet surmised, cutting to the chase.

"No, no – can't help you there. Listen – I better go and find my wife. I'll call you if she knows anything, OK?"

"Thanks, Andrew," Juliet murmured, putting the phone down. A horrible thought suddenly crossed her mind concerning Mark and Lara, but she dismissed it immediately as out of hand. He would never… but he had been watching her house through the binoculars, hadn't he?

As if he'd be that obvious if he was! Juliet told herself scornfully. And anyway, Mark would never do a thing like that. Their rock-solid marriage was a constant source of smug pride to both of them. Though Juliet could be volatile, she was always upfront with Mark about her feelings, and he in turn tried to reciprocate by not playing the Martian man, but by being as transparent as possible with her about matters of the heart. A good marriage was not, in their opinion, one where neither party played their hand and hid behind their respective shutters. It was easy to say you never argued if you never discussed your feelings in the first place… no, a good marriage was one where you could sit up half the night scouring your souls and maybe visit some dark places, but still emerge more or less intact in the morning, still united and determined to tough it out together.

No, Mark would not behave in such a furtive way, he would not do that to her.

But where was he? She wandered across the landing to the bedroom and looked down at the driveway. He had taken the car… that was odd. Perhaps he'd gone to check out something to do with the Haynes case, or the Bywater Farm business. But why wasn't he answering his mobile, if he had?

Maybe he had gone to discuss the Haynes case with the Bishop – that would mean a round trip to Foxburgh, which would account for his long absence and the missing car. But why drive all the way up there on a weekday evening? Why not just ring the Bishop?

She picked up the phone, but slammed it down immediately. This was silly. He had probably just parked somewhere and gone for a walk to mull things over. He'd left his mobile in the car and had lost track of time. Perhaps he'd decided to nip into the pub for a drink, after all. She tried his mobile again, but it was still ringing without the ansaphone clicking in.

When there was still no sign of Parlour at nine thirty, Juliet began to panic. She was just about to call the Bishop when the phone rang. *That could be Mark!* Exhaling in relief, she picked up the handset.

But it wasn't.

"Hello Juliet? Andrew here. Listen, I'm getting pretty worried, too. Nobody's seen Lara for a good two hours. Everyone just assumed she was elsewhere in the grounds. I thought she might have nipped out to get more wine or something – we rather underestimated the freeloading capabilities of most of our guests – but the car's in the driveway, and she hates driving anyway. I've called the Keltys and the Briscoes, but nobody's seen her. There was no reply at the vicarage. I don't think Beauville's answering the phone at the moment."

"Perhaps the three of them are having a jolly somewhere," Juliet said unconvincingly.

"Listen, I'll be over in a jiff," Andrew said briskly. "I think I can just about trust our guests not to trash the house or make off with the silverware."

"OK." Juliet put the phone down and looked up the Bishop's number. It was worth one last shot. Shadwell Allbright came to the phone immediately, doubtlessly fearing some catastrophe as it was now rather late to receive an unexpected phonecall. Juliet explained the situation.

"Oh dear," the Bishop replied gravely. "I do hope Mark hasn't come a cropper."

"What makes you say that?" Juliet asked sharply. Allbright reported his conversation with Parlour in the supermarket in Lexington Green that morning.

"I think I'd better come down to Deverton," he concluded, audibly worried. "I'll be with you in half an hour. And I'd call the police, if I were you."

"I think you're right," Juliet replied grimly. She knew Mark would not be best pleased were he to turn up on the doorstep in ten minutes time, but it really ought to be Leigh Blackman she contacted, as the Investigating Officer for the Haynes/Fostlewaite case. She located her husband's filofax and dialled DI Blackman's mobile. This time, her call was picked up immediately.

Juliet explained the disappearance of both her husband and Lara Monkton-Smith, as well as the Bishop's revelations about Parlour's recent activities.

Blackman asked her a few routine questions, but admitted that it was highly suspect given the Bishop's conversation with Parlour that morning and Parlour's rather bizarre antics with the binoculars that afternoon.

"I'll get a call out to look for his car," Blackman informed her, "and I'll be round asap. He better not be wasting police time, though," she added darkly.

"I'm sure Mark, of all people, is aware of the implications of that," Juliet replied dryly and put the phone down. The doorbell rang and she ran downstairs to admit a distraught Andrew Monkton-Smith.

Blackman arrived twenty minutes later, minus her side-kick.

"DS Robins not with you?" Juliet enquired.

"Can't get the whole team out of bed because your old man goes AWOL!" Blackman remarked, unbuttoning her overcoat.

"My wife as well, don't forget," Andrew Monkton-Smith frowned.

"Mm, funny that, wouldn't you say?" Blackman commented.

"I can assure you, there is nothing untoward going on," Juliet informed the Inspector hastily, "at least not between Lara and my husband."

Blackman noted how wives always referred to "my husband" rather than the name of the man in question when defending their marriage, even when the person was well known to both parties!

Juliet frowned, recalling Parlour's behaviour earlier that afternoon. Perhaps she should have put Andrew off coming round. It was difficult to speak honestly to Blackman with him there. Blackman spotted the expression that had come over Juliet's face and took her to one side when Andrew Monkton-Smith conveniently nipped out to the bathroom.

"You know something, don't you, Juliet?"

Juliet nodded miserably. "Mark's being working on the case for the Bishop – unofficially. He's still been doing his normal work, though," she added hastily, not wishing to dump her husband in it despite the somber circumstances.

"I knew it!" Blackman exclaimed, eyes glinting in anger.

"I think he'd worked out who killed Terence and Mary," Juliet informed her.

"Obviously one or both of the Monkton-Smiths, by the looks of it," Blackman frowned. "Chr***," she blasphemed, "why on earth have you invited *him* round here, then?"

She nodded in the direction of the bathroom to Andrew Monkton-Smith.

"I didn't think!" Juliet protested, frightened now. "Mark's good pals with Andrew, he was the obvious person to ring!"

She watched as Blackman punched some numbers into her mobile.

"What are you doing?" she asked.

"Getting some reinforcements!" Blackman replied. "Do you realise we could be holed up here with the murderer?"

"The Bishop will be here any minute," Juliet said weakly.

"Fat lot of good he'll be!" Blackman scorned. "Come on Dave, answer your bloody phone!"

She hastily went into the living room with her mobile telephone as Andrew Monkton-Smith rejoined Juliet in the kitchen, making sure she kept them both in her line of vision. She should have called Robins before she'd made the trip to Deverton, she chided herself. Her annoyance with Parlour for effing up her evening and her scepticism that anything serious was up, had clouded her judgment. Now she could have inadvertently placed Juliet Parlour and herself in grave danger.

Blackman returned to the kitchen a couple of minutes later, having requested DS Robins plus a squad car were sent to Parlour's house. Rossi and Singh had been sent up to Venison Row to check Parlour wasn't up there.

Was it her imagination, or did Andrew Monkton-Smith look decidedly nervous, over and above his obvious anxiety concerning his wife's safety?

The doorbell rang and Juliet gladly left the tense atmosphere of the kitchen to admit Shadwell Allbright. But he was immediately whisked to one side by Blackman.

"I understand from Mrs Parlour that you employed her husband in an unofficial capacity to investigate the death of Terence Haynes, Bishop."

"That's right," the Bishop replied firmly, refusing to be bullied into an apology by the discourteous Detective Inspector. "I wasn't satisfied with the line your enquiries were taking and felt Parlour stood a far better chance of catching our killer, being part of the local set-up here."

"Do you realise you may have put his life in danger?" Blackman enquired, too cross to achieve her favourite tone of silken sarcasm.

"I'm sure Parlour is best equipped of all of us to deal with such dangers, wouldn't you say, Inspector Blackman?" the Bishop replied, who did manage the desired effect.

"Juliet Parlour reckons Mark knew who the killer was, and that he may have given you some indication of who it might be."

"Does she now?" the Bishop remarked, stalling for time. Parlour, if he'd merely run out of petrol on some country road or something, would not be best pleased if he, the Bishop, revealed Parlour's suspicions to the Chief Inspector. On the other hand, if Mark was in trouble, any information he could supply may help the police track him down before it was too late.

"He had a suspicion one or both of the Monkton-Smiths were involved in the murder of Terence Haynes," the Bishop replied finally.

"One or both?" Blackman frowned.

"I really couldn't say for sure," the Bishop said, shaking his head. "He got me to keep Andrew occupied on Sunday afternoon while he searched their house. I gather he was looking for evidence of some sort to support a theory he had."

"But surely you must have an idea?" Blackman badgered him. She lowered her voice. "We could have a killer in the next room!"

"I have a feeling it was Lara he was more interested in," the Bishop admitted.

"That would make sense, given they've both gone AWOL," Blackman remarked. Her mobile rang and she hastily pressed the call receive button.

"Blackman… Yep. Yep. Deverton Industrial Estate, you say? Where? Right. With you in five."

Blackman marched into the kitchen.

"They've found Mark's car," she announced.

"And what about Mark?" Juliet asked shakily. The Bishop put a kindly hand on her shoulder.

"There were tyre marks on the gravel outside one of the lock-ups. The police broke into it and found Mark. He's received a blow to the head, but he should be OK," Blackman replied. "He's still unconscious, but the Paramedics are on their way."

"Thank God!" the Bishop replied, looking heavenwards, or at least at the kitchen ceiling. Juliet let slip a watery smile, trying to take comfort from the fact that though her husband was unconscious, he was at least alive.

"What about Lara, for Cripe's sake?" Andrew Monkton-Smith cried out, "doesn't anyone care about my wife? She could be lying in a ditch somewhere or run over by some idiot driver!"

Like Mary Fosthlewaite was, Blackman thought, trying to avoid his gaze. It was a very awkward situation. If he was involved, he was a very good actor. But then murderers had to be, didn't they? Still, given the circumstances, it was looking increasingly as if Lara Monkton-Smith was their man, so to speak.

Where the fudgecake are my reinforcements? Blackman grimaced. She could hardly nip down to the Industrial Estate to check out Parlour's car and leave a potential killer on the loose. Andrew Monkton-Smith could well be in cahoots with his wife, though what on earth their motive was, God only knew. *Damn Parlour!* Why did he have to get there first?

Finally she heard a beep outside. She opened the front door and noted with relief that Robins and the squad car had arrived in convoy.

"Dave, stay here with Monkton-Smith and the Bishop and call for assistance. Tell Billock CID they can stop patrolling the street corners in Foxburgh and get their butts up here. You two," she continued, addressing the two police officers in the marked car, "stay outside in case Dave has any hassle. Juliet, come with me."

Juliet followed her obediently to the car.

"You'll have to give me directions," Blackman informed her as she started the engine. Juliet obliged and they arrived a few minutes later.

"Follow the blue light, I guess," Blackman remarked, spotting a siren flashing in the distance. She drove through the estate to the wasteland at the end, where a small posse had gathered around the green and yellow ambulance and the familiar silver SLK saloon of Mark Parlour.

"What was Mark doing down here?" Juliet wondered, unfastening her seatbelt.

"That's what I intend to find out," Blackman replied and got out the car. She rushed over to where Parlour, covered by a red blanket, was being stretchered into the ambulance, closely followed by Juliet. He was clearly still unconscious.

"What's the prognosis?" Blackman asked Sean Denton, who had been first of her team to arrive at the scene of the crime.

"He's got a massive bump on the back of his head," Sean Denton replied grimly, guessing the anxious thirty-something woman at Blackman's side was Parlour's wife. "Looks like he was clubbed from behind by a cricket bat or something of that ilk."

Juliet let out a little cry.

"He'll be alright – Mrs Parlour, is it?" He hadn't been stationed at Billock that long.

Juliet nodded.

"Paramedics reckon he'll come round in an hour or two. He'll have a pretty bad headache, perhaps double vision and dizzy spells, but he'll be OK," Denton reassured her.

"An hour or two?" Blackman frowned. "I was hoping to get some info out of him!"

"No chance." Denton shook his head. "I can tell you that he was pursued by someone on foot. Looks like they hit him from behind then made off in a car, probably one stored in the lock-up as there's an empty tarpauline chucked to one side."

"And would that be a black car, by any chance?" Blackman grimaced. So Parlour had got it right while she'd been stumbling around in the dark trying to beat Martin Beauville into submission.

"Don't know, boss," Denton replied. "DI Parlour does have what appears to be a car registration written on the back of his hand, though. It's very faint – his attacker obviously tried to rub it off before leaving, but you can just about make it out."

"Well, what is it then?" Blackman asked impatiently. "Or do I have to get in the back of the ambulance and find out for myself?"

"It's Echo Charlie Foxtrot," Denton began reading from his notepad as Blackman jotted it down.

"No clues in the garage as to what make car it was?" Blackman enquired, her voice muffling as she wandered inside the lock-up to take a look herself.

"What do you mean?" Denton frowned.

"Touch-up paint? Logbooks? Car manuals?"

"Golf," Juliet Parlour suddenly called from inside the ambulance. "It's a VW Golf."

"What?" Blackman frowned, emerging from the garage and walking over to Parlour's wife.

"Don't you remember?" Juliet began excitedly. "On the day Terence died, Andrew Monkton-Smith disappeared off to the Post Office in Lexington Green to post a Haynes manual – oh dear – to his brother in Scotland. He said he had…"

"Just bought an old VW Golf like the one they used to have!" Blackman finished off gleefully. "Well, we'll see about that!"

She dialled Robins's mobile number.

"Dave – can you get Monkton-Smith on the phone, please…" she tapped her feet impatiently.

Andrew Monkton-Smith confirmed that his wife had indeed owned a Mark 1 black Volkswagen Golf 1.8 GTI a good fifteen years ago, but that it had long since been consigned to the scrapyard. Lara had arranged its funeral herself, albeit reluctantly. She had been very fond of the little black car, and had not driven a car since. He hesitated before confirming the vehicle registration as that jotted on the back of Parlour's limp hand, realising Blackman would get the relevant information from police computer records in any case. The threat of a custodial sentence for serving as an accessory to murder acted as a further inducement to aid their enquiries.

Blackman stuffed her phone back in her pocket. "Juliet was right – Sean, get an alert out to all airports and ferry ports for a Mrs Lara Monkton-Smith travelling in a black Golf, registration as noted – oh, and check she hasn't already been apprehended by the motorway police. The car may have been in a crash… the right wing and headlight could be damaged."

She slapped the bonnet of her car. "Yes!"

Meanwhile, the paramedics had secured the back doors of the ambulance and whisked Mark Parlour and his wife off to A&E at Billock General.

Blackman grimaced. She now had the unenviable task of informing Andrew Monkton-Smith that his wife was a double murderer. That was one job she couldn't foist off onto Robins.

22

The all-important call came through just after ten pm. A black Volkswagen Golf with a numberplate matching that confirmed by Andrew Monkton-Smith had been spotted in the Long Term carpark at Heathrow Airport. British Transport Police had broken into the car, but there was no indication of Lara Monkton-Smith's intended destination.

"I'm on my way right now," Blackman informed Robins outside Billock General, having been bleeped inside A&E, where she had been hoping against hope that Parlour would come round and supply her with some clue as to the whereabouts of his assailant.

She made her way quickly to the multi-storey, adrenalin pumping. Stopping off via Deverton Estate to pick up Robins, she headed for the motorway. British Transport Police based at Heathrow, in tandem with Airport Security, were already searching the check-in system and scouring the departure lounges for Lara Monkton-Smith.

"Right Dave, gotta drive like a maniac, there's no time to lose!"

Blackman wound down the window and shoved a portable siren on the roof then put her foot down hard on the accelerator.

"Where do you reckon she's heading?" Robins enquired, who had been filled in on the story so far by Blackman. "Monkton-Smith didn't know of any family or friends in foreign climes."

Blackman shrugged at the wheel. "As far as possible at a guess, best head for Terminal 4, that's long-haul, isn't it? First flight out, I reckon."

"So she could already be gone?" Robins frowned.

"Probably," Blackman nodded. "Don't think we got an alert out early enough. She'd have a good three hour headstart on us. But I hope not! Want my fifteen minutes of glory!"

"Can't believe she did it, can you, boss? She seemed so sweet-natured – butter wouldn't melt and all that."

"Can't believe it's not butter," Blackman murmured, leaving the M27 to join the M3 just beyond Foxburgh. They would hit the M25 in well under the hour at this rate, arriving at Heathrow soon after.

"What?"

"Nothing," Blackman replied. "Did you track down Beauville?"

She still hadn't ruled out the possibility that the vicar was somehow involved.

"Na," Robins shook his head. "His phone's just been ringing all night. Reckon he's ignoring it – his car's in the driveway."

"Or he's gone walkies," Blackman countered. "You'd take the phone off the hook if you didn't want to be disturbed, wouldn't you?"

"I suppose so," Robins mused. "But you don't still think Beauville's got something to do with this, do you – even after all that's happened tonight?"

"It's possible," Blackman replied, overtaking a convoy of red Norbert Dentressangle lorries. "They could be lovers. Who knows? Perhaps this whole thing was plotted years ago. Funny how the Monkton-Smiths moved to Deverton shortly after Beauville was appointed. Perhaps her flirting with him and his public rejection of her was just a smokescreen."

"Like *Death on the Nile*, boss?" Robins chuckled.

"Maybe Beauville met her at Heathrow and they're halfway to Egypt right now!" Blackman grinned.

"Make our lives easier, if Beauville *was* involved in some way," Robins commented.

"Yeah," Blackman agreed. "Can't believe bloody Pizza features got there before us!"

"Perhaps it was a divine revelation or something," Robins muttered.

"Get Sewell off my back, if it was," Blackman grimaced. "I have no idea how she did it – the peanut murder, I mean."

"You need to get ze leetle grey cells working!" Robins mimicked, tapping his temple in a Poirotesque gesture. "Do you think Parlour will call a meeting to reveal all?"

"Blimey, I hope not!" Blackman giggled.

Robins laughed. "Might need to borrow those binoculars of his!"

⧗⧗⧗

But the Police still hadn't traced Lara Monkton-Smith when Blackman and Robins arrived at the police desk at Terminal 4 an hour later. There was no sign of her anywhere on the airport's systems.

"Have you tried her maiden name, Lara Smith?" Blackman enquired.

"No joy there, either. We questioned six ladies similar to the photo you emailed us, but none of them were the suspect."

"What about Duty-Free, restaurants, toilets, etcetera?" Blackman frowned. He shook his head again.

"We've searched everywhere in all four terminals. But she can't go anywhere till she's checked in – and there's no Lara Monkton-Smith/Lara Smith on the system."

Blackman punched the wall in frustration.

"It's just an idea, boss," Robins said hesitantly, "but what if –"

He paused to think it through.

"What if what, Dave?" Blackman barked.

"What if," Robins began again, "she just dumped her car here to divert our attention? As a delaying tactic?"

"So where is she?" Blackman frowned.

"I don't know, but it would explain why she hasn't checked in," Robins replied. The phone in the police kiosk rang. The

Desk Seargent picked it up, banging it down excitedly a moment later.

"DI Blackman? One of the bus drivers reckons he took a lady matching your description to Gatwick on the Airport Shuttle bus about an hour and a half ago. She was carrying a small overnight bag and a laptop computer."

"Dave, you're a star!" Blackman exclaimed, slapping Robins around the chops in her glee.

"Which terminal?" Robins asked.

"North, long-haul," the Seargent replied.

"Ring Gatwick and see if she's checked in yet," Blackman commanded, regaining her composure. "Damn! We would nearly have been there by now!"

The Seargent nodded and picked up the phone.

Blackman looked at her watch then turned to Robins, looking worried. "It's eleven-thirty. We've wasted valuable time, Dave. I hope we're not too late."

⌛⌛⌛

They were met by a member of British Transport Police at Gatwick North Terminal some forty-five minutes later. Fortunately the M25 and M23 had been deserted in the early hours of the morning, enabling Blackman and Robins to make good time.

"Do you want the good news or the bad news?" An armed officer asked them.

"No more bad, please!" Blackman groaned.

"Well, the bad news is, our check-in system went down at nine-forty, so we've been unable to chase your Mrs Monkton-Smith. The good news is, due to the system going down, no flights have left here since nine forty-five."

"So she could still be in the terminal building, somewhere?" Blackman asked excitedly.

"Unless she decided to make a quick getaway," the officer replied. "But we've checked out the CCTV tapes and we've found no-one matching the e-fit carrying a black laptop in either terminal, or outbuildings."

"What about at the check-in desks?" Blackman frowned.

"Nope," he shook his head. "We've found nothing on tape, and we've run her photo by all the check-in assistants. No joy."

"Damn!" Blackman cursed.

"Could you have Left Luggage and bins checked for a black laptop. Also, could we ask all bog attendants if they've given anyone a cut and blowdry in the Ladies this evening."

"Understood, Ma-am," the officer replied.

"Also," Blackman continued, "could Dave here have a look at your tapes for the check-in desks. We've actually met this woman – we may recognise her, even if she's altered her appearance in some way."

The officer nodded.

"I'll do some sniffing around in the terminal myself," Blackman informed Robins. "It's likely she's planning on boarding one of the delayed flights, if she was aiming to get out of here ASAP."

Robins nodded in agreement and left with the officer.

⧗⧗⧗

Assuming Lara Monkton-Smith had indeed made it as far as Gatwick Airport, Blackman estimated she must have arrived some time between eight-thirty and nine pm. By this reckoning, Blackman reckoned Lara must have purchased a ticket for one of eleven delayed flights scheduled to leave from 21.45 onwards. She was just staring at the Departures board in the check-in hall when her mobile went off.

"Hello?"

"It's Dave. Listen – we've got her. She's got a bloody baseball cap on. She checked in with Aerolineas Argentinas at 20.42, flight number.."

"AR277 to Buenos Aires," Blackman read off the board. "Dave – Gate 43, pronto! Meet me outside!"

Just then a cheer went up around the Departures hall, and disgruntled passengers arose from their seats. The computer system had come back on. The slats on the Departures board rattled and gate numbers began to flash. Blackman rushed to Passport Control, and after a hurried exchange with the Customs officer, dashed through the Duty-Free boutiques and headed for Gates 40 to 50. Dodging a convoy of trolleys and sleepy passengers, Blackman finally arrived outside Gate 43.

"Come on Dave!" she moaned, noting desperately that the passengers, who had been ready and raring to go for the past hour, were already boarding the 747 to Buenos Aires. Much as she wanted to, she knew it was foolhardy to board the aeroplane armed only with her suspicions. She peered through the glass, and noted to her excitement that a tall woman with a pony-tail and baseball cap, dressed in a pale blue shirt, jeans and leather jacket, and carrying a slim black plastic case and an overnight bag, had just disappeared through the doors.

Deciding she could not afford to wait any longer, Blackman slipped into the room and walked over to the desk where two BA attendants still stood. She whipped her badge out.

"Detective Inspector Leigh Blackman, Foxburgh CID. I have reason to believe a murder suspect has just boarded that plane. We need to delay take-off until my men get here."

The attendants looked at each other, wide-eyed. This was the kind of thing that only happened on airport docusoaps, not in real life.

"Well, step to it!" Blackman barked, and one of them hastily contacted the Captain on board on their walkie-talkie.

Just then Robins and two armed policemen ran into the lounge.

"She's just boarded," Blackman informed them. She turned to the flight attendants. "Could I just check your list?"

They passed it to her. Blackman scanned down the list of names.

"Ms L Smith – got her! 38C – where's that?"

"Aisle seat, rear of economy," one of the attendants replied.

Blackman grinned at Robins. This was the moment they'd been waiting for. There were some hurried exchanges on the walkie-talkie between flight attendants, police and the Captain on board the plane, before Blackman was given the thumbs up.

"Alright – let's go!" she marched towards the door with the armed officer from the Transport Police.

Blackman felt her heart thump as she proceeded down the carpeted chute that linked the terminal building to the doorway of the 747. She stopped briefly once inside the plane for them to consult Robins and the other officer. They were at their station. Her armed companion issued their instruction to proceed then nodded at Blackman. She walked tentatively up the aisle, looking from side to side for the suspect, feeling eyes turn and stare as she approached the rear of Economy Class with the armed police officer. Then her steps grew bolder as she came within yards of her prize. She shook her mane of blonde hair from her forehead and put a hand inside her trenchcoat pockets. Her hand curled around her police badge as she approached 38C. *There she was, the evil bitch!* Her face was partially concealed by a copy of the in-flight magazine, blonde hair hidden beneath a navy baseball cap. But it was her alright. Blackman noted a centimetre of white flesh on the suspect's left hand where a sapphire engagement ring and white-gold wedding band had previously sat. Three hundred or so passengers sat with bated breath as Blackman waited for the suspect to raise her head and meet her eyes. The silence hung over the aeroplane like a mighty shroud, until, deafened by it, the suspect raised her pretty head.

"Lara Monkton-Smith," Blackman announced in her best public speaking voice, "I arrest you on suspicion of the murders of Terence Haynes and Mary Fosthlewaite. You do not have to say anything. But it may harm your defence if you do not mention when questioned something which you later rely on in court. Anything you do say may be given in evidence."

The passengers on board the 747 to Buenos Aires gasped. Lara Monkton-Smith froze, then quietly and slowly buried her head in her lap, as if adopting the crash landing position.

I did it for you, Jon, she mumbled as Blackman waited for her to arise.

⧗⧗⧗

Andrew Monkton-Smith had taken it very quietly in the end, supplying Blackman with all the information she required to arrive at what Parlour had already worked out:- namely, why Lara Monkton-Smith had seen fit to take the lives of Terence John Haynes and Mary Alice Fostlewaite. Parlour could supply the logistics of how she'd managed it later on.

It seemed Lara had never forgiven Commander Haynes for not managing to rescue her beloved younger brother, Jonathan Smith, from the debris around HMS Coventry that Saturday afternoon in May 1982, the 25th to be precise, Argentina's National Day.

Having tracked Haynes down to Deverton, she had egged her husband to trade in their pretty, yet labour-intensive thatched cottage in Lexington Green for a newer model in the designer town of Deverton.

Selecting one of the plots facing onto the handsome new vicar's newly appointed base, Lara Monkton-Smith had embarked upon a daring scheme to attain revenge for her brother's death and to obtain Martin Beauville for herself as the demands of Andrew, like their previous home, began to outweigh his charm. His paranoia that she would eventually leave him for a younger model was set to become a self-fulfilling prophecy, as Lara set about seducing the brilliant young clergyman in reaction to Andrew's increasing possessiveness. When Beauville rejected all efforts on her part to form a romantic attachment, Lara became embittered and decided to get back at him.

The Parochial Church Council away-day at Zion House provided an ideal opportunity to kill two birds with one stone – one literally, the other metaphorically through a character assassination.

On the day, everything had gone to plan. It was only later, when Mary Fosthlewaite turned up on her doorstep with a dangerous glint in her eye that Lara's carefully weaved web of deceit began to unravel. Fosthlewaite, following a grilling from Blackman and co, had later, in the sanctity of her own home, recalled a conversation her employer had casually had with her a couple of weeks back. Lara Monkton-Smith had managed to cajole Terence Haynes's burglar alarm combination out of her by enquiring whether it was standard practice to use one's date of birth for such things.

"Not necessarily," Mary had replied. "Most do, I admit, but Terence Haynes, for example, would never be so lax, being ex-Forces and all that."

"So what does he do, then?" Lara had asked, all innocence. "Use his late wife's birthdate?"

"No," Mary had replied, "he subtracts one from each digit of his date of birth. Simple, but clever, don't you think?"

"Very," Lara had agreed. Finding out Haynes's date of birth had been a piece of cake for the cunning wife of the local lawyer. A quick look at the church secretary's computer had revealed full personal details of both the wardens of Deverton Parish Church.

So Mary Fosthlewaite had to be silenced. At first, a new hairdo and vouchers for John Lewis was enough to keep the trap door shut. But as the murder hunt was stepped up, so

Mary's demands increased. Soon she was on her way to a car showroom in Billock with ten thousand pounds of Lara Monkton-Smith's savings sat safely in her Building Society account. Something would have to be done, before people began to question the cleaner's new-found wealth and before Lara's own cash reserves dried up completely. She might need them if things turned pear-shaped…

Andrew hadn't suspected a thing, and neither did he have any inkling of how his wife had managed to pull off such a stunt. That Lara had decided to hang onto his late brother-in-law's car didn't come as such a surprise, though. The well-preserved Golf had been one gigantic personal shrine to Jonathan. To be honest, that was why he had persuaded her – or so he thought – to get rid of it. It was fuelling what he considered an unhealthy obsession with the memory of her late brother. It was time to move on, not to forget him of course, but to get on with her life. So the car had to go.

But it seemed it hadn't gone very far.

23

"I get *why* she did it," Juliet said to her husband, back at Spatchcock Drive that Tuesday evening. She had invited the Bishop, Beauville and Blackman round to hear how Parlour arrived at his conclusion and the five of them were presently sat in the conservatory, enjoying an evening drink. Blackman, granted her five minutes of glory, was in a benevolent frame of mind, keen to hear how Parlour, head sporting a thick white bandage, had triumphed in solving the double murder case.

"What I don't get," Juliet continued, "is *how* she managed to murder Terence Haynes."

"That's what troubled me at first," Parlour admitted. "But I figured if I could just work out the mechanics behind Haynes's death, I would be able to fathom out who did it and work back from there."

"So how *was* Haynes murdered?" Blackman frowned, crossing one be-jeaned leg over the other. Juliet thought how much more attractive Leigh Blackman looked, casually dressed in 501s and a lambswool sweater, her blonde hair loose around her shoulders. Much softer around the edges.

"Lara Monkton-Smith put crushed peanuts in his flask, of course," Parlour replied.

"After she'd served the first coffee?" Juliet asked.

Parlour shook his head.

"Before the second round?" Blackman enquired.

Parlour shook his head again.

"Well, when then?" Juliet asked, frustrated.

"Before she even got there," he replied finally.

Blackman frowned this time. "How do you work that out? He would have died from the first cup of coffee, wouldn't he?"

Parlour just smiled with the serenity that only came from solving a double murder.

"Mark!" Juliet pleaded with him.

"The butler did it in the end," Parlour finally obliged.

"*What?*" Blackman snapped, reverting to type for a moment.

"Well, having got nowhere with my computer enquiries, I decided to pay Zion House another visit. I felt somehow it held the clue. So I decided to check out the kitchen and meeting room, in case I'd missed something. When I was looking in the kitchen cupboards, I came across four coffee butlers, the white ones with the screw lid like they use at meetings and conferences. I noticed that one of them looked a little newer than the others, and wondered if it had been introduced by an outside party –"

"And hidden in the kitchen afterwards amongst the others!" Blackman interrupted, slapping her knee.

"That was the theory, yes," Parlour continued, "but when I consulted the inventory on the cupboard door, I discovered that there were indeed meant to be four butlers in the cupboard."

"Lara could have taken one from the kitchen at the last PCC meeting held there," Blackman remarked.

"That was yonks ago, though," Juliet replied. "I can't believe she had it all planned that far in advance."

"Oh, it was planned in advance, alright," Parlour said, shaking his head. "But I agree, it seemed pretty incongruous that she should have taken it some six months previously, and I couldn't see her breaking into Zion House and risk getting caught to borrow a coffee butler!"

"So what was the score with the blasted butlers, then?" Blackman asked impatiently.

"I asked the Business Manager at Zion House if he had a more up-to-date inventory, as the one on the cupboard wall looked pretty old," Parlour continued. "He produces this sheet from his computer, and lo and behold, I find that there should only be three white coffee butlers in the kitchen as one had been broken and was never replaced. Bingo, I know how Haynes was killed. Someone had borrowed some of his coffee and made up a separate flaskful in a butler identical to those used at Zion House."

"The mysterious intruder to his house on Saturday morning!" Juliet exclaimed. "It was Lara!"

Parlour nodded. "Indeed. It would have been easy for her to smuggle it in, she would have put it in that giant *Givenchy* tote bag of hers. But what she didn't realise was that the inventory in the kitchen of Zion House was out of date, so the missing fourth butler wasn't just lying around in some other room at the centre, it didn't exist any more. Of course, she couldn't risk sneaking the fourth butler out with her or throwing it out the window or something, so she simply washed it up and popped it back in the cupboard with the others. She took a gamble that no-one would notice, even if the missing fourth one reappeared and a fifth one appeared in the cupboard. In any case, she probably knew the Centre would be closed for investigations for some days, and by the time any further cleaning or washing up was done, the police would have been finished there."

Parlour paused. The others were hanging on to his every word.

"I realised Lara had also been responsible for typing that letter from Haynes to the Bishop. Haynes's computer revealed that the letter to Bishop had been created on 24 May but last saved on the 25 May. She had saved it onto his PC on the Saturday morning to make it seem like Haynes's work, but printed it out with the original date on, Friday 24th, on Haynes's notepaper. I thought it was a little odd that Haynes would bother re-reading his letter and saving it the day after he had allegedly printed it out – but of course, it was a complete fabrication by Lara. She slipped up a little here – but I guess she felt it looked worse if she simply planted the letter in the study without saving it onto his PC, which of course, he would have done."

"So the whole technophobe thing was a smokescreen?" Blackman enquired.

Parlour nodded.

"All these committees she apparently sits on – nobody ever really checked them out. It would have been the easiest thing in the world for her to sign up for some daytime word processing and web design courses, and to have claimed she was elsewhere. She isn't an intellectual lady, but she's not thick either, she would have had no bother picking up the information she needed to carry out her plans, perhaps with the aid of some hapless male member of the species, not that anyone has come forward and admitted to helping her out."

"So was it Lara who called up and saved those dodgy websites on Martin's computer?" Juliet frowned, casting Beauville a sympathetic glance.

Parlour nodded. "It was easily done. Martin lost his electronic organiser containing all the passwords to his PC."

"I won't make that mistake again in a hurry," Beauville smiled ruefully.

"And it's common knowledge you keep the spare key to the vicarage under the kitchen window ledge, too," Parlour continued.

"Is it?" Beauville frowned. "Oh dear. I shall have to be a great deal more careful in future."

"Yes, you will," Parlour agreed soberly.

"So Lara framed Martin?" Blackman confirmed.

Parlour inclined his head. "Lara aimed to kill two birds with one stone by implicating Martin. She wasn't best pleased when Martin, here," he signified to the vicar, "rejected her advances. She was bored in her marriage and looking for a little excitement. When Martin didn't oblige, she took it rather badly. She retreated back into herself and the memory of her brother. So Lara reverted to plan A, which had brought her to Deverton in the first place – revenge on Terence Haynes for the death of her brother. She decided she might as well get revenge on Martin for turning her down while she was at it, so she framed him with the porn and gave him a motive for killing Terence by placing some fabricated news extracts on Haynes's computer, contained within a mocked-up website."

"The news articles were made up?" Juliet frowned. "But I thought…"

"I was Court Martialed alright," Beauville interjected hastily.

"But the extracts from the two newspapers were fakes," Parlour explained. "When the police investigated Terence Haynes's computer, they found he had called up a gay activist website that tried to "out" gays from the Forces. However, when I tried to call up the website a couple of days ago, it had been removed from the web. I called up the ISP under which the domain had been registered, but they refused to give me any personal information on its owner. They did tell me, however, that the web address had been first registered three months ago and that the website had been taken down two weeks ago. This seemed highly suspicious to me, and I realised the website was probably a fabrication."

Parlour paused for breath.

"My suspicions were confirmed when I called the Southern Regional Informer. They couldn't trace any such article on Beauville's Court Martial in their paper archives. Ditto the *Billock Courier* when I gave them a buzz about the other extract."

His audience shook their head in disbelief at Lara Monkton-Smith's duplicity.

"Lara certainly has a way with words, as well as a technically astute mind," Parlour continued. "I did some digging on her and it transpires she used to work as a messenger on the Foxburgh Herald, carrying copy from the journalists to the page setters in the days before computers. She probably read thousands and thousands of sleazy articles of this ilk and knew just how to phrase them."

"So she left the dummy website on Haynes's PC as well as the letter to the Bishop?" Blackman asked. She had been incredibly naïve about the newspaper articles, she now realised. Why did Parlour have to be so bloody informed on *everything*?

"She left files saved from the website, yes, and made sure we found them by placing a shortcut to them on the Desktop of his computer." Parlour nodded. "Lara designed the *Camping Out* website herself – I found a copy of *Webwhizz 5* on her laptop, it's a web design package, with all the information on it – then she temporarily registered the website on the worldwide web. She opened and saved the website on Haynes's computer that Saturday morning, but took down the website soon after, before someone complained about it – it was pretty inflammatory after all."

"What made you first suspect it was bogus?" Beauville enquired.

"It occurred to me that it was rather an odd thing for Terence to have done, and I smelt a rat."

"What do you mean?" Blackman looked puzzled, not for the first time.

"Well think about it. If Terence already knew about the Court Martial, by virtue of the fact that he was present at the actual event, why bother reading up on it on the internet? He could have simply provided the Bishop with information from public records, if he was seeking to back up his own eyewitness account."

"I see what you mean," Blackman nodded.

"Lara wanted to make sure we found out about the Court Martial you see, but resorted to a little bit of showmanship in doing so, a bit like with the eclairs on the table. She wasn't as clever as she thought."

"What I don't get, though," Juliet frowned, "is why did she bother deleting the homosexual websites from Martin's bookmarks on the computer? Why not just leave them on there?"

"Too obvious," Blackman snorted.

Parlour nodded. "She used a bit more savvy in Martin's case. She opened the articles on his PC, saved them, then deleted them, knowing he was a computer novice and wouldn't own or deploy the software necessary to entirely wipe them from his hard drive. This enabled the police to easily spot he'd been calling up dodgy websites – allegedly. Leigh's right, it would have appeared a bit suspicious, had she left them in his "last websites visited" box. Then it would have looked like an obvious set-up."

"Even given my proud status as a complete computer ninny?" Beauville enquired, bemused.

Parlour grinned. "You could argue that in your case, it would have been more realistic to have left the websites bookmarked!"

He paused for breath again. "However, I smelt another rat here. It occurred to me that it was a bit odd that so few websites had been saved and then each and every one of them deleted."

"I don't see what you're driving at," Beauville frowned, shaking his head.

"Think about it," Parlour replied. "To have stumbled "naturally" upon those websites, you would probably have to have been surfing the net a fair bit. There would be lots more web information and cookies stored on your computer alongside these deletions."

"I see what you mean – I think!" Beauville laughed self-deprecatingly.

"So how did Lara get into Haynes's house?" Blackman asked. "She bribed Fosthlewaite for the number?"

"I assume so," Parlour replied. "But when Mary started flaunting her blackmail money, she had to go."

"How awful!" Juliet shuddered. "To think she was sat here in the conservatory on Sunday afternoon! It's all so cold and calculated... I would never have thought it of her."

"And she relied on that reputation," Parlour nodded. "The pretty, blonde bit of Laura Ashley skirt from church."

Parlour recalled his conversation with Naz the florist the other week. She had described the lady sending flowers to South America in precisely those derogatory terms. It was pretty clear now who had been waving the plastic that morning at *Ring'O'Roses*.

"So she broke into Haynes's house while he was walking his dog that Saturday morning?" Blackman jogged him along.

Parlour nodded.

"So how come nobody saw her?" Blackman frowned.

"Now that's where she was very clever," he replied. He turned to his wife.

"Do you remember I had some bizarre dream last week about Julia Roberts and the postman?"

"What?" the Bishop and Blackman exclaimed at the same time.

Juliet nodded.

"I thought it was just my mind playing tricks on me, but I realised afterwards it was my subconscious giving me some clue as to how Lara pulled it off – putting the nuts in Terence's flask and fiddling around with his medipouch and his computer."

"I'm not with you," Blackman frowned.

"Well, Julia Roberts popped up because we were watching that film she was in on telly the other week. You know, the one where she pretends to drown but swims to shore to escape from her brutal husband. She then dons this ridiculous wig and escapes on a Greyhound bus!"

"Ah - *Sleeping with the Enemy*, you mean," Juliet said, enlightened.

"That's the one," Parlour nodded.

"I still don't get it," Blackman complained.

"Well, in the film, she learns to swim so that she can escape from her husband, who's a wife-beater," Parlour explained to his colleague. "He thought she was scared of water and couldn't swim, but she'd conquered her fear behind his back. Something I said to Daniel Kelty, when we thought Christine may be involved, suddenly struck me as rather important – namely, none of us are who we think we are. We tend to accept it at face value when someone tells us they can't do X or Y. But we only have *their* word for it. Who says Lara Monkton-Smith can't operate a computer for love or money, or that Lara hates driving so much, she doesn't own a second car?"

"Lara does!" Juliet exclaimed.

"Go on," Blackman commanded him, hooked now.

"Then there was the postman business. Clearly someone *had* entered Terence's house on the morning of his murder, yet nobody had been spotted entering the house by any of the neighbours. At first, I thought they had sneaked in through the back door, but that was pretty risky – any of the neighbours on Haynes's side of the road could have spotted someone entering via the back garden through their rear window. Then I hit upon an altogether simpler solution."

"What then?" Blackman asked impatiently.

"Well, who was the only person spotted in King Edward Mews between 7.45 and 8.25 that morning?" Parlour asked her.

"The postman, but.."

"And what was Lara Monkton-Smith wearing when you arrested her on board the plane?" Parlour interrupted her.

Blackman frowned, thinking hard. "Jeans and a leather jacket."

"What else?" Parlour pressed her.

"A baseball cap and a shirt - a pale blue shirt."

"And what do postman wear, especially in the summer?" Parlour enquired.

Blackman opened her eyes wide. "Oh my God! *She* was the bloody postman!"

"Oh, our resident Sleepy Head was doing the rounds as well," Parlour added, "but since punctuality and reliability aren't Wayne Shaughnessy's middle names, Lara knew no-one would suspect anything if the postman suddenly appeared at a different time to the previous day. So she slipped out the house while Andrew was still in bed, dressed in shorts, shirt and baseball cap. With her hair up, she could double as Wayne from a distance - they're around the same height and build. Fortunately for her, Terence has one of those open porches on the side of the house that you step into to post a letter. So she could let herself in, unseen, using a key she'd had copied from Mary Fosthlewaite's bunch, and disarming the burglar alarm with the number Fosthlewaite had unwittingly supplied to her. She slipped some nuts into his readily prepared flask of coffee, taking care not to get any on the flask cup itself. She then took some of his ground coffee away to make a fresh flask at home, which she brought to Zion House in her newly purchased white coffee butler – a clean cup of coffee that she would serve Terence Haynes first thing to deflect suspicion from herself."

"Oh my goodness, it fits," Juliet gasped.

"After that," Parlour continued, enjoying this immensely, "she must have found his Epipen® pouch lying around, ready to put on for his trip to Zion House. Either she came armed with an applicator tampon to swap the pen for, or she found one lying around at Terence's and decided it would do the job. This bothered me at first, as clearly Davinia would have stopped menstruating long before her death, and even if Terence hadn't cleared away some old applicator tampons of hers, they wouldn't be Melrose's latest hi-tech rounded edge design! But neither could I imagine she brought one with her just in case Terence was not wearing his pouch – she couldn't have guessed he would only put it on just before going to Zion House. Then I remembered that Terence had a god-daughter, Victoria, who used to come and stay at intervals, usually when some pop band were playing at The Foxburgh Rooms and she needed local digs for the night. She had visited quite recently, I remember Terence complaining about soggy towels lying everywhere and her mobile phone bleeping every ten seconds. Victoria probably left some female toiletries lying around and Lara decided on the spur of the moment that an applicator tampon would do the trick nicely."

"So where's the stolen Epipen® then?" Juliet frowned.

Parlour shrugged. "In a litter bin somewhere on Deverton Estate? It would be small and easy to hide, Lara would have just slipped it in her pocket and disposed of it on the way home, I guess."

Parlour took a slurp of his tea.

"After that, she rushed upstairs and quickly saved a letter from Terence to the Bishop on Haynes's computer, using the same number as his password. She also connected to the Internet and called up her website with fake news articles on his PC, saving them them so that the police would find them at a later date. She printed out the letter to the Bish and left it in an obvious place. She then left the house, reprogramming the burglar alarm. What she didn't bargain for, though, was that Haynes's burglar alarm kept a log of all entries. That, in a sense, was her downfall. She wasn't as technically astute as she thought."

Blackman, Beauville and the Bishop nodded in agreement.

"She then rushed back home, and took off the shorts and shirt. Underneath she was wearing her leotard."

"How do you know that?" Juliet enquired.

"When I looked at Leigh's notes from the second round of interviews, I was looking for someone who might feasibly have had time to dash round to Terence's and back before leaving for Zion House. Andrew Monkton-Smith said in his statement that he had been in bed sleeping while Lara was downstairs doing aerobics. When asked how he knew that, he stated that he had heard the video tape playing and that she had later appeared out of breath in the hallway in her aerobics gear. Operating on the Julia Roberts principle, that things aren't always what they seem, I subjected my wife to a little test."

"What test?" Juliet frowned.

"Don't you remember?" Parlour grinned. "I made you stay in the bedroom while I put the TV on and went outside. I came and asked you what I'd been up to, and you said, watching the TV of course. You assumed I was watching television because you heard it on in the background, when in fact I was standing in the middle of Spatchcock Drive counting to fifty. In the same way, Andrew Monkton-Smith assumed his wife was performing her morning exercise routine because he heard the tape playing, but in fact she had left it running while she nipped round to Terence's."

"Devious bitch!" Blackman commented.

"However, although I had worked out *how* Lara did it, and my theory was unfortunately reinforced by the death of Mary Fosthlewaite, I still didn't know *why* she had wanted Terence Haynes dead so badly. It struck me all along that whoever murdered Terence must have known him pretty well, or known someone who did, to have been aware of the peanut allergy. So I was looking for some kind of historical link to Terence, above and beyond the rather shallow relationships we have with one another at church. I decided to search Andrew and Lara's house – which is why I needed you to act as decoy," Parlour nodded at Shadwell Allbright.

"And needed me to keep Lara occupied," Juliet added.

"Yes. But I didn't find anything, except a photo of a rather handsome blonde chap on Lara's bedside table. This puzzled me, as I couldn't imagine Andrew letting her keep a picture of an ex in the room – especially with his jealous nature, but I put it to one side for the minute. I'd never heard her mention any brother, or anything about his death, so it never occurred to me he was family – I always assumed she was an only child. Since I didn't find anything incriminating in their house, I decided I'd follow Lara to one of her committee meetings. That was when I discovered the lock-up. I couldn't see what was in there, so I returned later that evening. I broke into the garage and discovered the black Golf with the laptop and clothes in the boot. I also found a letter from some naval bod. It contained references to a guy called Jonathan who had died at sea during the blast on HMS Coventry during the Falklands conflict. The writer of the letter, a James Mallinson, believed Jonathan had still been alive when the rest of the crew were airlifted to safety. But the Commander in charge had given the call to proceed without him. The Commander being, of course…"

"*Terence Haynes*!" the others chorused, enlightenment spreading across their faces.

"And Jonathan was the guy in Lara's photo," Juliet added excitedly.

Parlour nodded. "James Mallinson stated in the letter that he couldn't believe Haynes would intentionally leave a man behind, unless he was dead beyond a shadow of a doubt. However, Haynes had never been over fond of Jonathan Smith, as we now know him to be. Smith was a bit of a pretty boy, straight as a die apparently, but a bit too *glam* for our friend the Commander. He was also the ship's cook, which in Terence's eyes, made him a bit of a *nonce*. Haynes didn't rate him as a fully paid up action hero."

"Sounds like our Terence," Juliet commented darkly.

"Anyway, I immediately put two and two together and realised the Jonathan referred to in the letter must be the dashing blonde chap in the photo on Lara's bedside cabinet and that he must have been a relative of hers. There was a certain family resemblance. Lara had obviously discovered that Haynes was possibly responsible for her brother's death, though that is pure conjecture, and wanted vengeance. I've since checked out my theory online and it adds up. I found a memorial website for the Falklands online, and discovered an officer by the name of Jonathan Smith listed among the dead from HMS Coventry."

"He was killed on May 25th, wasn't he?" Blackman asked, remembering her chat with a shell-shocked Andrew Monkton-Smith in the early hours of that morning.

"That's right," Parlour nodded. "She murdered Terence on the 20th anniversary of her brother's death. I don't remember much after that."

"It *was* a cricket bat, by the way," Blackman commented. "We found it in the Golf along with the navy shorts and the book, with the initials AMS on it."

"He was the cook, huh?" Juliet murmured, her mind putting the remaining pieces of the puzzle together.

"Yes, you see you were on the right track, Leigh," Parlour nodded to her generously. "You were right that whoever killed Terence was someone who knew him very well indeed. After all, you don't know about a fatal allergy unless somebody either tells you, or it comes up in conversation, or, of course, they have an attack in front of you. Now Terence was essentially a very private man, though given to public outbursts of opinion. He didn't tell any of us about his peanut allergy. Therefore whoever knew must have been involved in some kind of *gastronomic* situation with him. Sorry Martin, but Leigh was right to investigate your time in the services. After all, you must have been in fairly close contact with Haynes, sharing the barracks with him."

"Though naturally I never sat down at the same table as him," Beauville replied.

"But Leigh was on the right track. Who's the main person you inform if you had a severe allergy?"

"The cook of course!" Juliet exclaimed.

Blackman nodded slowly.

"But what's so embarrassing about admitting an allergy?" Juliet enquired, looking puzzled.

Parlour shrugged. "It looks a bit poncey? You have to remember Haynes was a bit of a macho hero in his day. He would have seen it as a sign of weakness – and a potential means of personal attack, ironically he was right.”

“Silly old sod,” Juliet said sadly, a hint of fondness in her voice. He hadn’t been such a bad sort, after all. He had certainly run the PCC with military precision and would be sorely missed.

“What I don’t get is,” Blackman frowned, “why bother dumping her car at Heathrow then going all the way to bloomin’ Gatwick, when she could have been up and away on some flight from Heathrow? She didn’t gain any time trying to fool us she was there.”

“The airport transfer was her ultimate downfall,” Parlour acknowledged. “She didn’t actually do it to try and outwit us. She panicked, realising someone would soon be onto her once I regained consciousness. So she just jumped in the smashed up VW and tore up the motorway to Heathrow. Had she bothered to take a minute to ring the Departures Lounge at Heathrow, she would have discovered that the nightly BA flight to Buenos Aires had been cancelled. As it was, she only found this out once she got there. She discovered there was an Aerolineas flight going out later that evening from Gatwick and jumped on a bus immediately.”

“It had to be Buenos Aires?” Juliet queried.

“*En route* to the Falkands, to her brother’s grave, no doubt,” Beauville said sadly.

Parlour looked dubious. “I’m not so sure she would have risked making the long trip down there. She would have been rounded up pretty quickly if she’d headed straight for a British territory. My guess is, she just hoped to disappear in South America and avoid capture and maybe at some point in the future revisit the scene of his death. She had some links to civilians in Argentina. It seems she had, perversely as it may seem to us, developed a bit of an affinity for the country. She totally blamed Haynes for her brother’s death, not the real perpetrators of the crime, the Argies who bombed HMS Coventry.”

“The really awful thing about it all,” Parlour added, drumming his fingers on the chair arm, “is that it’s highly dubious that such a respected naval commander as Haynes would leave a man to die if he thought for a second he had a breath of life in him. It was probably all a ghastly mistake, Lara just couldn’t deal with her grief and had to find someone to blame.”

“Well well, what a sorry tale,” the Bishop said, shaking his head sorrowfully.

“It’s so sad,” Juliet said quietly, thinking of the well-heeled, confident blonde lady who had stood laughing in her own kitchen just the other day.

“But she was very devious,” Parlour remarked. “I shouldn’t have too much sympathy for her. This was a very carefully planned and cunning act of revenge. She even made sure the éclairs Martin had bought were placed right in front of him, so that he died in humiliating circumstances.”

“But she wasn’t cunning enough, huh?” Blackman grinned, slapping her colleague’s back generously. “Well done, Mark – you did a damn good job.”

“You saved my bacon, that’s for sure,” Beauville nodded, shaking his hand.

Parlour smiled, nodding at Blackman. “I couldn’t have done it without your help.”

“Boll - Billocks!” Blackman corrected herself in time. “I just made a late entry to steal the glory!”

“You certainly did that!” Juliet giggled. “Wish I could have been on that plane!”

“How’s Andrew taking it?” Beauville asked soberly.

“Pretty badly, poor bloke,” Blackman replied. “He had no idea. Thought she had turned the corner with this whole grief thing. Had no idea she was planning on eeking revenge on Terence.”

"What'll happen to her?" Juliet enquired, sadness overtaking her again. She had been a friend, albeit not a close one, and Juliet could not begin to imagine the depths of unresolved grief Lara must have been carrying around with her all that time to have engaged upon such a hideous course of action.

"She'll be locked up for a very long time," Parlour replied seriously. "She'll probably plead diminished responsibility, but I don't think she'll get off. Not when two lives have been lost in such a mean, calculated fashion. It's poor Andrew I'm sorry for. What'll he do? He doted on her…"

"Well I, for one, do not intend to turn my back on him," Juliet informed her husband.

"He's moving away," Blackman informed them. "He said so this morning. He's going to his brother's in Scotland - immediately. Escape the press. Said he'd never wanted to move to Deverton in the first place. It was all Lara's idea."

She got up as the theme from *Starsky & Hutch* emanated from her jacket, slung around the back of the chair. Blackman went into the garden to take the phone call. It was DI Lerwick calling from Foxburgh. Apparently the Red Light Killer had been identified and tracked down to a squat near the Railway Station. It was none other than Richard Bruton, the Delivery Manager Parlour had visited at Billock Sorting Office.

He whistled when he heard the news. "Cape Cod, it all fits. The early morning starts, the red car paint – van paint – in the victims' nails! I knew that man was a sleaze when I interviewed him about Wayne Shaughnessy!"

"Interfering in our investigations again?" Blackman mock tutted.

"Sorry, Leigh," Parlour grinned.

"Blimey," Juliet exclaimed, "This won't do the postal service's image much good! It seems they were involved in both murders!"

"Not really," Parlour demurred. "Lara was only impersonating a postman, after all."

Juliet giggled. "Much as Wayne does!"

There was a moment's silence as they all contemplated the fate of the Monkton-Smith's.

"So that's that?" Beauville asked finally.

"Hard to take in, I know, Vicar," Blackman smiled, "but you're off the hook."

"Does that mean I'll get a whole night's sleep in my own bed?" Beauville enquired, a twinkle in his eye.

"I'm sorry," Blackman apologised sincerely. "But you have to admit – she did a pretty good job of incriminating you!"

"She did, and apology accepted," Beauville smiled graciously, polishing off his glass of wine. "So, what next, Mark? Your own TV series?"

"*Parlour Investigates!*" Juliet giggled.

"I don't know," Parlour replied, "but by the time I've polished off this bottle of Champers, I'll be the *Singing Detective!*"

About the author

Carol A Shepherd is an author, college lecturer and LGBT faith activist from Eastleigh, near Southampton, UK. You can find her books at www.carolshepherdbooks.info

If you valued this book, the author would greatly appreciate a review to spread the word and support independent publishers.

You can also subscribe to Carol's newsletter, The Bi Christian Writer and claim a free novella: https://www.subscribepage.com/bichristianwriter

More titles from Easy Yoke Publishing can be found at www.easyyoke.org

Also in the series:

Allotment Affair (Parlour Mystery 2)
You Shop You Drop (Parlour Mystery 3)

9 781838 162047